W9-CAJ-150

Also by Caris Roane

ASCENSION

BURNING SKIES

WINGS OF FIRE

BORN OF ASHES

OBSIDIAN FLAME

GATES OF RAPTURE

CARIS ROANE

St. Martin's Paperbacks

This is a work of fiction. All of the characters, organizations, and events portrayed in this novel are either products of the author's imagination or are used fictitiously.

GATES OF RAPTURE

Copyright © 2013 by Caris Roane.

All rights reserved.

For information address St. Martin's Press, 175 Fifth Avenue, New York, NY 10010.

ISBN: 978-1-250-00995-1

Printed in the United States of America

St. Martin's Paperbacks edition / January 2013

St. Martin's Paperbacks are published by St. Martin's Press, 175 Fifth Avenue, New York, NY 10010.

10 9 8 7 6 5 4 3 2 1

To Kenra Daniels,
Fellow author,
Who knows how to "lay down her life" . . .

ACKNOWLEDGMENTS

Jennifer Schober, a gazillion thanks for all your hard work on my behalf.

Rose Hilliard, working with you is dynamite.

Danielle Fiorella, thanks for great covers—always.

Laurie Henderson and Laura Jorstad, thanks for the care you give my manuscripts.

Liz Edelstein, *Heroes and Heartbreakers* ROCKS!

My special thanks to Anne Marie Tallberg, Eileen Rothschild, and Brittney Kleinfelter for your continual support of my beloved warriors.

And once again, many thanks to Matthew Shear, Jen Enderlin, and the hardworking team at SMP.

My beloved held me in his arms
He whispered tender words
He spun golden thoughts through my mind
He moved quickly, his weight a beautiful anchor
I approached the gates of rapture trembling
The world exploded in a flash of brilliant light
And I was changed forever.

—Grace of Albion, "The Convent Years,"
from *Collected Poems*, Beatrice of Fourth

Understanding
Comes in its own time.

—*Collected Proverbs*, Beatrice of Fourth

CHAPTER 1

Leto Distra, out of the Eastern European tribes over three thousand years ago, was no longer just vampire, but something more, something he despised.

He was now part beast, a form that he couldn't control and which made a mockery of his life, his philosophies, and his civilized mind. At least he had a warning when the beast was about to emerge, a vibration that traveled down his left leg.

Sonofabitch, there it was. Very faint, which meant he had time—but not a lot—before he had to remove himself from everyone he knew.

He was dangerous in his beast-state, uncontrolled.

As he walked near the warrior-games contest grounds in the Seattle One hidden colony, he held a child in his arms. The toddler had his arm hooked around Leto's neck, a great comfort. Leto kept his right hand free for his sword. He'd been a warrior too many centuries not to sustain the basics, and for days now he'd been on edge. Something was in the wind, as though a decision had been made about the future of Second Earth and the war with Darian Greaves.

He glanced up at the blue sky. Early September in the Cascade Mountains was a beautiful time of year and perfect for the games.

A cluster of children, mostly under the age of seven, dogged his heels as he took one last tour of the contest grounds. For some reason, kids liked him, and the truth was he enjoyed their attention. They eased him. Not much did these days, not with Grace gone from his life these past five months. He missed her and he needed her. He was a beast clawing to break out of his cage.

Adjacent to the event grounds was a fair-like atmosphere that resembled something from medieval days, lots of colorful tents bearing handcrafted objects ready for sale. Other booths would soon become aromatic with food grown, slaughtered, steamed, and barbecued by the locals.

His stomach growled at the thought.

Hundreds of feet overhead, an innovative mist created a protective veil over the land that only the most powerful could see and which always confused the human mind. Anyone drawing near the dome of mist would experience disorientation and would turn to head in the opposite direction. In this manner, all the hidden colonies of Mortal Earth had escaped detection for three millennia, from the time the first colony was created.

The leader of the Seattle Colony, Diallo, had spent centuries perfecting his mossy-mist creation. He also checked the viability of the veil several times a day, especially since, only a few months ago, the colony had been breached by the enemy for the first time in its long history.

That breach, unfortunately, meant that a second attack wasn't so much a probability as an eventuality. One day, Greaves and his merry band of death vampires would find a way in. And then what?

He glanced at Brynna. She walked beside him, on his left, and just a little ahead of him.

How we doin'? he sent. It was easy to contact her telepathically, because over the past few months they'd become good friends.

Brynna was also in constant telepathic contact with the colony's Militia Warrior Section Leaders who were right now patrolling the external edges of the mist-dome, a thirty-mile perimeter.

She glanced at him, gave a single nod, then continued the telepathic communication. *Three of the squads are inbound with more discovery.*

Shit.

Exactly. This ain't good.

He looked up, his gaze shifting across an intense blue sky above, searching for a sign of death vampires. The Seattle Colony was hidden deep in the Cascade Range well to the east of the large city. All the hidden colonies were named for the largest cities or towns nearest them.

Greaves and his minions are getting closer, Leto sent.

Yep. There's no debating the situation anymore. Gideon said his team picked up five more little black boxes. The techs are working on them as we speak, but everyone agrees that they're probably transmitters of some kind.

The first black box had been discovered the day before. *It's just a matter of time, then. God help us. And if Greaves can subdue the colonies worldwide, he'll take all the refugee Seers and put them to work in his Second Earth facilities in South Africa, Colombia, and India. He'll finally have the advantage he's been working toward for the past fifteen years.*

Hey. A little perspective here, Leto. You've brought the Militia Warriors up to speed in every hidden colony around the globe, and we even have reinforcements from Second. Jean-Pierre's been bringing MW powers online, and that wouldn't have happened otherwise for another millennium. We're stronger than you think. We can protect our Seers from anything he throws at us.

I've just been uneasy for the past few days. Can't explain it, like I can feel forces moving into position.

You are so damn negative.

Tell me I'm wrong.

I'll do one better. I'll tell you what your real problem is: You need to get laid.

Okay, Brynna had a point. He chuckled.

That's better, asshole. Just remember, you built a strong force here on Mortal Earth and tied it to Thorne's army on Second. We're not helpless anymore. Trust in that, beast-man.

Beast-man.

He laughed. Brynna always made him laugh.

She smiled as she swept her gaze forward in the direction of the event grounds. *Do you see this obstacle set? I'm going to win it tonight.*

He shifted the child in his arms, getting a little more comfortable as he moved steadily forward. A stack of logs fifteen feet long, bark still on and braced by huge steel girders, climbed at a steep angle sixty feet into the air. Creating the obstacle-set had been a feat all by itself, but the Thunder God Warriors—the nickname for all Militia Warriors in any country—had outdone themselves.

The teamwork required to pull the games together had been an army-growing exercise. And if Leto knew one thing, it was how to build an army.

He stopped and stared up at the precise stack of logs. To win this set, a warrior would have to possess thighs of granite and speed, extraordinary speed, preternatural speed.

You haven't got a chance in hell, he sent. He loved poking the bear.

She turned and glared at him. *Like hell I don't.*

He merely smiled.

She rolled her eyes. *If all those brats weren't hanging on you, like you were Christ or something, I'd flip you off.*

Brynna learning restraint? he sent. *Impossible.*

She sighed. *I'm trying.*

Brynna had been one of the biggest surprises of his life, and a good one at that. She was tall, six-two, and had a couple of tattoos and piercings, straight black hair just past her shoulders, and steel-gray eyes. She was a refugee Seer, having escaped from a Seers Fortress a few centuries ago. Through the future streams, Diallo had found her and brought her to the colony to escape Second Earth Seer oppression.

She liked men, and more recently she'd discovered she liked making war. She was now a Militia Warrior.

She'd suggested more than once that they take their friendship to a much more productive level, but he'd refused. Sex with Brynna would have been wrong. She was his friend. No, she was more than that. She was his best friend. As much as he wanted to take a woman into his bed, he valued all that she was in his life way too much to dilute it with sex.

But there was another reason he'd refused.

His *breh* had shown up in the form of Warrior Thorne's sister: Grace Albion. Her surname was an ancient designation the family had all but dropped. Grace and Thorne's family originally came from the British Isles. Everyone knew her simply as Grace. But oh, God, even thinking about her brought a flush rising to his skin.

He took a few deep breaths. Thoughts of Grace tended to bring on his beast more quickly. Sure enough, the vibration strengthened, so shit.

But Grace was gone. She'd been gone all these months, having left with the Fourth ascender, Casimir, to who the hell knew where. Because no one could find her in the future streams, not even Marguerite, Thorne's powerful Seer *breh,* it was presumed Grace was off-dimension. He wouldn't be surprised if Casimir had taken her to his home world, Fourth Earth. Casimir wasn't a warrior, just some very powerful but worthless hedonist who had also caught Grace's *breh*-scent and somehow enticed her to go with him.

But all of it was a nightmare starting with the bizarre fact that Grace had caught the scent of not one but *two brehs:* himself and Casimir. The *breh-hedden* alone was such a new concept on Second Earth that no one could explain why Grace had actually ended up with two.

But Grace had taken it in stride, one of her many fine qualities, even if the situation had ruined something in Leto's heart. She seemed to have a strong intuition that her bizarre connection to Casimir was necessary, to Leto's survival as well as her own. So instead of completing the bonding ritual of the *breh-hedden* with Leto, she'd taken off with Casimir, convinced she had to for all their sakes.

He was still pissed off as hell about Grace leaving, but he couldn't exactly complain since she was better off with anyone other than his own sweet self. He had issues, maybe a hundred of them. But having served as a spy would do that to a man, split his soul deep, make him question everything. He was still recovering from that mission. Though well out of it, a century of living apart from his warrior brothers and of joining forces with a hated enemy had done a number on his mind.

That he was still alive seemed like some kind of cosmic joke. He deserved to die. He knew it, and there were way too many nights when, yeah, that was exactly what he wanted. He'd betrayed his warrior brothers and he'd betrayed Endelle, the leader of Second Earth, by building an army of two million on behalf of that bastard Darian Greaves.

Of course, he'd had no other choice. To have refused would have cost him his mission and his life. He'd agreed to become a spy on behalf of the Council of Sixth Earth because they needed a constant stream of data about Greaves in order to know when and how legally they could act in the affairs of Second Earth.

Leto's handler, James, had assured him that despite the army Leto had built for Greaves, all the information he'd gathered would more than compensate for his work as a spy. Leto wasn't convinced, but he had to trust that James, and all his Sixth Earth wisdom, would be able to shape the future in a way that prevented an annihilation of the innocent.

Maybe one day he'd know whether or not the horrendous things he'd done would be justified by lives saved in the future. He sure as hell hoped so, because right now his conscience was killing him.

He glanced at Brynna once more. She helped keep his head on straight. He owed her a lot. And when he went beast, which seemed to be happening more and more often, she made sure he got to the basement of his cabin so he couldn't accidentally hurt anyone.

One of the kids walking beside him said, "I'll be the champion of the warrior games one day."

Leto looked down at the boy, who was maybe seven years old. He held his shoulders back as though trying to measure up to warrior status. His eyes had a certain glow, a familiar light. Leto had been that age when he knew that what he wanted from life was to be the best warrior of his tribe. From the first, he longed to join the warriors on their hunts for food and in revenge assaults against their enemies.

The boy looked up at him and met his gaze. "I'm going to be a warrior."

Leto smiled and nodded. "And so you will be."

The boy smiled in return, then set his lips in a grim line and his face forward, into the future. Yes, he'd be a warrior.

He felt another vibration, stronger this time, like a nerve going haywire down his left leg from his hip to the sole of his foot. He took a deep breath. Tried not to panic.

A second tremor followed down his right leg.

So it had begun, and now he had a little over six minutes to get some shit done before heading to his goddam basement. Worse, he'd gone beast, as he liked to call it, only two days ago, which meant the frequency of the episodes had increased. But *why* was the question he couldn't answer.

Nor did he understand why he went beast in the first place.

He'd been helping to train the colony's Militia Warriors when his first real beast episode had occurred. He'd been working out in his basement, thank the Creator, when the whole thing had begun: the tingling down his leg followed a few minutes later by a transformation that bulked up his muscles an impossible forty pounds and increased his height another two inches. He'd been crazed during that time, unable to fold out of the basement, unable to leave because there were no doors. He'd built the damn thing as a private space, something he could only fold in and out of, but it had become a prison. In the end, he'd passed out. And when he woke up, he was back to normal.

After that, he'd suffered about every two weeks with the

same episode. He had no clear idea what brought it on, but he was convinced that the beast he now endured was connected to his use of dying blood for the past century.

There had been an earlier hint that something was wrong during the time he'd tried to reintegrate back into the Warriors of the Blood five months ago. He'd been at the Awatukee Borderland, battling death vampires, when he'd lost his mind and torn a death vampire to pieces with his bare hands, even breaking apart the rib cage to get to the heart.

Luken, now the leader of the Warriors of the Blood, had sent him here to the Seattle hidden colony to begin the long process of recovering from so many decades under Greaves's control and from the results of his long addiction to dying blood. For the most part, the assignment had worked. He was more himself than he'd been in a long time, despite his beast issue.

Brynna, he sent.

She turned toward him. *I can feel it, Leto. The change, I mean. Basement time?*

He nodded.

Aloud, she said, "We'd better get to HQ. Gideon will want to report in before you take off."

"Absolutely." Once he went beast, he could be out for hours.

He set the toddler down. The mothers and caregivers trailed at a distance. He turned to them and nodded.

They hurried forward and took over. Everyone knew of his disability and forgave him. The fact that they valued him made it all one big acid-on-skin experience.

A few moments later he and Brynna folded to the hidden colony's military HQ.

Grace stood on the balcony of Beatrice's floating palace, overlooking Denver Four half a mile below.

Everything had changed since her arrival five months ago with Casimir. Today, in just a few minutes, she would be leaving Fourth and returning to Leto. But how to say goodbye to both Casimir and Beatrice?

She held her spine straight, a reflection of her new determination. The hour had come for courage, and she meant to rise to the challenge. For her entire two thousand years of ascended life, she had kept herself apart from the war against Greaves. She had never wanted to engage in something that had hurt so many people she loved, most especially her brother, Thorne.

But today, all that changed. Today, she would begin her own campaign against Darian Greaves by returning to Second Earth and taking her place as the blue variety of obsidian flame. She had no idea whether she would bring something formidable against Greaves or not, but it didn't matter. He was the monster that had required Leto to take dying blood for a full century in order to prove his loyalty to Greaves's Coming Order. He had created a continual supply of death vampires to bolster his already massive army. Of course death vampires needed to be fed, so naturally Greaves had perfected the process of enslaving women to serve as blood slaves, an efficient method of creating dying blood through a process of killing the women off once a month then bringing them back to life with defibrillators. Heinous. Monstrous.

Greaves needed to be destroyed, and Grace had finally decided that she wanted more than anything to be part of that process.

She glanced down. Low clouds had begun to dissipate from around the dwelling so that she could finally see all of the city below. Many of the wealthier denizens of Fourth had homes built in the air, tethered to the earth by the sheer preternatural power of the owner.

In the same way that some Second ascenders could create and sustain microclimates in their gardens through the use of personal power, so Beatrice could keep her home floating in the air. The white marble palace literally floated in a fixed position above the earth, as did the attached land for the gardens and her rehabilitation pools. Even drastic changes in weather couldn't budge the airborne estate.

To the north, another mansion was preparing to launch in a few weeks. Grace had hoped to see the event, but the time

had come to put into effect a plan she had been forming for
the past several months.

"Come sit with me for a few minutes," Beatrice called out.
"I would like to finish these last two skeins of yarn, if you are
willing." Beatrice enjoyed knitting and other needlework.

Grace turned to her, wondering how much Beatrice already knew about Grace's intention to leave Fourth today.
The woman had tremendous power, so perhaps she had
known it from the first day of her arrival with Casimir.

She left her post by the balcony and strolled back into the
well-appointed marble receiving room. "Of course I'm willing to help. And what will you make this time?"

"Probably another meditation shawl."

Beatrice was a woman of endless good works, atoning for
a terrible decision she had made to allow her young son to
be fostered two thousand years ago. The tradition on Second
Earth at the time was for all children, once they reached the
age of five, to be sent to other tribal homes for care and raising. The result had been disastrous: The foster father had
sexually abused and physically tortured the boy for years,
ultimately releasing on Second Earth the psychopath known
as Commander Darian Greaves.

To the sound of Bach and the delicate tinkling of a gentle
nearby water fountain, therefore, Grace took her seat on an
old-fashioned needlepoint footstool across from Beatrice.
The large familiar round shape of the woman's eyes still
startled her, even after five months of living in Denver Four.
They were the same eyes that belonged to Greaves.

As Grace slipped a loop of soft lavender mohair yarn
over her arms, Beatrice picked up the growing ball, and the
fluttering of fine mohair began.

"You've been very quiet all morning." The woman's voice
was a lovely contralto, resonant, gentle, kind. Come to think
of it, Greaves spoke like that as well, as though speech patterns and word choices, despite his despotic nature, had been
transferred on a genetic level, from mother to son. Two ascenders could not have been more disparate, though, in terms
of motive, intent, and general kindness.

Beatrice was a healer and philosopher, a collector of ancient proverbs and poems, a woman of great spiritual insight, a woman of love. She was one of the finest women Grace had ever known.

Her son was a sociopath tyrant.

Grace's gaze fell and settled on one of the fine folds of light green silk of Beatrice's gown. Beatrice always dressed formally and wore her thick red curls in elegant waves separated by strips of gold. Her appearance was very Mortal Earth Grecian. Even her house had a Mediterranean feel, made as it was from all that marble. She was quite wealthy and served on the Council of Fourth. She was one of the most distinguished citizens of her world, honored in particular for the development of her redemption program that had the power, once completed by the participant, to absolve and transform even the most hardened criminal.

Though Beatrice had never stated her original purpose in designing the program, Grace believed she hoped above all things that her son might return to her and begin the series of excruciating baptisms in her five graded pools. Each pool forced the participant to face his or her crimes, to experience an almost intolerable sensation of remorse, to plan extensive future acts of atonement, and ultimately to be completely changed and made new.

Grace sighed.

"And now a sigh." The contralto blended seamlessly with the water, the music, and the light, but for a sudden moment Grace wanted to scream at all this perfection. What good was such a place on Fourth Earth when Greaves still lived, still continued to breed death vampires who in turn killed countless ascenders and mortals alike?

"So when are you leaving?"

Grace lifted her gaze to Beatrice. "Then you know?"

"I have felt it coming for days, and now you seem very much at peace yet removed at the same time."

"I intend to leave after Casimir completes his immersions today."

"You are changed, Grace, more determined than I have

ever known you. I have also felt that you intend to go after my son. Is this true?"

Grace nodded. "And I will bring him to you if I can."

"What made you come to this decision?"

As the yarn kept disappearing from around her hands, Grace said, "Many things, I suppose. Primarily that I can no longer ignore my obsidian flame power. It calls to me every day, like a burning flame in my soul. But I have watched so many suffer because of Greaves's ambitions and manipulations. I thought that if I join Fiona and Marguerite, who each bear the obsidian flame power, then maybe the triad can bring him down at long last."

Beatrice's fingers moved swiftly over the ball of yarn. "So you will finally embrace your obsidian flame power. Good. It is the right thing to do on many levels."

Grace nodded. "But it's not my heart's desire. I would prefer to stay here."

"But not necessarily with Casimir?"

"No. That part of our relationship is at an end."

"Have you even talked to him about leaving?"

"Not yet, but he suspects."

For the first two months upon arriving on Fourth Earth, she had joined Casimir in his bed and become his lover. She had savored his practiced lovemaking, his beautiful mulled wine scent, and his soul that she could see so clearly, a soul so different from the self-absorbed life he had led.

Oddly, neither she nor Casimir had felt compelled to complete the *breh-hedden* ritual in which the sharing of blood, body, and deep-mind engagement occurred at the same time. He had felt unworthy of her, and she had a second *breh* in Leto who still had a role to play out in her life.

Then he had entered Beatrice's program of redemption and her purpose in his life became clear to her. Casimir had needed to be redeemed, again for reasons she sensed would soon be revealed to her, but not here on Fourth Earth.

Beatrice had applauded her courage for leaving Second Earth with so notorious a figure as Casimir when everyone else would have condemned him as worthless.

Through one of Grace's strongest gifts, she had seen his soul. She had seen the wonderful man he would have become had earlier parts of his life not been riddled with sexual slavery. He had shared so many things with her, horrifying things, about how he was used during the first millennium of his life. What else could he have become except a careless hedonist?

When she had left Leto to be with Casimir, she had experienced a profound prescience that Casimir was destined to die and that if she didn't leave with him, Leto would die as well: To not love them both would be to lose them both.

She had no proof, just her ascender's powerful intuition.

Casimir had understood this to be his truth as well: that his future was tied to Leto's and in that intertwined fate, Casimir would surely die.

For that reason, she and Casimir had approached Beatrice about finding a way to prevent Casimir's impending demise. Beatrice had taken their request seriously, and after praying and meditating for several days, she had returned with the firm conviction that the only way Casimir could prevent his death was by entering the redemption program. "But you must see it through," she had said, "to the end, otherwise I can guarantee nothing for you. Do you understand?"

So Casimir had begun the program, hoping to alter his future.

But a surprise had followed, for from that first immersion into the initial graded baptismal pool, Grace had lost the ability to scent him and he could no longer smell what he called her meadow scent. At that point, she felt she understood something of the purpose of the *breh-hedden* between Casimir and herself: that she was the vehicle by which he could come to Fourth Earth and enter the redemption pools.

Grace had taken great comfort in this turn of events because leaving Leto behind had weighed down her heart. Her time with Casimir, despite how necessary it seemed to be, had been a betrayal of Leto. She could look at it no other way.

Yet in order to save them both, she'd had to align with Casimir first. Would Leto ever understand? Ever forgive her?

The process of being redeemed, however, had become a personal nightmare for Casimir. It involved a continual life review, and an exploration of every sin. Atonement was called for at each stage, and dear Creator, Casimir had so very much to atone for.

He had shaved off his beautiful dark curls as well, a sign of his determination. He was now bald and had tattooed his skull with Grace's name, as well as the names of his children, Kendrew and Sloane, in an elegant dark blue script.

Almost as quickly, therefore, as the affair had begun, it had ended, and all Casimir's energy had turned to the process of redeeming his life. Yet even though her desire for him had ended, still she loved him. She understood his worth and hoped that in time, he would at last be the man he was meant to be.

"In all of this," Beatrice asked, intruding on Grace's reveries, "what is your greatest concern?" Her fingers grew very still as she met Grace's gaze.

Grace removed one hand from the loop of yarn and pressed it against her chest. "That even though I have set for myself such strong goals, like returning and participating in obsidian flame and going after Greaves, I still don't feel real in my life, fully present."

"You're restrained," Beatrice said. "It's a very old habit of yours but not necessarily a bad one."

"I suppose at times restraint has advantages, but sometimes I feel like a ghost in my own life." She slipped her arm through the skein once more.

"What a strange thing to say. And yet I believe you are right. But are you sure you're ready to return to Leto?"

Grace felt her desire for him flow through her, a tender wave of sensation that ended with her heart beating a little harder. "Yes. I have missed him so much."

Beatrice smiled. "I believe you have loved him for a very long time. Centuries perhaps."

Grace thought it possible. Leto had been the true desire of her heart, even when she'd been in the Convent. During those decades when she'd been a novitiate, she had written hundreds of erotic poems with him in mind, as though her soul had been calling to him all those years.

She had been in the Convent when her obsidian power had first emerged and led her to Moscow Two. She had experienced the strangest sensation and had actually split into an apparition-form that had carried her straight to him. That he had been able to see her had been a miracle all in its own, for even Greaves, who was there, hadn't been able to see her.

She had saved him from certain death that night. Greaves had intended to kill him then and there. But Grace, in her apparition-form, had brought him safely back to the Convent. Later, she had taken him to the Seattle hidden colony. She then spent the next several days just keeping him alive by offering him her blood. Because Leto had been taking dying blood, at Greaves's insistence, he was in a profound state of withdrawal that threatened his life.

Only when given Havily's blood, which mimicked dying blood, did Leto finally begin to recover. Though the process remained a complete mystery, Havily's blood had cured his addiction to dying blood.

Beatrice's hands remained in her lap, her graceful fingers curled over the large lavender ball.

"You want to say something to me," Grace said. "I have sensed it all morning."

Beatrice's shoulders dipped. "It is so cliché, and I'm embarrassed at the choice of proverb. I've searched my mind a thousand times for better words, but cannot find them. And there is my greatest vanity; I always wish to appear wise."

Grace laughed, even though her heart was breaking. Her decision to leave had suddenly become very real, and she would miss both Beatrice and Casimir. She could feel change washing toward her, a break of endless waves that would not stop just because Grace wished it otherwise. "Just say it."

Beatrice sighed. "*Be true to yourself.* There. Now you may mock me for my lack of originality."

Grace wanted to laugh. "I want to do just that but I don't understand who I am?"

"Understanding comes in its own time." Beatrice put a

hand to her chest and breathed a sigh of relief. "Oh, that is much better. Don't you agree?"

"You are quite absurd, my friend."

"Yes. And I am vain. That I will admit. I am terribly vain. My greatest flaw. Something I am certain I passed on to my son."

Grace laughed again. She might even have asked how she could know herself better, but at that moment she heard the tinkling of a bell, which meant that one of the apprentices was moving at a quick, levitating pace up the long marble hall. Everyone on Fourth moved with advanced levitation. Very few walked about as Grace did. Her own levitation powers were minimal compared with others' on this world. But as the bell drew closer, Grace could sense that something was wrong. No one ever hurried as they moved about Beatrice's home.

Casimir was in trouble. She could feel it now. She released a heavy breath and drew in an even deeper one. He was still at the pools.

Grace rose just half a second before Beatrice. The ball of yarn slipped from her forearms to drop to the marble and bounced off to Beatrice's right.

The apprentice appeared, a petite black woman with diamonds laced through her braids.

"What is it, Eugenie?" Beatrice called out.

The woman put her palms together, her hands slanting toward the floor. "Forgive me, mistress, but Casimir says he must speak with Mistress Grace."

Grace wanted to run to him. Her lover, *her former lover,* was in such agony, day in and day out. By Casimir's account, the process was like having molten lava poured over his soul one minute out of every two.

"Where is he?" Beatrice asked.

"On the deck beside the third pool."

"The third pool," Beatrice cried. "Foolish vampire. He should not have done so. He had not even completed the proper sequence of baptisms for the second pool." She nodded. "We will come to him at once."

"Thank you, mistress. He . . . that is, we had to use the restraints."

Grace repressed the tears that rushed to her eyes. She wanted to run to him, to fold to him. She even started to, but Beatrice held up her hand. "You must calm yourself. More is gained in situations like this with a tranquil spirit."

Grace drew back then took yet another deep breath. Beatrice was right. She had learned one thing while sitting at Beatrice's knee: As restrained as Grace was, and as much as some of that restraint had to leave, there were times when it was necessary.

Grace nodded.

Beatrice rose a foot above the polished marble floor and began to move in that same form of levitated flight, but very slowly.

Grace, lacking the power to achieve the same kind of movement, walked beside her in a measured maddening cadence. But not for a second did she lose that terrible urge to run to him.

Leto sat in his executive chair in the Seattle Colony's Militia Warrior HQ at the far northern end of the narrow valley. The tremors were increasing. He had a little over four minutes.

Gideon stood in front of his desk wearing blood-spattered flight gear that also had bits of feathers and other debris stuck to it. He spoke quickly. He knew the drill with Leto. Everyone did. There weren't many secrets in the relatively small community.

"The death vamps are getting closer. We ran into a couple of squadrons and took care of business. We offed eight of them. Big motherfuckers. We collected several more transmitters."

Leto wanted to know more, but he spasmed deep in his gut and held up his hand. Thank the Creator that Gideon fell silent. This change was coming fast.

Leto rested his forearms on his chair and breathed through the agony that flowed within his veins, the latest turn in his splintered life. The addiction to dying blood was gone, at least the part that was like knives slicing up his intestines. When he had served as a spy and in order to sustain his mission, he took dying blood at Greaves's insistence. For decades, Greaves had turned numerous members of the ruling council of Second Earth, known as COPASS, into hypocritical versions of death vampires. Greaves provided the dying blood so that his followers wouldn't actually have to do the killing of mortals or ascenders themselves. He also provided the antidote, which served to halt the physical changes that dying blood created in the individual, even if the searing addiction remained.

A few months ago, when he'd been at the point of death, Leto had taken Havily's blood, which had miraculously cured him of his addiction. Havily was Warrior Marcus's *breh,* and the sharing of her unique blood with Leto had been a great kindness for which he would be forever grateful.

But something terrible remained, an incomprehensible residue that lived in his body. When the morphing occurred, he became like a tiger pacing the jungle floor, restless and starved, ready to attack.

He breathed again, but his shoulders strained forward and his spine arched.

The section leader wiped his forehead, which did little more than smear blood into his sweaty hairline. Gideon was a Militia Warrior operating at Warrior of the Blood status, thanks in part to his vampire DNA but in more recent months to Warrior Jean-Pierre's newly acquired ability to channel warrior powers.

Everything was changing.

Finally, Leto was able to speak again. He looked up at Gideon once more. "Give me details," he said, clenching his fists. He had maybe three minutes.

Gideon's nostrils flared. "We tracked them into the mountains. The mist-dome seems to be holding. At every juncture within ten feet of the dome, the detail would turn away, but each time they did, another one of their group, observing at a distance, would lay down another transmitter." He tossed the small black box onto the desk.

Leto stared at it. His cheeks cramped as a round of nausea swept over him. Still, he persevered. "Do we know exactly what this is yet?"

"The techs think it might be some kind of satellite mapping technology. We tried to get them all, but this is a huge perimeter."

"Shit," Leto muttered. "They're mapping the location of the colony through negative space."

"That's what it looks like. Maybe they can't see the mist, and maybe the mist turns them away, but laying out these transmitters will eventually create a map."

"It also means we've run out of time." He wasn't even sure they'd get through the three days set aside for the warrior games.

Gideon seemed to settle into himself as he said, "Agreed."

Leto turned the box over in his hand and breathed through another heavy vibration. This news wasn't good, but his current physical situation right now was even worse. His vision had started the paring-down process; soon he would see everything through a black tunnel.

Brynna sent, *You've got two minutes.*

Got it.

He turned back to Gideon. He was really feeling the change coming. His lips parted and he started breathing through his mouth. He leaned forward in his chair. Could he even get the next set of words out?

"You and your men get cleaned up and double the patrols. Let's get as many of these transmitters as we can. That should buy us some time."

Gideon nodded, turned, and left the room. Thank God.

His breathing grew rougher, heavier. This one had come on so fast.

Shit.

"Get up," Brynna said. "Now."

He pushed up from the chair. Sweat popped all over his body.

By the time he stood, he was hunched and shaking. "Get me out of here," he said, between clenched teeth.

He felt her palm on his shoulder. He cursed long and loud as the slide through nether-space began. He didn't know why, but it hurt like a bitch to dematerialize when the transformation started.

He arrived in the basement of his cabin. He'd built his home deep in the forest, at the edge of the mist-dome, to keep what he went through as private as possible. He collapsed on the hard stone floor, laid and mortared by his own hands. He curled up in a fetal position, trying to stop the process.

"You gotta let go," Brynna said. "Stop holding it in. Just let go, you idiot-bastard."

He huffed a laugh. "I . . . don't want . . . this."

"I don't know why not," she said sarcastically. "You look so comfortable on the floor sweating like a pig."

"Now get out of here. You know what happened last time."

"Hey, the scars are almost gone."

Again, he chuffed a laugh. Brynna was a powerful vampire. She'd stayed once, they'd fought, he'd cut her up some but she'd healed within an hour.

"Leave."

"Fine. Just don't soil yourself again."

He coughed and laughed at the same time. "Bryn, you're such a prick."

"Thank you. Best compliment ever. Adios."

As she dematerialized, he felt the faint movement of air over his boiling skin. The shaking started.

He breathed hard.

During the past few months, he'd tried everything under the sun to get over this condition, including weeks of therapy with Alison and even a blood transfusion.

When the shaking built so that he felt like every joint in his body would come apart, he let go of any hope that he could stop the process. In the hopelessness, however, came a kind of release, and he gave himself over to the change.

The shakes diminished as he pushed himself to his feet. He stripped off his clothes. They would be no good to him anyway in the next few minutes. They wouldn't fit. He'd learned that much—to get rid of his clothes before the change ripped them to shreds.

He bent over slightly and felt the inordinate swelling of his shoulders and arms, as though in an instant he'd packed on forty pounds of muscle. His thighs expanded and he grew from six-six to a powerful six-eight. Even his cheekbones spread slightly, giving him the look of a predator.

He tore the *cadroen* from his long black hair. His hair moved around his head in powerful emotional waves, settling at last to hang beside his face.

He was something greater, more powerful, yet more animal than he'd ever been. He hated this man-beast. He was a demonic version of the warrior he'd been and the opposite of the vampire he'd cultivated in himself for millennia. Warrior he might have been, but like Antony Medichi he considered himself a gentleman, with fairly refined tastes, a preference for an excellent port, long games of chess, and discussions of philosophy and religion.

That his centuries of service had led him here, to this beast-state, humiliated and infuriated him.

The next stage began, a vibration in his chest and throat, a new round of humiliation ready to come forth.

He chuffed. He even tried to restrain himself. But an image of Grace, folding away with Casimir and disappearing from his life all those months ago, streaked through his mind like a bolt of lightning. She was his woman, and she had left with that bastard, Casimir.

The ensuing roar came from so deep in his chest that he felt the sensation into his testicles. With his knees bent, he roared at the low basement ceiling, over and over, but this time the sound was different, full of a kind of resonance that had never been there before.

He felt as though he were calling from the distance of tens of thousands of years ago, when humans were swamp-creatures and battled in small territorial tribes. Was this what he was, a throwback to ancient times? Was this the result of the slavery to dying blood that Greaves had forced on him as a sign of his loyalty?

That he could form coherent thoughts was a complete mystery and an equal punishment, since he couldn't always act on those thoughts. And once he was well into the process, he wouldn't be able to fold.

His brain seemed to be split so that while he observed his conduct as if at a distance, the rest of him was locked into this barbarous state and equally barbarous feelings.

His right hand flexed, longing for his sword. He wanted to kill, but not in a general sense. His desire was more specific. He wanted to kill Casimir, to slay him for having taken his woman, having lured her with his scent and his power, having stolen her from him.

He moved in an oval in the small, dark basement. There was one ground-level window at ceiling height with steel mullions. He couldn't fit through the window, though God knew he'd tried to escape his self-imposed prison more than once during his episodes.

The healing of all the bruises and cuts had taken a couple of days. He'd even tried to tear through the stone and mortared walls so that his fingers were bleeding and torn down to the bone.

He was a beast.

Throwing his head back, he roared long and loud, sending shudders through his house and a trembling through the earth.

The beauty of the world
Is only appreciated
With arms opened wide.

—*Collected Proverbs*, Beatrice of Fourth

CHAPTER 2

The painfully slow, meditative walk to the pools took at least fifteen minutes, but just as Grace came within sight of Casimir, a terrible roar reached her ears and stopped her feet. She couldn't move. She could hardly think.

She'd heard Leto's roars before, even across three dimensions, but none of them had sounded like this one, like an animal with a leg caught in a trap, the metal teeth grinding against bone.

Beatrice continued on, the silk of her skirts rippling as she floated.

Grace knew Casimir needed her; she could feel his pain. But Leto's agony had been calling to her for months. So she paused where she was, unable to make her feet move.

Another roar reached her, full of anguish, a call of the wild that drove inside her chest and pummeled her. At the same time, the resonant sounds descended into the well of all that was female until she was weak with need.

What was she to do now?

She forced her feet forward.

Oh, dearest Creator, is it truly time to say good-bye to Casimir?

A few minutes later, Grace knelt beside him.

He was so different from the vampire she had known on Second Earth.

His spiritual reformation had turned him inside out. The guilt he lived with now was beyond anything she could have foreseen. She didn't know how he survived reliving portions of his life from the victim's point of view, experiencing just how much pain his selfishness and abuse had caused others.

He wept now and his body shook. He stared at her, unable to move. At first she thought the tremors held him captive, but with a start she understood that invisible restraints held him in place, pinning him over his hips, his knees, and his elbows.

His gaze implored her.

When the next roar reached her from Mortal Earth, however, she threw her head back. She felt Leto's pain this time, his need, his desperation, his call to her, soul-to-soul, *breh-to-breh*.

"Don't . . . Grace." Casimir's voice was hoarse. "Wait until I've completed the program."

Still kneeling, she once again looked down at him. "The time has come. I have to leave today. Now. I can't explain it."

"I have seen part of my future. If you could wait, it would be so much safer for me."

She couldn't hold back the tears. "I feel the need to fold to Leto deep within my bones. I have to go."

"Grace . . ." His voice was all breath and tremor as he extended a shaking hand to her.

"Why did you enter the third pool?" she asked.

His lips curved though his brow was crumpled in pain. "I thought to change the future. But today, probably because I entered a pool before I should have, I saw something about my destiny and about Leto."

Grace put a hand to her throat. "What did you see?"

"That you were right: Our destinies are intertwined with Leto's, and I have a task to fulfill."

She feared asking the question, but she had to know. "What task?"

His body relaxed. "It doesn't matter. You must do what is right for you, and I'll go where I've never gone before—" He actually smiled.

She squeezed his hand. "And where would that be?"

"Where my conscience leads me. How's that for a change?"

The next roar struck, still something only Grace could hear. She rose to her feet. Casimir turned to her and strained against the invisible binds. Grace saw Beatrice nod. The restraints disappeared, and he grabbed her ankles. She looked down at him. "I must go."

"I want you to know that you taught me about love. You loved me when you had no reason to. I will never forget that."

She backed up, and the weakness of his grip caused his fingers to slide over the tops of her feet and across her toes. She turned and moved as if in a terrible dream back across the gardens that separated the pools from Beatrice's home.

"My boys," he called after her. "You must promise to always be part of their lives, no matter what happens. You must promise."

She stopped for a moment. She had been a mother to them all this time, and now she had to leave. Mind-to-mind, she sent, *I will return and we will talk, very soon. I will not disappear from their lives. Please stay here, Caz. Please stay and live. Complete Beatrice's program. I fear more than life itself that you will die if you follow me.*

I have my own path to follow, he returned.

She couldn't bear it anymore. She lifted her arm and folded, one dimension, two, then three, traveling through nether-space straight through the pathway that Leto's roars had created for her, a shining blue pathway, like his eyes, lit and glowing, calling, begging, all the way from Mortal Earth.

When she arrived, when she materialized, the room was dark except for one small window. She adjusted her vision, turned, and saw a madman, wholly different from what she had expected. Leto was naked and so changed physically, she didn't recognize him at first.

He was also fully aroused, hunched, and moving like an animal, a beast. His long hair swirled around his shoulders as though it were alive. But he didn't seem to see her, so she called to him. "Leto."

He turned, his eyes widening. He seemed to freeze as he stared at her in disbelief. His nostrils flared then he closed his eyes, squeezing them shut as if in pain. His body shuddered.

Only then did the forest scent of him rush at her, forcing her to step back and back. This was so different from five months ago. She didn't understand what she was seeing or what was happening to him, what he had become. But the scent she recognized.

Oh, dear God in heaven, *that scent*!

She breathed in, taking a lung-expanding breath, drawing in the sweet, yet bitter and very male tendrils of herbs and fir resin. Desire moved through her, a wet wash of sensation. Her nipples hardened and puckered almost as though she had already orgasmed.

Her knees felt so weak. She ached fiercely and suddenly.

She felt a breath on her neck and opened her eyes.

The beast was in front of her, leaning down from his increased height, and sniffing. His breath came in hot swaths over her chest. He licked at her neck. His hands found her arms and pinned her then slid up to her shoulders and in a quick harsh movement ripped her gown from top to bottom.

"Leto," she whispered, but her voice sounded hoarse. She didn't know what it was she meant to say to him: to tell him to stop or to keep going, or to pause, or to take her.

Yet none of it mattered.

She also knew that he wasn't in control of himself and that the floor was made of stone. It seemed absurd, but just as he pushed her down—in a movement so hard that she was flying backward—in her sensible Grace way she folded a mattress beneath her, the one she had slept on in Beatrice's house.

Still she landed hard, with so much warrior, part beast, part vampire, on top of her that for a moment she couldn't breathe. Oh, but that stone would have hurt.

He had hold of her head now and shifted her in an abrupt movement so that her neck was exposed.

Oh, God.

She needed this.

He pushed her knees apart. She didn't resist. How could she? With every breath she took, more of his scent ripped through her brain. She spasmed deep within, needing him, ready for him. Her hands fumbled for him, reaching, and just as she took hold of him ready to guide him into her, the tips of his fangs paused on her skin.

Slowly, he drew back, as though the touch of her hand on his erection had stopped something. He looked at her, his blue eyes wild and intense. She knew those beautiful eyes, so sharp and clear, extraordinary. His eyes were the same. Leto's eyes.

He waited, trembling.

She understood. And in that understanding, that he was asking permission, more tears tracked down her cheeks. "Take me, Leto. Take me now."

He dipped down quickly. His fangs struck and as he began to drink, he pushed her hand away and pumped against her until he found her entrance, then he pushed hard. She cried out but it wasn't pain, it was a strange and wonderful kind of relief.

She was so wet and ready that as he began to drive into her and to drink from her, as she slid her hands up and down his swollen muscles and weeping wing-locks, as she sank her fingers into his strange long hair that moved restlessly about his shoulders, she came and screamed and came over and over again.

Leto felt as though he'd been on a long journey and had finally come home. Grace's blood was a sweet-meadow elixir down his throat that hit his stomach and fired his veins.

His beast-body had control. He wanted to pull back and hold her tenderly in his arms, cradle her, comfort her, apologize. But he couldn't, and her cries that sounded like a bird on the wing, and were full of pleasure, forced him to thrust harder still, to savor the way she gripped him as she came then eased up.

His stamina surprised him but now that he had her beneath him, like hell he was taking this fast. That he shouldn't be doing this at all was something he would grapple with later, but right now, with her meadow-sweet scent pouring in waves over his brain, he was doing what he was meant to do.

He drew out of her and pulled his fangs back. He hated leaving her neck, but he had other things in mind.

Her lids were at half-mast, her lips swollen, her cheeks a soft peach color. She groaned and her hips lifted up toward him, her hands clutched at him.

He chuffed and breathed at her. Her nostrils flared and her back arched. He moved down her body, biting his way so that she jerked from side to side, avoiding, begging. He reached her abdomen and the muscles rolled, her pelvis arching.

She smelled even more meadow-sweet, and he bit her hip bones and began his descent. She thrashed on the mattress. Oh, a mattress. Smart move.

He couldn't believe his brain functioned at all.

He reached her mons and opened his mouth wide. He took as much of her as he could and sucked hard.

The groan that left her was guttural and deep, resonant. He planted a hand between her breasts and held her flat. He was strong. He slid the other hand beneath her buttocks and pressed her into his mouth, lifting her up so that she could watch.

Her lips parted as she dragged in air. He slid his hand to the side, caught a nipple between thumb and forefinger, and squeezed. She threw her head back.

Watching her brought a chuff from his throat. His lungs worked like bellows until he was growling and huffing.

"That sound," she cried.

He couldn't help the sound he made but when he sucked harder and the chuffs strengthened, her legs locked around his back and he could tell by her cries she was once more caught in ecstasy.

Something inside him eased a little as he brought her over and over, resting between and taking her to the heights until she was limp, her eyes glazed, her breathing fast.

He moved over her again, moving up the bed, up and up

until he could position himself against her mouth. He pushed his cock against her lips, demanding.

She met his gaze then slowly parted her lips. When she was wide enough, he plunged into her and mouth-fucked her hard. She used her hands and her nails and scored his buttocks, and it felt just right.

He was taking possession of her. She knew it. He knew it.

He felt his balls grow tight, but he didn't want to come like this. He withdrew, suspending himself over her, waiting it out. He had to spend himself inside her.

He flipped her over and pulled her up onto her knees. She arched her back, which tilted her buttocks up. He dipped low and licked her until she was flowing wet again then he rose up and drove into her hard.

Damn, his wing-locks. They'd been burning and he had this feeling he would mount his wings, but he didn't want to. Shit.

As he began to pump into her, he chuffed hard.

"Come for me, Leto. You are so beautiful like this. Come for me."

Her words, her voice, her body, her scent. He supported himself on one arm and with his free hand he fondled her breasts, squeezing them hard. He bit down on the back of her neck and pumped fast.

Damn his wing-locks.

As he came, he roared because his wings released, adding to the intense pleasure. But would there be enough room for his entire wingspan? Or would he be maimed?

The sensation of releasing into Grace took over and pleasure came from every direction at once. He thrust hard, his wings flapped, and the sound of Grace crying out in pleasure spurred him on. He pumped harder, giving her every bit of who he was as a man. Pleasure rippled over his massive body, and some terrible pain inside him finally drifted away. Grace had come back. She had come home to him. He could breathe again.

He began to slow in his movements and to savor how she sighed and cooed, and that he was connected deep.

At last, his consciousness began to fade, and he fell down on her so that she collapsed under him and under the covering of his wings.

At first, Grace was too lethargic to move—but she wouldn't have been able to anyway. She was caught in some kind of postcoital bliss that rocked her eyes in her head. She smiled and savored. Her mouth was pressed into the mattress, making it even harder to breathe.

Everything was so very wrong, yet so right, which made no sense at all yet complete sense.

Leto had given her a choice.

She would always remember that as probably the most heroic thing he could ever have done with her. She had understood the depth of his need and she knew he'd been locked into some kind of primordial beast-mode. Yet somehow his rational self had shone through. No, she would never forget that he'd given her a choice.

So here she was buried beneath his wings and his massive, bruising body, and she couldn't move. She could barely breathe, he was so heavy on her. But she could draw just enough air to survive, which made her smile.

She was with Leto, the warrior she had known for the entire two thousand years of her long vampire life, from the time that Thorne had joined the Warriors of the Blood. Leto and Thorne had been battling death vampires together all these long centuries.

Leto was also the warrior she had written all her erotic poems about during her decades in the Prescott Two Creator's Convent. It was as though somehow her spiritual mind had known that one day she would be here, fulfilled by Leto's body.

But as she came down from the bliss of ecstasy, her rational mind began to explore all the implications of such irrational behavior. She wasn't afraid of pregnancy. For reasons she had never understood, she had been barren for almost her entire life. This was a great sadness to her, of course, but not something she'd been able to change in all these centuries. The one birth she had experienced, when she was young, had not ended well. She had always wondered if that was the cause of her inability to conceive.

She doubted she would ever know.

Her mind drifted very quickly to Fourth Earth and to the vampire she had left behind. How strange to think that just a little while ago, she had been living in a palace in Denver Four, caring for Casimir and his children, enjoying Beatrice's friendship, and now she was here.

She had left the clouds and had fallen hard to earth.

That her fate seemed inextricably bound to Leto's was clear. She knew his history, that he'd lost a mother to death vampires when he was very little. His soul had been closed off even longer than her own. But on some deep level, before these truths had been shared between them, she had known him and he had known her.

But what did this portend for her? Or, more accurately, what was she willing to do about it?

She was tired of not breathing deeply, so she pushed at Leto, giving him a hint.

"Hey," she said softly and pushed again, taking care not to disturb the feathers. A vampire's wings were strong but they were also in many ways fragile; even pulling on an individual feather too hard would cause pain.

But after a few more nudges, the last two quite firm, she realized he wasn't just asleep, he was unconscious.

She was about to remedy the situation, but something within her vibrated softly, like a chime deep within her soul, as though something must be understood and known in this very moment, before she took one more step into the future.

She grew very still, her face smashed into the mattress, Leto's body heavy and warm on top of her.

She searched through her mind and followed the sound of the soft chime, flowing down and down through a veil of dark clouds until her mind pulsed with blue light. She remained in that unearthly glow.

She had never been in this place before, but the color told her she was very close to her obsidian power, her blue flame power. Using her instincts, she wrapped herself in that power. As she focused, Leto's soul was simply there. She understood then that in some mysterious way, her power was related to her ability to read the souls of others, even to search them, something she had been able to do since she was very young.

This time, however, Leto's soul seemed sharper and clearer than ever before.

She sank deep into both his character and his past. She saw the battles he had waged, the thousands of conversations he'd had with Commander Greaves, his arguments with Greaves's generals. Then before his abdication of his Warrior of the Blood status, she saw his close connection to all his warrior brothers, especially to Thorne, and how Leto had once served as Thorne's mentor. She saw the women Leto had loved over the past century and beyond that, over the full course of his three thousand years. She saw him as a child, back and back until she was able to see what had prompted him to become a warrior. He had always wanted to be the very best warrior in his tribe. From a young age, he had prided himself on being the best. How much it must have hurt him to have been a spy. She moved forward swiftly in time until he was once more serving as a spy on behalf of the Sixth ascender James. She saw how James had explained how critical it was that Sixth Earth get extensive information on Greaves, something only a spy could deliver, and in the ensuing years just how much Leto had suffered as he performed his traitor's role.

She saw the arena battle in which Leto had been required to fight Alison, each bearing a sword. She felt how much the performance of this duty wounded the depths of his soul, how much he had hated setting his centuries of experience against an untried woman, even how hard he had fought. Then his surprise when her vast powers had emerged and Alison had defeated him using a pocket of time reversal. However, in this moment, Grace saw something more. She realized that Leto had a connection to Alison, a purpose to fulfill with her in the coming days, though Grace couldn't discern what that purpose was.

She knew that Alison was destined to open the Trough or portal to Third Earth, an unfathomable feat. This much Grace knew from conversations with Thorne over the past year and a half. No one knew the timing, only that when it happened, Second Earth would be changed forever. But what did it mean that Leto had this kind of connection to Alison?

She moved forward once more until she was now in the absolute present with Leto, still in his bizarre beast-form, crushing the air from her lungs, his weight growing heavier and heavier.

She was still locked into her blue flame power and was still rummaging around within Leto's soul. She saw the nobility of his character—that his loyalty, until the moment he'd become a spy, had defined him. Breaking that loyalty had caused a cancerous growth in his heart. He no longer felt worthy of life, of what was good in life. He especially didn't feel worthy of her. She also had the sense that the change he underwent with increasing frequency was permanent.

As she released Leto's soul, she returned to her reality and Leto's beautiful weight on her. She hated this war and what it did to fine, worthy ascenders, how Thorne had lived in pain for centuries, increasing when her twin sister, Patience, was taken; how a decent man like Leto had been turned into something almost unrecognizable.

Now she had returned to participate in the war in a way she had never imagined doing before. She was obsidian flame and had an opportunity to change the future.

Struggling to take her next breath, she knew the time had come to leave this dark place beneath the earth, to get some distance from Leto and chart the course she had set for herself.

Leto, you're very heavy. Can you move, please?

She gave him another push back with her shoulders and when he still didn't budge or respond to her telepathy, she simply folded from underneath him, hoping that his wings would lie flat afterward.

She materialized beside the mattress. The soft light blue

linen sheets hung over the sides and spread out like a lake on the dark gray stone of the floor.

She gasped. She had never seen Leto's wings so close before. She took a step forward, careful not to step on either the mesh superstructure that held the feathers in place or the feathers themselves. She had forgotten how beautiful Leto's wings were; upper and lower wings essentially created four panels. The feathers were a deep blue like sapphires.

He was so beautiful, even in his beast-form. She felt an almost overwhelming need to stretch out beside him and offer him what comfort she could.

Right now, however, what she needed was time to think about what coming back to Mortal Earth would mean for her in the coming days. She thought the thought, and folded to the bottom floor of Leto's cabin. A quick search through his home brought her to his expansive bathroom on the second floor and the sight of what she wanted now more than anything. A shower.

Endelle wasn't alone in her office, but she might as well have been; at least that's the way she felt. Thorne stood across the room by the east-facing windows, his back to her, talking quietly into his phone to his woman, his *breh,* Marguerite. Every once in a while, he'd laugh. Despite the passage of five months when Thorne had bonded with Marguerite, Endelle still had a rock in her chest that she couldn't seem to get rid of. The rock was Thorne-shaped. He had a new life now with his *breh* and as the Supreme High Commander of the Allied Ascender Forces, but that didn't change how much she missed him.

Thorne had been her right hand all these centuries, but he'd split from her and now lived his own life. She understood and respected that he had a new role to play. She just hadn't realized how much she had relied on him or how important he'd been to her.

She'd get over it, of course. But today was one of those days. She had a nasty gut feeling about the war, that something bad was on the wind. In former times, she'd have had a sit-down with Thorne; they'd talk it over, then strategize.

Now? He had other duties, important ones, like building her army.

He was powerful as hell now and actually served as part of the obsidian flame triad, not as a significant player but as the anchor. Between that, and adding to her massive Militia Warrior forces daily, he sure as hell didn't have time to soothe her shitty loneliness.

She rubbed the back of her neck, which reminded her of the other glorious part of her life right now, that she had permanent scars back there, also something she couldn't get rid of. That Sixth bastard, Braulio, had put them there, but she still didn't know what they were for or what he'd really done to her. She only knew she often woke up sweaty and nauseated and ready to do battle with anyone and anything.

Jesus H. Christ. Too much shit in her life.

She sat at her desk in her office, leaning back in her tall chair, her head pressed against the Appaloosa horsehide that hung over the back. With her elbows on the arms of the chair, she formed a steeple with her hands and tapped her fingertips together.

Her gaze shifted past Thorne. The windows had been re-placed since her last freak-out when she was sure Thorne was dead. She'd gone full-out, batshit crazy and demanded that James, another real Sixth Earth piece of work, get his ass down to her office on Second, bring healers with him, and restore Thorne's life. Hell, she'd threatened to destroy the planet if he hadn't.

So James had come, with the Sixth healers, and brought Thorne back.

And there Thorne stood, a changed man, his back to her, his Droid Ascender pressed to his ear. Marguerite was pregnant with twins, and he was playing the *concerned husband* role like he'd been born to it. God, staring at him was like looking at an amputated leg, the portion that had been re-moved. She kept wanting to reach for Thorne and reattach him somehow.

"So how are you doing?"

Endelle flipped around in her chair to find that Alison

had just folded into her office. "How the hell did you sneak in here without my knowing and why the hell are you grinning like that?"

"I have news."

Endelle waited to hear what it was. But Alison didn't say a word, she just kept grinning like someone was tickling her ass-crack.

"Okay, I am so not in the mood for any fucking games."

Alison lifted a brow then turned slowly around until Endelle had a perfect view of her bare back and what looked like wing-locks.

"Holy shit." She rose up from her chair and looked closer. "Alison, don't be shitting me. Does this mean you fucking got your wings?"

Alison turned back around, her expression euphoric. "Yes, Madame Endelle, I so fucking did. I woke up this morning, felt a little strange, then a vibration flowed through me like an electric current. The impulse to mount my wings was almost overwhelming. As soon as I told Kerrick what was going on, he folded me to the back lawn and I let them fly. I still can't believe it."

Neither could Endelle. Despite the fact that Alison was only recently ascended from Mortal Earth, Endelle had always known that Alison would mount her wings early. Anyone with that much power wouldn't wait decades to take to the skies.

Damn but wasn't she a beauty; about six feet, long blond hair pinned back this afternoon with a gold clip. Was it any wonder Kerrick had fallen hard for her? But then had he really had a choice? Her warriors were succumbing fast to the *breh-hedden*, one after the other, a bunch of overbuilt dominoes. She had long suspected that the appearance of the *breh-hedden* on Second Earth was a balancing force against Greaves, a set of dimensional scales working on behalf of ascenders everywhere to keep evil from triumphing.

Thorne was the latest victim of the *breh*-bond, and for the past five months she'd received reports from the Seattle Colony on Mortal Earth that Leto was still caught in the fist of that myth-that-wasn't-a-myth. Oddly, it was Thorne's sister, Grace, that Leto had lost it for.

But as she met Alison's gaze, she had a strong prescience that there was more to the sudden appearance of her wings than just flight capability. Endelle could feel it in every cell of her body.

Her heart started beating like a bird trying to get out of a cage. She put her hand to her chest.

Alison had ascended over a year ago, one freakishly powerful mortal who had carried with her just about every preternatural ability a Second ascender could ever possess. She had ended up serving as Endelle's executive assistant, even though she could have been anything in the second dimension, including a Warrior of the Blood. The woman, however, had the killing instinct of dandelion fluff, so executive assistant it was.

Endelle clapped her hands together. "This is some righteous shit. So are they white, blue, orange, what?"

Alison shook her head and her eyes glittered. "Emerald, like Kerrick's eyes. A beautiful deep green with black banding at the tips."

"Mount them for me."

Alison looked around then shook her head. "I can't."

Endelle smiled. "The wingspan is too big."

"Yep." Mounting wings in too small a space could cause damage.

Endelle narrowed her eyes. "Okay, spill the rest of it, because I know there's something else, right?"

Alison nodded. "My dreams have returned, the ones about opening the Trough to Third Earth."

"The portal to the third dimension," Endelle murmured. She put two fingers to her lips and sat down. Her heart was still that wild bird. Vampires didn't usually stroke out, but she thought if she didn't calm the hell down she might just be the first one. So Alison had mounted her wings and now her dreams had returned, the ones that placed her at White Lake with the blue spinning vortex above: the portal to Third Earth.

She swallowed hard. She had a feeling that everything relating to the war and to Greaves was coming to a head.

Then she felt something new slam into her from the direction of Mortal Earth and another *holy shit* shot through her mind.

When Thorne finally put his phone away and turned in her direction, she said, "You'd better get your woman over here, and while you're at it, I want to see Jean-Pierre and Fiona as well. Now. Within the next sixty seconds."

Thorne might have been the Supreme High Commander of the Allied Ascender Forces, but she was still in charge. He met her gaze, his hazel eyes clear and beautiful in a way they hadn't been in centuries. He was a new man thanks to the bonding of the *breh-hedden*. He nodded and withdrew his Droid from the pocket of his slacks, then started issuing orders.

"What's going on?" Alison asked.

Endelle looked up at her. "You'll find out, and it isn't just about your wings."

Marguerite arrived first. Her hair was short and platinum blond and her six-months-pregnant belly stuck straight out in front of her. She was a full foot shorter than Thorne. He slid his arm around her back and leaned down to kiss her. She wore a snug blouse, and his hand went to her stomach. She looked beautiful. Hell, together they could have been a pair of Mortal Earth movie stars.

Marguerite had turned out to be one big surprise in Endelle's world and in their small circle of über-powerful vampires. She had a mountain of power as a bona fide red variety of obsidian flame and as the most powerful Seer on the planet. Endelle had made her Supreme High Seer of Second Earth, a distinction that had no particular perks and a lot of responsibility. Marguerite had translated her job into a constant effort to secure global Seers rights for the frequently enslaved Seer population.

Near the east wall of windows, a shimmering brought Jean-Pierre and Fiona into the office, both wearing jeans with matching tanks and gazing at each other like no one else existed. Fiona had fang-marks on her neck. Oh, shit, the couple had been doin' the nasty when she pulled them in here. She was almost sorry she'd disturbed them, but she had more important stuff going on than a little nookie between *breh*-mates.

Jean-Pierre had a head of gold-streaked light brown hair that curled however the hell it wanted. She could tell he'd crammed it into the *cadroen,* another sign that he'd been busy when he got Thorne's call. He had eyes the color of the ocean, big teeth, and a big smile. Fucking gorgeous.

Fiona, the gold variety of obsidian flame, had silver-blue eyes and long chestnut hair. She'd at least combed her hair, but with the exception of some lip gloss, she wore no makeup. She didn't need to, though. She was in love and all aglow, maybe the best makeup a woman could ever wear.

"What is it, Endelle?" Jean-Pierre asked as he and Fiona drew close to her desk. His accent still carried a French lilt and drove the ladies wild. She often heard him speaking quietly to Fiona in French, after which of course she would end up wrapping her arms around his neck and kissing him. How many times had she seen the couple just take off from any old event once he started in with his mother tongue?

She glanced from one ascender to the next. "Have a couple of things to share, and before you start yelling at me about not sharing sooner, I just found out about both these things." She jerked her thumb at Alison. "This one got her wings this morning."

A round of congratulations flew from both couples in Alison's direction.

"We should have a party," Marguerite said. Her bonding to Thorne five months ago had released a hostess on the Warriors of the Blood. She often had everyone over to Thorne's Sedona house. Poker had become a big deal and even drew the unbonded warriors, like Zacharius and Santiago, out of that shithole of a rec room the boys called the Cave.

"Hold your horses, red flame," Endelle said. "There's more." When all eyes were fixed on her once more, she continued, "Alison has been dreaming about the portal to Third

Earth again and flying over White Lake. You know what that means, right?"

As one, everyone shifted to stare at Alison.

"Damn, Alison," Thorne said. "I didn't think it would be so soon."

"What?" Marguerite turned to Thorne. "Why don't I know what this means?"

He looked down at her and told her the story about Alison's ascension, how she'd had numerous dreams about flying over White Lake, about looking up and seeing the blue vortex that led to the third dimension, and that somehow she knew that her destiny was to open the Trough to Third.

Marguerite shifted to stare once more at Alison. "Holy motherfucker." She then clapped her hand over her mouth, patted her stomach, and said, "Sorry, kids."

Endelle laughed. But from the time Alison's daughter, Helena, arrived, they'd all started curbing warrior-speak. Alison scolded everyone because she said she didn't want baby Helena's first word to be *shit* or worse.

Fiona returned to the subject at hand. "Do you have a sense, an intuition, that you'll be opening the portal soon?"

At that, Endelle, swiveled in her chair to look up at Alison as well.

Alison blinked several times as though pondering the question. She then met Endelle's gaze. "Yes, it will be soon. But doesn't that mean the war will heat up? I always thought, or maybe felt, that once we had contact with Third Earth, the war with Greaves would end."

"We all thought that," Thorne said. He said to Endelle, "But how likely does this seem? I've been building the army, but we don't have anywhere near enough warriors to battle Greaves directly."

Endelle nodded. "I know. But now for my second bit of news, although"——here she glanced at Fiona and Marguerite——"I confess I'm a little surprised that the two of you don't have word for me as well." She then looked at their *brehs* and smiled. "I guess the pair of you have been too busy to notice that Grace is back."

"What?" At least three ascenders shouted that word at the same time.

Fiona shook her head. "I don't sense her at all."

"Well, hopefully it's because she's with Leto on Mortal Earth. Maybe the mist Diallo creates to protect the colony isn't allowing information to travel far. I felt her, though, just a few minutes ago, but then, well, I'm me and I have more power than the bunch of you combined." She didn't often brag but it felt kind of good right now. She then launched into exactly how she thought things should unfold, starting with Alison.

She looked up at the blond beauty again. "You'd better get to practicing your flight skills. I have a feeling they'll be needed within the next few days. Got it?"

"Absolutely. Kerrick has already been working with me. We're both feeling the urgency. My God, Endelle, do you think this is it? I mean, the war has gone on for so long."

"I won't say for sure, but I think it's possible." She clapped her hands together. "Now, the second thing is equally important. We'll need to bring obsidian flame up to speed as fast as possible." She looked from Thorne to Jean-Pierre. "If I remember correctly, though, most of the warriors will be out at the Borderlands. Both of you said you'd join Leto at the warrior games."

Marguerite said, "Yes, the four of us are going. So it looks like we'll see Grace there."

Endelle nodded. "Good. We'll get things rolling." She addressed Thorne. "I just hope your sister doesn't intend to pull any of her spiritual bullshit and refuse to participate because she needs to meditate or something."

He just stared at her, looking exasperated as he often did when she opened her mouth.

"Hey," she said. "Don't look at me like that. Grace was the one who took off with that good-for-nothing and left Leto flat-footed. Why should I trust that just because she's come back, she means to do her duty?"

Thorne leaned forward and held her gaze. "Because Grace has tremendous integrity and you know that. She also knows what obsidian flame will mean to you, to all of us. When she left like she did, I know she had a good reason, even if she didn't share it with us. Coming back, she'll have a better one."

"Do you have to be reasonable?"

He smiled. Thorne had a beautiful smile—maybe not quite as brilliant as Jean-Pierre's, but damn close.

"All right," she said, waving her hand in his direction. "The warrior games will start in a few hours. The four of you can take off, but, Thorne, please do what you can to impress your sister with all of this. Let both Leto and Grace know about Alison's wings as well."

When the two couples vanished, Endelle turned back to Alison, whose gaze dipped down to Endelle's chest. When Alison frowned, Endelle also glanced at her latest creation. She flipped the pinecones and the resin-coated monarch butterfly necklace. "You no like?"

Alison said, "Well, it's not in your usual style?"

"Lacks the glam I'm used to rocking. It's in honor of the warrior games. I'm telling you, though, that colony is so organic, it gives me the scratch. But I thought I should make an effort. I have bee-stilettos to die for."

"I'm not even gonna ask."

"Good. So how's Helena, anyway?" Warrior Kerrick had gotten his woman pregnant on about the third day of her rite of ascension. Talk about virile. Now baby Helena was ten months old, or something like that.

Alison shrugged. "She's got too many powers for an infant. It's hard to know what to do with her. She can communicate telepathically now, but hearing that baby gibberish in my head all day is driving me bonkers."

"Bonkers? That a new psychobabble expression?" Alison had been a therapist by profession before her ascension.

"It is today."

"Well, you should bring her by. It's good for morale." Endelle clasped her fingers together. She doubted she was fooling anyone, but she actually liked Helena. There was a kind of intelligence in her green eyes that Endelle approved of. She wasn't your ordinary kid.

"I'll do that."

Endelle was about to let Alison go, but she had one more person she wanted to alert to these sudden changes. She focused her thoughts on Marcus. *Get your ass in here,* she sent. She'd given up the complete futility of politeness, oh, about three millennia ago.

On my way. Marcus didn't complain. He was older than Leto and had a tough hide.

To Alison, she said, "Marcus is coming. I want to let him know what's doin'."

"Good idea."

Within a minute, Marcus appeared at the end of the long, glass-lined hallway. He was one good-looking sonofabitch. He had dark hair, which was now a few good inches down his back and secured in the *cadroen.* Two nights out of seven he battled at the Borderlands alongside his warrior brothers. The rest of the time he had an office down the hall where he worked his PR and administrative magic.

He was the High Administrator of Southwest Desert Two, but that was just a title. He was really in charge of global PR for Endelle's administration and had effectively staved off the defection of at least a dozen of her territorial High Administrators around the globe. This was no small thing. If Greaves had gotten his hooks into them, Endelle was pretty sure the self-styled Commander would have already taken the war to its inevitable conclusion and bombed the hell out of Metro Phoenix Two.

Marcus had become one of her numerous miracle workers. But whatever happened from this point forward, especially from a PR standpoint, Marcus would need to be included.

"So, what's going on?" he asked, glancing from Alison to Endelle. But he frowned as he looked back at Alison, his gaze running over her flight suit. "Is that what I think it is?"

Alison smiled and nodded.

"Shit, you got your wings."

"I did. This morning."

"Hot damn, that's good news."

Endelle told him the rest, about the dreams and about Grace returning. By the time she was finished, Marcus looked like she'd slapped him hard a few times.

"I'm fucking speechless," he said. "You know what all this means, or could mean, right?"

Endelle was smiling so hard that her cheeks hurt. "Damn straight I do."

Marcus put his hand on the top of his head and turned in a full circle. "Okay. Okay. Okay."

"You're repeating yourself."

"I'm in shock. This is amazing. Okay."

"You said that." But Endelle was enjoying herself. These moments that happened so rarely—when she took the time to savor what was a feeling of tremendous hope. She was sure there'd be more assfucking in the days to come, but right now the possibility that the war might just end had her heart still flying about wildly.

Once more, she looked up at Alison. "I want Kerrick off warrior duty. I'll let Luken know. Your man is now assigned to you indefinitely. Get your flight skills up, and be ready for anything. And in your off-hours, I want you to work with Grace like you did with Fiona. Help her get her obsidian power up to speed."

Alison tapped her pants pocket and said, "Call me when you need me. As soon as I get back to the house, Kerrick is taking me to White Lake. You'll find us there for the next several hours."

"Good. That's good. And let me know if you see any sign of the vortex."

Alison left, which meant Endelle was alone with Marcus, but she could do little more than grin, and he kept turning in a circle. She knew his mind. He was no doubt plotting all the ways he could make use of this information to tighten his hold on the High Administrators who'd been making noises about joining Greaves and his bullshit Coming Order.

She was not surprised when he suddenly took off running back down the hall, shouting over his shoulder, "I have calls to make."

Now that she was alone, Endelle let the moment play itself out. Her heart was on fire, revved up because for the first time in a long time, she had hope—beautiful, wild, shining hope.

Breathe, my beloved,
Take my essence into your soul,
That you might live
Forever in my arms.

—*Collected Poems,* Beatrice of Fourth

CHAPTER 3

Leto didn't understand where he was. He opened his eyes slowly and drew in a long breath, which of course brought a powerful memory flooding back, of coupling with Grace, of taking her while in his beast-state.

Oh, God.

He was facedown on some kind of mattress with extremely soft sheets. The light from the window was faint, even dull, very dull. He lifted up, glanced at his wings, and was stunned to see that he was still in full-mount.

He flexed his shoulders slightly and breathed a sigh of relief. He was no longer in his beast-state with his back and shoulders swelled to ridiculous sizes, like he'd been built to swing about five maces at once.

He levitated very carefully to his feet, taking pains not to tweak or bend his wings or feathers. He'd been fortunate that during the unexpected mount he hadn't broken any of the panels.

He drew in another deep breath, and with the practice of many centuries he began drawing his wings into his back. The feathers narrowed to super-fine points and the superstructure melted into the wing-locks as though being absorbed into his body. The process raked his nerves because it took longer now. Even his wings had changed. At least he could manipulate them whether he was in his regular vampire state or in his larger version.

He glanced at the pile of clothes. He'd had enough sense to disrobe before he transformed.

He looked around then back down at the sheet. There was blood near the head of the mattress. He'd savaged Grace's neck. That much he could remember.

He shuddered, remembering with pleasure the taste of her blood and the fire it put in his stomach. Her blood had given him stamina, and he had lasted long enough to bring her repeatedly. That she had thoroughly enjoyed herself was clear to him, so he wasn't too worried.

On the other hand, she'd left the basement.

He put a hand to his forehead. He had no idea how long he'd been out.

The light at the small window had dulled some. The day must have advanced.

More than anything, he wanted a shower. But before he left his basement prison, he sent a telepathic thread in multiple directions, hunting: *Grace, are you there?*

A moment later, her soft melodic voice returned within his mind. *I'm walking in the forest. Don't worry. I'm within the confines of the mist.* Had she sensed how tense he was? Or did she just know intuitively that he would worry?

She added, *I just let Marguerite and Fiona know that I'm back.*

We should talk.

I know. There's a lot of ground to cover. I'm going to swim in the hot spring at the rise above your cabin. Come to me when you're ready.

For a moment, he grew so still he wasn't sure he was even breathing. One of the reasons he had built the cabin in this location was because of the spring. He'd carved out a small bathing area, enough for him to relax in if not to swim laps. He often soaked there trying to forget his misdeeds, God help him.

But Grace was there now.

Naked.

Leto?

Yes?

Are you all right?

Was he all right? Dammit, he could barely breathe or think. The *breh-hedden* had done this to him, rendered him insensible.

I'm fine.

I'll wait for you here.

Good. Good. He nodded, even though she couldn't see him. He felt that she was no longer there, no longer connected telepathically. It was something that he could communicate with her at a distance, but then he was a vampire of power and she was the blue variety of obsidian flame.

His heart sank. What the hell was he supposed to do with all of this?

He lifted his arm, an unconscious gesture, and folded straight to his bathroom two stories up. The cabin had two floors and a basement. The upper floor consisted of a small study, a large bathroom, and a bedroom. He was a big man and he needed room.

Sometimes at night he would pace the length of the upper floor, from window to window, a distance of fifty feet. The bedroom had a fireplace. When he wasn't pacing, he sat in the nearby large leather chair and stared at the burning logs, at the flames rising, at the latent power of the wood being released in the form of heat.

He tried to spend part of each day chopping wood just to rid himself of some of the deep, unrelenting tension he felt.

With a thought, he turned on the shower. He looked into the mirror. Christ, he had Grace's blood spread over his lower face, his neck, his chest.

He feared going lower, examining more of his body, afraid of what he'd find.

But he had to know.

He glanced at his cock then drew in a deep shuddering breath. Oh, thank God. He had feared he would find blood, that in his beast-like state he would have hurt her, that he would have made her bleed. But he hadn't, thank you, Creator.

He turned and moved into the shower, the broad circular head slamming pinpricks of water against his hair and scalp. It felt so good. He wanted to get clean, to be cleansed of all that worried him, troubled him, and guilted him up. He took his time, using a loofah and shower gel. In his ritualistic way, he began at his forehead and scrubbed carefully down his body, one limb at a time, until even his toes were burnished.

He washed his long hair and used a healthy amount of crème rinse after, the only thing that kept his mass of hair in order. He had once told Greaves that his long hair would be a constant reminder to Endelle that Greaves had succeeded in turning a Warrior of the Blood to his cause.

The truth, however, had been very different. His warrior hair was the one thing he had held to symbolically as a hope that he would return to serve Endelle as he had served all the millennia of his life, as a dedicated warrior. Toweling off, he took a shortcut with his hair and modified his hand-blast to dry it out. Sometimes preternatural power could have an in-a-pinch application. Within a minute his hair was dry, if a little bit singed.

He wrapped a towel around his waist and headed downstairs. He grabbed a beer. Before he went to the hot spring, he needed to gather his thoughts. Mostly, he wondered who the hell he was.

His tribe had come from Eastern Europe. Though his name sounded Greek or even Italian, the root was farther north. At one time, he was called Leotrim d'Istra. Other versions existed as well.

Now he was Leto Distra.

Names morphed, but the old name still meant something to him. His tribe had been known as *the soulful ones,* and the name he'd earned in battle was *one who is brave.*

Those days, however, were long past, and the century with Greaves, betraying those he loved, had changed him. He was fractured inside. He didn't know himself anymore.

He didn't recognize himself. Parts, yes, like his warrior nature on one side, but this other part was big, demanding, even oppressive. Who was this beast?

In his three thousand years of ascended life, he'd never experienced anything like what he was going through. Was he part death vampire now and forever? He didn't know. But his last thoughts before passing out had been *Grace has come home. I'm safe now. I'll be okay.* And finally, *Oh, God, I can breathe again.*

He went downstairs and sat at the dining table in one of the tall-back chairs. He leaned his elbows on the carved wooden table and put his head in his hands.

The sex.

The sex had been magnificent, like every fantasy he'd had about Grace for the past five months all rolled into one.

But he'd been so damn rough. Had he hurt her? She hadn't seemed hurt. She'd seemed . . . *enrapt.* He smiled, just a small quirking up of his left cheek. Grace was such a pure soul; he would never have believed this of her, this complete abandon in her lovemaking.

He glanced at the clock, trying to determine just how long he'd been out.

It was nearly five. The games were due to start in two hours and he had a speech to make.

Duties to attend to.

He stood up. With a wave of his hand, and with long practice, he donned flight gear, all heavy, battle-worthy black leather, a kilt that was as familiar as air, battle sandals, shin guards, silver-studded wrist guards.

Time to speak with Grace. *May I fold to your position?* he sent.

There was a slight pause and his body tensed. Why the silence? Was something wrong? Was she in trouble?

Yes, of course you can come, but . . . I want to stay in the hot spring. Is that all right with you?

Even thinking about her in the spring to the north of his cabin brought pleasure gripping his cock. The location wasn't far, just a hundred yards, no more, in a cluster of rocks. And Grace had found it. He sighed. Perfect.

Leto?

I'm here. Sorry. The images. But I wish to speak with you before I head to the games, and later I'll want you to have a contingent of Militia Warriors around you while you fold to the landing platforms.

He heard a mental sigh. *As you wish.*

Sometimes the way she spoke, her word choices, surprised him. *As you wish,* for instance? But then she'd been convent-trained for a century.

See you in a few, he sent.

Grace floated in the small, decadent, heavenly pool of steaming water. The mountain air was cool in early September, the water hot and relaxing. Wisps of mist floated and swirled from the water in continuously moving patterns. The forest was beautiful at twilight. She ached in so many wonderful places that all she could do was smile up into the sky. She felt safe and free.

Leto had worked her neck fiercely, taking her blood. She touched her neck and rubbed a finger over the swollen tissue. She didn't want it to heal too fast. She wanted to savor the memories as long as she could.

She flapped her hands just a little and moved her body in a circle. There was enough room to stretch all the way out, and she would have done that now, but not with Leto coming. She thought it imprudent to greet him with her breasts bobbing above the waterline like two small islands, a pebble in the center of each.

The image made her smile.

Dear Leto.

She had missed him. She understood that now. She had missed him as much as life itself. She had known him all her two thousand years, even if their paths crossed infrequently. Even so, he'd been a constant in her life and an excellent friend to Thorne, having served as Thorne's mentor until recent decades. Leto had also inspired her erotic poetry at the Convent—the one signal, even to her own committed and devoted mind, that perhaps she needed a different life than the one ordered by the dogma of the church.

So here she was.

"Grace?"

Leto.

She turned in an easy circle, flapping one hand more than the other, her knees bent to keep her chest below the water. When she was in position to face him, she smiled and a soft vibration flowed through her body. She let loose another sigh, deep and carrying a slight groan. Was that her obsidian flame power or just her desire for her *breh*? How strange her life was right now.

Because of her heightened vision, she saw Leto as in a glow. Her man was in warrior gear. With his hair tight in the *cadroen,* he looked fierce, handsome, god-like, and powerful. Made for war.

He was an amazing vampire, a philosopher and a warrior combined.

Lest she get caught in his beauty, she asked, "You wanted to talk?"

"I thought we should." But his gaze drifted to her chin then her shoulders and chest. His lips parted and the air smelled even more of the forest than before. What an elegant scent.

She smiled. "Maybe you should sit down on the spring's edge." A hand-hewn stone shelf rimmed the entire pool.

He sat down with his back to her. His shoulders dipped a little. "Why did you return?" he asked. "Why now?"

So he wanted answers. She would try hard to be as honest with him as she could. "Because I heard you calling to me. I have all along, you know. From the time I left Second Earth five months ago."

"What do you mean?"

She remembered the sounds of his beastly roars. Even between dimensions that sound had reached her, burrowing into her heart, reminding her that she had left behind a warrior who carried a *breh*-scent meant just for her. "When you roared in your pain, I could hear you, all the way to Fourth. No one else could. Just me. But I heard you. That's why I came to you today. And . . . it was time."

She watched him nod. His leather *cadroen* bobbed. "You're very powerful."

"And we have a connection," she said. "Though I don't understand it."

"I don't, either, but there is something I must know. Did I . . . hurt you? Earlier, I mean."

Grace drew in a sharp breath. "Of course not. You must never think that what happened between us wasn't consensual, or that I didn't savor every second of it, or that you hurt me. I promise you, I'm uninjured."

"Good. I was so afraid."

"You needn't have been. But now I have a question for you, maybe a dozen, in fact. What is this that you've become, this extraordinary creature—all Leto, yet *more*."

"You mean this beast?"

"Yes." She chuckled. "This beautiful beast. The one I personally hope to see more of."

At that, his back tensed and he twisted his head slightly to look at her. His nostrils flared. "The entire forest smells like a sweet meadow right now. That's what I smell, you know, when I'm around you, your *breh-hedden* scent. But I can't believe you would speak well of this beast."

"He's *you*. Why wouldn't I speak well of something that is *more* of you?"

He looked away again. "That is your renowned compassion speaking, your acceptance of everyone around you. But this beast that you praise is a death vampire, or the remnant of one. At least that's what I think it is. How can you speak well of that?"

"Do you know for certain that these manifestations are a result of taking dying blood?"

He shook his head. "I'm really not sure. But it seems logical."

"Yes, I suppose it does. Did you ever seek treatment?"

"I stayed in the hospital in Metro Phoenix Two for a

couple of weeks for tests and observation. My beast even emerged for the staff once. The nurses wouldn't come near me but I could hardly blame them.

"After that, I had a complete blood transfusion and I spoke with Alison for hours. She thought there were three possibilities for this transformation: a consequence of having taken dying blood, an unheard-of emerging power, or possibly the results from having taken Havily's blood."

"Alison is very wise. So it is possible that what you're going through has nothing to do with dying blood."

"Yes, it's possible."

He was still facing away from her, bent over slightly. "There is something I must know," he said. "Why . . . *why* did you leave with Casimir five months ago? I've never understood. I mean I know you scented him, as you scent me, but how could you have chosen him, of all vampires?"

She paddled a little bit more, her knees still up, her gaze fixed on the small waves she created in front of her. But how to explain? "I had to go because of a powerful intuition I experienced about Casimir's future. Every cell of my body cried out that it was necessary, that I would not survive if I did not go with him; nor would you. What I believe, Leto, is that our fates, yours and mine, are intertwined with his, and I had to be with him to make sure we were all safe. When I left, it was with the certainty that if I didn't leave with him, I would lose you both, that you would both die."

"You believe you left to protect me."

"Yes, though I have no way of proving it. Marguerite had the same experience with Casimir once. She prevented his death some months ago because she knew, in the same way that I do now, that Casimir had to live, that he has some critical mission to perform in the future."

"But you don't know what it is?"

Grace shook her head, her long hair pulling to and fro beneath the water and causing more ripples. "No. Neither Marguerite nor I know. However, I am convinced it was about saving your life."

"How do you know that?"

She shook her head. "I just know. I think it's my obsidian power at work."

"So Casimir is no longer your *breh*?"

"No, he is not. I no longer scent him, nor does he scent me."

He rubbed his face with his hands as though working hard to make sense of the incomprehensible. "So why do you think you stopped scenting him?"

"It happened when he made the decision to enter Beatrice's pools of redemption." She explained about Beatrice's unique gift to redeem souls through extensive baptism in graded pools.

"I know of Casimir's exploits," Leto said. "He must have been in agony."

"I suppose you are making light of it, but he was in terrible pain, pushing himself hard as he went from one baptism to the next, working to change the future. We have both seen his death, but Beatrice said that if Casimir completed the program, he wouldn't die. He's so changed. More than anything in life he wants to be a proper father to his sons, to be worthy of them." She told him about not sharing Casimir's bed any longer as well. "Not for weeks."

She also spoke of her desire to fulfill her duty in the war against Greaves. "I just wish I was more powerful, like you and like Thorne, even like my twin, Patience."

At that, he laughed. "You're kidding, right? Grace, you can fold between dimensions, three of them. And if you'll remember, you appeared to me in Moscow Two, five months ago, in the form of what looked like a ghost. You took me away from Moscow in some mysterious preternatural stream of energy, back to your convent cell. You saved me from certain death. How is any of that *not* powerful?"

She shook her head, wanting to explain. "I guess I didn't mean preternaturally powerful. I meant a kind of internal fortitude. Warrior strength. My inclinations are more spiritual. I lived in a Buddhist monastery six centuries ago and more recently spent ten decades in a convent."

"I always thought you were unique, and perhaps if there

hadn't been a war, I might have done the same. And your brother speaks with such reverence when he talks about you. He has from the time he joined the Warriors of the Blood."

"But Thorne never really understood me."

"That much is true, but he envied you. He envied your freedom. I did, too. You were even free to choose a devotiate's life in the Creator's Convent."

"Free to give up my freedom."

"Exactly."

"And now my freedom seems to be disappearing." That was the truth she hated.

"I think you're right. For that, I wouldn't blame you for heading back to Fourth."

"I'll never go back. That much I know. I belong here." She could sense that he didn't fully believe her, but time would prove her intention.

"So I've wondered: In all the time you were gone, did you ever contact your obsidian flame sisters? Fiona or Marguerite?"

"No, I didn't."

"You never felt the desire?"

"On the contrary. I have never stopped wanting to reach for them. It's like a pressure in my chest, a need, a craving, almost an obsession.

"Sometimes I think I must be crazy to have come back. But now that I'm here, Leto, you should know that I'm determined to become part of the obsidian flame triad and to do all that I can to help Endelle and her administration bring Greaves down. More than anything, I despise how much he has hurt our world, especially those I love and care about, you and Thorne in particular. But now I'd like you to tell me something: What do *you* want of me?"

He stared at her and remained silent for several seconds. "I don't know. I seem to need you in this inexplicable, primal way, especially when my beast takes over. But right now, when I can be rational . . ."

She paddled over to him, close to where he sat. "When we are both rational, neither of us has answers."

He smiled. He leaned down and touched her face. "I'm glad you're here."

"Me, too. I'm going to leave the pool now. I just want you to be prepared."

When he nodded, she slowly levitated up and out in order to avoid the rough rocks that surrounded the edge of the pool. When she finally stood in front of him, she put her hands on his face. "But I will tell you this: I did not come back to torment you by playing a push-pull game about Casimir. I am not a cruel woman. My life with Casimir is over. I will not go back to him. Ever. Don't ask me how I know, I just do. Also, I know he's determined to follow me here, but when he comes, you must promise me to let him be. Can you do that?"

His jaw turned to flint and his eyes hardened. "If he touches you, I will go mad."

"I will not permit him to touch me. That is my promise to you. I will not be with Casimir again. Yet there is something I need you to know if we are ever to piece this whole mystery together and make sense of it. While I was with Caz, I became a mother to his children, to Kendrew and Sloane. No matter what happens here or on Fourth Earth, I intend to be part of their lives."

Leto saw Grace as in a glow. She was so beautiful, yet speaking of Casimir put hot coals in his blood. He felt ready to fight him to the death over having taken Grace away. Yet here was Grace demanding that he set his rage aside.

Time swam before him like a perpetual motion instrument, back and forth, back and forth, tormenting him, past–present, past–present.

He had been a powerful warrior, then a traitor-spy, once more a warrior, now a beast. He was jealous of Casimir.

Before him was all that he desired, yet he saw Grace through the haze of his pain and the depth of his rage. Mostly, he just felt unworthy of this woman.

She caught his arms. "Leto, please don't look at me like that. Please understand that I'm not a saint."

"But you are." His words were barely formed, just a whisper in the air.

She smiled suddenly. "How much of a saint does it make me when I want you so ferociously? Do you know that I wrote erotic poetry while I was in the Convent, and it was always about you? No, a saint I'm not."

"Are you saying that the whole time you were in the Convent, you were writing poetry about me?"

She smiled softly. "Very sexy poetry while thinking of you. And that was before I brought you out of Moscow Two."

When she shivered, he extended his arm straight out to his side and folded a fleece blanket into his hand. He wrapped her up then drew her close. His battle gear wouldn't exactly give her comfort, but she leaned into him anyway.

He searched her eyes. "I owe you my life, Grace. I was near death when you brought me into your convent cell and fed me your beautiful blood. You stayed with me over the next few days, and fed me a second time. I would have died but for you—and it wasn't just your blood. Your kindness fed me just as much, and your acceptance of me even though my service as a spy, as Greaves's right-hand man all those decades, helped to strengthen his hold on Second Earth. Your compassion saved my life."

"Leto, I know your soul and that you suffer with a profound sense of guilt over building Greaves's army. But I also know that you wouldn't have done it unless you felt it was necessary to complete your mission. So you have no reason to feel guilty. You were under orders, and like any good soldier, you did your duty."

He held her close. She was well named. A woman could not have had more grace than the woman in his arms. Her words were a balm to his tortured soul. "I wish that I had known you better all those centuries."

He felt her sigh. "I wasn't exactly present in my life then. All I was really doing was avoiding the war."

"Now you're here."

She drew back. "Now I'm here. And all I'm asking is that you forgive Casimir."

He sighed heavily because the mere mention of that hedonist's name brought shards of rage piercing his skull. "You'll have to give me time, Grace. I won't easily be able to forgive the man who took you away from me."

"I know. But you must try. Please. And trust in what I've told you; that our fates are secured together with Casimir's, that without him none of us will survive."

"You're asking me to forgive the past because of something that is going to happen in the future, something that required you to leave with Casimir all those months ago."

"Yes, that is exactly what I'm asking."

Leto knew she was right. That was the worst of it. He had been an ascended vampire for thirty-two hundred years and he knew how these emerging powers worked. Things were known, or not known. The future became very fluid. Faith had to be applied . . . and trust. Did he trust Grace, in this new obsidian power of hers, the absolute *knowing* that she experienced, even about Casimir?

The answer came to him in a strong *yes*. He trusted her and he believed in her, but that didn't mean that she would be loyal to him or even succeed in remaining alive. Both realities drove a stake through his heart.

Yes, he knew the score. Very little was permanent in ascension, so just how was he to commit himself to the woman in his arms?

The hell if he knew. "I have to give a speech at the opening ceremonies about an hour from now. Let me fold you back to the cabin and you can shower and dress. After I'm gone, I'll send two squads of Militia Warriors to guard you." When he felt her stiffen, he added, "And in this, my dear Grace, you will accept my orders. If I must overcome my bitterness toward Casimir"—the name came out laced with a little sulfur—"then you must accept what protection I can offer you. Greaves will soon know that you've come back, if he doesn't know already. I want you safe."

He felt her take a breath then sigh like she was swallowing a brick. "Fine."

"Yes. Fine. I'll fold us now."

"As you wish."

Actually, what he wished was to take her back to bed.

But that would have to wait. Hopefully, not for long. This first of three nights of the warrior games would only last a couple of hours. Then, if they weren't quarreling, he would make love to her again. And again.

Change is a mirror with many facets,
Always reflecting the soul's long journey.

—*Collected Proverbs*, Beatrice of Fourth

CHAPTER 4

Greaves sat at the head of his Geneva Round Table, in the throne-like chair he had designed to place him above any who would come to serve the Coming Order. The table represented his dreams of one day ruling Second Earth. He put his finger to his lips and plucked. He could feel the frown between his brows.

Earlier, he had felt the cosmic ripple indicating that Grace Albion, the blue variety of obsidian flame, had returned to the lower dimensions.

On the heels of this unwelcome sensation came the reports from his Seers Fortresses that had shrunk his testicles. Essentially, a decisive battle was coming. Thorne's army, supported by the obsidian flame triad, would be mobilizing soon. But that was all the reports had said—not when there would be a battle, or who the victor would be.

He sighed heavily, his gaze drifting over the table, back and forth. He had not gathered an assembly of High Administrators here in almost two years, from the time that Alison Wells had ascended to Second Earth and bonded with Warrior Kerrick. Her ascension had been the beginning of a long nightmare where his plans were concerned. Since her arrival, even more powerful women had risen to become bonded with several of the über-powerful Warriors of the Blood, ultimately changing the political landscape and forcing Greaves to shift his strategies again and again.

At present, the round table was empty and would remain so until the war was won. But for the first time in his long life, he knew that all his glorious dreams, including an administration that would meet here in Geneva and run the Coming Order, were in jeopardy.

He leaned an elbow on the well-padded arm of his chair and tugged once more at his lower lip.

Grace had finally returned from her little sojourn on Fourth, studying at his mother's knee while romping in Casimir's bed. His mother would have liked Grace's spiritual inclinations, and Casimir would have made liberal use of her body since apparently he had been her *breh*.

Now she was back, having left both Beatrice and Casimir behind.

Though he prided himself on his generally positive attitude, he couldn't help but feel morbid about her return. In point of fact, he had been dreading this moment for one simple reason: He would now have to deal with obsidian flame, because Grace would complete the triad.

The truth was that Greaves simply didn't know what obsidian flame would be capable of once it launched. Two of the pieces were already in place. Fiona Gaines, now *breh* to Warrior Jean-Pierre, was the gold variety, and Marguerite Dresner, *breh* to Thorne, was the red variety. Add blue, as in Grace, and who knew what level of power the three women could achieve. It was even rumored that Thorne, himself, was obsidian flame, but Greaves didn't know what his role was, or possibly could be. So the whole thing was just one giant assfuck waiting to happen.

Five months ago when Grace had taken off with Casimir, she had disappeared from the future streams, which had then forced Greaves into a holding pattern. Unable to learn *when* she was most likely to return, he knew that any attempt to take over Second Earth risked the possibility that she could show up, engage with obsidian flame, and destroy his plans.

However, he still had the advantage over Endelle in terms of the size of his army. At two million strong, thanks to Leto, he could subdue Endelle's forces any day of the week. In addition, he had some sway with COPASS, since at least a third of the members were addicted to dying blood. It wasn't a perfect situation, but he could frequently manipulate international politics to side with him.

On the other hand, Endelle still had the majority of territories aligned with her. Of course, she was now losing them at a rate of one a week because Greaves had been impressing the High Administrators with his army as well as offering all sorts of incentives to align with the Coming Order.

But Grace was back, and he would have to start dealing with her. She and Leto would be his primary targets over the next few days. His secondary object was to destroy the hidden colony network on Mortal Earth. His Seers Fortresses had relayed a constant stream of prophetic information about that network, which indicated Leto had built up a formidable army among what turned out to be a thousand hidden colonies worldwide on Mortal Earth. According to Seer information some of those colonies had over ten thousand residents.

But finding the colonies had been a bitch. However, with the first location mapped and his teams reporting great success with his transmitter concept, he knew that within days all of the colonies would be visible on his electronic grid.

For that reason alone—that the hidden colony network was nearly in his grasp—the timing of Grace's return frustrated the hell out of him. Once he knew the exact locations of each colony, he had planned on destroying them one by one and thereby the army that Leto had built within the Militia Warrior population of each colony. After each community was brought under his control, he would then extract what he believed was a vast wealth of Seers and force them into his various Seers Fortresses. He dared even the powerful Marguerite to best him then.

But now Grace was back, which would no doubt put obsidian flame into play. The timing was an absolute bitch.

He closed his eyes and calmed his spirit. He would need to keep a cool head to face the challenges of the next few days and weeks. He developed a new mantra: *Stay focused, capture and eradicate Grace, destroy the hidden colonies.*

As he rose from his chair, he decided it was time to put to work his most powerful Seer: Owen Stannett.

He focused on Stannett and found him in his private meditation room, where he knew the pervert liked to cruise the future streams and do his own form of porn viewing: real couples, future time. He gave him a mental nudge as a warning, waited a few seconds, then simply folded from Geneva Two all the way to the inner depths of the Illinois Two Seers Fortress.

He found Stannett on his chaise longue, zipping up his pants and rising to a sitting position. "Master," Stannett said, looking up at him. His cheeks were flushed as he patted the immaculately coiffed wave alongside his head.

"Enjoying yourself I see."

At that, Stannett smiled. "Always, but to what do I owe the honor of your visit?" He turned and slid his legs over the side of the chaise.

"Well, my friend, if you had not been so busy beneath your leathers, you might have noticed a slight wavering in the fabric of space and time, a rumbling as it were in the order of the entire universe."

Stannett frowned.

"Grace has returned."

His eyes went wide. "Well, finally. What do you intend to do?"

"To find her and separate her from the herd if I can. Then I'll give her to one of my Third Earth death vampires as a snack."

Stannett eyed him carefully. "I've always wondered how you managed to bring Third Earth death vampires down here to Second Earth when the portal to Third has been closed all this time."

At that, Greaves smiled. He had his own secrets, and since he didn't really trust Stannett, he said, "I have many powers, my friend."

Stannett chuckled. "Well, I do like the idea of giving Grace to your vampires to feed on."

Stannett was not a squeamish vampire, but then a man who had raped his own Seers when he was the High Administrator of the Superstition Mountain Seers Fortress did not have the loftiest morals.

"I want you to recommence your experiments harnessing yourself to six Seers. I must have *pure vision*."

"But, master, you know the difficulty. The Seers keep dying."

"I no longer care. I shall have the best Seers from my Mumbai, Johannesburg, and Bogotá Fortresses shipped here as needed. From all your experiments over the past several months, we both know that a more powerful Seer has a greater chance of surviving the process. The Coming Order is in grave danger because of obsidian flame and because of the colonial militia. Grace completes the triad, as you well know. I must have the most perfect visions of the progress of the triad over the coming days. Are you still unable to track any of the Warriors of the Blood?"

"Marguerite guards them all from me while in the future streams. She has great power. Greater than mine."

"But I know that you have the power to block her in the future streams as well, right?"

Stannett nodded.

"Then do so going forward. But right now, I'd like a little information." He directed Stannett to recline once more on his chaise longue. "I want you to enter the future streams and as you do, I will join my mind with yours so that I can see what you see. I want you to focus on Grace. At the very least, I want to know where she has gone, though I already suspect she is with Leto at the Seattle Colony."

Stannett stretched out once more, folded his hands over his stomach, and closed his eyes.

Greaves put his hand on Stannett's forehead and slipped

within. He ignored the chaos that came at him from all quarters, all that Stannett was as an ascended vampire. He joined his mind to Stannett's as the Seer began to focus. He had done this a handful of times over the centuries so he knew what to expect. But he was still surprised at the beauty of the future stream ribbons that flowed endlessly away from the eye and stretched in an infinite range of colors.

Stannett centered his mind on Grace, and a lot of the chaos disappeared.

The line of ribbons began to move rapidly for several seconds, then slowed until an iridescent blue ribbon of light appeared, bearing a central stream of red and gold. Greaves could feel that the ribbon belonged to Grace.

Stannett picked up Grace's ribbon again and felt his way into the immediate future. How curious that Greaves could tell that what he saw would happen this very evening. Though he had not been to the Seattle hidden colony, he could sense the location. How absurdly quaint. Beyond the rows of cottage-like homes, each with attached vegetable gardens, was a massive setup like a medieval fair with canvas booths. Opposite the booths was an oval track set up for runners with lanes. In the center of the racetrack were all sorts of jumbles of logs and blocks and old used tires, like you'd find in army training camps. This his Seers had prophesied; he recognized the warrior games.

The vision moved suddenly to Grace, who sat in the grandstands near the oval track beside Leto. She held his arm and looked up at him. She wore a long loose skirt, jewelry on both her wrists, her hair curled and hanging in a golden cloud around her shoulders and down her back. An array of silver stars crowned her head.

She looked different, changed, more womanly, less like a convent devotiate. But then she'd shared Casimir's bed. Maybe he'd brought her up to speed.

The vision panned back even farther, but what Greaves saw sent a chill straight through him. On Grace's left were Marguerite and Thorne, and on Leto's right sat Fiona and Warrior Jean-Pierre.

In other words, obsidian flame would start coming together tonight.

He had seen enough of the warrior games. To Stannett's mind, he sent, *I want you to focus on the hidden colony we mapped at Nazca in Peru.*

Stannett merely shifted his focus. The ribbons began to move rapidly for a few seconds, this time in the opposite direction, then slowed. A sand-colored ribbon rose. Stannett dove within so that Greaves saw the very small colony, with just a few hundred ascenders in residence. Above the mossy dome of mist, now partially burned away, dozens of death vampires appeared in flight, beautiful black wings flapping. They descended on the colonists below, in close-mount, wings pulled in tight. When the screaming started, Greaves smiled.

He watched the entire vision play out until the moment Leto arrived; then the vision faded, blocked by Marguerite. But he was left with an idea that involved Leto and at least ten of his Third Earth death vampires. He was still very unhappy that Leto had proved to be so disloyal. He wanted his skin and if he could get it, he would. Given that he knew where Leto would be, this seemed as good an opportunity as any to make an effort.

As he drew out from the vision, he had his next course of action in hand. He would destroy the first of the colonies, a good beginning. And in the process, maybe he could take Leto down as well. No doubt Endelle would retaliate, which he hoped would mean that she would make some sort of use of obsidian flame. More than anything else, he needed to figure out what the triad could do if he had any hopes of winning the coming battle.

He reiterated that he wanted Stannett to put all his effort in to harnessing Seers, as many as it would take to achieve pure vision. "This is your top priority. I must have the best possible information that you can provide me. The next several days will be critical to the Coming Order. Do you understand?"

Stannett nodded gravely. "I understand, master."

"Good."

With his plans set in place, Greaves smiled the entire distance back to Geneva.

"But I miss Grace already." Kendrew's brow tightened.

"All will be well," Casimir said. "She had to return to Mortal Earth to help a friend, but she will be back. She promised me she would."

Kendrew didn't look convinced, but why would he trust anything Casimir said? He hadn't exactly provided his boys with the most stable environment—except of course for these several idyllic months with Grace, in Beatrice's palace. He'd actually watched his boys start to relax, even to run and play as boys should.

Casimir lay on the soft silks of his bed, in the redemption gown of white linen that he wore day and night since entering Beatrice's program. His skin felt as though it should be blistered because he was in such terrible pain, his soul no less so, but he knew the pain he felt was of a spiritual nature and would soon pass.

For now, he had much to think about.

Beatrice had tried to warn him to follow the program and to not hurry his steps. But from the time he'd made the decision to enter the program in hopes of preserving his precious hide, he'd experienced a terrible urgency to move forward as quickly as he could.

He had arrived as Grace's *breh* and had taken her into his bed, making love to her for the first few weeks. He'd fallen in love with her and couldn't imagine a life without her, yet he knew that part of his journey was over as well.

But it was when he felt his impending death as strongly as Grace did that he'd made the decision to do the impossible and to attempt to redeem his soul. He wanted to live. More than anything, he wanted to live to raise his boys, to make up for the self-absorbed behavior that had cost them their mother's life.

How odd, though, that the call of the *breh-hedden* had disappeared as quickly as a sigh the moment his toe hit the water of the first pool. He had lost his ability to scent Grace and she him. Their moment of shared passion had passed.

He had never blamed Grace for the disappearance of the *breh-hedden*. She had simply been a light he could not hold. She had saved him by coming with him to Fourth and by encouraging him to enter Beatrice's program. Her presence in his life had made him a better father and a better man and quite possibly had returned his life to him.

He knew the sacrifice she had made in leaving Leto behind. But at the time, he hadn't given a blind bat's testicle about how she felt, only that she was with him and that he'd been able to take her to bed. Now, after experiencing true remorse, and seeing from the perspective of those he'd hurt, he would give anything to undo the deed.

But here was the true punishment of remorse: that nothing could be taken back.

His only consolation was in the nature of the task he'd foreseen accomplishing in the lower dimensions. Grace had sacrificed for him, and now he must return the favor. If only he'd been able to complete the redemption program, he would be home free.

Not so now. Despite his hurrying the process today, he now faced his mortality as surely as he'd let the Grim Reaper in the door himself.

But if there was any way that he could come out of this alive, he'd do it. He didn't care what it took.

Both Kendrew and Sloane stood by the side of his bed. The windows were open and the sheer drapes billowed, letting in the fresh Denver Four evening air.

He reached a hand toward Kendrew and smoothed his fingers over the small wrinkles on his son's forehead. He could sense Kendrew's confusion. Sloane stood beside him, younger and much less certain about all that was happening. His lips were turned down and he leaned into Kendrew. He relied heavily on his older brother, another point of remorse for Casimir.

"I miss Grace, too," Sloane said.

He smiled at Sloane. "I know you do."

Because of Beatrice's program he had a sensitivity to others he'd never known before, so he could feel now all that his boys had suffered because of his narcissistic lifestyle. He had not done right by his children, the first he'd ever had in his five millennia of vampire life. But he would make it up to them, so help him God.

He looked into Kendrew's eyes and held his gaze firmly. "You will be with Grace again, I promise you that with all my heart."

"How do you know, Papa, when everyone leaves?"

His chest hurt as though a boulder now sat on top of him. "Because I saw it in a vision, that you would be camping with her one day."

"When did you see the vision?"

"While I was in Auntie Beatrice's pool. And you know how wise and powerful your auntie is."

At that, the wrinkles began to soften. "She can make butterflies appear with a wave of her hands."

Casimir smiled, but the smile cost him because it stretched the skin of his face. He didn't stop, though. What a small price to pay, this pain he was feeling, for all that he had done in his long wretched life, for the way he had failed to protect their mother from something so simple as a car accident on Mortal Earth. He had heard her screams between dimensions, but because he'd been enjoying himself with another woman, he'd ignored her and she had died.

Oh, yes, his sins were legion.

But he was atoning, and he would continue to atone until the last second of his life, so help him Creator. He opened his arms therefore to his boys. "Come to me. Let me kiss those beautiful foreheads."

They were too young to understand that he was in pain, so as they scrambled over him, he took deep breaths and refused to release the bellows that hung low in the depths of his lungs. He could have screamed for the agony, but he didn't.

Instead he drew his sons close, one to each side, and cradled them, ignoring the fire on his skin and instead savoring that what he loved the most was close to him in this moment.

He talked with them and laughed with them, until they began to slumber. He saw the stars through the sheer drapes. He gave thanks for the beauty of this night and for the path he was on. He ignored the darkness of the future. Above all, he promised himself that he would fulfill the destiny he had foreseen. In a few hours, when he was better recovered, he would pay a visit to Endelle, offering his services as a Guardian of Ascension.

As he slumbered, a dream came to him. He saw an elderly man sitting on a park bench feeding sunflower seeds to pigeons clustered around his feet. The man looked up at him with eyes that shone as he said, "Well met, Casimir. You will attend me tomorrow at the portal to Third Earth."

"How do I find the portal when it's been closed for so long?"

"It's above White Lake on Second Earth, but you have sufficient power to follow the coordinates I give you now. You will awaken in a few hours completely healed. You must come to me then." Casimir felt the information drop into his brain. He bowed to the old man, and the dream faded.

Grace stood in front of the mirror in Leto's upstairs bathroom. She'd taken her time showering, then afterward drying and curling her hair, dressing, putting on makeup, just being a girl. She lifted a hand to flick her eyebrows a little, shaping them. All the silver bracelets jangled, the ones she had crafted herself during her stay at Beatrice's home.

The bracelets made a pretty sound, a relatively new sound in her ascended life.

She was nervous. Leto hadn't exactly seen her like this but she thought maybe she needed to be forthright—not just about Casimir and Fourth and her intentions now that she was back, but about everything.

She'd changed her manner of dress, something Leto wouldn't have noticed since he'd been in his beast-state when she arrived in his basement. Later, at the hot spring, her makeup was gone and her hair plastered to her head, no curls, no beads, no stars, no blue sapphire, no adornments.

She moved to the window of the bedroom and looked down into the open backyard. Two Militia Warriors were standing close together and laughing. If she extended her hearing, she'd be able to hear the gist. But then they were warriors. She probably didn't want to know what they were talking about.

Okay, so she was stalling.

She put a hand to her stomach. Her *bare* stomach. The full-length muslin skirt hung low on her hips, and the top was cut long at the sides but high at the middle of the waist to allow a peekaboo of her navel. Though the blouse had long sleeves, the neckline plunged and she was very much on display. She fingered the small sapphire in the loop just above her belly button.

Her heart tapped a little tremolo.

Would Leto even like this version of her?

"Move it, Grace," she murmured.

She could have folded outside to the warriors, but they'd probably all draw their swords. If she understood their positions, they'd surrounded the house. Also, Leto had talked about folding to the landing platforms, which meant that dematerializing in the colony right now was being monitored carefully.

So she walked down the stairs and loosened up by shaking her hands a few times.

She opened the front door, and four warriors turned in her direction. The nearest was almost as tall as Leto. His brows rose and he seemed to freeze as he stared at her. The rest did as well.

"I'm ready," she said. When no one said anything, she felt a slight blush rise on her cheeks. She'd spent a hundred years in a convent, covered from neck to ankle. She often forgot what the display of a certain amount of skin could do to a man.

She also knew that for this event and among the colonists, she was dressed properly for an outdoor, festive occasion, held at night.

The tallest one, who seemed to be in charge, blinked a couple of times and lifted his chin as though studiously refusing to drop his gaze lower. Yes, she was definitely showing some cleavage, and, yes, her stomach was bare.

"Good evening, ma'am. I'm Warrior Gideon. My squad will see you safely to the landing platforms in the valley proper. I understand you're familiar with the valley and with the Seattle hidden colony?"

"Yes, I am."

"Warrior Leto wanted me to tell you that platforms have been set up on the far western side of the competition zone. That's where we'll be going from here."

She smiled. As though she hadn't been folding all her two thousand years and into tens of thousands of different localities, including Fourth Earth. "You're very kind, but I think I can handle a little fold through the forest and across a fairly narrow glade."

At that, a glimmer shone in the warrior's eye and his lips twitched. "I might have made mention of that fact to Warrior Leto."

"And?"

"He might have scowled at me."

Grace smiled. "Then allow me to take your arm for the fold."

He moved with that easy lethal stride that most athletes and warriors possessed. When she took his proffered arm, he spoke into his com. His squad of eight, from all around the building, folded to his position, assumed a large V-formation flight pattern. A moment later she felt that swift glide of nothingness through nether-space. But despite her confidence, she landed a little unsteadily.

Gideon caught her. He glanced down at her with a questioning brow.

She shrugged. "And after I boasted about my abilities. I do have an excuse, though. My last fold was from Fourth. I forgot how short this one would be."

He chuckled. "Show-off."

She was laughing when half the warriors behind moved

forward and started to march down the ramp in front of her. The rest would no doubt follow. Leto would have arranged this. He had said he would do his utmost to protect her.

Lifting her gaze, she took everything in at a glance. From the elevated position of the landing platforms, she could see that the warrior games were about ready to start. The entire colony had to be present as well as competitors from all over the world. She could hear various languages float across the air.

To the left of the platforms, which was north in this case, were dozens of tents selling clothes, food, trinkets, and jewelry. She'd have to check out the latter, but the smell of grilled meat made her stomach rumble.

To the right were what looked like a number of massive structures that no doubt tested various warrior skills. Arranged throughout were tall poles on which sat metal-sculpted baskets full of wood. A crude form of lighting, perhaps? There were a couple dozen of them arranged down both sides of the event grid. In addition, lines of torches were everywhere, guarded and kept lit by teen ascenders all wearing matching bright orange T-shirts and jeans.

She knew that the Seattle One hidden colony had a strict policy of keeping electricity-based light usage low in order to sustain the colony's secrecy. The overhead web of moss-based mist could only go so far in cloaking the colony.

Excitement permeated the air.

When the first four Militia Warriors parted, she had a view of the ascenders waiting for her at the bottom of the platform. There were two women and four men, and she smiled since she knew them all.

Jean-Pierre stood with his arm draped over Fiona's shoulder, his fingers laced through hers. They were both listening to Jean-Pierre's great-grandson Arthur tell a story of some kind. She still couldn't get over how much Arthur could have been Jean-Pierre's twin.

Thorne stood slightly turned away from Fiona, his hand on Marguerite's hip. She faced Leto and punched a finger into his weapons harness at pec height and was telling him something quite firmly. Thorne didn't look happy. He kept batting her finger away from Leto.

Leto backed up a step. Grace thought she knew what was going on, so she extended her hearing; sure enough, Thorne had set up a possessive growl. Yep, her brother was growling at Leto.

Marguerite whirled on Thorne and shoved at his chest with both hands, but he didn't budge. He just glared at Leto over her head until she finally reached up and kissed him flush on the lips. She had to reach pretty far since Marguerite was the short one of the group at only five-five. She was also very pregnant. Thorne froze and kind of melted all over her, apologizing and kissing her neck and her chin.

Leto stood back from them, but he was smiling and shaking his head.

She heard Arthur's voice as he said, "Holy shit, is that Grace?"

She glanced in his direction and once more felt a sudden heat rise on her cheeks.

"Grace?" Thorne's gravelly voice cut through all the chatter. "Is that you?"

She shifted to meet Thorne's surprised gaze. He was looking her up and down. She nodded.

He ran toward her and her heart warmed up. Was this Thorne? He actually smiled. He was holding her in his arms and twirling her in a circle until her legs and fairly full skirt flowed away from her. She must have looked like a large flag.

When at last she was begging him to stop, he set her down and he was grinning from ear to ear. She quickly adjusted her clothes, pulling the waist of her skirt up and the hem of her top down.

Leto moved up next to her. She heard him giving orders to Gideon and his men, but Grace was focused on her brother. "Thorne, you look so different—and can I say, wow, you actually look happy."

Thorne extended his arm to Marguerite. "I *am* happy, and here's the reason why."

Marguerite led with her belly. Her hair was still short and

very blond, which seemed to enhance her large brown eyes. She looked adorable. Grace greeted her with a hug, though she had to lean down to do it. They'd been cellmates in the Convent, and good friends. She'd missed Marguerite.

Thorne's arm was immediately around his *breh*'s waist, part protective, part possessive, and a big part just wonderful affection. Marguerite put her hand on Thorne's.

"So you've come home," Marguerite said. "I heard you were on Fourth."

"I was."

"What's it like up there?"

"Beautiful. I stayed at Beatrice's palace. It was similar to Endelle's palace but practical, with more hallways and private rooms, a lovely and very large central courtyard with plants from all over the world. And a hanging garden off the second-story balconies." She felt shy again, since everyone was staring at her. "Oh, I guess I forgot the most important part. Many of the homes, like Beatrice's, float in the air."

"No shit," Marguerite said. She then patted her belly. "Sorry, kids." She glanced back at Grace and lowered her voice. "We're trying to curb warrior-speak. But, hey, I'm so glad you're back. We all are."

"It's good to be back."

Thorne brought Fiona forward next. She was the gold variety of obsidian flame, the first to discover her power. Jean-Pierre and Arthur rounded out the half circle on the left, next to Thorne, with Leto on the right.

As Fiona drew close, Grace felt her obsidian power begin to vibrate and rise through the bottoms of her feet as though originating from deep in the earth.

"What's happening?" Thorne asked.

Since Marguerite was already close, Grace glanced at each of them. Power vibrated from one to the next, flowing and rippling. As though they'd always done so, they touched shoulders and formed a circle.

"Oh, the babies are kicking like crazy now," Marguerite murmured.

Grace's power really began to flow, and she knew it was the same for both Fiona and Marguerite. Without warning, their powers combined, though Grace could tell hers was weak since it still hadn't been fully released. She had a sense that the men had moved back a couple of steps, taking it in.

Power swirled and rose. She looked up and three flames of color twirled together; gold, red, and blue.

But the sensation began to feel uncomfortable for Grace and not quite right. "No," she said. A headache crawled up the back of her skull and nearly imploded her brain. "No," she said louder. "Please stop."

"I . . . can't," Marguerite whispered.

"Jean-Pierre," Fiona called out. "Help us."

But it was Thorne who pushed between Marguerite and Fiona and broke the circle. All that power that had been flowing around and building now seemed to flow into him.

Thorne ended up glowing, but apparently that wasn't unusual for his version of obsidian flame. Fiona, too, would glow. Grace remembered stories about Fiona—that when she was first learning to use her power, she would light up the Militia Warrior grid room in Apache Junction Two with her golden aura.

At least Grace could breathe again.

She stepped away from Thorne to look at him, to enjoy the silver light of his aura. She hadn't seen him since his own obsidian power had emerged so many months ago. He lifted his arms wide and turned in a circle. "This feels like heaven."

Grace's headache worsened so that she half fell, half collapsed to a sitting position on the sawdust that covered the event grounds. Leto immediately dropped to his knees beside her. "What's wrong?"

"My head. It really hurts."

"Gideon," Leto called out sharply. "Get one of the healers over here. Now."

"You're barking," she said. She turned her head slightly and looked up at him, offering him a smile.

"You deserve a bark or two. You're scaring me."

"It's just a headache, but it was so sudden. I don't know what's wrong."

Marguerite looked down at her. "I do. You need Leto to bust open your obsidian flame power. It's no picnic to get it opened up, though." She glanced up at Thorne, whose glowing skin was finally settling down. "But it has its perks."

When Thorne's eyes fell to half-mast and he once more cuddled with Marguerite, Grace looked away. The sight of her brother so much in love warmed her heart, but her head still really hurt.

Thank goodness the healer arrived. The woman dropped to her knees and asked Grace to describe the pain. When Grace told her, the healer put her hands just above Grace's head; the result was almost instantaneous. Soothing waves of healing warmth began to flow through her mind, and the pain drifted away. Her lungs opened fully and she breathed deep.

She looked up at the healer and smiled. "That was wonderful. And fast. Thank you so much."

"I'm training to work with the Militia Warriors. They don't have enough women in the healers division yet, but we're getting more assigned to the training program every day."

Grace smiled. Things were changing everywhere. She knew that Horace, who took care of the Warriors of the Blood every night at the Borderland battlegrounds, had mostly men on his teams.

Leto offered her a hand and helped her to her feet. She swatted sawdust off the back of her skirt.

She was about to apologize when a short male ascender, bearing a clipboard and a headset, approached Leto. "Five minutes, Warrior Leto. All is ready for you."

Leto thanked him then glanced around the group. "Ready for opening ceremonies?"

When Casimir folded to the gateway to Third Earth, he had half expected to see the park bench from his dreams. But no such thing. He stood in a large room with windows across one wall that had the capacity to see through a dimensional Trough, something he'd never experienced before.

He turned to look at the opposite wall, which held a set of thick-looking steel gates like something borrowed from a Mortal Earth maximum-security prison. Instinctively he knew that no one could fold into the space without prior permission, undoubtedly from the Sixth Earth gatekeeper.

The side walls of the space were paneled in a fine-grained wood but had no other adornments. The wall to his left, however, had a door that led to another room.

He moved back to the windows, which were curved and created part of the flooring. This portion of the windows could actually be walked on.

He moved there now and below, at a great distance, perhaps a mile, was what he knew to be the extensive White Lake Resort Colony that stretched the length of White Lake on both sides of the man-made body of water. Located on the west side of the White Tank Mountains, the lake was lined with over a hundred hotels and public gardens.

As he looked around, however, he caught a scent, something similar to Grace's scent, yet different. He could smell a meadow now, yet this one seemed richer—as though it had blossomed with a thousand wildflowers all at once.

The trouble was, he liked the scent and the scent liked him so that he began to be aroused. He shook his head. He'd already had one difficult experience with the *breh-hedden*. He didn't want another. But beyond that, what was the likelihood that he would be given a second chance at having something so profound as a *breh*?

He chose therefore to ignore the scent, believing it must be his imagination. As he looked through the window once more, he felt the presence of the Sixth ascender before he saw him.

When the old man materialized, he inclined his head to Casimir. "How do you do? I'm James of Sixth Earth. I've been the gatekeeper here for a few millennia."

Casimir extended his hand, and James shook it.

He'd heard of James. Grace had told him the stories of

Alison, who had met him during her rite of ascension. Apparently, this was the same ascender who had persuaded Leto to serve as a spy for the sixth dimension by appearing to defect to Greaves's camp.

Casimir had several questions, most having to do with the portal to Third, so he launched in. "Were you the one who sealed off the third dimension from all the others?"

James shook his head. "No, that was Luchianne's call. A bit before my time." Luchianne was the first vampire ever and had ascended to Second Earth eleven thousand years ago. "When she saw the danger Third Earth presented to the rest of the dimensions, she made sure the portal was sealed."

"Grace told me that Alison was destined to open the portal," Casimir said. "Has the danger that Third Earth previously posed to the dimensions diminished?"

"No, the danger remains as grave as ever. However, what will be needed to secure Second Earth from the difficulties of Third is to have the portal fully opened. Your former friend Greaves has been slipping Third Earth death vampires through a breach in the portal that we've been unable to locate. If we open the portal, we can seal the breach and thereby ensure that no more of these extremely powerful death vampires can pass through the Trough from this point forward."

Casimir frowned. "But if Luchianne closed the portal, why doesn't she open it back up to set it straight?"

"Luchianne is a stickler for the niceties. She wants a Second ascender to open the portal, which sets a precedent that only Second Earth can open or shut the portal. She doesn't want Upper ascenders to have command over any of the lower dimensional Troughs."

Casimir thought that made sense. Autonomy from dimension to dimension had always been the law. "When I was in Beatrice's redemption pool, I saw that I was to become a Guardian of Ascension—but who am I guarding?"

At that, James smiled. "Haven't you guessed?"

"I haven't got a clue."

The smile broadened to a grin. "Leto, of course."

Casimir's jaw unhinged and his mouth fell open. "Holy

fuck." How the hell did he end up as a guardian to a man whose woman he'd stolen? He sighed. Sometimes Fate had a twisted sense of humor.

"All right, so I'm Leto's guardian. How will this work? Am I supposed to rent a house on Second or something?"

"You can use this space if you like. Nothing can touch you here, although I should warn you that there is a female, a Third ascender who has worked for me for the past century, making sure the gate isn't tampered with. She'll show up from time to time. She serves as a Militia Warrior here on Third, so she's very busy helping to keep the peace."

Casimir thought about the scent he'd smelled earlier. Maybe it was hers. If so, she wore a very strong perfume.

"As for how you manage your guardian job, I presume you have a voyeur window, right?"

"Of course." What Fourth ascender didn't? "Are you saying you expect me to spy on Leto?"

"Yes, to a degree. I can see that you're a changed man, so I hope you'll show some good sense where both Leto and Grace are concerned. And by *good sense,* I mean discretion."

Casimir smiled, though his lips tugged up a little higher on one side of his mouth than the other. In earlier times, he would have kept the window open constantly and savored every naked ass, male or female, he could find, the more action the better.

But now he knew what remorse felt like, and he knew that Grace would be appalled if she even suspected he'd been tagging after her with a voyeur window hoping to catch a glimpse of her locked in a joining with Leto. He couldn't help repress a sigh. "A few months ago, this would have been a dream assignment."

"Kind of sucks to be reformed, doesn't it?" James offered.

Casimir met James's gaze. He was short for an ascender, and all that gray hair led Caz to believe he wasn't looking at James in his usual form. "You sound like you know where of you speak."

James sighed. "I do. But I also know everything will work out just fine as long as I do what I need to do."

"Are those words for the wise?"

James nodded.

"Fine. I'll be respectful and stay focused on my mission." He glanced around once more. "And I'll make this area my home base."

"It's a good space. The door to your left leads to a comfortable suite with a bed, a kitchen, a living area, the usual."

"Thanks."

James gripped his arm suddenly. "Guard Leto. This is most important. Use your Fourth Earth hand-blast capability if you need to and don't let him get killed. He's critical for the future of Second Earth."

"Understood."

"And as soon as you can, present yourself to Madame Endelle as Leto's guardian. Protocol demands that she accept your services."

Leto held Grace's arm pressed around his own as he led the group to the eastern side of the games where several sets of grandstands had been built. Diallo, who oversaw all administrative aspects of the colony, had designated a box for Leto's use throughout the three days. Militia Warriors were posted at each end of the box as well.

As he walked, he kept glancing at Grace. She was so changed. She wore a crown of several small silver stars, and her hair was in a beautiful cloud that floated over her shoulders and down her back. She wore makeup and jewelry but it was her outfit that had his body in an uproar.

The top was sexy as hell and cut low enough to make his tongue tingle. Her cleavage was exquisite. Her skirt rode low on her hips so that more than once, when he reached for her, his hand hit bare flesh. He found himself grateful for a pair of snug briefs and a kilt. Both hid a multitude of sins, big sins.

He leaned forward and looked down to once more catch sight of the blue gem at her navel. His tongue tingled again. The sensation this time sent a vibration streaking down his left leg. He hissed softly, waiting for the mirror sensation to attack his other leg. If it did, he had six minutes to get to his basement; Diallo would have to take over the opening of the warrior games.

Shit.

"What's wrong?" Grace asked. She leaned close. He released her, but only to slide his arm around her. "Nothing. That is . . ." He squeezed his eyes shut for a moment, then took a deep breath. "I'm okay."

Your beast? she sent discreetly.

He met her gaze. *Yes. I'm susceptible right now because you're next to me.*

She smiled, but in her eye was an unholy glint. *I like your beast.*

He guided her around a group of children. *Your skirt and your blouse have my body desiring things I shouldn't be thinking about right now.*

She smiled again. *Good.*

Was this Grace?

He let go of her waist, because she felt too damn wonderful right now. He once more took her arm and was grateful to be distracted by all the well-wishers as he guided her toward the grandstands.

Several enormous screens, a PA system, and a number of cameras were set up to cover the events all up and down the valley as well as to send a secure live feed to the rest of the worldwide hidden colonies.

There were, however, no electric lights anywhere. Though Diallo, the creator of the system of hidden colonies, had perfected over hundreds of years the mossy mist that covered and protected all the colonies around the world, electrical usage was kept as low as possible. Dishes were washed by hand and clothes hung on lines to dry. Gas stoves were used instead of electric. Gas generators were the order of the day, and solar was gradually being implemented as the products improved. But mostly it was the light signatures themselves that were avoided. The grounds, therefore, were lit by torchlight.

That the games were filmed and sent overseas had required a team of advanced mist-makers to get the job done. But Diallo knew his stuff and so far, so good.

When he escorted Grace to the top of the grandstands, he led her first to the box on the left in which Diallo and his wife, Mei-Amadi, were seated. Diallo rose and took Grace's hand. "I remember you well from your visit a few months back, but I don't think you met my wife." He placed his hand on Mei-Amadi's back. The woman bowed slightly. She had lovely Asian eyes that gave her brown skin an exotic look. Overall, she was lighter-skinned than Diallo. Her hair was piled high on top of her head. She looked regal.

"It's very nice to meet you," Grace said. "You both must be so pleased with the event tonight."

"It is wonderful," Mei-Amadi said, her hands spread wide. "To see competitors from all over the globe, from all the colonies. I never thought to see such a thing happen. But we have Leto to thank for this. He has unified our world here in a way neither Diallo nor I thought possible. Truly magical."

The assistant with the headset interrupted. "Please forgive me, Warrior Leto, but it's time."

"Yes," Diallo said. "Get the games started or we will have many unhappy warriors shaking fists at us in a minute or two."

Leto nodded. "You're right. The competitors' nerves will be jumping right now."

Once Grace was settled in his box, he approached the microphone. He took a long, slow breath. The entire fairgrounds had fallen silent. Crying babies were soothed by caregivers and children ordered to hush. Only a breeze set a few flags flapping here and there.

For a long moment, Leto was overcome by the respect he was being paid. Not long ago, he'd been a despised traitor, but all that had changed when Grace had brought him almost magically out of Moscow Two and away from Commander Greaves permanently.

Now he was a resident of the hidden colony and everyone waited to hear what he had to say.

He had taken great pains to prepare a speech with which

to open the games, focusing on how proud he was of the contestants and the hidden colony Militia Warriors, on his gratitude for having a place in their lives. All good stuff.

But as he surveyed the crowd, his heart began to expand. He saw the families he had come to know and love over the past five months, all those ascenders who had embraced him and forgiven him, who had helped him build his cabin. He saw, lined up by colony, the hundreds of warriors, both male and female, who had trained hard under his leadership in preparation not only for the games over the next three days but for the ongoing war against Greaves as well.

He felt a strong need to say something different from his practiced praises. Making use of his most powerful voice, he began, "We're on the brink of war, my fellow ascenders." He heard a rippling murmur pass through the crowd but most remained silent. "We all know it and we all know that this is the reason our warriors have trained as hard as they have, pushed themselves, male and female alike, gotten hurt in the process then pushed harder still."

Several small cheers went up and down the narrow valley.

"But at heart, we are all warriors no matter what role we play in our society. Whether we raise our children to be well loved and strong or whether we teach in our schools or labor in the fields to put food on every table, or build a business to serve the community. This is the war we make, to care for those we love day in and day out. This is the true battlefield of life."

More cheers went up, louder this time. He let his gaze ride the scene from the north where all colorful tents were laid out, all the way south across the event obstacles designed to test the mettle of the assembled competitors.

"Hold fast to the job you were designed for. Do that service to your community and to your world with every ounce of strength the Creator has given you. This is the note you sing in the choir of humanity. Hold that note so that the chorus we create together, backed by the angels of heaven, will prevail against the enemy, wherever evil is found. Tonight, we are all warriors."

A great cheering rose into the dark night sky. Knowing that his words had hit the mark, he cried out very simply, "Let the games begin!"

Jealousy casts a wide net,
But who gets caught in the web?

—*Collected Proverbs,* Beatrice of Fourth

CHAPTER 5

Endelle levitated just at the top of the tree line on the western side of the forest. She wore tight black leather pants and a forest-green embroidered bustier but kept herself cloaked in her own private mist. She had intended just to check in for a moment, to see what the colony had put together for this worldwide event.

She wore the same necklace of miniature pinecones, adorned with preserved monarch butterflies. This was her nod to the natural surroundings even if she'd had the insects' wings dipped in resin to keep them from busting apart.

But it was her stilettos that claimed the prize. She had worked diligently to attach wires to various parts of the shoes; at the end of each wire was a black-and-yellow bumblebee. The wires came to various heights so that it looked as though a cloud of bees buzzed around her. Her design even included shields that kept the bees from getting all tangled up.

Of course the whole ensemble was more frivolous than serious, but given the homespun nature of the event, she thought she fit right in.

The air rippled beside her. She might have been worried,

but she felt the flavor of a Fourth ascender. Maybe Beatrice had come to watch the festivities.

However, as she turned in the direction of the moving air, who should appear but that worthless piece of shit, Casimir. Only he looked really different. "Holy hell, what the fuck happened to you?"

Casimir wore a white robe and was completely bald. She moved in close, still levitating, but scooted up higher in the air and put both her hands on his head. She read the names inked on his skull. "These your kids?"

"My sons, yes."

"Imagine you having children."

"I was shocked myself."

"So, you slumming it or what?"

His gaze took in the the fair-like atmosphere. "I take it these are the warrior games."

"If you're looking for Grace, she's in the stands with Leto, but I suspect he won't give you much of a welcome. He lost it when Grace left and went through some kind of change none of us has figured out."

Casimir glanced at her. She couldn't get used to what he looked like without all his long curly hair. He was still a handsome bastard, though.

"How has Leto changed?"

"Bigger at times, then not."

"Cryptic."

"You can see for yourself if you stick around long enough. So, did you come here hoping to bust up my latest power couple?"

He shook his head. "No, but I have a feeling that my being here won't exactly be welcomed or understood."

"Now who's being cryptic? Cut the shit, Caz. What's going on?"

"I'm here to serve as a Guardian of Ascension to one of your warriors. This particular warrior, it would seem, is ascending to Third Earth."

"What?" Endelle had always had a good sense of things,

especially when a major ascension was in progress. "Who the hell is ascending to Third?"

He swept a hand in the direction of the grandstands. "Why, Leto, of course."

Even the air around her seemed to slow to a halt. Her mind got stuck in neutral and wouldn't budge. She just kept staring at Casimir. Finally, she said, "That make no sense at all."

"Are you sure? You said Leto has gone through a change. Could it be Third Earth–related?"

She frowned because certain things started making sense. Was that why Leto could change into something that resembled Greaves's Third Earth death vampires? Maybe Leto's ability to shift into an über-warrior wasn't about his former addiction to dying blood after all.

But if he was ascending to Third, what about Grace? Usually, if an ascender was married, his or her better half emerged with new powers at the same time. Unless of course you counted obsidian flame as a power matching Leto's ability to morph into Leto-the-Hulk.

A sudden loud thumping drew her attention to the south.

"Fireworks," Casimir said. "How nice."

"Sweet Christ, if you intend to start showing some manners, I might just puke."

Casimir met her gaze and smiled.

At the distant end of the valley, fireworks shot into the air. These were not quite as high or as magnificent as the usual display, probably because they had to be contained within the dome of Diallo's mist.

However, the effect wasn't diminished in the slightest. Music blared through a number of loudspeakers, a kind of brisk Sousa march, and sure enough, at least a hundred DNA-altered swans and geese took to the skies in strict formation, guided by their handlers. Instead of flying straight over, however, they flew in spirals, around and around, in order to draw out the moment. At the same time, all those equally well-trained teens began climbing the poles and lighting the massive bowls of wood. Before long, the field was lit in a startling amount of fire-based light.

It might have been home-spun spectacle, but damn, it worked.

She knew Leto and Diallo had cooked something up as a competition for all the hard training the hidden colonies' warriors had done all around the globe. But she hadn't expected to find fairly grand spectacle and some goddam righteous oratory at the games as well. Leto had somehow reached into the hearts of every ascended vampire present, caught their souls in his hands, and squeezed hard until cries of near-ecstasy filled the valley.

Even she had been moved by his speech, ready to take up arms, or to do whatever she could against Greaves. Leto had moved her, had made her believe that they would win, somehow, and that it rested not on the might of an army, but on the convictions and lives of the average, everyday ascender.

Leto had spoken the truth as well, more than even he knew.

War was close.

The flying squadrons of geese and swans, and a smaller one of ducks, were opposite her now. The music had changed to something by Debussy so that the flying spirals had taken almost elegant and certainly more complicated patterns. Even the fireworks had slowed to match the music. A series of red whales swam in blue-and-gold fireworks off to the south. Magnificent.

And now Leto. My God, was Casimir right? Was he really ascending to Third?

As she extended her gaze to Grace and the crown of silver stars over her long blond hair, she wondered if obsidian flame would be enough, or Thorne's army, or the secret colonial militia that Leto had built.

She spun in the air to face Casimir. "So, you're here to protect Leto until he ascends to Third, have I got that right?"

He nodded.

She looked him up and down. "In a weird-ass, Fourth Earth white robe? You know most of my Guardians know how to use a sword."

"I have other powers. Hand-blast is my specialty."

"And you're going to need it because if you get anywhere near Grace, I have no doubt Leto will aim to kill."

But Casimir didn't rise to the bait. Instead, he remained silent and turned in his newly acquired serene manner to watch the fireworks.

"You know, you're kinda freakin' me out here." Then it dawned on her. "Holy hell, Caz, did you enter Beatrice's redemption program?"

"Her lake of fire? Yes, I did. But I didn't complete it."

"Then there's still time for you to become a more normal version of yourself."

But he merely smiled. "When the hell was I ever normal?"

She exaggerated a big sigh of relief. "That's more like it. You had me shaking in my stilettos for a minute there."

At that he turned to her. "Endelle, never have I known you to shake in your stilettos or boots or anything you've ever worn in your nine thousand years of vampire life."

Endelle grinned, "Damn straight. I'm not the Supreme High Administrator of Second Earth for nothing."

"I believe protocol demands that I request permission from you to serve as Leto's Guardian of Ascension. Do I have that permission?"

Endelle couldn't help but smile. "Never did I think to see the day that you would either serve as a guardian or ask my permission for anything."

Casimir chuckled. "Ditto. So, is that a yes?"

"Hells, yeah! Guard away. And if you have a chance to blast Greaves's testicles off his cock-stalk, don't debate the issue, just do it."

Casimir laughed. "Don't ever change."

"Don't plan to."

He then gestured with a sweep of his hand over the contest grounds. "Are you joining in the fun?"

She shook her head. "Nope. Just came to see the kickoff. I'm setting up a command HQ at the palace. I take it I'll be seeing more of you."

He nodded.

Endelle couldn't believe this strange turn of events: Leto ascending to Third and Casimir, of all vampires, serving as his Guardian of Ascension.

Well, she had her own issues to deal with right now, like setting up an HQ for what might just turn out to be one helluva showdown with Greaves.

"Later," she murmured, then folded back to her palace.

Grace thought Leto's speech was absolutely perfect. She was proud to be seated beside him. She had her arm hooked around his and had begun to feel a little more at ease.

He leaned forward, his gaze fixed on the runners in the mile-long race that ran in an oval around the entire field. He never let his eyes leave the field as he leaned down and spoke to Grace. "The man in the lead is from the Republic of Chad Two. A powerful Seer. He's very fast and one of our best swordsmen. Jean-Pierre thinks that with a little work, and some of Jean-Pierre's power, he could be brought up to WhatBee status."

So this was the world Leto had built since she'd left. Yes, everything had changed.

All those months ago, he had been near-death because of his refusal to take dying blood anymore. He'd also been severely depressed.

Now he was a different man, a new man.

And at times, a beast-man.

She glanced at Fiona to her right. Jean-Pierre had his long fingers massaging the back of Fiona's neck and he was kissing her and murmuring things in her ear that sounded like French. They were so in love.

She looked up at Leto again. She knew she loved him, but could they truly have a forever kind of love? He had been through so much, and she could once more sense in him a holding back, even a sense of guilt and unworthiness, that kept him in a tense state. She felt his restraint, even toward her, even as he desired her. Could they build a life together with so much between them?

Grace felt the bench move. She glanced to her left at

Marguerite, who bounced next to Thorne. His hands never seemed to leave her, always touching her shoulders, her arms, her hands, and sometimes her belly. And when she asked for popcorn, he leaped up and moved so fast, the vendor at the bottom of the grandstand stumbled and would have fallen backward if Thorne hadn't caught him.

How much her brother had changed. And he had made her an aunt-to-be. He was in love, too. *Breh-hedden* love.

She turned back to Leto. She had her arm around his, her hand on his arm. An intense desire to belong washed over her—not just to be Leto's *breh,* but to have a place in this community. And yet this group of ascenders disturbed her, because the men were warriors and she had always loathed the war. Patience's disappearance had driven a final wedge between her and a willingness to be involved.

Yet even her former refusal to participate in the war had changed. She had come back, determined to do what she could to bring Greaves's reign of terror to an end. She wished she was more like Marguerite, however, who rarely flinched at a challenge.

Part of her wanted to rise from the grandstand, walk back to the landing platform, then fold anywhere else, to any other dimension. Another part, however, seemed to be calling to her from the depths of her soul to stay, to see this through, maybe even to become more than she had ever dreamed of becoming.

"Hey." Leto's voice was a soft hush as he broke through the overwhelming nature of her thoughts. "What's wrong?"

She blinked up at him and realized that the entire crowd was roaring their cheers as the runner from Chad took a victory lap.

"Oh," she murmured. The noise was profound, and Marguerite was jumping up and down on the wooden floor support, so Grace slipped into telepathy. *Sorry, I was thinking about obsidian flame and the war.*

He moved his arm from beneath hers, but slid it instead around her waist and pulled her close. *Oh, that's all . . . just the war and your emerging powers. Well, as long as it's nothing serious.*

She smiled, and he was so close that it seemed the most natural thing to do to reach up and place her lips on his. He turned into her and kissed her back until his tongue was in her mouth and his forest scent drenched her. In this moment, held within the circle of his powerful arms, savoring his body close to hers, feeling lightning streaks of pleasure penetrating her abdomen, she thought there was no place she would rather be, or even ought to be, than here, with Leto.

He drew back and shuddered. *You work me up so fast.*

It's the breh-hedden.

But at that he smiled and pinched her chin. *No, Grace, it's you.*

She smiled back. *You sure about that? After all, we've known each other for centuries. Why now?*

His thumb touched her lips. He shook his head. *Maybe the* breh-hedden *brought us together, but it can't be the whole picture. I value who you are, I always have. But hey. Try not to worry so much.*

She smiled. *Not sure that's possible right now.*

The noise of the crowd died down and a second race started, this time with massive hurdles that would require some levitation skill added to the running. Grace leaned into Leto and for once just tried to relax and enjoy herself.

Leto didn't quite understand what he was feeling, but it was like grabbing at air. He couldn't pin it down. Happiness? Contentment? A strangling fear that something would happen to Grace? Maybe it was everything: fear, hope, desire, anguish, all combined.

He held Grace against his side, one hand on her bare waist, the long sides of her blouse covering his fingers as he kneaded her skin, thumbing low into her hip then up to rub the underside of her breast. That her meadow scent kept flowing over him in waves sustained the certainty that he was pleasing her as well as forming a most inappropriate erection. He was hard as a rock and was grateful that the light from the torches and the tall, pole bonfires didn't exactly reach the depths of their grandstand box.

The shadows were covering all sorts of misdeeds. In particular, he was ignoring how Jean-Pierre had been making out off and on with his *breh* for the last half hour. He and Fiona had been together for over six months, and it was clear the pleasure they took in each other hadn't dimmed much if at all. He wondered how soon the two of them would take off.

But Leto was enjoying the games, despite the fact that his thoughts were fixed on just how soon he could get Grace back to his house, into his bed, and make love to her again.

Of course, these were unfortunate thoughts because now he was in pain. He gritted his teeth and breathed hard through his nose a couple of times. He pulled his hand out from under her blouse and went back to just offering her his arm.

That she chuckled softly told him she understood. He looked down at her. She looked up.

All I can think about is your bed, she sent.

He sighed. *Same here. Soon enough.*

He forced himself to look away. It helped that Brynna's event was up next. The woman had powerful thighs and the log climb was one of her favorite exercises while in training, never mind the contest. But she was also competitive by nature.

He said as much to Grace then sent, *She took me under her wing when you left.* He shared with her their camaraderie and that he considered Brynna his best friend.

The loudspeakers blared as the introductions were made for all the contestants, including a fiery Aussie from the hidden Brisbane One Colony and a Japanese competitor from the hidden colony outside Kyoto One.

As the warriors took up their places, he realized Grace had grown very still next to him. He looked at her, but her head was bent. She held her hands together on her lap, which was a little awkward since her right arm was still wrapped around his.

What is it, Grace?

She shook her head. *This is ridiculous. I feel so . . . angry, but I shouldn't. I left you, and she obviously took care of you.*

She was upset about his relationship with Brynna? Jealous? He tried not to smile but he couldn't help it. And damn, wasn't he a bastard for liking it.

He tried to explain Brynna's value to him. *She made sure that I didn't hurt anyone when I turned beast. She would come into the basement with me.*

At that Grace looked up at him, her eyes wide and her expression hard. The starting pistol fired at the exact same moment that she said aloud, "She did *what*?" The last word held resonance, which brought a sort of yelp from Fiona behind him.

Jean-Pierre leaned around Leto and said, "I am sorry, Grace, but Fiona's ears are sensitive to resonance. If you would go easy with it?"

Grace nodded. "Of course. Sorry."

When Jean-Pierre shifted back, Leto stared down at her and again his response was way too male. His eyelids felt heavy as he slid his hands down her arms. "So you're thinking about the basement, huh?"

"That's not what I meant, and you know it."

"Oh, I know what you meant. You're jealous of Brynna, but I love that you're jealous. I just wish I could get you back there right now, take some of the sting out of the situation."

When the crowd started shouting, only then did he slide his gaze back to the event, seeking out the nearest screen. Brynna was neck and neck with the Aussie.

He rose from the bench and started cheering her on, punching his fist in the air. Marguerite knew Brynna well, so she joined in. Thorne, too.

Grace remained seated and frozen in place. She held her arms tight around her chest. This was ridiculous. She wasn't this woman, but she could feel her fangs in her mouth and a rumbling in her throat. Her legs shook. She felt a profound need to sink her fangs just about anywhere into Leto, to mark him and to let him know that what he was doing was wrong.

She had a rational mind somewhere, but for this moment all she could think was that his focus was on another woman, that he had a great deal of affection for this other woman, and that Grace couldn't stand it.

She had to leave. She feared what she would start doing if she stayed. And, yes, it involved her fangs, and more resonance in her voice than Fiona could tolerate, and maybe word choices that would more comfortably come out of Endelle's mouth than her own.

When the cheers became shouts of triumph because Brynna won her event, Grace raced from the box and down the stairs, half levitating the entire distance. She would have folded, but the rules for the event forbade dematerializing of any kind.

She ran past the grandstands, pushed her way through the crowds, and increased her speed, which was significant. She ran straight into the forest. She ran and ran, her mind screaming the whole time, and her fangs protruding unladylike from her mouth.

She could vaguely discern someone running behind her, but her mind was a whirl of angry mush, so she kept pushing on, heading in the direction of Leto's cabin, pushing past fir branches, hopping over big stumps and logs, flying over shrubs and ferns.

Suddenly powerful arms clamped around her and carefully brought all her forward momentum to a stop.

"Grace, what the fuck?" Leto was breathing hard as he turned her in his arms.

She didn't want him to see her like this. She struggled against him, but he was bigger and more powerful so he caught her wrists and held them wide.

Forced to stop fighting, she panted against him, glaring at him from underneath her brows. She could feel her fangs heavy on her lips. His gaze slid to her fangs, and he drew in a sharp hiss.

"Shit," he murmured. His *cadroen* had come out, and his long black hair hung around his shoulders, over his arms and chest. He released one wrist; she squirmed trying to wrench herself from his grasp but he didn't let go. Instead, he pulled his hair over to one side. When she caught sight of his exposed throat and the vein throbbing there, beckoning to her, she grew very still.

She truly hated that this was who she was in this moment, but Leto didn't seem to mind. He caught her around the waist and pulled her close. He even lifted her up off her feet so that her mouth was at his chin level. He leaned into her slightly and whispered, *"Do it. Take what you need."*

Maybe it was his use of resonance when he spoke, she wasn't sure, but she leaned back, planted her hands on his shoulders, and drove her fangs hard into the vein waiting for her. She began to suck on his neck, deep pulls, taking his blood into her mouth and down her throat.

He held her in place, her legs dangling as she worked his throat. He adjusted slightly to hold her with one arm around her waist. With his free hand he glided down her back, slipped beneath the low waistband of her skirt, and when his fingers found flesh—because she wore only a thong—he groaned and pressed her against him.

She slowed her drinking, because what she needed now shifted. He was a hard length against her abdomen. With his blood in her belly and firing her veins, desire streaked through her body, pinching at her breasts, teasing between her legs.

She needed Leto and she needed him now.

Leto had never experienced anything like this in his long vampire life. The last thing he'd expected was for Grace to become so jealous that she'd actually had to leave the games. But as soon as he saw her fangs, he'd understood that she was completely and beautifully out of control.

So here he was, having her draw on his neck. Though her deep pulls had slowed and it was clear her original ferocity was dialing down, everything about this moment was so at odds with the sweet, reverential woman he'd always known Grace to be.

The truth was, he loved it, and the beast in him was yelling at him to finish this the way he needed it finished.

At last, Grace removed her fangs and pulled back enough

to meet his gaze. Her gold-green eyes glinted in the dark forest night. She had run far enough away from the games that silence surrounded them. He was alone with her.

Very alone.

"My turn," he said, his voice deep.

She nodded. He pulled her up against the nearest tree. The rough bark would hurt her but he had a plan. "Get rid of your skirt and thong."

"Okay." A moment later he felt only flesh against the palm of his hand.

With a thought, he lost his kilt and briefs. "Put your arms around my neck and hold on."

She did. "God, I need you."

"Same here."

With one hand, he lifted her left thigh. She lifted her other leg and he supported her underneath. He angled himself and pushed. He found her so wet that his knees buckled as he groaned.

"Don't worry," he said, his voice hoarse. "I'm strong and I can hold you like this."

"I know."

Bending his knees, he began to drive into her. It wasn't the most elegant position but by God it worked, because he was inside her and that's exactly where he needed to be.

She moaned against his ear, then his temple and his neck. There was nothing like strong muscles to get something organized and working just right.

But he needed just a little more resistance so he folded his kilt into his hand, placed the kilt behind Grace, backed her up against the tree, then seated her against the leather. He moved into her again.

Yes, that's better, she sent.

Reassured and with her anchored, he could push the way he wanted to. She kissed him. He tasted his blood, and because she was crying into his mouth, he started pumping hard.

Leto, come. Please. Aloud, she said, "Please. Now."

She threw her head back and then he understood. She

was coming, and that brought his orgasm streaking through his cock. She gripped his hair and grunted, holding back her cries because anyone could be in the forest right now.

He came and came. His cock jerked inside her, and she threw her head back again, hitting the tree and resting there.

She was breathing hard. So was he. He could feel her clench around him, and it was a wonderful sensation: that he was inside her when he hadn't planned to be there quite yet, that he was connected to her like this, to Grace, to his *breh*, that she had been so overcome with jealous rage that she had run from the games, into the forest, probably trying to escape all those possessive feelings.

He knew how she felt. The *breh-hedden* was a tough master. If he'd been able to follow after Casimir, he was pretty sure he would have killed him for taking Grace away.

Kissing the side of her neck, he said softly, "If the situation had been reversed, if you had been cheering for another man, I don't think I could have borne it. I will try to temper my actions toward Brynna."

But Grace pulled back. "I don't want you to have to do that. I feel like such a cretin. I don't even know myself. It's the *breh-hedden*."

He shook his head. "Not entirely. I've talked to both Thorne and Jean-Pierre. They've both said that essentially you just become *more* of who you really are."

At that, she seemed to relax, though she frowned. "Is this who I am? A jealous monster?"

But he gripped her around the waist a little more and pumped his hips once to make his point. "I like this part of you. No, I love that you got so worked up. You can do this for me anytime."

She just shook her head. "How am I supposed to do that and still remain a civilized part of our society?"

He shrugged then kissed her. When he drew back, he said, "Well, I'm not sure. Maybe it's something we'll just have to work on, set some boundaries, have a couple of signals."

"Oh, you mean like when you see my fangs emerge, you'll know I intend to run off into the forest?"

She was sarcastic, but he pumped his hips again, and she groaned against him. "And I'll follow you every time."

He began sucking on her neck. Then he had new idea. "I think turnabout's fair play, don't you?"

"We should get back," she said, but her voice was little more than a whisper.

He licked her neck and what do you know, her vein rose for him. The thought of taking her down his throat brought his cock to attention once more and she groaned again. "Do it, Leto. Just do it."

He bit her and sucked, then went to work on her, driving his hips hard once more.

A couple of hours later, Grace congratulated Brynna on her win. The warrior had a gold medal around her neck suspended on a purple silk ribbon. She was taller than Grace by at least two inches and couldn't seem to stop smiling.

Grace took deep breaths as Leto slapped Brynna on her back and fawned over her. She could see the level of friendship they shared: best friends. Just terrific.

Grace wasn't used to having a boyfriend but she really didn't like that she was so ridiculously jealous.

Marguerite drew close and elbowed her softly. "Hey, do you want me to boil her in oil for you?"

Grace glanced down at her, startled. "I . . . uh . . . what do you mean? Why would you say that?" She tried to laugh, but the sound came out a little strangled.

"You look like you're ready to kill her."

Grace sighed and looked away. "I'm going out of my mind. I mean, he had a life while I was gone."

"Leto wasn't sleeping with her. I know that for a fact. Bryn and I are good friends. She's good people. You can trust her."

Grace looked down at Marguerite and turned a shoulder to the warm exchange five feet away that was driving her crazy. "I know and I wasn't exactly a saint while I was gone. The whole thing is too ridiculous for words. I just can't seem to control how I feel. It's the *breh-hedden*."

"You know, usually it's the other way around. The men

get horribly possessive, although I did see it once with Parisa when I hit on Medichi."

"Wait, you hit on Antony? When? Oh, my God, Thorne must have gone ballistic."

"Yeah, you could say that."

"And Parisa?"

"She wanted to tear my face off. She had just launched herself at me, and was ready to get into a serious catfight, when Endelle intervened and used her stasis skill to stop the action." Marguerite sighed. "I admit I was behaving badly but in my defense, I didn't quite understand at the time what the *breh-hedden* meant."

"But you had been with Thorne all that time in the Convent."

"Yeah, I know. But I was also intent on making my escape to Mortal Earth and living my own life."

"You changed pretty soon after that."

Marguerite glanced at Thorne, who was deep in conversation with Jean-Pierre and Fiona. "Everything changed. I did, my obsidian power emerged, and Thorne really changed. He's spent the last five months building Endelle's army. He's done an amazing job."

"He looks wonderful. Do you remember how red-rimmed his eyes used to be?"

"Too much Ketel One."

"Yes." She met Marguerite's gaze once more. "I wanted to thank you again for being there for Thorne all those years. I was so grateful to you and I know I thanked you, but it never felt like enough. I think you saved his life."

"Well, he saved mine, too. Maybe that's why we were meant to be together—because we ended up saving each other, repeatedly."

Grace looked at Leto, who was still praising Brynna and laughing with her. She thought about what Marguerite had said. Was she meant to be with Leto because they could save each other? And in her case, exactly what would that look like?

Leto glanced at Brynna. "Do you need to report somewhere?"

"Yeah, the coordinator wants all the participants to sign in then head to bed. I'll catch up with you tomorrow."

Leto nodded. "Good. I'll see you then."

Brynna shifted her gaze to Grace and drew close. "It's great to see you again. I'm so glad you've come home to us." She slid her gaze briefly toward Leto, then back. "We've needed you here."

Brynna was being too nice, which made Grace feel guilty and very foolish. "Again, congratulations on winning your event."

Her smile broadened to a grin and she fingered her medal once more. "Thanks. It was a thrill. Well, I need to do some serious stretching, then find my bed. Good night."

"Night, Bryn." Leto's voice carried a hint of affection, which brought Grace's beast rising once more.

As Brynna walked away, however, Grace felt vibrations from deep within the earth that had nothing to do with jealousy. Instead, her obsidian flame power was coming online very suddenly.

Her skirt flowed around her ankles, and as the power rose it moved the long sides of her blouse, then lifted the tips of her hair. She glanced from Thorne to Marguerite to Fiona and back. Each turned toward her.

She didn't understand what was happening. She remembered earlier that something similar had occurred when all three of them were together, yet this still felt different.

Leto's eyes popped wide and he drew close. "You have a blue aura, Grace. What's going on?"

She lifted her hand, waiting. She felt something or someone calling to her, calling for help. By now the power was flowing uninterrupted through the top of her head. She lifted both hands palms up, as if in supplication. A sense of urgency flew through her now in rippling waves, but urgency for what?

She closed her eyes and focused on the call, for she could think of it no other way, as though forces out there were summoning her. Unfortunately it hurt, because her obsidian power wasn't opened all the way yet.

Despite the pain, she kept her focus. She opened her eyes and became fixed on Marguerite. "Check the future streams. Now. I think one of the other hidden colonies is in trouble, but I don't know which one."

Marguerite nodded then turned to Thorne. "I can feel it as well. I need to drop into the future streams and find out what's going on. But this feels big and it feels really bad. Come support me?"

"You got it." He moved to stand beside her, an arm around her waist.

Fiona moved in close as well, Jean-Pierre behind her. "Yes, it feels very big," Fiona said. "My obsidian power is vibrating like crazy."

Thorne addressed Leto. "Get Diallo and Endelle over here. Now."

Choosing the courageous path,
Even while trapped in fear,
Honors the Creator.

—Collected Proverbs, Beatrice of Fourth

CHAPTER 6

As Grace stood in the middle of the event grounds, she swore the very air among the small group took on a tactile quality that could actually be touched.

Leto took command.

He whipped his phone from the deep pocket of his kilt and punched a couple of times. "Hey, Diallo, sorry to intrude, there's a problem and we need you. Can you fold to the landing platforms? We'll meet you there." He nodded as though Diallo could see him. "Good."

He then changed phones, whipping his warrior phone from the top slit in his flight battle kilt. He called Jeannie and issued the order to get Endelle to the colony immediately. "To my position." He then contacted the colony's Militia Warrior HQ. He authorized Madame Endelle's fold, then added, "I want all the Pacific Northwest warriors on alert. Let the Section Leaders know. We'll be assembling teams at the landing platforms ASAP."

Grace held her power steady, uncertain what she was doing, but she went with her instincts. Something big was happening, something dangerous, that much she could sense.

The problem was, her head was really starting to hurt. She took deep breaths.

She fixed her gaze on Marguerite and continued to hold her palms up. Thorne turned to Marguerite. "Are you ready to do this?"

She nodded, then closed her eyes. A second later her body jerked, but Thorne kept her steady so that she didn't fall. Her eyes moved rapidly beneath her eyelids, back and forth, as though she was reading something. Her body jerked again and her hand went to her stomach as she opened her eyes.

She looked at Grace then at Thorne. "We have maybe ten minutes, but I don't know where this is. It's an attack on one of the hidden colonies. The top of the mossy-mist dome just like this one"—she pointed up—"looked as though it had been burned off and was still burning. Death vampires, maybe two hundred of them, were flying into the colony from all directions."

Leto nodded. "Okay," he said quietly. He held his warrior phone and issued orders.

Grace glanced in the direction of the landing platforms. It was amazing to watch all the Militia Warriors, dozens of them, start gathering in squadrons, off to the left of the platforms as though by long habit. Leto's drilling, no doubt.

Leto addressed the group. "I'm sounding the alarm." He spoke into the phone; the next moment a series of tones hit the air in groups of three. The colonists and the foreign contestants all stopped what they were doing. The contest grounds fell completely silent.

To Grace's complete shock, everyone began moving in prearranged directions away from the grounds. Within seconds, only Militia Warriors remained, and all of them were assembling with amazing speed by the landing platforms.

"Leto," Jean-Pierre murmured. "You have worked miracles here."

Leto nodded, but he set his gaze on Thorne.

Thorne was the man in charge, the one who was building Endelle's army and working with dozens of Militia Warrior Section Leaders to formulate battle plans. He said, "It's clear we're looking at trouble with a hidden colony here on Mortal Earth, so I'm deferring to Leto on this. He's set up the global defense system for this dimension."

Leto glanced toward the landing platforms. "My men know what to do. What we need is the location of the attack."

A moment later, Endelle folded right next to Thorne, adjusting a strange necklace of pinecones and butterflies. She twisted her neck and gave the necklace one more turn. "Just got the call from Jeannie that we have some deep shit going on here." She caught sight of Grace. "And why does our latest obsidian flame look like a goddam glowing Smurf?"

A few nervous barks of laughter followed.

Grace couldn't help herself. She laughed as well, then sobered instantly. Dear Creator, her head really hurt.

"We've got trouble." Leto said. He glanced at Marguerite then back. "Future streams just told us one of the colonies will be under attack in a few minutes."

"Which colony?"

"We don't know."

Endelle turned to Thorne, "Well, you're obsidian flame. Can't you find out?" She planted her hands on her hips, which drew Grace's gaze back to the pinecone-butterfly necklace, then to the bees that appeared to be buzzing around Endelle's calves and knees.

Grace was convinced that no one was as absurd as the ruler of Second Earth. She might even have laughed at the strange outfit, but her obsidian power set up a new wave and her head really started to pound. She winced.

Then she understood. "I think I can find the colony. I remember now that when Leto was in trouble in Moscow, my obsidian flame power led me to him through my split-self apparition. I believe I can do it again here. Marguerite, why don't you show me what you saw in the future streams, and we'll see what happens."

"Okay."

Grace crossed to Marguerite and put her hands on her face. "Show me," she said quietly.

The vision flew through her mind swiftly and seemed to

resonate with her obsidian power. The next moment she was flying through space in that same split-self, her ghost-like apparition, the one she'd used to bring Leto out of Moscow Two. She could sense that she was heading south, as in South America.

When she arrived at the vision's destination, she looked around. She could see both the limited farmland and the nearby barren hills. She saw a small town, maybe ten or twenty thousand people. Not far, and to the east of a dry riverbed, lay the colony, all secure and locked down with Diallo's mossy-mist creation protecting the location. However, as she turned in every direction, she could see death vampires on each horizon all headed toward the colony.

She dipped her apparition-self toward the lights of the town and found the name on a couple of storefronts: Nazca. She knew this place. The entire world was fascinated with the famous lines that an ancient culture had drawn in the sand, which could still be viewed, all these hundreds of years later, from high in the air. A spider and a humming-bird were the most famous designs.

Satisfied, she thought the thought and her apparition-self began flying back to the Seattle Colony. When she re-connected with herself, it took a moment to adjust. She opened her eyes and found everyone staring at her with wide eyes. Leto had shifted to support her, holding her by the waist.

She blinked a couple of times. "I'm sure that must have seemed strange but I have the location. Nazca, Peru." At the same moment, however, her headache tore through her skull. She dropped to her knees, clutching the sides of her head. She felt Leto's strong hands on her shoulders and as if at a distance she could hear his voice, but she couldn't re-spond. Tears streamed down her face. "Grace, I'm here. What's wrong?"

Marguerite said, "She has to get that sheath sliced, Leto. It's her power. It's trying to break through. Better do it soon."

"Understood."

* * *

Leto couldn't just leave Grace in so much pain, but he had his teams to lead. He stood up and looked at Endelle. "I need to get my warriors down to Peru now. Can you help Grace?"

Endelle smiled. "Leave her to me, Warrior. Get your men to Nazca." When Endelle drew her phone into her hand and a moment later started barking orders at Alison, telling her to get her ass down to the Seattle Colony, Leto knew he could trust the situation.

He turned and headed to the landing platform. He wasn't surprised that Thorne, Jean-Pierre, and Arthur followed him. Diallo was waiting for him and Leto filled him in.

Diallo frowned. "The Nazca Colony only has a population of four hundred and you say several hundred death vampires will be attacking?"

"Yes."

"It would be a slaughter."

"Not if we can help it. I'm sending the squadrons now." He glanced at the top of the ramp. Gideon stood there awaiting orders. Leto placed a call to the colony's Militia HQ and folding coordinates were laid in within seconds.

Leto met Gideon's gaze and let the orders fly. "To Nazca. Now."

The squads began to fold in brisk succession, eight at a time. Within one minute a hundred warriors had folded to Peru, and the second hundred began folding equally as fast.

Leto nodded to Diallo. Glancing over his shoulder, he saw that Alison was already with Grace.

He turned and ran up the ramp with what he now thought of as his own squad. Once he reached the top, he, Thorne, Jean-Pierre, and Arthur folded to Nazca. Gideon would remain behind to keep the warriors en route to the battle zone until at least a thousand Militia Warriors were doing battle.

Once Leto touched down, and thanks to long training, he moved swiftly away from the landing site, mounted his wings, folded his sword into his hand, and took to the night skies.

Out in the desert, the moon lit up the skies like a beacon.

It was so bright that the ground seemed to be covered in snow.

His warriors, male and female, battled death vampires all over the sky, but it was to the colony that Leto headed. He knew that any colonists attacked by death vampires would die within seconds. No mercy would be shown.

He pulled his wings in tight, dipped and corrected to miss battling squadrons. He aimed for the now visible world of the colony. There was a main street and low simple buildings made of stone blocks, carved out of the land.

He could hear screams coming from houses and alleys between. Once he reached the ground, however, he retracted his wings and entered the first house he came to. There was a lot of blood and too many bodies. He raced through and found a death vampire in the back room with a teen ascender, drinking her down, raping her.

He threw a dagger into his kidney, which brought the death vamp arching back and off the young woman. Leto moved swiftly and with his sword took the bastard's head.

The girl pushed away from the monster, then crawled to the other side of the room. He didn't want to leave her, but he had to go. "Hide," he said.

She held her neck and nodded. She slid quickly beneath the bed.

He left by way of the window, jumping out.

His night progressed in exactly that way. He went from house to house hunting for evil, finding it, striking it down.

He came upon four death vamps in a house on a hill near a small dry streambed. These pretty-boys were huge, and he recognized them for what they were. They belonged to a group of recruits brought from Third Earth, something Greaves had been doing for the past year. No one knew exactly how he'd been doing it, but Greaves was a vampire with many tricks.

Leto knew he wasn't a match for these vamps in his current state. When three of them turned and stared at him indifferently, while the other continued drinking a woman to death, Leto felt the vibration go down his left leg, then his right.

For the first time, he did exactly what Brynna had been encouraging him to do all along: He let his beast take over. At the same moment he mentally adjusted the belt of his kilt as well as the buckles of his shin guards and battle sandals. He got rid of his weapons harness altogether.

"Motherfucker" came out of one of the oversized death vamps. "Where the hell did you learn to do that, traitor?"

Leto smiled. Now, there was one of the great ironies of his life—that a death vampire would call him traitor.

His sword almost felt small in his beast-sized hand. "What's the matter, pretty-boy? You afraid of me?"

"Just because you can morph like a Third Earth warrior? Hell, no. There are still four of us and only one of you."

"Bring it, asshole. Let's see what you've got."

Leto felt more powerful than he ever had before. He held out the palm of his left hand and let a hand-blast fly. The sound was almost deafening in the small house.

The death vamp on the left took it in the chest. He flew backward, hard into the wall. His ribs were smashed in. He wouldn't be breathing anymore.

Leto aimed another hand-blast at the second death vamp, but since the bastard had decided to deliver his own deadly blast, the searing energy met in the middle, soared upward, and blew part of the roof off.

All this activity had the advantage of getting the fourth death vamp off the woman. But knowing the power of these Third Earth death vamps as he did, Leto was still no match for their combined strength and skill, so he used his primary advantage: his battle experience.

He folded behind them, shoved a dagger through the back of one, then folded outside the building and waited.

Two to go.

"Get him" came from inside. "He's out there. I can smell him."

Leto cloaked himself in mist. He listened. He felt the air move behind him. He swung his sword and took the bastard's head off. It hit the stone lane with a terrible thump.

Only one left.

Leto looked up the lane. He extended his vision and saw a number of colonists rising up to look at him. He waved them down and they disappeared.

Good. The people were hiding. Part of the strategy among all the colonies was to teach the people to move the most vulnerable well way from the buildings when the death vampires came.

He smiled, remembering something Arthur had done to taunt death vampires. He made a raspberry sound with his lips. "Come out and play," he shouted, letting his mist melt away.

He wasn't going to hide this time.

The last death vamp leaped through the window, and it was game on. He was huge, like Leto, and had Third Earth skills. But Leto had been a warrior for three millennia while it seemed this bastard had been relying on size alone to win his battles.

Leto circled, his sword held out and away from his body. He watched the bastard's eyes; when they shifted he lunged, blocked, stepped back, then whirled. With another swift lunge, he caught the pretty-boy up through soft part of the belly.

His scream swallowed up the night air.

Leto withdrew his sword. The death vamp fell forward and Leto, also with the practice of millennia, took his head.

He leaned back, bent his knees, and roared into the air.

He pivoted and headed back to the main street on a run, his gaze strafing the sky above, then every shadow nearby. By now, a thousand militia warriors were swarming the town. There were bodies of death vampires everywhere, some moving slightly, others inert.

Gideon had the north end secured and Diallo had already arrived to begin repairing the mist that had been burned away.

The air smelled of smoke and blood and fear.

The fighting was thickest now at the southern end, but the battle was almost over. His warriors were steadily collecting death vampire bodies and moving them to Gideon's position.

Standing off to the side, Leto watched Gideon direct traffic. He had his warrior phone to his ear, issuing removal orders either to the morgue at Apache Junction Two or to the one at Central Command. Headless bodies and the detached heads began disappearing as fast as they were collected.

The mission proceeded with great speed, all the warriors moving on lightning feet. Months of training had paid off.

Gideon kept sending repeat details to scour each house, each garden, each nearby ravine, and especially the underground cisterns, hunting for the enemy. There was no way they were leaving a single death vamp behind.

Leto approached Gideon, knowing that he would look strange to the warrior, but it couldn't be helped. Besides, in this form, Leto had vanquished four Third Earth death vamps. Not half bad for a beast-man.

Gideon's eyes widened a little, as did the eyes of a number of the Militia Warriors near him.

Leto shrugged. "Better get used to it. Apparently, this is my new look."

Gideon glanced around and ordered everyone back to work. "We're bringing in backup squads to patrol through the night."

"How many?"

"Twenty."

"Good." That would put eighty warriors on the ground. "And the healers?"

"As soon as the fighting in the south is done, we're bringing them in. Horace has forty ready to go. But, Leto, we have at least twenty dead colonists, and several of our warriors didn't make it."

It could have been worse. It could have been a disaster. That's what he thought but that's not what he said. "We'll need counselors in here as well."

Gideon nodded. "Mei-Amadi will take charge of that."

"Do we know how the colony was identified by the enemy? Did any of your men find transmitters?"

"Yes," Gideon said. "They're everywhere. But we knew it was just a matter of time." He looked up. "Diallo feels confident this renewed layer of mist will eradicate the position of the colony. If Greaves's army wants to come back, they'll have to work for it."

Several hours later, the Nazca One Colony was well in hand. Gideon sent dozens of Militia Warriors to search out the last of the transmitters.

Leto folded back to the landing platforms. He was the only one at that location. The grounds were quiet, as they should be. The hour had to be near two in the morning.

He was about to fold when he sensed something behind him. He turned around and watched a large shimmering appear in the desert. He drew his sword into his hand and was about to sound the alarm all over again when Greaves appeared with a contingent of ten Third Earth death vampires. On top of that, Greaves held both hands out in front of him. Leto could feel the hand-blast gearing up.

He saw his death in this moment as sure as Greaves was standing there. He couldn't legally kill Leto, but he could wound him as near to fatal as he could get, then order his death vamps to finish him off.

Leto had only one thought: *But Grace just got back.*

Like hell, however, he would take this lying down. He lowered his chin and built up his shields as fast as he could. He drew a dagger from his weapons harness.

Greaves just smiled. "I've been waiting for this moment for months now." He let loose with a hand-blast that roared at Leto like a freight train.

Leto's shields buckled, and he was thrown off the platform and rolled downhill. The whole time, he worked at rebuilding his shields, but it was as though they'd been melted. Still, he had to try.

He glanced in Gideon's direction, but he couldn't see him. Greaves had put a mist around the battle. Of course.

Leto had just gained his feet when another blast hit, but to his surprise, it didn't even touch him.

Another shimmering brought a new entity between Leto and Greaves. He was tall and bald but with writing on his skull—tattoos, maybe.

"Casimir," Greaves called out. "What are you doing here?"

"Making sure Leto stays alive."

This was Casimir? And he was here to defend Leto? What the hell?

What Leto saw next was a shower of energy that met in the middle between both men. Light and sparks flew up into the sky.

"I can do this for hours, Darian, and I have permission from Endelle to engage however I can to protect Leto. I suggest you get the hell out of here and take your pretty-boys with you before I blast your mist to hell and the rest of the Militia Warriors below decide to take on your men. What do you say?"

When he finished this speech with a flick of his wrist that sent a wave of energy piercing Greaves's shoulder, Greaves waved his arm. Just like that, he and his death vamps were gone.

Leto had too much adrenaline in his system. He held his sword in a tight fist, and his whole arm shook. He'd faced death and would have died just now except for the aid of the one vampire he despised the most: Casimir.

The bastard turned around and faced Leto. He looked so different without his long hair. But there was something more. His dark eyes held a light Leto had never seen before.

"What the fuck are you doing here?" Leto asked. "And what do you mean you're here to protect me?"

Casimir's smile quirked. "Is that any way to address the vampire who just saved your ass?" He looked Leto up and down. "Like the new look you're sporting. Bigger."

Leto took two deep breaths. "Grace is mine."

At that, something of the old Casimir showed through. He rubbed the top of his head. "We'll see about that. I think she should have a choice."

Leto would have launched on him, but Casimir just held up his hand and Leto couldn't move, which made him mad as hell. He roared.

"Relax, beast-man. I'm here as your Guardian of Ascension. That's all. I relinquished Grace months ago. She's yours."

Leto had no reason to believe Casimir. "Shut it, asshole, and please just return to Fourth Earth."

"No can do. Greaves wants your ass in a sling—or did you not notice that he outpowers you about a hundred-to-one?"

Leto noticed.

"Yeah," Casimir drawled. "I think he was a little ticked off that you oh-so-easily dispatched the other Third Earth vampires he'd sent to get this job done. Oh, and maybe because you defected back to Endelle's side."

Leto knew many definitions for the word *nightmare*, but right now, this situation in which Leto owed Casimir his life, had just created a new meaning. "What about Grace? Are you here to guard her as well?"

"Nope. Just you."

Yep, nightmare. Leto was many things, but he wasn't a fool. If Greaves had targeted him and had staked Leto out in order to finish him off, Leto was in for it.

He needed Casimir. Nothing could have put a fire on his nerves worse than that.

"You're not staying in my house."

Casimir just lifted a brow. "I'm not staying anywhere on Second Earth." With that, he vanished, though Leto could sense he hadn't dematerialized. As a Fourth ascender, he had powers that Leto couldn't relate to, like going invisible—which he was pretty sure Casimir had just done.

Leto turned in a circle. He still held his sword in his hand. He focused and sure enough, he could sense Casimir's presence.

Don't be an idiot, Casimir sent. *You need me right now, and I'm sticking around. I owe Grace at least that much, to keep you alive. Adios. At least for now.*

This time, Leto knew that Casimir had gone. So had Greaves's mist. He glanced down in Gideon's direction, but no one seemed the wiser about what had just happened.

He let out a heavy sigh and headed back up the hill. Once at the landing platform, he folded to the Seattle Colony's landing area then headed to HQ. The Militia Warriors on duty reported that the colonists were all in their homes; no lights were on anywhere since they were still on high alert. The warriors folding back from battle were immediately sent home to clean up and recoup.

He glanced out the window at the contest grounds, visible beyond the empty tents.

"Have all the competitors returned to their continents?"

"Diallo gave the order shortly after the last of the Militia Warriors folded to Nazca."

Leto nodded, but his heart was heavy. So much for the warrior games.

He wasn't under the illusion that Greaves had actually started the war, not by attacking one insignificant colony on Mortal Earth. Greaves had probably been testing the waters. But whatever this attack had been, it was just the beginning. The transmitters had been all around Nazca, one small colony in a relatively insignificant corner of the world. That meant that Greaves was probably tracking all the colonies.

He sent out a telepathic thread toward Grace. *Where are you?*

Leto? Are you back?

Yes.

He heard her sigh, or at least he thought he did.

Thank God. When you're done with all your duties, I'm at the cabin, having a glass of a very nice German wine I found in your fridge.

Listen, I'm going to fold straight to the shower, but I don't want you to join me. I don't want you to see me like this because I've been battling.

Well, I confess you won't have to twist my arm on this one. But, Leto, when you get here, I really need you to break open my obsidian flame power. I'm done with these headaches, and as I told you before, I'm done holding back from my role in the triad.

He felt a jolt go through him, an awareness that what Grace had just said to him was no small thing. Grace was staying. That's what went through his mind. If she meant to embrace her obsidian flame power, it meant she was staying.

Something in his chest opened up, and he released a deep sigh. Relief washed through him. Grace was staying. He wouldn't have to bid her good-bye anytime soon. Maybe things weren't completely settled between them, but until this moment he had felt she could easily walk away.

On the other hand, would Casimir's sudden return have an effect on her? Would the *breh* return? Jesus H. Christ, a Guardian of Ascension. What exactly did that mean? He wasn't, that is, he couldn't possibly be in a call to ascension to Third Earth, could he?

Battle fatigue had started settling in, however. He set aside this new development in his bizarre life and focused on Grace.

I'll fold there after I've taken care of a couple of things.

Okay. I'll be waiting.

He left orders that HQ was to contact him at his cabin if he was needed for anything. When he felt confident that the situation was stable, he thought the thought. The next moment he was washing blood and debris down the drain of his shower.

But as he washed his hair, and had to bend to get beneath the spray of water because he was still in his beast-state, he rose upright and looked at his arms and hands.

He wondered. In the midst of battle, he had so easily morphed into this state—and what do you know, he hadn't passed out. And another thing, he'd folded without any repercussion.

As he thought about the situation, he realized that the major difference had been his level of acceptance. He'd wanted his beast to come, he'd focused on the change, and the next moment he'd become his beast-form. But could he return as easily?

He relaxed every muscle of his body, and as the hot water beat on his skin, he focused on his normal vampire state.

In stages, he felt the change come, a gradual reduction, an easing into his regular body. He held his hands and arms up and watched the transformation. This couldn't just be a condition of having once been a death vampire—and what had the Third Earth pretty-boy said about morphing like a Third Earth warrior?

Not a Third Earth death vamp, but a Third Earth warrior. Huh.

Much of Third Earth was a mystery, apparently even to the Upper Dimensions beyond Third. Third was cloaked in some kind of nearly impenetrable fog so it wasn't clear what was going on in that world.

And here he was, having been described as a Third Earth warrior. He suddenly felt hopeful that his beast-like condition could mean something good for Second Earth. It certainly had in terms of battling Third Earth death vamps.

When he was dressed in jeans and a long-sleeved ribbed T-shirt, he made his way downstairs. Much to his surprise, Grace sat at the dining table with a meal she'd prepared for him. She had a platter of cheese, fruit, and some cold fried chicken piled on a plate.

And suddenly he was starved. He apologized as he dove in, but he hadn't known he was hungry until he'd seen the food.

She smiled at him and laughed a couple of times. She leaned back in her chair and sipped her white wine. "I'm so glad you're back. I was worried."

He nodded, swallowed, wiped his mouth. "It must be hard sitting around waiting to get word on something like this." He took a nice swig of wine.

Grace sipped and smiled some more. "Go ahead and eat."

He took her at her word and made quick work of his meal.

When only a few bones remained, he sat back. "I forgot what it was like. I haven't been in a battle like that in a while." He looked at her and held out his hand. Shit. He would have to tell her about Casimir. The bastard.

She took his hand. "You okay?"

He hardly knew what to say. "What happened tonight is just the beginning. I think we're in for it."

"Was it as bad as I think it was?"

"Parts were, yes. But in reality we had very few casualties and we took care of a lot of death vampires tonight who will never again harm a mortal or an ascender."

"Did we . . . did we lose many colonists tonight?"

"Gideon set the number at around twenty. But, Grace, if obsidian flame hadn't acted, it would have meant complete devastation."

"That's what I thought."

"But there's something else, and I have no idea what it means or how you're going to feel about this. I know I'm pissed as hell." He fell silent thinking about what Casimir had just done for him and the announcement he'd made.

"Hey, don't leave me hanging."

He blinked at least once. "Sorry. I think I'm still in a state of shock. Casimir showed up. In Nazca."

She leaned forward in her chair, but she was frowning. "He did?"

Leto nodded.

"What was he there for? I mean, did you get into a fight with him?"

"No." He shook his head because he was still in disbelief. "Actually, he saved my life." He told her about Greaves arriving armed with a large squad of Third Earth death vampires. Then he dropped the bomb. "I don't know exactly what this means, but Casimir said he was now my Guardian of Ascension, that he had it all arranged with Endelle."

"What?" She tilted her head and narrowed her eyes. Her lips moved as though she was trying to form a few words. "I don't understand. Casimir said he's *your* Guardian of Ascension?"

Leto nodded. "Yeah." He scrubbed his face with his hand. "I don't know the why of it, but I do know if he hadn't shown up when he did, I'd be toast."

Her head bobbed, and she set her glass of wine on the table. "I guess this is real. I mean, I knew the war would heat up once I returned because of obsidian flame, but it never occurred to me that Greaves would go after you. I thought it was all about me." Her mouth then fell open. "Leto, tell me you're not in your call to ascension to Third Earth."

He shook his head. "I can't be. You just came back and

usually couples ascend together, at least if they've been married awhile. This doesn't make sense." He paused then met her gaze squarely. "Except for one thing. While I was out battling tonight, a Third Earth death vampire said that I was morphing like a Third Earth warrior."

Her shoulders fell. "Leto, no. You can't be ascending."

She rose, and before he knew what she meant to do, she crawled into his lap, slipped her arms around his neck, and held on. "Leto, I'm trying to be brave, I really am. But this is one of those moments when I wish I was like Thorne and Patience." He felt her trembling so he held her tight. He kissed her neck. "I don't want to lose you," she said.

"Well, first, I don't know if I am ascending. Second, you could come with me. I mean, if you could stay on Fourth, why not Third?"

She leaned back and looked at him. "But the portal's closed. I couldn't visit you on Third if I wanted to, which means you couldn't return to the lower dimensions, either."

"Shit." He rocked her and kissed her. He held back the storm of feelings that threatened him right now. The thought that he could be separated from Grace for any length of time tightened his chest until he could hardly breathe.

After a long moment, and once her trembling had subsided, she drew back and met his gaze. She kissed his forehead, his eyelids, his nose, then his mouth. She lingered and he savored, letting her do what she wanted.

Finally, she leaned back and drew a deep breath. "Okay, I guess we should deal with this one step at a time. First, we need to take care of my little problem."

Grace led the way upstairs to Leto's bedroom. She had been thinking about this moment from the time she'd left the contest grounds and returned to his cabin to wait for him. She'd drawn some hard conclusions.

Mostly, she wanted her blue flame powerfully expressed so that she wasn't hindered by these terrible headaches. After that—well, she didn't know what exactly would happen, but she did know that events tonight had brought her right next to the war, and given the number of colonists that had been saved, she was glad she'd come back when she did.

Once in the bedroom, she looked up at the unusual bed. "I've never seen anything like this."

"It was handcrafted by a local artisan." Dried branches, scraped clean and oiled, formed a canopy over the massive king-size-plus bed, which seemed like a fitting choice for a cabin deep in the Cascade Mountains.

"I couldn't say no to the bed," he explained. "The woman who made it lost her Militia Warrior husband last year. She needed the money to support her family."

"I think it's lovely." She ran her hand over some of the smooth branches, letting her fingers glide over nubs and arches. "And the sentiment is equally beautiful."

Opposite the bed was a large fireplace, enough for a roaring fire in winter. But in September, not so much.

He slid his arms around her. "How's your head?"

"Much better, thanks to Alison. And did you know that her wings have emerged? She spent the day flying over White Lake with Kerrick."

"Wait, that has significance, doesn't it? When I tried to rejoin the Warriors of the Blood, Luken brought me up to speed about everything, especially about Alison and that she would one day open the portal to Third. Holy shit, do you think we're headed there?"

Shivers suddenly chased down Grace's shoulders and arms. "I hadn't thought about that when I heard her wings had emerged. It would cast a new light on your possible ascension to Third as well."

He leaned down and kissed her, then drew back. "I think you might be the missing piece of the puzzle, Grace. It can't be a coincidence that your return here, to be involved in the war, has coincided with Alison's wings."

Grace felt overwhelmed suddenly, and the part of her that was deeply intuitive knew Leto was right. Her return was connected to Alison, even as much as her presence here would affect the war against Greaves.

"You did good tonight, Grace. I don't want to think what would have happened if you hadn't embraced your obsidian power, despite your headache, and gotten the Nazca location for us. It was some quick thinking, too."

She looked up at the branches and once more let her fingers glide over a bend and a smooth knot. She shook her head. "I've avoided the war my entire life. Now here I am right in the middle of it. But then I ask myself, why should I be spared these fears and sufferings? War has afflicted human- and vampire-kind for most of history. I hid out in the Convent, sent there by my sister's disappearance. I can see that now. I'm not exactly sure that I'm worthy of you, Leto. I think I've been a coward."

He drew close and put a hand on her shoulder. "No one likes war, Grace. Those of us who are built for it serve because it's the right thing to do. But when lives are destroyed, as they were tonight, there is no real solace. So why would you choose that, especially when it's clear you're built for other things?"

"I want to help, that much I know. I didn't understand how much being of use would actually mean to me especially in this situation. But because Greaves won't hesitate to slaughter millions of people if it suits his purposes, and if I can stop him, then I have a responsibility to do what I can."

As she stared up into Leto's clear blue eyes, at least one thing crystallized for her. He had been in her life a long, long time and she loved him. She knew his soul, his infinite worth, even if he didn't. If having her obsidian flame power opened and utilized fully would help her to keep him safe, then whatever sacrifices she must endure would be worth it.

"So, how would you like to do this?" he asked.

She glanced at the bed. "Right here, lying on the bed, with you beside me."

He smiled. "Then let's do it."

> *To set a course and stay the path*
> *Sets the angels of heaven to rejoicing.*

> —*Collected Proverbs*, Beatrice of Fourth

CHAPTER 7

Grace stretched out on the bed and folded her hands over her stomach. Leto joined her.

Ready? he sent.

She smiled. "Absolutely."

Leto was a powerful vampire, and within seconds he had pushed inside her mind. She could feel him at the outer boundaries of her thoughts, seeking, finding his way.

She took deep breaths and made sure that all her mental shields lay flat.

What am I looking for? he sent.

Wow, your voice is so clear because you're inside my head. It always surprises me that there's a difference.

I know. And you sound like you're shouting.

Sorry, Grace sent. *I'll tone it down.*

Leto chuckled, but she wasn't sure if it was audible or within her mind. His presence was like warm water, very soothing. That surprised her as well. He was so physically strong that she had been certain once inside her mind he would feel like a bear pushing around and foraging for things. Instead, his presence reflected the gentleness and kindness of his character.

You seem to be thinking very hard, he sent.

Oh, sorry. Have I made it impossible for you to find my obsidian power?

Yes. I'm blocked at every turn.

She forced herself to relax and once more lowered her shields. He moved through her mind back and forth, searching her thoughts and memories, hunting. *Grace, I can't seem to locate the seat of your power.*

Marguerite said that her power was deep within her mind, down a long tunnel.

I've been through your mind. There's nothing there that I would call a tunnel, just your memories and a sense of who you are, your thoughts. But I don't see a tunnel or an opening of any kind.

You don't see anything? No glow of light?

Nothing.

Both Marguerite and Fiona had spoken to her of long tunnels at the end of which were the vessels that contained their power. Fiona's had been filled with gold light and Marguerite's with red. Marguerite had also told her that for whatever reason, these aspects of power were very sexual in nature and that they had strong sheaths that had to be broken to release the power.

Yet apparently Grace didn't share such a structure. *Where do you think it could be, Leto, if not within my mind?*

What about your soul? You have to admit that you're unique in our world, Grace. Among all these powerful ascenders, you have always charted your own path, followed your own passion, served your communities in different ways. Essentially, you lead with your soul and you're able to see into the souls of others.

I think you're right, and I can sense what you would need to do to reach my soul. But the truth of it frightened her.

What's wrong? I can feel that you're afraid.

She would have to open herself up as she had never opened herself up to anyone in the entire course of her life. In essence, Leto would know all of her secrets—and there was at least one that still haunted her.

Not surprisingly, Leto withdrew from her mind. The sensation felt a little rubbery, and as she opened her eyes, she had to blink several times before she could see him clearly.

He leaned up on one elbow and rubbed her shoulder. "I know you didn't want me to go there with you. I could feel how much it troubled you. We don't have to do this."

There it was again, his light hands with her, his kindness, his patience. If he had been strident, she might have recoiled, even made other decisions. She might have worked to protect herself instead of moving forward.

Instead, she gripped his arm and nodded once. "It's okay. I still want to do this. I must do this. I'm not going back to the life I knew. I know this changes things, but so be it. This is my path."

He leaned over and kissed her full on the mouth. "I'm so grateful that you're here with me and that you're so accepting of my beast-state. I confess I don't understand all that's going on with the *breh-hedden* right now or with you and your obsidian soul-based power, but I want to be here for you as much as I can."

She rolled toward him slightly and kissed him back. "This is new ground for both of us."

He looked so worried, his brow heavily furrowed. "I just don't want you to have expectations of me. We're being pushed toward this profound degree of connection, but I'm not sure how much of a heart I have to give."

She sensed how troubled he was because of all he'd been through. The guilt he carried with him was a constant companion.

She smiled and placed her hand on his cheek. "How about we take everything one step at time, no matter how messy or strange it gets."

He nodded, stroking her cheek with his thumb. "Okay."

"But I do have one suggestion."

"Sure. Anything."

"Why don't we lose the clothes."

His eyes went wide and he grinned. His expression was so male right now that she laughed. Not a bad thing to lighten the mood. "I'm in no way opposed to the idea, but why?"

She shrugged but felt her cheeks growing warm. "For the closeness, I think, and maybe even the vulnerability. If I can be open physically right now, I think it will help the rest of the process. Besides, I've heard the whole thing becomes pretty exciting."

He leaned over and kissed her, drew back, then waved a hand the length of his body. Clothes gone.

She let her gaze drift over him. He was so beautiful, his arms heavily muscled, his pecs thick, his abs sculpted.

She returned the favor, also waving her hand to encompass her clothes. When they disappeared, he let out a solid groan. He reached over and put his hand on her stomach, touching the sapphire-studded ring at her navel. But she caught his hand then rolled onto her back. She chuckled. "Try to focus, if you can."

"What? I didn't quite hear what you said."

She met his gaze. His beautiful blue eyes were suddenly alive with laughter. She once more put her hand on his cheek. "Okay, beast-man, come bust open my obsidian power, then I'll let you do whatever you want to me."

His body did a full shudder. "Okay, so what do we do now?" he asked.

"Try diving into my mind again, and this time I want you to go soul hunting and not tunnel searching. I think I'm built a little differently than either Marguerite or Fiona."

She closed her eyes and lowered every mental shield she could find.

Leto turned into her to lie on his side. He took hold of her upper arm in a gentle clasp. Mentally, he pushed at the edges of her mind and slid within, because again her shields were down.

He loved being naked beside her and he loved being inside her mind. His body reacted, firming up. Because he was so close, the tip of his cock touched her. She smiled, but didn't open her eyes. Instead, her hand searched for him and found him, closing around his stalk and thumbing just the tip. Then she sighed and the frown disappeared.

He laid his head down on the bed. *I love being inside your mind.*

I love you being here. Her fingers played with him and his hips flexed, moving a little closer.

I'm not sure this is going to help, he said. He pumped a couple of times, so that his cock moved against her palm.

Does it make me a strange woman that holding you like this eases me?

I think it makes you the perfect woman. This time he released a sigh. He could get used to this. He really could, the intimacy, the touch of Grace's hand on him, the pleasure of being in her mind.

Leto, this time, I'm going to do something different. Just be ready.

Okay. I'll be as careful as I can.

Sink, she sent.

Sink?

Yes. Just sink. Let yourself fall deep into my mind, and I'll hold my mind open. I can't explain more than that. Just try.

Leto took deep breaths. Being within another person's mind was always a strange experience. Memories tended to fly past the intruder, thoughts as well, streaking by like wind.

Within her mind, he looked down, but what his mind's eye could see was something vague, grayish, almost mist-like. Without trying too hard to make sense of her instructions, he drew in another deep breath and let himself fall, although she was right, *sink* was the better word.

It was like easing into a dark fog. He looked up and saw the memories streaking by one after another. Soon, all that color and activity disappeared. Yet his awareness of Grace increased, of who she was as a person and as a woman, even as an ascended vampire.

The only trouble was, the more he sank, the more physically aroused he became.

Grace?

But she didn't respond. He had the feeling that she couldn't, that holding this gateway open was requiring tremendous effort on her part.

Suddenly he felt how afraid she was of being known, of experiencing this much intimacy. She trembled beside him. All that fear, decades and centuries of fear. And damn him for how aroused he was. But being connected to her like this was a turn-on like nothing he'd experienced before. He wanted to be inside her in the same way that he was penetrating the outer regions of her soul.

He took another deep breath and tried not to stroke himself within her hand. She still held him in a firm grip, not too tight, just right.

Grace, you're so beautiful.

From a distance, as though far below, he heard her. *I'm not beautiful. I've done something terrible.*

He couldn't imagine what Grace would consider terrible. Telling a lie? Not being polite?

The dark gray mist began to give way to a blue glow, which made sense since she was the blue variety of obsidian flame.

Suddenly he was surrounded by all that blue light but he couldn't exactly *see* anything, just light. He turned in a circle and as he stopped trying to *see,* as he just let the experience happen, he felt all that Grace was surrounding him. She was goodness, she was woman, she was hunger, need, fear, and quiet strength. More than anything she was afraid of the war, of death, of losing those she loved, of giving herself completely to anyone, of being known.

Yet here he was knowing her, sensing her, feeling her.

Then he felt a new sensation begin to flow, of guilt, her guilt, a terrible kind of guilt, and it beat on him in waves, so that all the blue dimmed and swirled through him in a kind of heavy dark wave. He saw how divided she was and that to some degree all the restraint she showed to the world was because of this seemingly infinite divide in her soul. She wanted to step forward, but guilt held her back, a deep feeling of unworthiness.

He could relate.

Mostly, she feared the discovery of what she was about to reveal. She trembled against him now.

Grace, let go, please. It's okay. He pressed himself against her hip, pushing his cock up her fist. He overlaid her breasts with his arm and leaned in to kiss her neck. He tried to help her know that it was okay, whatever it was, it didn't matter, would never matter to him. Every human, every vampire, no matter how noble, made mistakes.

He felt her release an agonized sigh, and what had been withheld, perhaps shielded deep in her memories, was of a child, an infant whom she had placed in the hands of another woman. Grace's face was red and swollen from weeping.

You gave up a child.

Yes.

The blue glow turned pitch black and swirled around him. He felt her agony at this one act, which he could feel was early in her life when she was just a young woman.

But something didn't seem right or feel right about this to Leto. There had to be more. He pressed her. *There is more, I can feel it. Tell me. There's nothing you can tell me that will change my feelings toward you or my good opinion of you.*

She spoke within his mind, but the words rushed at him, too fast for him to catch each individual one. However, the context was clear. She'd been raped by death vampires when she was a young woman. They were drinking her to death when Thorne found her. He'd slaughtered them all and saved her life, but she'd become pregnant. All of it had been too much for her. She'd given the baby away. She never knew what became of the little girl. She hadn't wanted to know.

So many pieces of Grace's life fell into place for Leto, the choices she'd made, her incessant spiritual journey that never seemed to end. She'd been seeking absolution for the abandonment of a child; or perhaps she'd never adjusted from having been violated by what was truly evil.

He was wise enough to know that there was nothing he could say to ease her agony, her guilt, her pain. All of those dark feelings were part of her path, the one she had to travel alone. So he remained silent, his body still attached to hers, her hand still a gentle, firm touch.

No woman deserved such horror.

But how to offer comfort? What could he possibly do for her now? What did she need from him?

I am sorrier than you can possibly know that you've had to bear this, Grace. There are no words. I know that. Tell me what you would have me do now.

Maybe he'd said the right things because something in her seemed to relax or possibly to relent.

The color changed, lightening, and returning to her beautiful blue.

I just want to move forward. I want you to find the source of my obsidian power and break the sheath so that I can serve as I should have been serving all these centuries.

He turned in another circle. *I can see nothing here, nothing like a tunnel. What if you tried to access the power? Meet me here, be with me here?*

It felt like a strange request but he felt a shift within her body and her mind, because that's the only way he could describe it. He felt her mind descend toward him.

Leto, I can see you within my soul, just a darker blue than my obsidian flame power. We share the same color.

A tremendous sensation of pleasure flowed through him as she approached.

He heard her moan aloud.

Are you feeling what I'm feeling, he asked.

Desire?

Yes. Can you sense what I want to do?

She didn't answer. Instead, from what felt like a great distance now, she tugged on his arm and pulled him over on top of her. She made her intention clear as she spread her legs. He entered her swiftly.

Then he understood just how close they were in this moment and that breaking her power open would be extraordinary.

As he moved into her physically, she joined him within her soul. He felt her reach for her power, down and down, very deep until he could hear and feel the rumblings of the earth. Was it in his mind or beneath his cabin? He couldn't tell.

But her obsidian flame power, connected to the earth, began to flow upward. He pushed into her body, harder now. He could feel her grabbing at his buttocks, his waist, his back, his shoulders. Her fingers glided over his sensitive wing-locks.

He moaned.

The power of the earth rose.

It's coming. Leto, can you feel that? My power?

Yes, God yes.

Up it rose, then it caught him, a warm rush of heat and light that swept over him, through him, around him, Grace with him. He saw the tunnel now but only as an exit point. He must have come from that direction, which meant he'd already entered the seat of her power, which was the seat of her soul.

His mind or his soul, or whatever combination of himself he was in this moment, separated from Grace and he began to glide faster and faster through the channel, up and up, into her mind where her memories and thoughts pummeled him anew, then out, up, and away. At the same time, he pumped hard into her. Pleasure rode his cock as he released into her and as she screamed her ecstasy at the same time.

He trembled at the pleasure that kept going, kept riding him, that seemed to flow back and forth from mind to soul to body and back, an endless whirlwind of sensation. He roared and once more she cried out. The bed shook, or maybe it was the house.

He came again and again, something so impossible yet possible. His mind was full of her beauty and her power. It was her power that held the sensations on this seemingly endless ride.

At last, the end came, and with it a sense of satisfaction he had never known in his entire existence. He felt her body grow lax as well. He lowered himself down on her, savoring the feel of her breasts, her hips, her legs as she stretched out beneath him.

He kissed her lips and opened his eyes.

Only then did he realize her body glowed an exquisite shade of blue, just as she had glowed at the event grounds earlier when she had accessed her obsidian power.

He kissed her. "Headache?"

She smiled, offering a soft curve of her lips. "Not at all." She pushed at his hair and reached up to kiss him. "Can I say how amazing that was?"

He nodded and kept nodding, like an idiot. "Incredible, but you didn't experience pain?"

"No, but as you left, the tunnel took shape, as though you created it."

"Is that what happened?"

"I think so."

"Then you were right. Your power is very different from that of your obsidian sisters. And very erotic and very beautiful."

Grace was changed.

She could feel it deep within her body, her mind, and, yes, even her soul.

Her obsidian power was fully expressed now, though she could hardly guess at the implications for the triad.

She looked at Leto as with new eyes, clearer eyes. She petted his back and stroked his wing-locks. Who was this man who had been able to sink into her soul, to see her, to know her worst deeds and most heinous secrets? He hadn't judged her at all, even though she still judged herself, still hated that she had rejected the infant because of the baby's sire.

A clarity came to Grace, about herself and her life and the illusion she'd sustained all these centuries.

After the death vampires had taken her innocence and almost her life, she had withdrawn into a hard shell full of piety, restraint, even propriety. These were the walls behind which she had hidden for the past two millennia. She just hadn't seen it.

She'd always admired Thorne and Patience, their warrior-like qualities, even their shared exuberance for life. What her life could have been had died the day she had given up her daughter. That was what she knew right now. For nearly two thousand years, she hadn't lived, not really.

Oh, she'd performed good works, she'd made use of her intellect and studied hard, she'd prayed and meditated, she'd eased the sufferings of the less fortunate and righted wrongs wherever she had found them.

But she had never lived, not as she was meant to live, not as a woman of power and strength and formidable preternatural ability ought to live. She also knew this was why she was connected to Leto, even physically in this moment with his male part anchored in her femaleness.

"I don't know what to make of this," he said.

She leaned up and kissed him. "We're both being called to stand up and fight, Leto. I get that now."

Her power suddenly rumbled very deep in the earth, then spread upward through her legs once more.

"I can feel that," he whispered.

She stared into his eyes, nodding in return. A prescience came to her, powerful and frightening. "There is something we must do," she said.

"I can sense it as well." He squeezed his eyes shut. "Something is on the horizon, something very bad. If we're to survive—" He let the words hang.

She knew the answer. She felt it in her bones. "We must complete the *breh-hedden* right now. We have to be connected for what's coming."

"Yes." He put his hands on her face, pushed her hair back. He kissed her hard.

"You feel it, too," she stated. "The necessity of it."

"We're about to go through hell."

"Greaves is on the move. Everything that's happened tonight tells us that something terrible is afoot."

"But are you sure you want to do this?" he asked. "I've heard the bonded warriors talk. Completing the *breh-hedden* always takes place later, when the couple is more attuned or something, I'm not sure."

"I know," Grace said. "On one level, we shouldn't be doing this, but I think the only way we'll survive the next few days is if we're bonded. Tell me you understand."

"I understand."

"Then you're willing?"

He drew a deep breath and dipped his chin. "I'm willing."

Even as he spoke the words, she knew she was asking for trouble of another kind by engaging the *breh-hedden* before the time was right. On the other hand, her instincts were also shouting at her to do this thing and do it now, that their lives depended on it.

Therein lay the frequent paradox of life: that what was instinctual was often much more important than what could be seen by the eye.

Leto knew that this was both a mistake and a necessity. He felt what she felt, he believed what she believed, that if they didn't seal this bond, death would follow.

He understood the mechanics of completing the *breh-hedden:* being joined as they were now with him buried inside her, a simultaneous sharing of blood, then a back-and-forth possession of each other's minds. Jean-Pierre had given him the details. He shared them now with Grace.

She nodded, smoothing her thumb over his cheek. "I'm ready."

He kissed her, but this time didn't draw back. Her lips parted and her sweet-meadow scent quite suddenly perfumed the air between them. He groaned and his hips moved so that he was once more thrusting in and out of her.

The *breh-hedden.* Now that he had begun the process, his body reacted powerfully.

"Leto," she whispered against his mouth. He kissed her again. Hard.

Her body writhed beneath his. *Take me at my wrist,* he sent.

Yes. Her voice was a sweet murmur through his mind, which further ignited his body.

He lifted his arm, and she shifted her head to bring his wrist to her mouth. She didn't wait, but struck to just the

right level, then began to suck. This action alone almost
brought him.

But there was more to be done. While she worked his
wrist and he pushed into her and felt her hips rise up to meet
him, he used his other hand and pushed her hair away from
her neck.

She groaned, and again he almost came.

He waited for just a moment, easing back on his thrusts.
He closed his eyes and counted out a few innocuous numbers. When he'd calmed down, he leaned forward and began
licking her neck above her vein.

He could feel her vein rise for him, asking him to do what
he loved to do. A sense of reverence overcame him suddenly, that once he started to take her blood, he was close to
making Grace his *breh* forever.

Take me, Leto.

The words drove his head down and he bit her then began
to suck, strong pulls on her neck. The moment her blood
flowed down his throat, the demands of his body increased.

We must do this now.

She understood and pushed her mind against his. He lowered his shields and she all but fell in. As she suckled his
wrist, she cried out, her voice muffled with her lips pressed
to his skin.

He loved her being inside his mind. She was a warm
presence, soothing his loneliness. But it was time. He could
barely hold back. *My turn. Just be prepared when I push past
your shields.*

Understood.

He sucked her neck and his hips moved swiftly now. He
found the edge of her mind and shoved hard so that he was
just there.

We've done it, he said.

Leto, I can't wait any longer.

He felt her begin to clench around him, tugging at him.

He released his fangs, she released hers. He rose above
her, pounding hard now, staring down into her beautiful
gold-green eyes. She held his shoulders and began to cry

out, throaty sounds that caused pleasure to begin flowing through his cock. His orgasm was brisk, sharper than earlier because he'd come already.

But even as his body settled down, hers as well, he could feel something massive waiting as though just offshore.

"Do you feel that?" she asked.

He nodded. "Like something's coming."

He leaned close, as though a magnet drew him to her. He placed his lips on hers.

He felt something click deep within, a lock turning and sliding into place. She was his, and he was hers. Truly one.

He drew back and looked at her. He moved inside her but there were two sensations now, not just one. He felt the small jolts of pleasure it gave her and then his own pleasure.

She gasped.

He withdrew then plunged.

The dual sensation caused him to shout.

"Do it," she cried out.

He began to stroke her again. "Oh, my God. The way you feel me."

"The way *you* feel *me*." She added, "More."

He became a hard, driving machine once more and pumped. The pleasure felt magnified a hundred times because he felt her pleasure as well as his own. He hadn't thought he'd be able to become aroused so quickly again, but there he was.

He kissed her neck, only he felt what it was like for her to have his lips pressed against her skin, how moist they felt. The sensation was strange but exhilarating. He wanted to know the rest, what it would feel like for her to come.

All his efforts became focused on what she was experiencing, what his cock felt like deep inside her, all the pleasure building in a line, it seemed, from the outer part of her to areas almost indefinable inside.

All that sensation made him harder and readier, which increased her sensation, which made her grip him . . . and back and forth it went. Her nails dug into his shoulders and that made her cry out. He could feel all her external sensations. He couldn't feel things like her heart beating, but anywhere that he could touch her, even with his cock, that he could feel.

He kissed her and slid his tongue into her mouth, and, yes, he could feel the way she experienced his tongue.

But that seemed to be what caused her to fly once more over the edge because she cried out, "Your tongue. Oh, God." Her neck arched and she was coming. Her pleasure seemed infinite and it brought him, which increased her cries until she was screaming and screaming.

He started seeing black spots before his eyes as he came, as his cock jerked, as her pleasure finally began to recede, as her body grew lax and eased against the sheets. Her head lolled to one side, her eyes closed, her lips parted. She was breathing hard.

He breathed hard as well but now he was frozen above her, staring down at her.

She had become something new to him, wondrous, surprising, extraordinary. "Grace," he whispered.

She shifted her head, then looked up at him. She smiled. "You're so beautiful, Leto. Have I told you that?"

"I can feel your body everywhere, the way we're connected, the feel of the sheet beneath your head, your arms, your bottom."

She lifted a hand and rubbed her thumb across her lower lip. He turned and kissed her thumb. "Do you think it's possible we'll never leave this bed again?" she asked.

He laughed. "So this is what it's like. It's so strange."

"It is. I can feel what it's like for you to be inside me."

He pressed a finger between her brows. "I can feel that frown, how it pinches together. What's wrong?"

"I'm not sure. This has been wonderful, but I'm uneasy, even afraid. Leto, we weren't really ready."

"I know. But we both agreed it had to be done."

She nodded. "This was amazing."

He kissed her again, and she kissed him back. He felt her tension leave.

After a long moment, he withdrew from her body and

was surprised at how empty she felt when he left her. He'd never imagined what that must be like for a woman, to be so filled up, then so empty.

He rolled onto his back and lay looking up at the arch of branches overhead. Grace turned on her side, lifted his arm, and settled her head on his shoulder. He wrapped his arm around her. It was heaven to have her so close.

"I wish this moment would never end," he said.

He felt her sigh.

A well-trained army
Can overcome astonishing odds.

—*Collected Proverbs,* Beatrice of Fourth

CHAPTER 8

As dawn crested the McDowell Mountains in the east, Greaves stood on the round patio located in the middle of his famous peach orchard. The microclimates he had created in order to grow and ripen peaches every month of the year had won numerous horticultural awards. He had been pleased at the time to have been so honored.

Right now, however, he could not have cared less. What good was an award-winning peach orchard when his kingdom hung in the balance?

He moved in a slow circle, pondering the nightmare that, in a matter of just hours, had become his life.

His spies had observed Alison, during the previous day, in flight over White Lake, her emerald wings glinting beneath the sun. Her *breh,* Warrior Kerrick, had flown with her, instructing her, protecting her, eventually surrounding her with a dense mist.

The portal to Third Earth was over White Lake, and Greaves had learned from his Seers Fortresses that Alison was destined to open the portal to Third sometime in the next few days.

In the next few days.

His mind still reeled. As far as he knew, no one on Second Earth was aware of the truth about his dealings with Third Earth and what he had done to the portal. A year ago, he'd created a breach that had allowed him to bring Third Earth death vampires through the Borderland to his Estrella Complex without anyone knowing.

But over the past week, he'd succeeded in widening the breach, which would make it possible to bring a large contingent through on command, at least a hundred Third Earth pretty-boys.

If Alison opened the portal, the breach would be discovered and closed. He was a vampire who liked known outcomes, and a regiment made up of primarily Third Earth death vampires would have ensured his success because, in sufficient numbers, they'd be able to wipe the Warriors of the Blood off the face of Second Earth.

Worse, of course, was that the portal and Alison weren't even his largest concern. Alison was only a wedge of this shit-pie.

Casimir had returned to serve as Leto's fucking Guardian of Ascension. Leto, that two-faced traitor, who should be strung up by his balls for eternity. Of course having a guardian meant only one thing: Leto was ascending. And yet Greaves had an uncomfortable knot at the center of his stomach that told him this would not be an ordinary ascension to Third Earth.

He pressed his hands to his face and breathed deeply. The orchard had just been watered so that the air was humid and cool as it entered his lungs.

He moved to sit down on one of the stone benches that bordered the patio. Then there was Grace's abrupt return to the arms of her other *breh,* Leto. And if what he felt was true, she was the real source of his every concern. She had returned to take up her place as the third key to obsidian flame. It was almost as though her decision had somehow triggered Alison's wings and Leto's ascension.

If his recent plan to eliminate Leto at Nazca had succeeded, he would have been able to unravel this terrible synchronicity of events. But Casimir had shown up, fresh from his baptismal rites, and had met his own powerful hand-blasts with equal, if not stronger, skills.

As Greaves pondered his situation, he knew he had only one hope of coming out of this a victor: He must attain pure vision in which the absolute future was laid out before him and he could prepare and act accordingly. But would Stannett be able to curtail his pleasures sufficiently to get him the information he needed?

Casimir sat in a very comfortable recliner. He'd changed to jeans and a T-shirt, but the shirt was pretty snug. He smiled. One advantage of having participated in Beatrice's redemption program was the absolute requirement of regular exercise, in a gym, including weight lifting. He was looking better than he had most of his life. And the truth was he felt better.

He even munched on an apple.

The suite came with a full bar, and he had been tempted, just for the hell of it, to make a peach blow, that absurd drink he'd made a few months ago in an attempt to seduce Greaves. He'd even pulled out the fresh peach and the soda water and was hunting around for the cream when he realized he'd lost interest. All he wanted was an apple and to cruise some Mortal Earth TV channels. He liked watching *The View* just to keep up.

Yes, he really had changed.

He took another bite of apple and was trying to figure out how to DVR *Criminal Minds* when he heard the steel gate in the observation room glide open.

His heart set up a racket. James had said a female Militia Warrior often came to the portal to do some work for him. He hoped to hell that was her.

He set his apple down and went invisible. If this wasn't the woman, then he'd fold the hell out of there. Third Earth had some strange goings-on, and he wasn't a warrior, not by a long shot. He also didn't know what one of his powerful hand-blasts would do to the portal to Third if he had to use that skill to defend himself.

The door opened, and a woman crossed the threshold, a very beautiful, curvaceous woman.

"Is that you, James? Are you in the bathroom? Jesus, I can smell you. Did you bathe in wine or what?"

Casimir weaved on his feet. The scent was back, that intense wildflower scent, the one he had first smelled when he arrived at the observation deck.

And the scent belonged to this woman.

Oh, my God, it was a *breh* scent. He couldn't be mistaken about that, because right now all he could think about was how to get this woman on her back. Worse, her scent was about a hundred times stronger than he'd ever experienced with Grace.

She wore jeans and a snug tank top that displayed beautiful breasts. She was as tall as Grace, which was perfect for sex. Her hips flared and her lips were full, two of his favorite attributes in the female form. She had a deeply sensuous look. Her hazel eyes looked familiar somehow, but he couldn't quite place her. Her long light brown hair lay in waves over her shoulders.

Some of his former hedonism took root, and for a long moment all he could think about was stripping her down and taking her to bed.

But the newer part of who he was asserted itself. He forced himself to calm down, then he made himself visible.

Her eyes widened when he appeared, but she didn't look too shocked, like maybe invisibility was more normal on Third Earth. "Who are you?" she asked. "And what are you doing here and did you bust up a bottle of vino or what? The entire room reeks of it."

A wine scent. Grace had said he smelled of mulled wine.

He wondered what this woman would think of *breh*-scents.

He moved forward holding her gaze. "I'm Casimir of Fourth Earth. James brought me here to guard Warrior Leto."

She blinked several times as though processing what he'd just told her. "So, you're Casimir. I mean, I know of you because James and I talk a lot. And you took Grace to Fourth Earth as your *breh*."

So she did know about the *breh-hedden*. "Then you know all about Leto and Grace? And you know about me, about events of five months ago?"

She nodded. "I felt so bad for my Grace. She was so torn, but James assured me that there were strong reasons for your presence in her life. I hear you entered Beatrice's redemption program?"

He nodded. "I did. It's been extremely difficult but the right path for me absolutely. I have two little boys—"

"Kendrew and Sloane."

He smiled; he couldn't help it. "Yes, apparently James does talk a lot."

"But what's this about you guarding Leto?"

"Apparently, he's in his rite of ascension to Third and for some reason I was chosen to get the job done, I think because Greaves wants him dead."

"Leto's ascending to Third? But won't that change things for Grace?"

"I don't think any of us understands what's going on. Leto's supposed ascension just isn't following the norm— starting with the fact that I was assigned to guard him. How does that make sense?"

"I see what you mean. So while you're guarding him, you're staying here?"

"James's idea."

She looked around. "Exactly how are you guarding him if you're up here?"

He tapped his head. "I have my voyeur window tracking him constantly. I wasn't going to follow him around at the Seattle Colony or wherever else he happened to go. Besides, he and Grace are engaging with the *breh-hedden* now, and I don't want to intrude."

At that, she cocked her head. "James told me a lot about you. All I can say is that Beatrice's program really must be working for you to be staying out of their business."

He smiled wryly. "Then you really do understand my previous reputation. And you called it exactly right. In fact,

I would have made a point of annoying the hell out of him by constantly suggesting that we make it a threesome."

At that, the woman laughed, a full-out laugh that made his heart soar. "And that would have bugged Grace as well."

He felt himself drifting back into dangerous waters, because right now he wanted to tease this woman, say some risqué things, see if he could get her worked up. Given that she was still cascading her wildflower scent in his direction, it wouldn't take much.

He turned to stare at the wall just to gain some perspective. He wanted to stay on the right path.

When he glanced back, he could see that she was eyeing him. He shrugged. "I'm trying to be good."

"You know, this is really strange that I've caught your scent like this." She blinked twice and enlightenment dawned. "Holy shit," she said, eyes wide. "Are you my *breh*?"

"I think it's possible that I am. You smell of wildflowers, by the way."

She waved her hand in the air. "Sorry, but your wine scent is getting to me." Her cheeks were flushed, her eyes dilated, her lips swollen. She fanned her face and looked around.

This time she glanced at the wall, but she said, "I know there's a Murphy bed in there. Were you aware of that?"

"Yes." The word came out strangled.

Casimir knew temptation, because her wildflower scent was really working him. His jeans were feeling as though they'd shrunk. He also knew how easy it would be to take her to bed.

"So, how do you know Grace?" he asked.

She laughed that bright laughter of hers again. She slapped a hand against her chest. "I'm Patience, Grace's twin sister."

"Holy shit. Holy, holy shit."

"Yeah, and double that."

He stared at her for a long, long moment. The nature of her scent, so similar to Grace's, now made sense. And that she said he smelled of wine. He also marveled at what he considered a significant twist of fate—the kind of synchronicity he'd never really believed in, yet here was some kind of proof.

"As for the bed," he began, "believe me, Patience, if I'd caught your scent even three months ago, that bed would already be out of the wall. But I'm not that man, or I'm trying not to be that man. If you are my *breh,* and I'm yours, then fate has brought us together and I don't want to screw it up."

She nodded. "I get where you're coming from. But I hardly know what to think. Third Earth is a shitfest, and the last hundred years have been a trial. The one good thing that has come of it is that I was able to serve as a Militia Warrior, something Thorne fought against my whole life.

"But I never felt like I belonged here. I never quite fit in, probably because I have no family in this world. I'm not anchored." She then tossed her hands in the air. "But, hey, you've got a lot on your mind and I just came over to check on the portal. And I have to get back to my barracks. Maybe we can reconnect once you get Leto ascended. How does that sound?"

He took a few steps toward her. "Are you okay?"

She shook her head. "No, I'm not. I'm lonely as hell, but that's not your problem."

"James shouldn't have brought you here. I can see that it's taken a toll on you."

She laughed. "Well, that was my fault. He asked me, and I jumped at the chance to do something different. I haven't lived the most stable life, just so you know."

She returned to the observation deck, and he followed.

She touched a panel on the wall and a computer emerged. She fired it up, took several looks at the portal, then typed in what Casimir supposed was her report.

She then moved to the steel gates.

He didn't want to let her go. He could see that she was hurting, maybe even embarrassed. He wanted to do something for her, at least to reassure her, but she waved her hand over the steel lock to the left of the door, and the gate slid open. He reached a hand out to her, but she stepped through and waved. The gate closed.

He realized that his millennia of seduction hadn't exactly prepared him for handling a real relationship with a woman.

"Well, shit," he muttered.

That afternoon, Grace had just finished her first meal of the day when Leto got word that Endelle wanted them both at the palace. Alison was ready to work with Grace on her obsidian flame power, and Thorne was busy setting up a temporary command HQ in the middle of the palace's central rotunda. It would seem that Endelle and Thorne both believed a decisive battle with Greaves was on the horizon.

After dressing in soft black yoga pants and a loose blue cotton top that gathered at the hips, Grace folded with Leto to the palace. He held her hand the entire way, and it was so strange to feel what her hand felt like *to him.* She could sense his external sensations, which had been a bizarre experience upon awakening. His arm had been draped over her waist and stomach, so that when he began touching her, she could feel how soft her skin was to his callused warrior fingers.

Of course, he had made love to her, a very quick and erotic experience because of the extraordinary nature of the *breh-hedden.* It seemed to take so little to become thoroughly aroused, which she could see had terrific benefits. But at other times, she had no doubt it would be very inconvenient.

As Grace materialized on the landing platform in what she recognized as the dining room rotunda of the palace, Alison was there to greet them both. The blond beauty looked tall and elegant as always, her hair pulled back in a twist. She wore navy slacks and a lavender silk blouse. She gave Grace a hug. "Welcome home," she said. "You were in so much pain at the contest grounds that I'm not even sure I welcomed you home."

Grace smiled. "Yes, my head really hurt, and you helped me so much. Thank you again."

"How are you feeling now?"

"I'm fine now, really." She glanced up at Leto. "We've taken care of the problem."

"Good. I'm glad."

Grace felt Alison's compassion like a wave flowing toward her. Everything about Alison brought a sense of peace and rightness with the world.

Alison turned to Leto and extended her hand to him. When he took it, she grew very still as she searched his face. "It's wonderful to see you like this, Leto, so relaxed. And like Thorne, you've lost that pinched look about the eyes that both of you carried all those years."

He glanced at Grace. "My *breh* has come home."

Alison glanced from one to the other, still holding Leto's hand, perhaps reading him as an empath might. "Oh, I see what it is. I almost missed it, but you've completed the *breh-hedden,* haven't you?"

"Yes," Leto said. "We both felt it was necessary."

She nodded, releasing his hand. "This is the time to go with your instincts."

Leto dipped his chin, and his expression grew serious. "Alison, I know that we've never spoken of it, but I can't tell you how sorry I was that Greaves forced you to do battle with me in the Tolleson Two arena. My duties serving Greaves had always been a nightmare, but I think from that moment, when I saw you standing opposite me, so inexperienced, so frightened yet brave, I knew I had to end my tour of duty under his command. I'm just so sorry it had to happen at all."

Alison's eyes welled with tears. "It was a beginning for both of us, Leto. But I have to say that despite the horror of that battle, given all the wonderful things that followed, I wouldn't change a thing. Knowing and loving Kerrick, having a baby with him, being close to all the warriors and their *brehs* as I am, even having a place in this world that makes sense to me because of my powers, no, I don't regret any of it. Not even battling you in that arena."

Grace watched Leto smile. She even felt some of the tension ease from his body. And as hard as it was for her to speak the words into his mind, Grace sent them anyway: *You should hug her, Leto. I think just this one time it would be very acceptable and good for you both.*

Leto glanced at her, brows raised. *Are you sure?*

Grace nodded.

Leto turned back to Alison and opened his arms. She stepped into them and held him tight. Grace ignored the fiery rise of her *breh* jealousy. Instead, she focused on the healing that she could feel happening between them. Leto had been through so much, and given his deepest character, the trial of battling Alison like that would have cut him to the quick.

Of course, it was no surprise that the landing platform came alive and Kerrick's voice boomed over them all. "What the fuck is going on here?" He stomped down the ramp, his green eyes flashing with anger.

Grace instinctively drew close to Leto.

As for Alison, she pulled away from Leto wiping her eyes and laughing. "I suppose it was too much to hope for." She went straight to her *breh,* however, cutting off his hostile approach. She surrounded him with her arms and kissed him deeply.

Grace turned toward them and watched Alison shoving her fingers into Kerrick's hair, dislodging his *cadroen,* kissing him again. Undoubtedly, she was speaking a long string of words into his mind.

At last, Kerrick released her. He had calmed down quite a bit. He took her arm, after which Alison brought him back to Leto.

Leto just shook his head. "We were talking about the arena battle. I was apologizing."

Kerrick nodded, his eyes haunted. "It was a hard day."

"I'm so sorry, Kerrick," Leto said.

"I wanted your death, but Alison wouldn't have it. She was much wiser than all of us that day."

Grace slipped her arm around Leto's. She could feel that he stood on some terrible precipice as he stared at Kerrick. "It ruined something in me to betray the warriors, to betray

Second Earth." He began to shake as though his century of being viewed as a traitor, in that moment, had just caught up with him.

Grace glanced at Alison. Alison stared back and shrugged as though even she didn't know what to do.

But it was Kerrick who suddenly stepped into Leto. He grabbed him, hugged him, and held on. Maybe it was a warrior thing, something only another warrior could truly understand. "You're back with us now," Kerrick said. "That's all that matters, brother." He all but pounded on Leto's back.

Leto settled down and pulled away. He nodded several times, then offered a smile. "Thank you for that."

Kerrick nodded in like manner and cleared his throat. He swept his arm around Alison, who leaned up and kissed his cheek. "Okay. Well, that's settled. Good. Good. Uh, but just in case you didn't know, it isn't wise to go around hugging other warriors' *brehs*."

Leto laughed. "Oh, I know." He slid his arm around Grace. "And I wouldn't have, but Grace gave me permission."

Kerrick shifted to smile ruefully at Grace. "Yeah, that's what Alison said." He laughed and shook his head. "Damn *breh-hedden*. It's always charging down on me when I least expect it." He nodded a few more times, then jerked his head in the direction of the landing platform. "Well, I better get back." He drew away from Alison and reset his thick wavy black hair in his *cadroen*. "I'm working with Seriffe through the afternoon. Luken, Zach, and Santiago are at Apache Junction Two as well. Come say hi if you get a break later today."

"I will."

He leaned down and kissed Alison again, then headed up the shallow ramp. Alison walked with him to the top of the platform.

Grace slipped her arm around Leto's waist. "You okay?" she asked quietly.

He turned into her and drew her into his arms. He held her in a tight embrace. *I feel lost,* he sent. *I can't help it, I just do. What I did robbed me of something, a feeling that I'll never really belong, never feel whole again.*

There were no real words to make things right, so Grace continued to hold him, to stroke his arms and back. To kiss his neck above his vein over and over, to whisper her love and to remind him that she knew him deeply and valued all that he was.

Thorne called out, "Hey, I didn't know you two were here."

Grace pulled away and turned toward her brother, who stood in the archway that led to the large central rotunda. "Kerrick was just here," she said.

She glanced at Leto, but his gaze was fixed on Thorne, his expression intent.

"Looks like we've got a battle coming," Thorne said. He glanced at Alison, who had rejoined them. "And I think it's because we have a major convergence among the three of you."

Grace couldn't help but agree. Both Leto and Alison had some connection to Third Earth, especially if it turned out Leto really was ascending. And she, of course, was the missing piece of the obsidian flame puzzle.

"Where do you want me?" Leto asked.

"Here, at the palace, or in Apache Junction Two at Militia Warrior HQ. We'll both float between the two places. I'll want you to liaison with the colonies' militia."

He turned and waved a hand forward then led them into the large central rotunda.

Grace was surprised to find that the usually empty room was now laden with long tables, dozens of swivel chairs, computers, and cords running every which way. A massive and familiar grid that mapped the entire globe sat at the center of everything.

Leto looked around. "This looks damn familiar, the way Greaves's HQ looked at the Estrella Mountain Complex."

Thorne took him on a tour and introduced him to the various techs and Militia Warriors he'd chosen to work at the palace with him. Grace followed behind, savoring the wonderful changes in Thorne that had occurred since she had last seen him. He was even taller than she remembered, maybe by a full inch, a result of the recent transformation he had been through as he took on the mantle as anchor to the obsidian triad. His beautiful hazel eyes were clear and full of fire. He even had a faint silver aura and overall, he just *felt* more powerful.

When Thorne reached the last table, he said, "Endelle wanted me to bring all of you through to her private suite once you got here." He waved them forward and led them through two smaller adjoining rotundas.

Endelle met them outside another large archway that undoubtedly opened onto her rooms. Her skin had the beautiful olive tones of the Middle East. Despite her garish fashion sense, and her unmatched profane mouth, she was an Arabian beauty, out of Mesopotamia nine thousand years ago. Her eyes might have at one time been a rich chocolate brown, but they had grown strangely wooded in appearance over the millennia, as though the deep struggles of her life, of having lived alone as the ruler of Second Earth for such a long time, had left her scarred.

She wore a pair of pants in striped black-and-white leather topped with a cherry-red bustier. Her low-hanging belt was made of tiny silver scorpions. Grace was a little surprised, because even though most women would never wear such an outfit, this actually had to be one of Endelle's most subdued ensembles ever. She frowned as she greeted them. Grace could sense her distress.

Endelle's sitting room was filled with purple velvet couches and chairs all arranged on a huge pure white shag rug. Glass tables were scattered around. As with much of the palace, instead of a window, the wall was open to the air and led to a small terrace and low wall.

She gestured for everyone to sit down, even though she remained standing.

Thorne took a seat in a big chair that faced away from the terrace. Alison sat opposite him, which gave Grace the chance to sit with Leto on the couch, which suited her. Maybe it was the *breh-hedden*, but she wanted to be close to him right now.

Endelle paced the length of the room, the scorpion belt

jingling. She called over her shoulder, "Havily brought in Starbucks, and I drank three grandes all by myself. I'm either peeing or pacing." Her hair moved as well in response to her emotions. She was definitely keyed up.

"I was about to tell them what's going on," Thorne said.

"Fine," she responded, but without her usual sarcasm.

That was new. Normally, especially with Thorne, she would have laid on the attitude. Apparently not today, maybe not anymore.

Though his expression grew somber, Thorne spelled it out. "We're headed for a battle against Greaves. Marguerite has been in the future streams and she's seen parts of it. It will take place over White Lake."

"But there's a resort colony over there," Leto said, frowning, "with over a hundred world-class hotels and public gardens."

Thorne shrugged. "Just reporting what she's seen. Apparently part of the battle takes place over White Lake, and obsidian flame is at the center of things, along with Endelle. And, no, she wasn't able to determine the outcome. She wanted to emphasize that she's only gotten glimpses, not even enough to plan a strategy."

He huffed a sigh then continued. "There was, however, an anomaly, in that she's had another vision of obsidian flame in flight, together, as in some kind of demonstration. So we're going on the assumption that everything is going to happen fast, and we want to be prepared. And to answer the question that I'm sure is on all your minds, yes, Owen Stannett is blocking her in the future streams. But to be fair, she and her Seers work to block him just as much. To some degree, they've been canceling each other out, but as far as I'm concerned that's fine by me. I'd rather there was an absence of information than that the enemy had a Seer advantage right now."

Grace's stomach flip-flopped. Was this really happening? The war had been going on for centuries, and had been steadily escalating for the past fifteen years. Was it really about to reach some kind of sudden, abrupt conclusion? It didn't seem possible. For as long as she had been alive, all two thousand years, Greaves had been creating death vampires and causing a mountain of trouble, from one century to the next, in anticipation of taking over Second and Mortal Earths.

"So Marguerite isn't working alone on this?" Grace asked.

Thorne shook his head. "No, not at all. She learned from some of Diallo's refugee Seers that working in teams improves accuracy. She has a setup out at the rehab center, a nice lounge, in which Seers work in shifts and in groups of four." He inclined his head toward Alison. "Of course you know by now that Alison has mounted her wings and has been having dreams about the Third Earth portal."

"Yes," Leto said, but he dipped his chin frowning. "I suppose Endelle told you about Casimir's arrival."

Thorne nodded. "This has to be a shitfest for you on several levels."

"Especially since he saved my ass out at Nazca."

Endelle stopped her pacing. Thorne leaned forward in his chair, a deep crease between his brows. "I didn't know Casimir had been out there?"

"Me neither," Endelle said, resuming her movement back and forth. "What the fuck happened?"

"It was well after the battle and after the colony had been secured." He then related the tale of Greaves's arrival with his Third Earth death vampires.

Endelle moved to stand near Thorne. "Are you telling us Greaves was there, himself, in Nazca, and meant to kill you with a hand-blast?"

"Knowing Greaves, I'm sure he meant only to disable me, but his death vampires would have finished the job. Greaves would never go against that particular COPASS directive, the one that forbids him to kill anyone by his own hand. He wouldn't risk it because he only owns about a third of the committee."

"But it was clear to you," Thorne said, "that he meant for you to die."

"No question. But as you can imagine, he holds a certain

animosity toward me. I betrayed him by leaving his service and returning to Endelle."

"Leto," Endelle said, her voice sharp. "Are you in your call to ascension to Third?"

He held his hands wide. "I don't know. I don't think so, except for my beast-state. I haven't experienced the usual longings or dreams, nothing like that. Although one of the death vamps said I was morphing the way Third Earth warriors morph."

"A Third Earth warrior?" Thorne asked.

"That's what he said."

Thorne exchanged a look with Endelle. She shrugged and said, "I don't know what to make of it. We know so little about Third Earth other than that it's having its own share of growing pains. I suppose it's possible that warriors there do what you do. This is a strange dimensional world. Anything's possible."

Thorne scratched his forehead with his thumb. "Despite all the unknowns, your possible ascension to Third, or whatever the hell this turns out to be, was one more reason we decided to set up the war room here at the palace."

Endelle nodded, then gestured from Leto to Alison. "You know, there's a bit of symmetry here between you two. You battled each other in the arena, and now Alison got her wings and more dreams of White Lake, and you have a Guardian of Ascension sent here to protect you during your ascent to Third."

Thorne fixed his gaze on Grace. "Endelle and I believe that Greaves has been waiting for your return before making his move. I've been tracking the location of his army for some time now, for months. Almost within the hour of your return, he began moving a massive portion of his force here to his extensive underground bunkers near Estrella."

"How do you know?" Grace asked. "I mean, the bunkers are partly under Greaves's peach orchard and partly deep beneath the Estrella Mountains."

But it was Leto who answered the question. "Because I

created a back door to the facility, and told your brother all about it."

"A back door?" Grace asked.

"A computer program linked up with hidden surveillance units in just about every main room of the compound. I couldn't do anything about the rooms Greaves used—he was too smart for that. But the concealed aboveground landing platforms and the underground bunkers, yes."

Thorne smiled. "Leto has shifted the balance of power in our direction. We know so much more about Greaves and about his operation than we ever would have known if he hadn't served as a spy." To Leto he said, "I want you to work with me at the command center, specifically on strategy. If Greaves intends to attack at White Lake, with all those gardens and hotels lined up on both banks, we'll need a plan in place with orders ready to deliver to all the Militia Warrior Section Leaders."

He rose, and because there was command in his manner, everyone rose along with him.

Leto could breathe. Between Kerrick's earlier demonstration of warrior acceptance, and Thorne's obvious trust in Leto, yes, he was beginning to breathe. "Where do you want me?" he asked.

Thorne smiled. "Right next to me for now. We have some planning to do."

Leto nodded.

What might have happened next was disrupted by a shimmering that appeared next to Endelle.

Both warriors drew swords, but the man who materialized looked about as harmless as a librarian. Leto knew him well.

James.

He had gray hair, a novelty in any ascended world. He was short given the relative height of everyone in the room, and there was laughter in his shining light blue eyes.

As Thorne and Leto folded their swords away, Endelle addressed the newcomer. "Hey, shorty, long time no see. What the fuck are you doing here?"

He drew close. "How about a date?" he asked.

"In your dreams."

He laughed as he turned to face not Thorne, or even Alison whom he had known since her rite of ascension, but rather Leto.

"The time has come, my boy," James said. "I have a directive from Sixth Earth at long last. I know you always questioned whether all the difficult things you had to do serving Greaves would be worth the sacrifice: becoming a death vampire, providing us with thousands of documents, building an army for Greaves."

Every muscle of Leto's body tensed. Grace must have felt it because she slipped her hand into his, a great comfort. He didn't say anything, though; he just waited, as they all did, hanging on what James would next say.

James's lips curved slightly. "So you know that army you built?"

"All two million of it? Yes, and the knowledge is painful."

"Well, sometime in the next forty-eight hours, I want you to start taking back as much of Greaves's army as you can. Not the death vampires, of course, they're beyond reasoning. But the hundreds of thousands of Militia Warriors will follow you, if you but ask. That's what we know to be true."

Leto was stunned. "Why will they follow me?" he asked.

"Because you're a Warrior of the Blood, and you carried those values with you when you built that army. The same values now live in all those men and women. You treated Greaves's Militia Warriors, especially your Division and Section Leaders, with great respect. Your reputation among them is unequaled.

"Greaves's generals, on the other hand, are struggling to maintain control because they failed to continue the structure you put in place, the one built on honor and decent treatment. Thousands have deserted, and an equal number have been executed at the whims of the generals.

"When you left, several of Greaves's top men fought for control so that the army is now split under three separate men. Believe me, you have an opportunity to win them to

Endelle's side. As you know, the Council of Sixth Earth can never act outright, but we can offer guidance. Just please take what I've said very seriously."

Leto had known James for a century. Though he had the appearance of a mild, humble man, at times he spoke like an ancient warrior, like someone who knew what battling was, how hard it was on the dedicated soldier, how much discipline was required to get through each day, especially when the days were filled with war. At other times, like now, he talked like a man who had served on a council for centuries. He was two men, but perhaps everyone was.

Leto drew in a deep breath. "If there is even the smallest chance that I could turn the army, or any part of the army, I'll do it. I swear it on my life."

James stepped toward Leto and clapped him on the shoulder. "I know all that your service took from you, every ounce of hope at times, and how far into despair your activities plummeted you. But that life is over, and this new one has begun. So don't hold back, Leto, not in any sense. We have a chance now. We have a chance."

Then James smiled, a very broad smile, and a sheaf of papers appeared in his hands. "Remember all those files you stole for us?"

Leto glanced at the papers. "Yes." His heart began to vibrate softly, as though he already knew what James was about to say.

"Well, right here are the private cell phone numbers for every Division and Regiment Leader of Greaves's army. We broke the code for you, so you needn't worry about that. Also, we suggest you start with the divisions out of Mongolia Two and Australia Two."

Leto took the papers and his heart began to sing. Here was justification, something specific that could be drawn from his years as a spy, that could help the ones he'd betrayed. He could bring a fully operational army and lay it at Endelle's feet.

"Hot damn," Endelle said. She even slugged James's arm. "You finally came through for us."

James did the unthinkable. He reached high, planted his hand on the back of Endelle's neck, drew her toward him as he reached up, then planted a kiss on her lips.

As she recoiled in protest, James laughed then vanished.

Endelle wiped her mouth with the back of her hand. "That little bastard. I'll get him for that. And why the fuck did he just take off? I have a thousand questions he needs to answer. One day, I'm going to sit on him and force him to cough up all the information I want, and Sixth Earth can just suck it."

Transformation
Begins in the soul.

—*Collected Proverbs,* Beatrice of Fourth

CHAPTER 9

After James left, Thorne suggested that he and Leto move to the command center so that Alison could work with Grace on her obsidian flame skills.

But as Thorne headed back to the central rotunda, Grace took Leto's hand, holding him back. "This is fantastic news."

He nodded. He had a wind-blasted look. "I just can't believe it." He glanced at the papers in his hand. "Well, I know what I'll be doing for the next few hours." He met her gaze again. "To think I could win them over."

Grace was ready to agree, but it was Endelle who came forward and put her hand on his shoulder. "The man who gave that speech at the opening ceremonies of the warrior games could win back the entire army, given enough time. Shit, Leto, I'm fucking glad you're home." She looked down at her feet. "Hold on a second."

She folded off her stilettos and what do you know, Leto was actually taller than Her Supremeness. She held out her arms. "Welcome home."

As Leto returned Endelle's embrace, Grace put her fingers to her lips. Her eyes burned like crazy. She wasn't even jealous, but then she could count on one hand the times

Endelle had demonstrated anything close to something as impractical as sentiment.

When she let him go, she still gripped his arms. "I hated that you left when you did."

"Did you truly believe I'd gone traitor?"

She shrugged. "When you've lived as long as I have, you really have seen everything. But I was damn glad when James finally showed up and told Alison here what was going on with you." She smiled. "All right, go get me an army."

He chuckled, but instead of just leaving, he turned to Grace and dipped down to kiss her. She kissed him back, wanting him to know how proud she was of him.

"Oh, for Christ's sake," Endelle barked. "Do I have to get a hose?"

But for some reason, this only made Leto move into Grace and take her more fully in his arms. Maybe he was just trying to provoke the scorpion queen, but Grace thought it was genius. She let him kiss her for as long as he wanted. After all, the man had just gotten the validation he'd needed for the past century.

She sent, *You know if anyone else had built that army . . .* She let her thought rest.

I know. He deepened the kiss and held her tighter still. Celebration came in many forms.

When he finally did pull back, Endelle was rolling her eyes.

"Get to work, beast-man."

Leto saluted her and left.

Grace wondered if Endelle meant to watch her work with Alison, but once Leto left she said she had a meeting with Marcus and that she'd be at her administrative HQ for the rest of the day if she was needed.

Grace had no idea what her session with Alison would be like, but was a little surprised when Alison made a space on the white shag rug by pushing the nearest chair and a couple of the smaller tables off to the side. After pushing the coffee table into the couch, she then sat down cross-legged on the rug and asked Grace to join her.

As Grace seated herself opposite Alison, she felt a certain amount of relief that Alison was taking the lead. She had helped Fiona a few months ago to find her channeling gift.

Grace's heart was beating hard all over again at the thought of exploring her obsidian power. Somehow, it made the potential of the triad more real.

The only thing she knew to tell Alison, however, was what it had been like for Leto to open her power up, how he'd had to reach deep into her soul. She added, "I suppose I should tell you that from the time I was young I had the ability to read souls, to see into the deepest parts of people and to find their essential goodness, to discover all they were meant to be."

Alison tilted her head, her eyes narrowing slightly. "I think I understand. That's why you were able to leave with Casimir, isn't it? You saw all that he could be."

Grace nodded. She experienced waves of Alison's compassion flowing toward her, and some of her nervousness subsided. She took a deep breath and promised herself she would hold nothing back. In order to do what needed to be done, especially with speed, she would have to share her deepest thoughts and concerns with the woman opposite her.

But then Alison, through her empathy, made the process so easy.

Grace spoke first of Casimir, of having read his soul in the Convent when he'd brought a death vampire attack against Leto on behalf of Greaves. "That was when I first realized that I had two *brehs*."

"It must have been frightening."

"And overwhelming, because I was so drawn to them both. But while on Fourth with Casimir I looked into his soul. I saw all that he could have become but for the horror of the early centuries of his life. He'd been used as a sex slave. I think, or at least I would like to believe, that my real purpose in his life was to lead him to Beatrice's pools of redemption. He changed so much after his first baptism. He was becoming a new man. Every day I saw a difference."

"And now?"

"I worry that he'll die." Grace shared all that she knew of

Casimir's destiny, how it was linked to both Grace and Leto. "Before I chose him, I saw his death. But we asked Beatrice if the future might be changed. She said only if he completed her program."

"But he didn't?"

"No, and for that I feel sick at heart. I felt compelled to return to Leto yesterday, and now here I am. And of course you know the rest, that Casimir is serving as Leto's Guardian of Ascension."

Alison nodded. "We don't always know the twists and turns of our paths. And thank the Creator for that. If I had known what would transpire during my rite of ascension, that I would be required to battle Leto with sword in hand, I probably would have crawled beneath my bed on Mortal Earth and stayed there."

At that, Grace laughed. "You're exactly right. We would all do that."

Alison searched her eyes. "What I sense from you is the tremendous courage that you have shown in coming forward to join the triad. I'm very proud of you. It's not easy having so much natural power yet not wanting it. That was exactly my life from the first time, as a child, that I dematerialized. I was human, and there was no one in my mortal life to help me or to guide me. So I do understand what it is not to be made of warrior material yet saddled with more power than you ever wanted."

Grace released perhaps the deepest sigh of her life. "You have no idea how good it feels to hear you say that. My twin and Thorne were always ready for any adventure. But I liked my books."

Alison smiled. "I so get you, Grace. I really do. And it also couldn't have helped to share a convent cell with Marguerite, who is also in Thorne's mold."

"I admire her so much; I guess because she has all the pluck I never will."

But Alison only smiled. "Let me tell you something. Pluck comes in many forms. Just because you're not a wildcat doesn't mean that you don't have pluck. Your being right here with me, for instance, is huge. You're just different, that's all, and you have a different role to play."

Grace couldn't remember the last time she'd heard such wonderful encouragement. "Thank you for letting me see myself in a new way."

"You're welcome. Okay, so let me understand. From everything you've told me, I take it that you've held back exploring your soul-reading power, correct?"

"Yes. But now I believe it's the key to my obsidian flame power. When Leto opened my power, it was very different from what Fiona and Marguerite experienced. He had to go deep into my own soul. The problem is that I've spent much of my life learning not to invade the lives of others in that way."

"So it feels like an invasion."

"It's too much knowledge. It overwhelms me with a sense of responsibility and at the same time a feeling of complete impotence, as though I can really be of no use."

"Maybe that's the key. Maybe your gift has a use, in the same way that both Fiona and Marguerite have specific purposes for their gifts separate from obsidian flame."

Grace shook her head. "I can't even begin to imagine what I could possibly do with this soul-reading gift."

"Well, why don't you begin with me? Why don't you read my soul, as an experiment, and we'll see where it leads us."

"You're okay with that?"

Alison smiled. "Of course. I trust you implicitly."

Grace's brows rose. She had never been more surprised. "But you hardly know me."

"You forget that I'm empathic and that I've been trained to *know* people just by conversing with them. Also, in your case, I know you by your reputation. Marguerite always praises you to the skies, and Thorne has you on a pedestal. In that sense, I've come here today greatly prejudiced in your favor."

Grace couldn't help but smile, and yet she felt she didn't deserve such praise.

"That look you have right now is the one I want to understand the most. I can sense how unworthy of life you feel. Maybe through this process, I can help you with that."

"Maybe," Grace said. But she realized there was a good chance that Alison was about to learn the hardest truth of Grace's life.

Still, there was nothing for it. "All right, then," Grace said. "Give me your hand and let me read your soul."

When Alison extended her hand, Grace took it. She closed her eyes, and after at least one deep breath, she fell into Alison's mind. She felt Alison's hand jerk beneath her own. She pressed on through her mind to the deepest layers, letting herself fall until she was swimming in the absolute beauty of Alison's self, her soul.

She grew very still, until she realized she was being drawn toward the source of Alison's ability to heal the mind. The source felt like a door with a lock and for which she somehow had the key.

Using her intuition, she extended her power into the lock, like a blue flame key, and the door flew open. Grace then drew Alison's healing ability into her body in long sweeping waves, a complete sharing. Once the process was complete, she drew out of Alison's soul and her mind. Leaving her was a very strange rubbery sensation. She blinked. Alison smiled, but she shook her head.

"What exactly happened?" Alison asked. "I mean I could feel you, but what were you doing?"

Grace sat staring at Alison. She was filled with a sense of wonder at what she had just done. "I believe I acquired your ability to heal the mind." She related all that she had experienced to the last detail.

Alison grinned. "What an amazing gift this is. I mean, if I understand it, you could acquire any power. *Any power.* Just think about that. The implications are astonishing. But we should test it."

At that, Grace smiled. "But how could I test your ability to heal the mind." Then it was as though Grace knew, and she put her hand on Alison's forehead and let the healing waves flow.

The experience was like having something warm at the center of her palm.

Alison closed her eyes and sighed. Her shoulders even dropped a little. "Oh, that's wonderful. So that's what everyone else feels."

"Yes, it is," Grace said. "I've felt it from you many times, like soothing warm waves just easing over the mind. That's what happened when you came to help me at the Seattle warrior games."

Alison opened her eyes. "Wow. And thank you. I actually feel more relaxed."

"So you think this is it, then?" Grace asked. "That I can acquire abilities?"

"I do."

"So, now what?"

"I think you have to work this out with obsidian flame."

Grace realized she had taken the first step toward forging the obsidian flame triad. For just a moment, she wondered if she should go forward. She felt as though she had come to a crossroads—but she could still retreat if she wanted to. She could return to a former life and ease back into her more spiritual pursuits.

Yet even as the thought went through her mind, she knew she couldn't. In the same way that she was the sort of person who could commit happily to life in a convent for a hundred years, she knew she wouldn't go back. She had made her decision while on Fourth Earth to embrace her calling as obsidian flame, and so she would.

She mentally contacted Fiona and Marguerite and arranged to meet them in half an hour at the Militia HQ workout room. With the arrangements made, Grace walked Alison to the landing platform. She was headed to Endelle's office and would let Endelle know the results of her time with Grace.

After Alison left, Grace hunted Leto down to tell him her news. She found him in a quiet corner of one of the lesser-used rotundas. He had James's papers on his lap and his phone in hand. "How's it going?" she asked.

He looked up at her and smiled. "Incredible. It didn't even occur to me how things would be for my warriors when I left."

For *his* warriors. Grace loved the sound of that.

He leaned forward slightly and took her fingers in a light clasp. "How's it going with Alison?"

"I think we're done."

"You're done? So soon?"

She nodded then told him what had happened. Leto's brows rose. "You can acquire any ability?"

"That's what it feels like to me."

"Huh. Like the ability to fold masses of people?"

This time her brows rose. "You mean like warriors?"

He nodded slowly.

"Oh. Well." She squeezed his fingers. "Looks like I have some work to do with obsidian flame." She told him where she was headed. "You can let Thorne know what's going on as well. I know he has a role in obsidian flame so we might need him. I'm just not sure." She glanced behind her.

"I will."

"Walk me to the landing platform?"

He rose so fast from his chair that she took a step back and laughed. He put his arm around her and squeezed, then put them both in motion. She felt very young right now, like she was just a girl with her boyfriend and he was walking her to class. It was a nice feeling and in this moment, not far from the truth.

Her class, however, involved obsidian flame.

Once near the platform, Leto kissed her. She let the kiss linger.

I don't want to let you go, he sent, his lips hovering just over hers.

I don't want to leave.

The kiss deepened until she was swaying. Finally, she had to push him away.

He drew back and smiled ruefully. She always forgot how beautiful his eyes were until she was this close. They were the color of clear blue water. She gave him another quick kiss, and because she had the feeling if she didn't just take off, she'd stay for another hour with her hands fondling his biceps, she ran up the landing platform ramp.

He waited where she had left him, smiling and looking better than ever, more relaxed, more at ease.

She waved as she dematerialized and was still waving when she arrived at Militia Warrior HQ.

The Militia Warriors on duty looked at her with serious expressions then nodded as she started down the ramp.

She hadn't been to HQ in a long time and had to get directions to the workout room. In the past couple of years, the complex had been expanded; it actually took her several minutes to walk the distance to the room. No folding whatsoever was allowed within the complex. In previous years, before the addition of the current state-of-the-art security system, death vamps had been known to fold inside the facility and take the lives of dozens of Militia Warriors, often before anyone even knew what was happening.

Now the whole complex was locked down tight.

Once at the workout center, Marguerite waved to her from across the room.

Grace had missed her. Though they were opposites, a hundred years sharing a convent cell had created a warm bond. She would always consider Marguerite one of her closest friends.

Marguerite wore stretchy black pants and a crisp white maternity blouse. She was barefoot, leading with her belly, all full of Grace's niece and nephew. Fiona was there as well in flats, jeans, and a tank. Her long chestnut hair was drawn into a ponytail. She looked beautiful.

"How pretty you look," Marguerite said, holding her hands out to Grace.

She took them. "Thank you and so do you. Glowing, actually, although I have to say it's still strange to see you with short blond hair." For the ten decades Grace had been with Marguerite in the Convent, her hair had been very long and dark brown.

"So what happened with Alison earlier?" Fiona asked. "I know she helped me tremendously. What did you find out?"

Grace shared her experience.

Marguerite's large brown eyes went very wide. "Any power?"

Grace shrugged. "That's what I'm sensing. Any soul, any power."

"Wow," Fiona murmured.

Marguerite whistled then looked around. "Well, I guess this place is big enough for us to do some practicing."

The room was huge, and Colonel Seriffe had cleared the space for them, moving all the machines and workout equipment to one side.

Grace laughed. "Well, I hope it's big enough. I mean, what if we have enough combined power to blow the roof off?"

As if on cue, all three women looked straight up at an interlacing of steel girders, then back at one another. When Marguerite and Fiona laughed, Grace joined them, and something tight within her chest started to unwind.

"This seems so strange," Fiona said. "Six months ago I was a blood slave. Now I'm here, with powers I'd never dreamed of." Fiona could channel powers and enhance them at the same time. She could even be possessed by another person, which really enhanced the power level. She reached one hand toward Grace and one toward Marguerite. Even without touching their obsidian power flared.

Fiona jumped back and laughed. "There it is again, just like at the Seattle Colony."

Grace rubbed her arms. "It's always so strange. I wonder if we'll ever get used to it."

"Hey," Marguerite said, her voice lowered almost conspiratorially. "Let's try creating a circle like we did by accident before the warrior games. Remember?"

Grace nodded at the same time as Fiona. Grace put her hand on Fiona's shoulder. Fiona did the same to Marguerite, and even without the circle being completed the vibrations were strong.

Marguerite's dark brown eyes glittered with delight, which made Grace smile. Marguerite's hand would close the circle but she aimed her fingers at Grace's shoulder, holding back, then inch by inch crept toward her.

What a tease, but it helped to lighten the mood.

The moment contact was made, however, Grace flew backward, as did each of the women. Not far, but it was unsettling to sit up and watch Fiona do so as well. Marguerite had a little more trouble. She rolled to the side and pushed her heavy body up.

Once upright, Grace moved back toward the other women.

When they were together again and the same level of power surged even before they touched, Marguerite said, "I think we're going to need Thorne here to anchor us. If it's all right with you, I'm going to ask him to come over. Maybe he can get us started or something."

"I totally agree," Fiona said.

Grace nodded her acquiescence as well.

Marguerite strolled away, one hand touching her cheek as she moved. Grace could sense that she was communicating telepathically with Thorne. She even knew when the conversation ended.

When she turned back around, she called out, "He'll be here shortly."

Grace recalled seeing Thorne bent over the grid when she walked Alison to the landing platform. She wondered how he would feel about leaving his command center.

When Thorne arrived, Marguerite explained what had happened.

He glanced down at her belly. "Are you all right?"

"I'm fine. I'm tougher than I look."

His expression softened, and he dipped down to kiss her. When he rose back up, he was all business. "Okay, well I never quite understood my role, but it seems that I'm an anchor here, at least for now. Why don't you try touching again, but I'll keep a hand on Marguerite's shoulder."

Once more, Fiona began and connected with both Marguerite and Grace. The power vibrated among them like crazy.

"This is really something," Thorne said.

Sure enough, as Grace put her hand on Marguerite's shoulder, closing the circle, the power surged. But this time the excess traveled through Thorne.

"Doesn't that bother you?" Grace asked. He was lit up and glowing with the most beautiful silver aura.

"Not at all. In fact it's pleasant." He nodded a couple of times and narrowed his eyes. "So, Leto told me that you have the ability to secure the powers of others by doing some soul diving. Do I have it right?"

"Yes."

His silver aura began to diminish and soften, and finally disappeared. "All right, so how exactly do you think the process works then?"

But it was Marguerite who answered the question. "I think it means that when any of us experiences a profound intuition that something is wrong, like what happened at Nazca, then I look into the future streams. When I get a solid vision, the three of us can determine what power is needed to resolve whatever situation appears. Grace then learns the skill from whatever ascender would be best for acquiring the ability. She takes possession of Fiona because Fiona has the power to exponentially amplify any power. And that's how we get the job done. But the amazing thing is you, Grace. If you can enter the soul of any individual in the entire world and you can learn any ability, then there is no real limit to what we can accomplish."

And there it was, the identification of what this triad could do.

Grace thought for a moment, and let herself rest deeply within her obsidian power. She felt it vibrate softly. "If our ability as a triad to accomplish a task rests with me, then maybe we should practice exactly that: I should acquire an ability and we should apply it. How does that sound?"

"Perfect," Fiona said.

Marguerite nodded her assent.

"What power would you like to explore, then?"

Grace addressed Thorne. "I have an idea because I think

it would make a great test. I'd like to acquire Leto's ability with the sword. Then I'd like to possess Fiona and have her do battle with Jean-Pierre."

"That sounds dangerous."

"Have Jean-Pierre here as well as Leto. Because of the *breh*-bond, I think some of what we do will have to include the other men, don't you agree?"

"You're absolutely right, especially in these early stages."

"What's my role?" Marguerite asked. "I mean, if my job is to choose the task through the future streams, how do I fit in here?"

Grace tilted her head. "Actually, I think in order to really see what the triad can do, we need to be connected when I take possession of Fiona—we need to be functioning as a triad. I mean, I know that Fiona and I could do our parts alone, but I have a feeling that the triad adds something extra."

An intuited consensus followed.

Grace contacted Leto and asked him to come to the workout center while Fiona did the same with Jean-Pierre. Because of the folding regulations, both warriors had to fold straight to the landing platforms then walk the considerable distance to the workout room.

When Leto and Jean-Pierre finally entered the room, Grace's vision narrowed to a fine point focused exclusively on her *breh*. His hair was tight in the *cadroen,* which set his sharp angled cheekbones in strong relief. He walked with a lethal athletic stride, and because he wore a snug T-shirt, her gaze drifted to his pecs. She blinked a couple of times and wished for a moment that she was alone with him.

Her heart rate soared at the sight of him. Because of the *breh-hedden,* she could feel the give in the black mats as he crossed toward her, the brush of his fingertips against the sides of his jeans, and the way the muscles of his face moved as he smiled crookedly at her.

Hello, beautiful, he sent.

She had only one real thought, that she wanted to be alone with him. "Hey," she murmured when he drew near. She was a little embarrassed, but out of the corner of her eye she saw that Jean-Pierre was holding Fiona in a warm embrace and Thorne had taken Marguerite at least twenty feet away.

She wasn't alone in what she was feeling.

Leto put his arms around her, and she put her hands on his chest. "So what's this idea you have?" he asked.

"I want to acquire your swordsmanship." She explained how the triad worked.

"You'll enter my soul, acquire this ability, then take possession of Fiona."

She nodded. "Yes, but we'll be connected as a triad with Thorne anchoring the early part of the process. We thought it would be best if Jean-Pierre participated just in case we need some outside corralling of the sword battle."

"If you take possession of Fiona, then you won't exactly be in your body."

"I think it will be like when I do an apparition-split. I'm in both places at once, just more present in the apparition form."

"You made the right call," he said. "Until the triad has everything worked out, I'm glad I'm here."

After a few minutes, Marguerite and Thorne strolled back toward the group and Jean-Pierre released Fiona.

"Is everyone up to speed?" Thorne asked.

A series of assents went around the group. Grace then asked Leto to remain where he was; she would enter his soul before the triad fired up its power.

She took three deep breaths, closed her eyes, and entered his mind. His shields were already flat, a point of trust that warmed her heart as she began to fall deep into all that was Leto. She passed into his soul, and because her intention was fixed, her blue flame power forged a key and found the lock that contained his ability to use a sword.

All that experience and skill flowed through Grace. She flew up and out of Leto's soul very fast and was suddenly within her own mind. Her arm felt different, her shoulders, her back. She could feel how her hand was ready to receive a sword.

She glanced at Jean-Pierre who smiled, showing his large gorgeous teeth. He held up a sword and tossed it to her.

Both Marguerite and Thorne gasped. Even Leto moved to intervene, but it was as though Grace had been a warrior for three millennia. She caught it by the grip and went through a variety of training motions, ones that had been passed down through generations of warriors.

When she was done, she faced the group. "This is astonishing."

"Holy shit," Leto said. "It certainly is."

Then she smiled. "What amazes me the most is how the muscles of my arm just reach for the movements." She stared at Leto for a long moment. "How much you must have loved this part of it—the training, then the use of your skill in battle when you fought the enemy."

"Everything you've said is exactly right."

Grace turned toward her obsidian sisters. She handed the sword to Fiona. "You'll need this in a few seconds."

Fiona swiped the blade through the air. Jean-Pierre wisely gave her some space, but he said in the lilt of his French accent, "How strange to think that I will be battling my *breh*."

The moment of truth had arrived, the truth of exactly what obsidian flame could do. This was a very small test, to pit the triad against Jean-Pierre's ability as a swordsman.

Of all three men, Leto had the smallest role in what was to unfold in the next few minutes. He drew his iPhone from the pocket of his jeans and backed up about thirty feet so that he could make a video of this first test run.

He felt the scowl on his face. He wasn't thrilled that there was a sharp blade involved in this first venture. But he thought that might be because his woman would be near the battle. He didn't like the idea of her getting accidentally hurt.

He watched the women join together, hands to shoulders. Even as far away as he was, he could feel their power expand suddenly, like a whip through the room.

He held the phone steady with both hands elevated at shoulder level. He could see events unfold. Grace's neck arched, then she left the circle and began backing up and away, at a right angle to Leto's position, and stood very still.

He shifted his gaze to Fiona. Her eyes were wide open and she had a gold aura as she turned toward Jean-Pierre. She held her sword in the ready position, her knees slightly bent, her chin down, her eyes up, both hands on the grip.

He had to remind himself to keep filming because all he really wanted to do was to watch the battle. What followed startled him. Fiona's skills were at Warrior of the Blood level, a perfect reflection of his own ability as well as his centuries of training and use.

Jean-Pierre worked hard to keep up with her, and yet Leto had the sense that Fiona was holding back.

He shifted his gaze to both Marguerite and Grace, then he saw what he hoped the camera would pick up as well. Rivers of faint light flowed between the women, moving strands of blue, gold, and red.

Fiona—or was it Grace?—began to move faster and faster. She flew through the air with levitation power alone; she tumbled through exotic rolls and kept Jean-Pierre completely off balance. Her speed increased as the triad flexed its power, until at last she was a long blur of speed and Jean-Pierre finally stood still, his sword pointed toward the black mats.

The sound like the roaring of a wind rushed through the room—and then the moment ended. The blur that was Fiona stopped midair, arms outstretched as she floated back to the black mats.

The room fell silent. No one spoke.

Fiona touched down and walked toward her obsidian sisters. Leto saw when Grace returned to herself since her neck arched in the same way as when she left. She walked back in Marguerite and Fiona's direction.

When they came together, they touched shoulders again and formed another circle. Power flowed once more. A vast beam of white light filled the space in front of each of them and flowed in a massive stream up to the ceiling.

Leto had to shade his eyes.

At last the light faded and the circle broke.

He stopped filming and returned to the triad.

Thorne glowed his silver aura.

As they spoke about their experiences, Leto confirmed what each said with his own observations. Thorne did as well. Because they had video, it was decided to return to the palace and watch the feed on the large screen.

When the video had been reviewed about ten times with Endelle, she summed it up succinctly. "Well, damn."

Seduction comes in many forms.

—*Collected Proverbs,* Beatrice of Fourth

CHAPTER 10

Twenty-four hours had passed since Greaves had last seen Stannett. He entered the heart of the new Seers Fortress in Illinois Two, instead of Stannett's private room. The surroundings were lovely: black marble on the ceiling, part of the walls and floors, black leather padding on the rest of the walls, a few dim inset lights around the perimeter to cast the inner sanctum in a nice glow. The Seers' chaise longues were actually set in a lower level and reached by a flight of stairs at either end, almost like an orchestra pit. The viewing platform was quite large and finished with a fine polished mahogany.

Doors on either side of the inner sanctum led to an outer hall and the rest of the Seers palace.

From the platform, Greaves could watch Stannett and his bound Seers in action.

The chaise longues were arranged in a straight row, but each was tilted ever so slightly, almost imperceptibly. The concept behind the tilt was to keep the body slightly off balance and therefore the mind better focused.

Greaves moved to the edge of the stage and stared down into the pit. Stannett had his Seers strapped in place. His eyes were closed, and he had a sublime expression on his face. No doubt he had just filled his embroidered, red leather pants.

The vampire was hopeless.

"Stannett, we need to talk."

The Seer opened his eyes. "Hello, Greaves." He blinked rapidly several times. "I suppose you'd like an update." He sat up, then glanced at the three women bound to his right and the three to his left. "None of them is conscious yet. The power we just shared has put each in a stupor. Not a bad place to be. At least, they're not dead."

Greaves glanced at the women and noted the dark brown skin. "From Mumbai?"

"Yes. Some of your most powerful Seers."

"How long have you been working them?"

"Not long, about an hour. I allow them to rest for two afterward and make them drink lots of water. I've only had two die on me since last night."

Greaves repressed a sigh. "And what have you discovered about our present difficulties?"

Stannett looked up at him wide-eyed. "Nothing yet. I have kept these early trial runs relegated to less strenuous matters."

"You mean you've been hunting for future stream tail?"

"Well, yes. It seemed the most sensible way to get the women accustomed. I assure you, I haven't been the only one enjoying the process. If you'd arrived earlier, you would have heard a great deal of delighted moaning."

"And this is meant to reassure me?"

Greaves knew it was impossible for Stannett to comprehend the difficulties Greaves faced, but he began to suspect that the man was an idiot. Or if not a complete imbecile, then so given to his own pleasure that nothing else seemed to matter.

Greaves folded to his position in the pit. He put a finger beneath Stannett's chin and used resonance. *"Have I not told you how badly I need pure vision? That I must have the best possible information from moment to moment over the next several days?"* He could feel Stannett tremble. *"Why have you not done as I asked?"*

"I . . . I thought I did," Stannett said, wincing. Greaves had used resonance and he meant for it to hurt. "You didn't tell me to start amassing information. You told me to work the skills of your Seers."

"Then let me be very clear right now. I need an abundance of prophetic material as close to pure vision as you can achieve." Greaves swept a hand over both sets of women. "Go back in and find me some useful information for tonight. And I do mean tonight."

Stannett didn't hesitate. He stretched back out and began the process. Greaves folded back up to the platform. He could feel Stannett's power moving through the women. He wasn't surprised when many of them cried out as if in pain.

Good.

He waited for a moment, then when the Seers relaxed, he drove his mental power straight at Stannett, pierced his mind, and found himself in what looked like great chaos. A battle of some sort. Greaves recognized the Seattle hidden colony and the warrior games setup. He watched his death vampires flowing over the citizens and striking them down.

Peace moved through Greaves because he could feel that this was pure vision. If his enemy did not interfere, if Marguerite did not catch wind of the prophecy, then the Seattle Colony would be reduced to rubble. He sought for the timing of the event and knew that he had at least two hours to prepare. But he wanted to see the outcome. He was delighted when he saw his death vampires cheering and drinking people to death, chasing their victims into the forest.

When the stream ended, Greaves's heart beat strong in his chest. He would strike a blow against the opposition that would leave Endelle reeling. Right now it looked like Marguerite had failed to intervene by blocking Stannett, or maybe Stannett and the six Seers were just too damn powerful.

Either way, he rejoiced.

He was about to fold when he looked down and realized Stannett was trying to rouse the Seer to his left. The woman was dead.

Stannett looked up at him. "When the power begins to flow, they can't take it without rest, just as I said."

"But you have no problem with that level of power?"

Stannett laughed. "Of course not. Did you think I would?"

"No. You have many failings, my friend, but the inability to handle a power surge is not one of them." He glanced at the remaining women. "Are any of the rest dead?"

"Yes." Stannett looked from one to the next. "Three altogether."

"Pity." He rocked on his heels slightly. "Get rid of these, harness more, and forge a path through the future streams. And lest you mistake me again, I need as much information as you can gather, despite how hard Marguerite blocks you."

"Understood," Stannett responded.

That evening, after dinner at the palace, Leto returned with Grace to the bedroom of his cabin. He was still reeling from the hundred-plus conversations he'd had with the Division Leaders earlier in the day. His initial effort had been to test the waters as subtly as possible. To take anything further, to ask for commitments, was out of the question until he had a plan in place. His largest concern, about executing a mass fold, was just as Grace had suggested. He had no idea how he was going to physically move even one division, not to mention several, without Greaves finding out and stopping him.

He had finished his shower and had a towel around his waist. With another towel, he was drying his hair. Grace was sitting cross-legged on the side of the bed, staring at the wall. She was still in her yoga pants and shirt.

"What's going on?" he asked.

"I'm still stunned by that experience of possessing Fiona and battling Jean-Pierre with a sword. And when I allowed the triad's power to really infuse my movements, then I became a blur of speed."

"Were you ever afraid you would wound Jean-Pierre?"

"No, never. You can't imagine the amount of control the triad has. It was amazing. I'm still in shock." She looked around.

"Now what's wrong?"

She shook her head. "I don't know if it's just a residual effect from all the practice today, but my obsidian power is vibrating. I keep trying to intuit the problem, but I'm getting nothing. I just have this feeling . . ."

He moved to stand in front of her. "What can I do?"

She looked up and put her hand on his hip. "That's exactly what I needed to hear. Thank you. The funny thing is, I'm not sure. I feel like I'm supposed to do something, but I don't know what. I guess I'm a little wound up."

"Why don't you try contacting either Fiona or Marguerite?"

"I've been thinking about it, but it was such a long day for everyone."

"I think you should anyway."

She nodded, then closed her eyes. Her shoulders rose and fell, and she grew very still. He didn't move, either. He didn't want to disrupt the communication.

Finally, she seemed to relax and opened her eyes. "It was so easy to reach Marguerite. I just thought her name, and suddenly she was there. I wish you could have heard her. She was practically screaming at me, 'What's wrong, what's wrong?' " Grace laughed.

"What did you tell her?"

"Actually, I asked her to hop in the future streams because I was feeling uneasy. She said that was good enough for her and that she'd get back to me."

"Good, that's good."

Grace rose to her feet. "It's probably nothing. I'll go take my shower, but don't go far." She leaned up on her tiptoes and kissed him.

"I'll be right here." His chest felt warm and very full. He could see by the light in her eye that she had something cozy on her mind. He was definitely game.

He almost suggested he join her in the shower, but he had a few things to check out first. He looked around the room. Then he felt it, too. Something didn't feel right. He wondered if Casimir was around causing some sort of mischief.

He heard the shower running. Grace started humming,

and the sound gripped his heart in the nicest way. He could feel the water on her skin, her hands soaping up, then rubbing over her shoulders, her arms, her breasts . . .

Okay, he had to shut that down because he knew if he didn't, he'd be heading back to the bathroom. He ordered his mind and found that with a little effort, he could block some of her physical sensations. He really did need to check in with the colony's Militia Warrior HQ to see how things were going.

But as he folded his phone into his hand, his sense of uneasiness increased, though he couldn't say why. His cabin was a significant distance from the main portion of the village.

He turned the lamps off in the bedroom so that the only light in the room was the glow from the bathroom.

Grace was suddenly in his mind. *Marguerite said the Seattle Colony will be under attack.*

When?

Anytime.

I'll let HQ know.

He moved to the large window to the left of the bed and pushed back the curtain to look outside. No movement except the wind in the fir trees. He looked down at his phone. It was only eight in the evening. He thumbed, then located the colony's HQ phone and tapped the screen.

The phone rang.

The hidden colony HQ had a small working grid that constantly checked the perimeter throughout the mountainous terrain. A second grid checked the space beneath Diallo's dome of moss-based mist.

There was no answer.

There was no answer.

He scrolled for Thorne's number. The phone rang. Thorne picked up. "Marguerite just told me. I'm letting Seriffe know. We'll mobilize. Get up here to Second as soon as you can, and make sure Grace is safe."

"Shit. You must be right, and I think it's already started. I couldn't reach HQ."

"Got it."

When he tossed his phone on the bed, he realized that Grace had shut the water off and she no longer hummed.

Everything felt quiet.

Too quiet.

He turned to face the bathroom.

A shimmering next to Leto caused him to bring his sword into his hand.

Casimir.

"Thank the Creator. We're under attack."

"I'm here," Casimir said.

Leto had blocked Grace's sensations so he quickly reestablished his *breh*-connection. Then he knew. He could now feel the cold line of tiles that pressed against both sides of her back as well as her bottom, which meant she had backed up into the corner of the shower.

Leto. Her voice was suddenly in his mind. *Bring your sword,* she added. *We have company.*

To Casimir, he sent, *Death vamp in the bathroom.*

I've got your back. Casimir held his hands wide, and Leto could feel the power start to build.

Leto moved with blinding speed to the bathroom. Yet at the exact same moment, he felt three more large bodies fold into the bedroom, into the space he had just vacated.

He didn't wait to see what happened, but he could hear the vibrations of the hand-blast. Bodies fell to the floor.

He found Grace pressed up against the tile, staring into the face of a warrior-sized death vampire.

Leto used the tip of his sword and pricked the death vampire right on the ass.

The pretty-boy turned around. "What the fuck," he muttered, perhaps thinking one of his comrades was giving him a hard time.

Surprise.

Dropping into a fighting stance, Leto kept his gaze pinned on the death vamp. At the same time, he sent, *Grace, fold to the basement. Then get dressed. I'll meet you there in about three seconds.*

She vanished. A moment later he felt the cold of the basement touch her wet skin and hair.

He raised his sword, which drew the death vamp's arm up to meet steel with steel. But Leto had been a warrior a few thousand years longer than this sonofabitch. Folding his dagger into his left hand, he let it fly and caught the bastard straight through the neck.

At the same moment, he folded down to the basement. Grace wore jeans and a long green sweater that ended mid-thigh. She had on leather loafers. Good.

With a wave of his hand, he changed into clean flight battle gear.

To Casimir, he sent, *I'm taking Grace to Diallo's house, deep into the courtyard garden. Meet us there.*

Done, Casimir returned.

He took Grace's arm. "We're going to fold to Diallo's house, to the garden. I can't raise the colony's HQ on my phone. Casimir will join us there. I'll block my trace so that we won't be followed by any other death vampires who arrive here after we're gone. Okay?"

She nodded.

Leto folded her in a quick flash through nether-space. He felt her feet touch down just as his did. They were where he wanted them to be, hidden by foliage. He blocked his trace. However, Diallo's central courtyard was crawling with even more death vampires.

Holy shit, while he and Grace had been battling in his cabin, the colony had been attacked by death vampires. Why the fuck hadn't the alarms sounded?

Crouch, he sent.

She was quick and ducked.

Leto, what happened here?

He looked up at the dome of mist. *It's simple. Greaves mapped and breached the colony.*

The top had been burned away, just like at Nazca.

Another couple of seconds passed, and Casimir folded next to Grace. She looked up at him and nodded. There was nothing of the vampire Leto had known all those months ago. Casimir had been absurd, always taunting with sexual innuendo, always easy in his smiles. Now he was serious, even somber.

Casimir looked at Grace, but without flirtation. Right now, he even looked a little confused. Leto saw nothing to challenge in his demeanor toward Grace. He could only imagine what the redemption pools had been like to have taken the casual smirk from his face.

A number of sensations struck Grace all at once: Casimir's odd presence beside her, the humidity of the garden, the terrible number of death vampires milling about and ready to fight. She could feel Leto crouching without even looking at him because of the *breh-hedden*. Earlier, while she was waiting for Leto in the basement, she had felt him throw his dagger at the death vampire. Right now, when he pivoted on his heels to scan every inch of the garden, she could feel his battle sandals grinding against the hard pavers.

She peered through the shrubbery and started counting the number of death vampires, all restless, all moving as though they were hunting, even if their current job was to guard the courtyard. There had to be at least fifteen in the relatively small space. None of them spoke.

The war again.

She looked up. Remnants of the mist remained but mostly it was just gone, destroyed. In the distance, she could hear screams coming from the lane beyond Diallo's house as well as the sound of a rhythmic drumbeat. Why was there the sound of a drum?

Creator help them.

To Leto, she sent, *What do we do?*

I'm not sure, he responded. *I talked to Thorne. He said he was contacting Seriffe and would mobilize the Militia Warrior contingent at Apache Two. But I have a bad feeling about Diallo and Mei-Amadi.*

When she shivered, he slid his arm around her waist. *Sorry,* he sent. *But I think this is about to get worse.*

It's okay. I'll manage. She thought for a moment. *Do you think they have Diallo and his wife?*

That's what I think. Greaves would have ordered them to be either apprehended or killed.

Do you want me to look for them? She met his gaze. His blue eyes glittered in the garden shadows.

How will you look for them? Wait, I can feel your obsidian power rising, up through your legs.

She nodded. *Yes, that's it exactly. I can do what I did for you in Moscow Two and when I searched out Nazca One. I can use the apparition part of this power to travel the house.*

Won't you be seen?

She shook her head. *Don't you remember? Even Greaves couldn't see me. Just you and . . . Casimir.*

She felt him tense then relax. She could feel him swallow, which was a strange experience all in itself.

He nodded, but turned to stare once more through the leaves. *Do it.*

She leaned over and kissed him on the cheek. *Steady me while I do this thing.*

You got it. He tightened his arm around her. *I'll let Thorne know what's going on.*

Grace let her obsidian power flow. Because her blue flame was now fully opened, the rush of energy was like a flood.

She glanced up at Casimir and telepathically told him what was going on.

Be careful, he sent. He reached for her, glanced at Leto, then withdrew his hand.

Grace turned toward the house. She thought of Mei-Amadi, and her apparition-self moved swiftly through the shrubs and even past the death vampires.

She sped into the hall. To the left was the kitchen and dining room and another major hall leading to the bedrooms.

Shifting to face forward, she saw that the largest gathering of death vampires was in the front living room where she had sat with Leto all those months ago. They were making a lot of noise, even cheering. She found the pretty-boys grouped around a single death vampire on the floor. He was engaged in copulation and was drinking a woman to death.

Oh, God. Mei-Amadi.

She froze for a moment as visceral memories pummeled her. She knew exactly what the woman was experiencing, the terror, the pain, and the rage combined. She felt ill.

Grace, are you all right? Leto sent. *You're trembling in my arms.*

His voice eased her. *Yes,* she responded. She drew close and saw that the lovely African-Asian woman was white-faced, near death. *They have Diallo's wife.* But she knew what to do. She put her apparition-hand on the woman's forehead.

Grace simply took her with her so that Mei-Amadi vanished from beneath the death vamp. With a rush of energy, she headed back to Leto. At the same time she gave him a brisk mental warning of what she had done.

When she arrived and Mei-Amadi materialized beside her, she collapsed on Grace. She was naked, bruised, and bloody. She was also weeping. Her sounds would bring the death vamps.

We've got to get her out of here, Grace sent to Leto.

He drew Mei-Amadi into his arms and sent, *We're folding to the Militia Warrior HQ in Apache Junction Two. The landing platforms.* He glanced past her, and she could tell that he was sending Casimir a similar message.

Take her, Grace sent. *I'll follow.*

As he dematerialized, he was shouting into her head. *Grace, come with us now. This is too dangerous.*

She shifted to meet Casimir's gaze. He frowned heavily. *You need to go with him, don't you?*

He nodded, but he looked pained. *I hate to leave you here, but I'm Leto's guardian. Will you be safe?*

Yes. But I must find Diallo. She noticed movement to her right and saw that a couple of death vampires were headed in her direction. She couldn't stay in the garden.

She considered all her options and looked up. *I'm going to the roof. Come with me.*

She folded to the rooftop and blocked her trace. She'd half expected to meet up with a couple of death vamps here on top of the house, but none was present. She lay down on the shingle roof, making herself almost invisible since the sky was dark overhead.

Casimir materialized next to her. *What are you doing?*

I'm going to remain prone while I do my split-self. Don't worry. I feel very secure here. Go to Leto. I can feel your need to guard him.

He put a hand on her shoulder, then vanished.

Once more she let her obsidian power flow. She moved in apparition-form and began searching through the house room by room. A great deal of angry shouting was going on in the living room. She pressed on.

She found Diallo in the middle of his large master bedroom, beaten around his head and face, his arms cut up. A death vampire was behind him, his fangs in deep and drinking him down at his neck. Another was in front, and had attacked him in the groin, sucking from the vein. There were other fang-marks as well. Diallo's beautiful brown skin had actually paled.

Grace hurried toward him and he met her gaze. Diallo had so much power that he could see her when even Greaves couldn't. She put her hand on his forehead, and he simply vanished with her as she flew back to the roof and reentered her physical self. He collapsed facedown on the roof next to her.

"Lie still," she whispered. "I'm going to fold us to safety, but it will hurt like hell because you're wounded."

Diallo merely smiled.

She folded him to the landing platforms at the Militia Warrior HQ. He arrived facedown on the platform, screaming. In addition to the many cuts, it now became apparent that he had broken bones as well. After a few seconds, his back arched and he passed out.

Not long after, probably because of Leto's advance warning, several healers arrived. They moved Diallo off the platform, but not very far, as they began healing him.

Thorne arrived running up the ramp toward her. He drew her into his arms. "Are you all right?"

She nodded, then looked around. "Where's Leto?"

"He took Mei-Amadi straight to the hospital from here."

She could sense that Leto's arms were wrapped around his stomach and that he was blinking rapidly. *Leto, I'm at the landing platform. I've got Diallo. He's alive.*

Oh, thank God. I could feel that you had folded and that you had him with you. The breh-hedden *is really something, but who the hell is hugging you?*

Grace didn't know whether to laugh or cry. The whole situation was so horrible, yet Leto had time to be jealous? *Thorne. Just Thorne.*

Okay. Sorry about that. Diallo's wife has been calling for him. What can I tell her?

We got him in time. The healers are with him. He's really messed up: drained, cut up, some broken bones. I'm going to wait here with Thorne. Come to us when you can.

I'll come back as soon as Alison gets here, probably just a minute or two.

Okay, that's good. Is Casimir with you?

There was a slight pause, then *He just left. I told him you were with Thorne.*

She knew he was angry, and she knew exactly why, so she sent, *Leto, you must not fault him for not staying with me. He is your guardian. You know how critical that feels. You've served as a Guardian of Ascension in centuries past. You know he did what he had to do.*

I know. But I don't have to like it. I'll leave here shortly.

She turned to Thorne and told him what she'd seen. "The mist was destroyed and the colonists are being slaughtered. Diallo's house was crawling with death vampires."

"We're getting ready to launch. Donna, who works the grid here at HQ, moved the grid to the colony's location. Seriffe is with her. He has his eye on everything as well. He sent out a general call for Militia Warriors fifteen minutes ago. We're assembling the squadrons in the flight hangar now. They've already started arriving. A couple dozen squads are just about ready to fold."

As if his words were magic, the landing platform officer called out, "Incoming. Friendlies."

More squadrons folded in from all over the Metro Phoenix Two area. By long habit of drilling and preparation, the
Thunder God Warriors marched off to the left toward a
large departure hangar.

Thorne took her hand. "I want you to see this."

Grace went with him to the double doors. Within were
dozens of tight squads of four, repeated over and over. Wherever a squad awaited one of theirs, the warriors stood grouped
at the back. Once a squad had all four members, they moved
into position to the fore awaiting orders on several sets of
departure platforms.

Thorne leaned close. "We have a reconnaissance team,
couched in Endelle's mist, over the colony right now. We'll
have a report within seconds."

As if on cue, the large screens came to life and the horror
of the attack on the colony caused Grace to list. A moment
later, Leto arrived and slid his arm around her waist to support her. "Alison is with Mei-Amadi now. God, I felt you
start to fall. What is it?" But his gaze found the screens soon
enough, and he murmured, "Creator help us."

Hundreds of death vampires roamed what had been the
fair-like atmosphere of the warrior games. The bodies of
several colonists could be seen lying prone on the sawdust,
but fewer than Grace had expected. A number of death
vamps were using them, going after dying blood. The enemy appeared to be celebrating, gathering around the feeding spots, shouting, raising their fists in the air.

"I thought there would be more casualties," Grace said.

Leto squeezed her waist. "The colonists are well trained.
Remember the drums?"

"Yes. I didn't know what they were."

"That was the secondary alarm. Once the electronic
alarm failed, the HQ warriors would have started pounding
the drums. The death vamps would have had no idea what
that was."

"So you're saying a lot of the colonists would have gotten
away?"

"Yes, as many as heard the drums would have folded to the Portland Colony. We should have a report soon."

"Thank the Creator for that. Leto, were the drums your idea?"

He nodded. "It seemed like a logical precaution. And something the enemy wouldn't have expected. I made sure that every colony drilled with drums."

A voice came over the loudspeaker. "None of the death vampires is watching the skies." The image on the screen pivoted to what Grace knew to be a position in the west because she'd been there herself earlier in the evening. The voice added, "The landing platforms are clear and unguarded."

Thorne leaned in her direction. "Gideon has several reconnaissance warriors in flight and cloaked in mist. They're over the colony now. You're hearing one of them reporting."

Grace could make out the flapping of the warrior's wings, the one who apparently wore the camera strapped to his head. She could also see the fine lace-like appearance of mist surrounding the warrior. None of the death vampires had the power to see the mist or to perceive the Militia Warrior's flight over the battle site.

She felt heat radiating from Thorne and glanced up at him. He was glowing, his obsidian flame power lighting him up. He looked god-like and in control. He touched his com. "Gideon, start sending the squads."

Gideon's voice broke over the heads of the warriors at the lead spots. "On my mark to the Seattle One Colony platforms. I want an eight-squad fold pattern. You know the drill. Get me some blue skin."

The air in the hanger heated up, now charged with anticipation and intent. The first thirty-two Thunder God Warriors sped to the folding line and simply vanished. The next eight squads were on their heels with only a five-second interval between.

On the screen, the reconnaissance warrior held his camera aimed at the platforms.

"Thorne," Leto called out. "This is some righteous shit."

"Yes, it is," he said.

Grace glanced up at her brother. "You created this, didn't you?"

Thorne shook his head. "No, this is Seriffe's work in partnership with Leto. I'd take credit if I could." As the Militia Warriors continued to fold to Mortal Earth, Thorne turned to Leto. "So how did you save Diallo and his wife? What happened?"

Leto spoke in a clipped manner, as though giving a report to a commanding officer, which Grace supposed was exactly what he was doing. He spoke of death vampires coming to his cabin, which was their first knowledge that the colony was under attack.

Thorne put a hand on Grace's shoulder and very quietly sent, *When Mei-Amadi arrived, we could see that she had been badly used. I'm so sorry.*

He was remembering.

It was a long time ago, Thorne.

I know, but I have a feeling it still feels like yesterday for you.

Grace realized she'd never given her brother enough credit. *Yes. Sometimes, like tonight, it does.*

Leto turned toward Grace. "I have to get out there. My place is at the colony, but I think you should stay here, stay with your brother. I'll be back as soon as I can."

"Do you think it's wise," she asked, "if you and I are separated right now?"

He took her hand. "I'm not sure, but I have to be part of securing the colony." He glanced at Thorne. "I think we'll need Endelle to work on restoring the mist. Diallo won't be fit for duty for a few more hours yet, though I made sure Horace was with him."

"Good," Thorne said. Horace was the strongest healer on Second Earth. He glanced at Grace then back to Leto. "I'll take Grace to the palace with me. Endelle will want to know everything, and I'll get her started on the mist. Just report in as soon as the colony is secured."

* * *

Casimir stood at the observation window over the portal to Third. It felt so strange being with Grace and Leto just now. He knew they had completed the *breh-hedden*. He could feel their bond as though it had strings he could touch.

Though she had parted from him, still he loved her. How strange to know she was with another vampire and that his duty was to keep that vampire alive.

After having been with Patience earlier, he wondered if he would scent Grace again, but he had smelled nothing from her.

He glanced around the deck. He sniffed; the wildflower scent that belonged to Patience was still very much present in the space.

He focused on his voyeur window, holding Leto's image in his mind. He saw the warrior running through the Seattle Colony. Casimir used his window as a tracking device, and since he knew there were death vampires at the colony, he simply folded with a thought to Leto's position but kept himself invisible.

He watched Leto drop to his knees as he tended to a wounded colonist who was still breathing. He lifted up and called for a healer.

Casimir had enjoyed both men and women in his long life, and Leto was one of the finest-looking warriors he had ever seen. His eyes were an exquisite shade of blue and very intense, a heady combination. He was built, too. He would make a wonderful lover for Grace, for anyone really.

He kept out of the way and just watched him work. His view of life was so different now that what he began to feel for Leto wasn't so much lust as it was respect. Leto deserved a woman like Grace, whose heart was pure and compassionate, who saw the best in everyone she met.

With a piercing sense of self-awareness, he knew Grace was with the man who deserved her.

He had made a promise to his boys that he would bring Grace back to them, but there had been a part of him still hoping that she would return as his *breh*. That was now over, especially because Patience had suddenly arrived in his life. Yet deep in his heart, he knew Grace would fulfill her promise to be a part of his sons' lives. Just knowing that eased his heart.

The healer arrived and began taking care of the colonist. Leto moved on. Remaining invisible, Casimir trailed after him as he worked with three squads of Militia Warriors, hunting deep into the forest for death vampires.

Endelle stood before the mirror in her bedroom and un-hooked the scorpion belt. She let it fall to the floor. She had just gotten word that the Seattle Colony had been attacked and that Seriffe and Thorne were sending her Militia Warriors after Greaves's death vampires.

She opened her closet door and pulled out a black flight suit, nothing special. She waved a hand and with nine thousand years of experience switched outfits within the blink of an eye. She drew a leather piece from her closet, something she had never worn before, and for the first time in centuries there was absolutely nothing silly or absurd about this garment. She'd had it made about fifteen years ago when Greaves had started turning up the heat. She slid it on the old-fashioned way then buckled the belt in front and adjusted the side fittings. She felt for the dagger at her waist with a left-hand draw. She'd need her right hand for her sword if it came to that.

"You look perfect, Endelle. You were made to wear a weapons harness."

She turned slowly. Braulio was there, that handsome bastard, standing near her bed. But she'd give him this, he wasn't sporting his usual teasing come-fuck-me smile.

"I think this might be it," she said.

Braulio nodded. He looked very serious, more than he ever had.

"So, you gonna tell me what you did to me?" She reached up and rubbed the ripple of scars over her neck.

"Not yet. But soon."

She didn't bother to argue. With the war ramping up, nothing else seemed to matter. Besides, Braulio wouldn't tell her a damn thing until he was ready.

"I'm with you, Endelle," he said. "I'll be close by when you need me."

"Are you talking future stream shit?"

He nodded.

"Fine. Whatever."

He offered her half a smile, then just vanished.

She headed back to Thorne's command center since she really wanted to see what was happening in the Seattle Colony.

So Greaves had finally figured out how to locate the hidden colonies. She had a feeling that Nazca and Seattle were just the beginning, and she suspected he meant to move fast. One more flank to cover.

Once at the center, she moved to stand in front of the largest central screen. A few seconds later, Thorne arrived with Grace on his arm. When he reached Endelle, he smiled down at Grace then kissed her on the cheek.

Jesus, he looked so different. He was a new man—but maybe that's what happened to any man when he got laid on a solid, regular basis. Marguerite was good for him, and so was the *breh-hedden*.

When Thorne inclined his head to Endelle and took his seat in front of the same screen, Endelle said, "Thought I'd watch the action from here."

Thorne tapped a few buttons and spoke softly into his com. "Donna, we're ready to link up." He waited for a moment. The screen suddenly came alive. "Thanks, we've got it."

He shifted slightly and spoke to Endelle over his shoulder. "Once we had a visual at Apache Junction Two, which started up about ten minutes ago, we gathered two hundred squadrons and began folding them down to Mortal Earth."

Endelle stood back and watched Thorne work. He was all business these days, more sure of himself, relaxed, willing to take criticism in the name of building a stronger administration and army, and still he battled at the Borderlands a few hours every night. "Just to stay fit," he'd told her a couple of weeks ago.

She crossed her arms over her chest and took a couple of deep breaths. Her gaze was fixed to the back of his head. Yep, like an amputee watching a limb walk around by itself. She wondered if she'd ever get over the absence of the mind-link she had once shared with him.

Grace moved to stand off to Thorne's left.

Endelle glanced at her. Grace stared back then sent, *They were raping Diallo's wife when I found her. She'd almost bled out by then.*

Shit.

Exactly.

But you brought her out?

Grace nodded.

Endelle narrowed her eyes. *How?*

The explanation involved Grace's obsidian power, the same power she'd employed to locate the attack at Nazca.

"Love that you can split into an apparition. Reminds me of my darkening work, although it sounds more powerful and more versatile, like you can go just about anywhere."

Thorne was tapping away at the computer, and the next moment the screen split into four segments, each a live feed from the in-flight video crews that were flying over the colony.

To her infinite pleasure, the Thunder God Warriors were making mincemeat of a bunch of blue-skinned, black-winged sociopaths.

"Hot damn," Thorne shouted. The room, which had a dozen techs on different monitors, burst into shouts and applause.

Endelle could see Militia Warriors engaging four-to-one against each death vamp. Militia Warriors were limited in that way—it was the rare warrior who could take on a death vamp by himself. Her Warriors of the Blood were the truly gifted and could battle as many as eight at a time. Luken, the biggest of her warriors, often battled nine or more on a regular basis. He was one fit brute.

But the squads of four Militia Warriors were brilliantly

trained and took down the enemy like dominoes falling one after the other.

As new squads peeled off the colony's landing platform, at least three Section Leaders were directing the action, speaking into their coms and aiming traffic as needed. Many of the squads headed south into the valley's grain fields, but more and more of them were sent into the forest. Their activity would be difficult to track, but guerrilla work was part of the training.

"Are you streaming any of this to Marcus?" Endelle asked. "He'll want to send this out to our allied High Administrators all around the globe."

"He was my third phone call after you and Seriffe."

"Good." Something inside Endelle began to ease. She had hated her break with Thorne when Marguerite entered the picture, but right now she saw the results. Thorne in this position, essentially commanding all aspects of the war against Greaves, was exactly what she had needed.

As for Marcus, who headed up her PR, he would be eating up the videos. Ever since he'd returned from a two-hundred-year vacay on Mortal Earth, he'd been piling the electronics. She now saw one of the results: He could mobilize his PR crews within seconds of any situation. She approved. On the other hand, one of the other results bugged the shit out of her since she now had a website called MadameEndelle.com, and all the other crap that Marcus called "a critical social media platform." Thanks to a thing called "tweets" that Marcus and his *breh,* Havily, formulated on her behalf, Endelle was enjoying a surge in popularity.

How fucking precious.

"So what do we think all this means?" Endelle asked.

Thorne turned to meet her gaze. "Besides the obvious?"

"That's right, besides the fact that Greaves has attacked two of the colonies on Mortal Earth two nights in a row and risked our world becoming known to the human population. Besides all that, what the fuck is the bastard up to?"

But it was Grace who answered. "He's testing everything without showing his hand on Second Earth: the strength of Diallo's mist, response time of the Militia Warrior army, what, if anything, obsidian flame would do if he attacks, perhaps even my own power."

"She's right," Thorne said. "This isn't an overt battle. If Greaves had wanted to do that, he would have launched at Apache Junction Two at any of your allied Territories around the world. But he knows if he does that, he opens the war. He's not ready yet to go full-out, but I don't think he's going to wait very long."

Endelle turned to Grace. "Where's your man right now? Alison said you completed the *breh-hedden*. Can you find him?"

Grace nodded, then blinked a couple of times as if she was concentrating. Finally, she said, "He's just sent a squad of sixteen deep into the forest after three death vamps. He also said to alert Jeannie that he'd want to start moving corpses and clearing debris in small bursts. I told him I'd relay the message."

Thorne held the mouthpiece of his headset, clicked a couple more buttons, and Jeannie's voice filled the space. "Jeannie here."

Thorne gave her Leto's instructions. "Shall I let Gideon know?" he asked.

"I've got it," she said. "Later."

Endelle heard the softest click. She was fucking impressed. This was a massive team that Thorne had built. "What do we think Greaves's next move will be?"

Thorne turned around to face her. "This worries me the most because we just don't know, and according to Marguerite, that bastard Stannett is working his ass off blocking Greaves's movements in the future streams. She has four teams of Seers working with high rates of accuracy, but none of them is able to find out much about Greaves or his generals or his army. I can tell you what my biggest concerns are."

But Endelle already knew them. "You're worried about the colonies falling to Greaves, because Leto a built a force of a hundred thousand."

He nodded then glanced at Grace. His brow was furrowed. "And I'm worried as hell about obsidian flame."

Peace, though sought from every corner of the universe,
Can only be found deep in the heart.

—*Collected Proverbs*, Beatrice of Fourth

CHAPTER 11

Greaves once more stood on the viewing platform. Stannett reclined with his hands behind his head, staring up at the ceiling, waiting for Greaves's orders. He had a new set of Seers strapped down on the chaise longues. He was such a powerful bastard that the women were dying right and left, literally, and yet he looked refreshed.

Greaves recognized some of the women from Johannesburg. All had their eyes closed. Apparently Stannett kept them in a stupor in order to control them. Smart thinking, but then Stannett had been in charge of Seers for centuries. He knew what to do.

Greaves was disappointed that the attack at the Seattle Colony had unraveled as it did and now cleanup was in progress. He had watched events from a levitating position in the sky behind his mist. He had to admit that Thorne and Leto had created a tremendous amount of discipline in their forces, and especially in the citizenry of the colony.

Though Greaves had effectively eliminated the security system's electronic alarm, he had not been prepared for the pounding of drums that had alerted most of the citizens to his attack. He'd been stunned to observe how many colonists simply vanished—all prearranged, of course.

Despite the achievement of pure vision, no doubt Marguerite had somehow discovered the attack as well and alerted the colony. Earlier, he had spent time with his generals, setting his strategies—especially where the hidden colonies were concerned. He knew that Leto would have trained all the Militia Warriors in all the colonies. He knew Leto's mind and his skills. He would have been perfect for the task. The warrior games had no doubt been a culmination of his work.

Greaves wasn't certain exactly how large a force the hidden colonies had, but his generals had put the estimate near eighty thousand and Greaves really didn't want to be surprised once a battle began. He hadn't come this far to lose to something as ridiculous as an army built of colonists. More than anything, he wanted to eliminate the colonies as a factor in what would become a major showdown over the next several days.

His other concern, of course, was obsidian flame.

He'd decided to shift his strategy just a little and try one last time to eliminate the triad as a force in the upcoming confrontations. All he needed to do to solve this problem was to render Grace harmless, and he'd formed a plan that might just work. But he thought he'd check it out with Stannett first. Maybe the future streams could give him an edge on this one. That's all he needed, just a slight edge.

He called down to Stannett. "Are you ready?"

Stannett unloosened his hands and met Greaves's gaze. "Yes, master."

"Good. I want you to search for a time when I'm alone with Grace and I want to know where and when."

Stannett nodded. The women on either side of him tensed almost at the same time, then relaxed one by one. How many times Greaves had wished that he had Seer ability. Given his level of ambition, he'd always felt it a cruel trick of fate that he'd been denied the gift. Ah, well.

No more than a minute later, Stannett opened his eyes and smiled. "I found Grace alone and unprotected in Diallo's

Seattle courtyard garden. You were speaking very tenderly to her with all the gifts in your power. You were offering her things."

"What kind of *things*?"

"Nothing that couldn't be withdrawn should necessity dictate, things like world peace. She was falling beneath your spell, despite the fact that she is already *breh*-bonded to Leto, a sign of your power, no doubt. For that reason, I pulled back, getting a larger bird's-eye view until I could see into the lane near the house.

"The vision expanded, and I could see Leto battling more of your Third Earth death vampires in that location."

"Good." Greaves actually smiled. "Was Casimir visible?"

"Unfortunately, that's when the vision ended."

"And when does all this take place?"

"Sometime this evening, though I couldn't ascertain the hour. But it's not yet dawn in the region. In fact, it didn't even feel close to midnight." He frowned slightly.

"What is it?"

"It would follow that you have already been planning this kind of tactic, but what do you intend to do with her?"

"It's simple. I want to disrupt her thinking and have her return with me to Geneva."

"Where you will have more Third Earth death vampires waiting?"

Greaves smiled. "Of course."

He then issued orders to continue searching the future streams for signs of the colonies or of anything having to do with obsidian flame.

Hopeful once more, he dematerialized to his Estrella compound, where he chose from among his most powerful Third Earth death vampires. He suspected Casimir would intervene again, but it didn't matter. Greaves just needed to distract Leto for the few minutes he would require to take control of Grace's mind.

Casimir waited near Leto, still invisible. The forest had grown quiet. He glanced up at the night sky, barely visible beyond the layer of mist that Endelle had built to cover the colony.

He sighed. He understood why he'd been given this job: He understood Greaves's mind better than anyone. Greaves didn't have a conscience, and until recently, Casimir hadn't had one, either. So how could Leto, with his hypersensitivity to right and wrong, ever truly know how devious Greaves could be?

His instincts were humming a warning tune. He made himself visible to Leto, which caused the warrior to take a step back. "What the fuck? Why didn't I see a shimmering?"

"I've been here since you folded down to the colony. I can go invisible, or did you not know that?"

He scratched his chin with the edge of his thumb. "I keep forgetting that you're even around. So what's going on?"

"I have an uneasy feeling that Greaves is about to shake things up again."

Leto looked up at the dome of mist and frowned. "Even with such a strong cloak over the colony?"

"Yeah, even with all this."

Leto looked up at the house. "Gideon cleaned up the death vamps in and around the house. Grace is there now, in the courtyard. I'd say there are three squads of Militia Warriors in there now."

"She should be all right then."

Another squad of warriors reported to Leto, and he directed them into the south pastures. "Make sure there isn't a wounded death vampire hiding in any of the haystacks, barns, or fields."

The men took off. Leto planted his hands on his hips and looked up and down the lane. Casimir followed his gaze. What did the warrior see? What was he looking for? Was this who Patience was? Always looking for the enemy, trying to get one step ahead.

He wished to hell she'd come back to the observation deck. For maybe the first time in his life, despite how desperately attracted to her he was, he just wanted to talk to a woman.

* * *

With the hidden colonies secured and a new layer of powerful mist over the land, Grace returned to Diallo's house to
wait for Leto to finish his duties. She felt a strong need to be
near her *breh* as much as possible right now.

The corpses were long gone, and all the colonists had
been accounted for—either those few in the morgue or the
rest at the Portland Colony.

She reclined in one of the chaise longues in the lush
courtyard. The temperature in the garden was very comfortable, and because of the thick shrubs, flowers, and trees, a
wonderful humidity eased the dryness of the mountain environment.

Leto was in the lane below Diallo's house finishing up
with the Militia Warrior Section Leaders and going over the
numbers one last time. At least a dozen squads were still doing a house-to-house search just to be sure.

She had long since started blocking Leto's external physical sensations. She had learned from chatting with both
Fiona and Marguerite that blocking those sensations became a critical survival skill for the *breh*-bonded couples. It
was a very doable skill, and she was learning fast.

Even though the colony had been secured, Grace had
begun to feel uneasy, but she didn't know why. She half expected her obsidian power to rise, but the earth remained
quiet beneath her.

A chill went down her neck, and she rubbed her arms. She
looked around. Something had disturbed her, but what? All
the shrubbery remained still, unmoving. She had the jitters,
but then why wouldn't she after all that she'd been through?

She looked up at the dome of mist that once more covered
the colony. Endelle had created it as a temporary solution
until Diallo could recover and repair the damage. She had
even worked to add her own moss to help with the disguise.
But if the colony had been mapped, and if Greaves had
enough power to burn the mossy mist away, then in what
manner could the colony ever be secure again?

She wrapped her arms around her stomach and held herself. She wanted to crawl into bed and forget everything at

least for a little while, but which bed? Where? She couldn't go back to the cabin, Leto's wonderful cabin, not for some time at least. On the other hand, if either she or Leto could cloak the cabin in an additional layer of mist, the combination might just work.

She thought the thought and instantly, because of the *breh-hedden,* she was in Leto's mind. *I'd like to sleep in your cabin tonight,* she sent.

Hey, sweetheart, he responded instantly. *I'd like nothing better as well, but I'm not sure it's safe.*

Are you almost done?

Just a few more minutes. I just sent the Section Leaders to bring in their teams, then we'll head out. So give me a few minutes . . . that is . . . He fell silent.

Grace waited but that uneasy feeling returned.

Oh, shit. His voice was suddenly loud in her head. *More Third Earth death vampires just arrived. Casimir's with me.*

Because she was completely open to all his external physical sensations, she could feel him turn in a complete circle, and within a split second he had his sword in hand. She sensed a vibration all along his skin and knew he was letting his beast-man out.

Grace, you should get back to Second. Now.

Grace sat up. She was in danger. She could feel it.

She lifted her hand to fold, but couldn't. She didn't understand. Her heart rate kicked up a few notches.

Then, just as quickly as her fears rose, they retreated. Very odd. Yet she felt sublime waves of peace begin to pour over her. She didn't need to worry about anything.

She folded her hands over her stomach and closed her eyes. She felt the air move near her, but she was too tired to care who it was. Probably Leto, which would be nice. She wanted to open her eyes and smile at him, but she couldn't. How heavy her eyelids felt.

Lips touched her cheek several times. As if from a great distance, she heard a stream of words, murmured very softly in a kind of chant. The lips moved and covered her mouth.

Come with me, Grace. The words now flowed through

her mind with the most beautiful resonance. *We will build a new world together, one without war. Isn't that what you want above all things?*

This wasn't Leto, but why wasn't she afraid? Was she being enthralled?

Somehow, she didn't care.

She felt so at peace, as though she never wanted to be anywhere else in her life than right here with this man's voice in her head and his lips touching hers.

Tell me you want what I want.

Yes, I want a world without war. Yes. Yes.

Then come with me. Say you will join me. I will make you my empress, and you will have the power to order the world exactly how you desire it to be.

At last, she opened her eyes. Some part of her mind truly did realize that she was looking at Greaves, that he sat on the side of the chaise and petted her head in soft soothing strokes, and that he had been kissing her.

He must have enthralled her. She wondered why he didn't just take her away with him. He had her in his power—that much her rational mind could make sense of. But she knew that by the rules of COPASS, both he and Endelle were limited in what each could do, all those rules set up a hundred years ago to regulate two powerful ascenders. No, Greaves couldn't just take her. He would have to persuade her to leave with him.

All she had to do was say yes.

She put her hand on his face. She wanted to. Very badly. Yet she resisted.

His eyes were lit with a strange, unearthly glow. He looked so beautiful. That was one of the most surprising things about Darian Greaves, just how beautiful he was. He had thick, perfectly shaped dark brows, full lips, and large brown eyes, just like his mother's. He also possessed the best manners. She had always liked his manners.

He slid his arms behind her back and pulled her against him. He kissed her again. Even his mouth was beautiful and tasted of the sweetest peaches. She licked his lips and heard him groan.

I could love you, Grace. I didn't know that, but holding you in my arms like this, love is what comes to mind. You are the earth. I can feel that in you. Your power would anchor me and change me. I would be made new. Will you do that for me, Grace? Will you make me a new creature through your goodness and purity? My mother would like that. Beatrice would be indebted to you forever.

She loved Beatrice. How wonderful if she could give her such a gift as renewing her son's soul.

Come with me. Say you'll come with me.

She wanted to say yes. More than anything in her life, she wanted to say yes. But there was a part of her that couldn't do it.

She struggled to find the word, to make her mouth move. "No," she murmured at last.

The soft chanting resumed.

Leto had his sword in his right hand and one of his daggers in his left as he battled three Third Earth death vampires, all cloaked behind what must have been Greaves's mist. He'd already killed three of the bastards.

Casimir had his own problems with the remaining four, who apparently specialized in hand-blast capability. Greaves had clearly learned from the failure at Nazca. Sparks showered everywhere. Casimir kept working the vampires away from Leto, protecting him as he battled sword-to-sword. One hit with a Third Earth hand-blast and Leto wasn't sure he'd survive.

His opponents were damn experienced. More than once he'd gotten a mild skin burn because one of the pretty-boys would fold behind him and slice at his calves. He could feel that his battle sandals were partly cut away and that blood dripped into the soles. His feet were slippery.

When two folded at once, he lunged under the raised arm of the death vamp in front of him, caught him in his kidneys with his dagger, and took him down. He'd made the right call. The other two materialized in the exact spot where he'd originally stood.

He increased his speed, darting forward and swinging his sword at the same time. He took the hand of one of the vamps, who now rolled on the ground screaming.

The last bastard wasn't about to be distracted. Leto folded well beyond the prone death vamp, and before he even noticed, Leto brought his sword down hard and took his head. The vamp still standing was almost on him. Leto lifted his sword, and the weight of his opponent's downward strike sent heavy, almost paralyzing vibrations down his arm.

At the same time, he caught movement to his left. One of the death vamps had broken from Casimir and was lifting his hand in Leto's direction.

Again Leto lunged, rolling on the ground below the closer vamp.

The hand-blast was ill placed and hit his opponent, sending him screaming into the air and flying backward about ten feet.

Leto was now exposed and on the ground. He waited for a moment while the hand-blast geared up. Then just as he saw the pretty-boy's smile widen, Leto pivoted, folded, arrived behind the vamp, and thrust his sword through the spine.

Turning, he saw that the three remaining death vamps had moved in tighter on Casimir and that the Fourth ascender had started to struggle. Casimir was not a warrior.

Leto used his speed, and took two heads. The final death vamp standing, turned at the commotion, which was a fatal mistake because Casimir lifted his hand and caught the bastard in the throat with a hand-blast. His head lolled and he toppled over, his skull crunching hard against one of the severed heads.

Leto bent over at the waist, breathing hard. He still had his sword in hand. His gaze drifted back and forth. If Greaves intended to add to the party, he was ready.

"Thank you," Casimir said.

Leto glanced at him. He was trying to be mature about the presence of the Fourth ascender since it was clear the whole situation was an ascended convergence, but he still resented

Casimir for having taken Grace away. He nodded, then reverted his attention to the corpses. Three of the death vamps
needed finishing, so he moved swiftly and took heads.

He took one more long look around, but everything
seemed quiet. Satisfied that he wasn't still under attack, he
glanced up at the mist.

Greaves.

Did he really think he could take Leto this way? Was that
his purpose?

Then his chest tightened with one simple thought: Grace
might be alone in the garden.

He folded to the lane beyond the mist, but the moment he
did, his mind felt as though it had just been struck down by
a mallet. He couldn't give shape to his thoughts. Even his
body felt heavy and unmovable. But why? What was happening to him?

Casimir materialized next to him. "Are you all right?
What's wrong?"

Leto struggled to find the words. "Help Grace. Protect her."

"No can do. I stay with you, Leto. Sorry. And it looks like
Greaves is using his thrall power on you."

"Fuck." He had to get to Grace. He could sense she was
in danger. For one thing, he couldn't *feel* her anymore, not
any of her physical sensations.

With great difficulty, he rose from the dirt lane and
peered up at Diallo's large house that overlooked the valley.
She was up there, waiting for him. She had agreed to wait, to
stay in the garden. At least three squads of Militia Warriors
had set up a command center in the house, and Gideon had
just gone up there a few minutes ago. She should be safe.

Yet somehow, he knew she wasn't.

He called to her, mind-to-mind. *Grace, Grace.*

No answer, which was not possible. They were bonded.

He tried to fold up to the house but couldn't. He began to
walk the long driveway, one uphill step in front of the other.
He focused on Grace, but thinking about her only made his
mind muddier.

Instead, he focused on Gideon.

That was better. Gideon. One foot in front of the other.

Casimir walked beside him. He glanced at him, even though it was difficult. He sent, *Can you fold me to the house?*

"I'll try." Casimir put his hand on Leto's shoulder. He could feel the attempt to fold him, but Casimir couldn't do it, either. *Sorry, Leto. This is Greaves's party.*

Greaves. That asshole.

But the moment he thought of the Commander, he fell to his knees and a terrible pain sliced through his mind.

Oh, shit. Once more he shifted his focus to thoughts of Gideon. He kept what was left of his mind centered on the Militia Warrior. Gideon was tall. Yes. He was at Warrior of the Blood level now, but he refused to leave the Thunder God Warriors. Jean-Pierre had brought Gideon's powers on-line. Yes, his brother warrior, Jean-Pierre, had developed new powers once he completed the *breh-hedden* with Fiona. He could now lift other warriors up to higher levels. Yes, that was what Jean-Pierre could do, and that was what he had done for Gideon.

He just had to keep thinking about Gideon or Jean-Pierre.

His feet were so heavy, but it didn't matter. He understood that his *breh* was in trouble, but he wouldn't think her name.

On and on he pressed, but it was like moving through a nightmare. Finally, he made it to the front walk. At last, he pushed the door open. Two Militia Warriors drew their swords to challenge him, though they immediately backed off when they recognized who he was.

"Forgive us, Warrior Leto." Each looked him up and down because he was still in his beast-form.

"Gideon," he whispered. His voice sounded hoarse, and he'd barely been able to get the word out.

They called for Gideon. He came running. He had blond hair, but not so dark as Jean-Pierre's, nor so light as Luken's.

"Warrior Leto, what's wrong? You're covered in blood. Are you injured?"

He put his hand on Gideon's shoulder and breathed hard as he said, "Grace. Danger."

"She's in the garden. Shit, what the fuck has happened?"

"Go to her."

Gideon called his men in close, and as one powerful unit they marched into the garden calling Grace's name.

Greaves was sweating and exhausted. The effort to mind-control two such powerful ascenders, in two separate locations, was costing him. But he was close to shutting Grace's mind down, getting her to agree to go with him, and the longer he worked her mind, the more he could feel her resistance breaking down.

Come with me. Say the word out loud, and I will fold you to my home in Geneva. Say that you agree to come with me.

Her lips moved. Her jaw worked. She lifted her face to him. *I want . . .*

The next moment he heard Militia Warriors shouting. They were calling for Grace. He was out of time. Though he had mist around himself and Grace, the garden was small and the most any of the warriors had to do was to just push through. Or fold.

"Over here."

Greaves heard Casimir directing traffic. Shit.

"Gideon, break through here."

Grace, say you'll come with me.

Grace was growing weary, fighting against Greaves. She knew if she said yes, it would feel so good. But something deep inside her, perhaps even her soul, refused to give up. If only she could open her eyes.

She felt a strange sliding up and down her arms, and she heard her name called as if from a great distance.

She wouldn't go with him. "No," she said, and her voice sounded stronger. "No. I won't go with you."

"Come back to me."

"No." She began to struggle against the arms now gripping and shaking her. She slashed out at Greaves with her fingernails and screamed at him.

Then suddenly, Leto was in her mind. *Grace. Grace. Can you hear me?*

Leto?

I'm here.

She fought harder and flew at Greaves. She started screaming and pushing at him, clawing at his face, kicking him. She wouldn't go. She would never go with him willingly.

"Open your eyes."

But it wasn't Greaves's voice that she heard.

She forced herself to obey. Finally, she popped her eyes wide. Leto was in his beast-state standing beside the chaise, next to her. She was safe, but he had blood running down his face in deep scratches. "What happened to you?" she cried. Then she understood. "Oh, Creator help me, did I do that to you?"

"It's okay. I will heal very fast." He dragged her into his arms and held her tight. "He almost had us. Both of us. He used some kind of mind control. I couldn't think straight. I barely made it up the hill to get to you."

Grace pushed back. "He promised me so many wonderful things, to bring peace to Second Earth, no more war, if I would just go with him. He had me in thrall." She shuddered.

"He's gone. But we can't stay here. He got through Endelle's mist."

"How could he have known where I was?" Even as she spoke the words, she understood. "Stannett and the future streams." She shook her head and slid her arms around Leto's neck. "Leto, we're in trouble. Greaves divided us, even though we're bonded. He found me because of the future streams. I . . . I don't know what to do. Where do we go? Where do we hide that he can't find us?"

Greaves folded back to his penthouse in Geneva and collapsed on the floor in the living room, facedown. His fingers grasped the thick carpet, and he squeezed. He experienced a profound preternatural exhaustion. He couldn't remember the last time he'd exerted so much effort. Trying to gain control over two extremely powerful ascenders at the same time had used him up.

So much power. His body vibrated with what he'd felt from both Grace and Leto. Greaves had power, but he'd just attempted the impossible, to wrest a woman from her *breh*.

Maybe he would have succeeded if Casimir hadn't joined Leto in his fight against the death vampires. Even then, the shield he'd put around Leto should have kept him immobile. But Leto wasn't himself anymore. He had somehow gained the power to transform into a Third Earth warrior.

The entire time he'd been working at breaking Grace's will, he had felt Leto's impossible walk up the hill to Diallo's house. At least Casimir had been unable to help him fold to Greaves's position.

Grace. My God.

There was something within Grace's power structure, because it was anchored by the earth, that was both highly compassionate and at the same time incredibly erotic, unlike anything he'd ever known. He panted as he lay on his carpet.

Grace would never be sadistic, but she had power that vibrated along the insides of his thighs and up through his testicles. For a woman who espoused all things spiritual, she was surely a reincarnation of Aphrodite. She could command him if she understood her power. That she didn't and probably never would was the only real advantage he had in this situation. He couldn't be manipulated by her because it would never occur to her to make the attempt.

Greaves had been so close with Grace, so close to getting her to surrender. By the rules of COPASS, neither he nor Endelle could kill anyone outright or abduct them. And though he had over a third of COPASS in his pocket, he knew an outright abduction wouldn't be overlooked by those members of the ruling committee who still held to their morals.

For just a moment, however, he had debated taking her and having her killed immediately, which would have ended the obsidian flame threat.

But the repercussions would have been swift. Endelle would have gone to Prague and argued against him in front of the entire COPASS committee. He was simply unwilling to take that kind of risk at this late hour, not with a decisive battle looming before him.

He could feel the battle coming now, and with it his chance at securing his ambitions. In so many ways, he was fully prepared. He even had an ace up his sleeve, something no one knew about. If all else failed, he would use this specialized power and hopefully overcome whatever odds presented themselves.

Yet because of a mere woman, the key to obsidian flame, he was living a nightmare. All his plans had come down to Grace and her ability to fulfill the power latent in the triad. He understood that once a triad came together, there was always one member who could acquire the abilities of other ascenders. The nature of the power or ability didn't matter—from wielding a sword to healing the mind to throwing hand-blasts. Once that triad member learned the skill, obsidian flame could then magnify that skill a thousandfold. He knew for a fact that there was at least one triad operating on Third Earth. He had witnessed for himself a valley of warriors slain by a single hand-blast, and in turn he had seen a hundred thousand people folded out of the path of a flash flood.

If only he'd had been able to persuade Grace to surrender to him, he could have turned her over to his favorite death vampires and let them dispose of her.

But she had held steady to the end. He had failed.

His blood finally settled down so that he could ease himself up off the floor. He showered and changed into a fresh Hugo Boss suit. He put on his pinkie ring of black onyx. He would head to Estrella next and continue working military strategies with his generals.

Before leaving, Greaves checked on Julianna, his current love-slave. She was facedown on the bed, naked, a sheet just covering her buttocks. Her wing-locks were torn but healing well. Their last session had been one of the best yet. Despite his arousal while feeling Grace's earth-based power, Julianna was his preference. The claw that he could bring forth from his DNA-altered left hand tingled at the thought that she might be healed as early as noon, at which time they could enjoy another energetic half hour or so.

He glanced at her nightstand and frowned. There was a vase with at least two dozen long-stemmed peach-colored roses in it. He saw a card on the table.

He wondered if someone was attempting to seduce his woman. Casimir had once held Julianna captive in his Paris One apartment. Maybe he wasn't as reformed as he appeared.

Greaves moved to the table and read the card. He couldn't help but smile. Sometimes he thought he and Stannett were brothers. The words on the card, in Stannett's hand, were very simple, "Grace has come home. Casimir, too."

He saw something gleam behind the vase. Ah, a half-empty bottle of Jack Daniel's. Julianna had needed some solace.

He leaned down and kissed one of the upper shredded wing-locks. "Patience," he whispered. "You will have your chance to destroy one or both of them, I have no doubt."

Grace had stolen Caz away from her, and to a woman of Julianna's temperament, that was an unforgiveable sin.

Grace sat across from Leto in the Apache Two conference room, her arms folded over her chest. It was past midnight now, and all the events of the day and evening had taken a toll. She was beyond exhausted. But no decision had been made yet about where they would settle down for the rest of the night. Leto had reverted to his normal size, and he'd changed from his stained battle gear into jeans and a dark T-shirt. He'd even showered in the Militia Warriors locker room.

The recent encounter with Greaves had shaken her. The bastard, for she could think of him as nothing less in this moment, had almost taken possession of her. She'd almost given herself into his power. She shuddered. She had no doubt that once she'd agreed to go with him, he would have had her killed.

She chewed on the inside of her lip.

Leto met her gaze. "Grace, please talk to me." He leaned forward with his elbows on his knees, his hands clasped loosely between his legs. He looked so beautiful, and so different from Greaves. Leto had wonderful thick raven-black hair. She loved feeling his hair. She reached out and touched it now.

Greaves was bald. That circumstance alone should have made her fight him. She still couldn't believe that he'd been able to place her in thrall like that.

"I don't know what happened, and I'm frightened. He almost had me." She shivered and hugged herself tighter.

"Grace, I can feel how tense you are. I just wish I could have gotten to you sooner. But as soon as Casimir and I defeated the death vampires and I folded out of Greaves's mist, I could hardly move. If I thought about you, I experienced such pain."

Grace rose from her chair and started to pace. "He has so much power. My God, his power." That's what struck her as she walked the length of the Militia Warrior conference room. The vastness of his power. That's what she could recall and what truly frightened her.

"But he didn't succeed," Leto said. "With either of us, and it cost him to do what he did. Mentally, I mean. To hold both of us in some kind of thrall like that, for at least twenty minutes, to keep us separated though we share this bond, means that he's not all-powerful. He would be drained and even vulnerable right now."

"He was after me, intent on destroying obsidian flame."

"No doubt."

She met Leto's gaze. "I'm the real threat here. I've never wanted to admit it to myself. I shouldn't be surprised that he came after me. But you know what I really don't understand? What does a soul-based power have to do with destroying armies? I'm like Alison. I don't want to kill anyone. I don't think I could."

Leto shook his head. "I don't know. I don't have anything close to your power, nothing like obsidian flame. I'm just a recovering death vampire who can get big enough to give you a good ride."

Grace stared at him, then laughed. "I can't believe you just said that." She laughed some more. "Give me a good ride?"

Then he smiled, and before long he had joined her. She sat down opposite him again and laughed until tears streamed down her cheeks. She couldn't seem to stop. For Leto to have reduced everything to his ability to pleasure her when he grew into his beast-state seemed so funny. She wished Marguerite were here. Her Convent cellmate would have found what Leto said hilarious.

"I shouldn't have said that." He palmed his eyes and laughed some more. "I know what we have is more than just sex."

Grace went to him and sank down to the side of his knees. She put her head in his lap. She giggled some more then looked up at him. "Well, it is pretty awesome that you can change size. I mean, isn't that something most men dream about?"

"Oh, shit, I've become a cliché."

"I guess you have." But she kissed his knees, then his thighs, and again laid her head down. "Leto, I'm really tired. Where can we go? I need sleep more than anything right now. The last couple of days have really drained me."

He tilted sideways and slipped his phone from his pants pocket. He thumbed, and a moment later she heard him talking to her brother. The conversation lasted a couple of minutes as one location after another was suggested and discarded.

Finally it was settled that they would go to Medichi's villa. Antony had recently installed a new security system, and Endelle sustained mist over the property. She'd done so ever since Havily and Marcus had lived there over a year ago.

Maybe the enhanced security system would be enough, but at this point, with fatigue settling like an ache into her bones, Grace didn't care. She just wanted her head on a pillow, any pillow.

A moment more and Leto had her flying through netherspace.

Once at the villa, Leto stared at the couch in Medichi's formal living room and the memories flooded back.

Five months ago, Luken had supported him, half-carrying him to the sofa where Leto had thought he would breathe his last. Though Grace had fed him twice from her vein, it hadn't been enough, and Leto had been near death. He'd been taking dying blood a long time, a hundred years, but he'd made the decision: no more. If he had stayed the course, he would have died, probably that very night.

But his brother warriors and their *brehs* had stepped in and changed everything. Havily donated her powerful, unusual blood, and he had been permanently healed from his addiction. He never again experienced the severe cramping that occurred at the withdrawal of dying blood. He owed his life to Havily, and to her *breh,* Marcus, who had allowed him to take her blood, and to their small group for providing all the extra support he'd needed.

Seeing the couch now brought it all back, how his life had changed forever in that moment. Glancing at Grace and giving her hand a squeeze, he was grateful.

She met his gaze and smiled. He just wished that he could see the future more clearly, especially the why of his beast-state and just what role he was meant to play in Grace's life, even in his world. And what would happen if he really was in his ascension to Third Earth?

Grace had spoken more than once about how she had gone through life as a ghost. The truth was, he could relate. Even though they'd completed the *breh-hedden* and even though they had amazing sex together, he didn't feel a complete connection to her.

But he didn't blame her. He blamed himself. He was as much a ghost as she was. In all his long life, he'd never truly given his heart to another ascender for safekeeping, not once. Maybe the death of his mother had ruined him in that way, but he kept an invisible emotional barrier all around his heart, always protecting himself, always working hard to be the best warrior, perhaps unwilling to love until the last death vampire was slain.

It was in this way that neither he nor Grace had been ready to complete the *breh-hedden*. It felt strange to be able to feel the pressure of his palm against hers, to know what his skin and the squeeze of his hand felt like from her point of view. They were so close, and yet still so far apart. He wondered if he could ever truly let go with her, truly give his heart completely, truly yield to all that the *breh-hedden* could be.

Parisa appeared from a side hall at the southern end of the villa. She carried several black towels folded over her arms. "I found some extras in the second suite. I'm putting you in the room closer to the library." When she reached a rectangular table in the center of the hall, she waved them forward, then gestured to her left.

Leto put his arm loosely around Grace's waist as he walked beside her down the hall.

Parisa was another beauty, Antony's *breh*. She wasn't as tall as Grace, perhaps an inch or so shorter. Her hair was long, dark brown, and layered. She had extraordinary violet eyes.

She led them to a room on the left, and as she pushed the door open, she said, "Antony won't be home until dawn. He's out battling at the New River Borderland. Of course, as soon as he gets back, I'll be putting him to bed." A faint blush climbed her cheeks as she held the door wide.

Grace passed into the room, and Leto followed her. The bed was a massive carved mahogany and looked bigger than a king, which was a real plus, especially if Leto went beast. Grace moved to stand near the doorway leading to the bathroom, her arms folded across her chest.

"I know this has been a long night," Parisa said, her voice quiet. "I just wanted to say how sorry we are about the Seattle Colony. There simply are no words."

Leto nodded. "Most of the colonists were able to fold to the Portland hidden colony."

She nodded. "Thank goodness for that. Well, you both

must be exhausted so I'll leave you now. Also, Endelle said she was adding a smaller dome of mist over the villa itself, which should make it impossible for Greaves to get to you." She glanced toward the window. "Antony insisted on several squads of Militia Warriors as well. They'll be patrolling the grounds nearest the house day and night. I think there are eighty warriors out there right now."

"So many," Grace murmured, but she actually took a deep breath and her arms fell away to hang loose at her sides.

Even Leto felt it, a sense of security, at least for now. "Parisa, thank you so much. We'll be very comfortable here."

She smiled. "I'm basically on Antony's schedule for now, so I'll be sleeping away the day with him when he comes home at dawn. Just make the villa your home, especially the kitchen. Have anything you like." She glanced from one to the other. "Sleep well."

She closed the door.

Leto turned to find that Grace was staring at the carpet and blinking. He went to her, took her hand, and kissed her fingers. "Take your shower. You'll feel better."

She nodded and headed for the bathroom.

All good things know a proper time of fulfillment.

—*Collected Proverbs,* Beatrice of Fourth

CHAPTER 12

Several hours later, Grace awoke to a strange sensation that
she couldn't place at first: a kind of rumbling. She thought,
Tank, maybe? But as she came more fully awake, she realized that Leto was snoring, his head facedown on his pillow.

She smiled and rubbed his shoulder gently. How normal
this seemed.

The snoring jerked to a stop, and he lifted his head. He
blinked a couple of times, then rubbed his face with both
hands. "I couldn't breathe. I was dreaming I was flying way
too high and there wasn't enough oxygen." His eyes rolled as
he turned to look at her. He blinked some more.

She continued to rub his shoulder slowly back and forth.
"I'm not surprised. I think you were suffocating against your
pillow."

He dropped his head back down on the pillow. He chuckled, shifting to look up at her. "I sure hope I wasn't snoring."

"Not at all." She didn't mind lying.

The wrinkle between his brows relaxed. "That would be
wretched, indeed. Nothing so unromantic as a loud snore.
But I must say, you're a terrible liar."

She chuckled, stretched, and turned to look out the back

window. Dawn had broken. "I always forget how high up in the foothills of the White Tank Mountains Antony's villa is. I can see a lot of the peaks from here. Oh, look, there's a deer on the lawn. A doe."

Leto shifted on his side. Because of the *breh*-bond, she could feel the sheet tug at his legs until he kicked the tangle away. He moved closer and stretched out beside her. He draped his arm over her stomach.

His forest scent drifted up and teased her nostrils. Desire, always so close to the surface because of the *breh-hedden*, swirled through her body.

"Meadow," he whispered. He leaned over and kissed her cheek, then her throat, and moved lower to her breasts.

She didn't protest when he pushed the sheet to her waist and began to feast. It was so strange to experience what he felt, just how soft her breast was against his lips, and the feel of her hardening nipple when he began to suckle.

All the dual sensations increased her need.

With one hand she held on to the headboard. She used the other to pet his head. He suckled her breast, tugging on the nipple. His hands pushed at both breasts. His shoulders hunched. *God, I love feeling what this feels like to you.*

"I know what you mean." She drifted her hand down the back of his head, over his long hair, the exposed and always sensitive wing-locks.

She slid the tips of her fingernails over a lock, and he writhed. She did, too, because she could experience what that felt like. She added just a little pressure, and he sucked harder on her breast.

I can feel the sensation of my mouth on your breast, what it feels like to you, he sent. One more suck and she clenched.

Experiencing both at the same time brought desire rushing, but she didn't want to rush. So she worked at blocking his experiences, which helped her to settle down a little.

But an idea slipped through her mind, one she couldn't resist. "Leto, there's something I want to do to you."

That got his attention, and he popped off her breast, looking up at her. He didn't smile, though. Instead, a beautiful dark glitter filled his blue eyes. "Anything," he said, his voice as low as she'd ever heard it.

She smiled and pinched his wing-lock. His body writhed beneath hers. Wing-locks were extremely sensitive, and the act of mounting wings was very close to sexual release.

"On your stomach," she said.

He groaned as he shifted to lie down beside her. He pushed the pillows out of the way.

"And now, I need your beast." She kissed his shoulder. "Will you give me your beast?"

"You want my beast? As in, you want me to change into the larger version of myself."

She sighed deeply. "Yes." The word left her with a soft rush of air. "I mean, if you want to. Do you want to?"

He groaned. "If you want me to, God, yes."

She felt him take a couple of deep breaths. She could feel the vibration slide down one of his legs, then the other.

When his muscles began to enlarge everywhere, she sat back on her heels and watched the transformation. Her lips parted. Her breaths grew uneven. She realized that this was pure sex to her, that he grew, got bigger, became more of what he already was. Only instead of just his cock growing, his entire body grew, becoming more heavily muscled and gaining a couple of inches in height.

Meadow, Grace. Does this turn you on?

More than you will ever know.

I don't know if that's true, because I can feel all your responses. He groaned again.

She put her lips on his shoulder, kissing him softly, moving back and forth over his skin. She could feel the muscles swelling. A soft vibration passed through her.

He hissed softly. "Your scent."

"Your skin, your muscles." She slid her hand from the inside of his elbow up his arm slowly.

Chuffs left his throat, and she shivered. Her fingers touched more swelling flesh. She overlaid his bicep with her hand and licked his shoulder as everything beneath her continued to grow, shift, change, become larger.

She loved it. The feel of all this movement and energy beneath her hands and her mouth. His skin was hot. She licked. All that warmth and flavor, of Leto tasting like the forest, sent ripples down her body, little waves lapping at the shore, teasing her, tempting her.

He trembled.

"What's wrong?" She licked again.

I want—

She cut him off. "Use your words, Leto. I need to hear your voice in this state. It's much deeper, sexier. It gives me a thrill."

"I want to flip you over, throw you on your back."

She massaged the growing bicep. "I know. Don't care. You have to do as I say, at least for now."

A small piece of laughter, like it had broken off from the rest, barked from his throat. He sighed.

His shoulder pushed at her lips, dragging away from her. She opened her eyes. Leto was getting taller. She licked down his arm and nursed on his bicep. He grunted. She knew this was torture. Again, she didn't care.

This was her turn.

She left his bicep, then, using both hands, she began at the top of his back and slowly descended, stroking each weeping wing-lock, taking all that moisture with her, down and down to his waist until her hands were sopping.

He gave a shout and whirled to face her. But she moved with her newly acquired speed and was fifteen feet away, at the door of the bedroom. He was off the bed before she could blink, but she held up one hand and he stopped.

"What are you doing to me?" His voice was so low, so resonant, she found it hard to remain where she was. "Let me come to you."

She wept from between her legs. She wanted to run to him, throw her arms around him, and sink herself on what was very hard and very big.

Her hands were dripping with the moisture from his wing-locks. The scent tempted her. With one hand held out to him to keep him away, she lifted the other to her lips. She settled her gaze on him and licked her palm.

The flavor seemed to reach inside her and give a hard tug. "Oh, Leto, you taste of heaven to me."

He palmed his erection and slowly stroked himself. She could feel what his hand felt like touching his cock, and her body clenched with need.

Her gaze fell to what belonged only to her, and her lips parted as she dragged air into her lungs. She put her moist hands on her breasts. Her nipples drew into hard beads. She drifted her hands lower over her sensitive navel, and lower still.

His hand moved faster as she descended.

"Please, let me come to you," he said, his gaze almost frantic.

She didn't answer him. She couldn't. She was enjoying this too much, having this kind of control over him. She felt heady as her fingers slid into her pubic hair and pushed. The sensation was delightful.

He closed his eyes and groaned. "I can feel what that's like for you, the pressure of your fingers, the pleasure it gives you." He was close.

She had an idea. With a burst of speed, she was on her knees in front of him and her lips closed around the crown of his cock.

He gave a strangled cry. His hands suddenly on her head, he pushed his cock into her mouth. She took him as deep as she could. Using both her hands, she sucked and stroked him at the same time.

Leto, how wonderful my mouth feels to you.

"I can't wait."

Let it all go, Leto. Give me what you've got.

His body jerked forward as he began to pulse. She kept stroking and stroking. His cock released into her, and she drank what tasted of the forest and of Leto. She drank and drank.

But she knew him and she knew that he wasn't done,

even when his movements slowed and he pulled out of her mouth.

"You're glowing," he said.

She smiled up at him. "Why wouldn't I be?"

"I mean your skin. You're glowing. You have a blue aura."

She rose slowly to her feet and looked at her arm. She laughed. "So I am. It's almost iridescent."

He dipped down and kissed her, driving his tongue deep. Her hands found a pair of biceps that were huge. *I taste myself in you.*

It's so beautiful, making love like this.

And I'm not repulsive to you in this state?

Sexy, Leto. You're sexy. She pushed her tongue into his mouth and his heavy arms embraced her, pulling her off her feet and against him.

She worked her arms to slide them around his neck and held him fast. *Your hair is moving over my arms.* Even his hair was different.

He pulled back and met her gaze. His eyes were so blue, so intense, his black lashes thick. His cheeks were more prominent in this state, and as he held her dangling above the floor, she pressed her forearms into his shoulders to give herself a little leverage. She lifted up just enough to run her tongue across the increased line of his cheek. "You're bigger everywhere."

She dropped down that couple of inches and saw that he was smiling, a crooked smile. "Everywhere?"

She nodded. "Oh, yes." She let her arms fall away and arched her head back so that he was holding her without her help.

He chuckled and swung her in a circle, then another and another. Here was all this man, all this sex, all this enormous body, and she felt light and feminine, all six feet of her in his arms as he continued to swing her.

He stopped and drew her in close once more, pressing her head into his shoulder, still holding her off the floor. "You have made me so happy," he said. "I didn't think I could be this happy in this beast-state. I thought it was a curse, but how can it be a curse when you seem to like me like this?"

"Leto, here's the truth that I know about who you are: You could turn into a raving ghoul, and you would still be the finest man I have ever known."

He grew very still suddenly, so she continued, "I can remember the first day I met you. Of course, this was so long ago, but I was fighting with Thorne, begging him to be more careful. He had just joined the Warriors of the Blood, and I feared for him every day because he was reckless. He had come home, and just as I punched his arm, you folded into the room, into my home in Rome Two, so many years ago. Do you remember?"

"I do," he said. "You were so angry and you glared at me."

"I blamed you for introducing him to Endelle, for making him a Warrior of the Blood."

" 'So you must be Warrior Leto.' I'll never forget your icy tone," he said.

"But you merely smiled and looked at me, and I looked back. I . . . I've never told anyone this, but I had the worst crush on you."

"You did not." His eyes were wide, disbelieving.

"I did, and it lasted decades," Grace said. "I made excuses to be near you. Did you ever think of me—back then, I mean?"

"Yes, I admit I did. Don't you remember that I would always talk to you? Always ask how you were doing?"

"I thought you were being polite," she said, smiling.

"I was smitten. You were so beautiful and so compassionate even then. But you were young, so very young. It wasn't right. By then I was twelve hundred years old."

And there was another truth of his character as he held her a foot off the floor, his body altered into the beast-state. He hadn't pursued her because she was young.

With a rueful smile, he added, "And you know Thorne would have taken me apart if I'd courted you."

She chuckled against his shoulder. "Yes, he would have. He was always very protective of me. Of both Patience and me."

He held her tight, his arms compressing some of her wing-locks in the nicest way. She felt secure, even safe. Now, there was a novelty—that she felt safe, if for just this moment, in a world at war.

He drew back and let her slide to plant her feet on the floor. He smiled. He was so beautiful. He kissed her, then said, "I want to feel the backs of your knees over my shoulders. How does that sound?"

She blinked very slowly, and as soon as she understood his meaning, she squeezed her eyes shut and shuddered, a full-body shudder that went all the way down into her heels. She opened her eyes. "I would like that, Leto, very much."

He kissed her again, and his tongue pierced her mouth. He moved in and out seductively. He sent, *Can you feel that even my tongue is bigger*?

She didn't have time to answer him because suddenly she was airborne as he lifted her over his shoulder. He thumped across the floor to the bed and tossed her on her back. She bounced and laughed, but he didn't so much as smile. He caught her ankles, and as he pulled her toward him, he dropped to his knees beside the bed and split her legs wide.

Her laughter drifted away because suddenly the room was full once more of forest scent and his head was easing down in the right direction until he was chuffing, making that resonant growling, huffing sound that somehow relaxed her pelvis. He brought her legs across the new breadth of each shoulder, and the fit was perfect.

She threw her arms back and closed her eyes, drowning in his scent.

Then he went to work on her.

Leto was being educated right now. When his beast-state had begun to rise five months ago, he would never have believed that it would have led him here, to a point that he felt comfortable in his skin. He was relaxed in his beast-state as his tongue plowed his woman, his *breh*.

He was getting used to the feel of his body, and, yes, parts were bigger. His tongue felt thicker, which made talking a challenge, but there was definitely an advantage as he licked in a wide slow path over Grace's flesh, pressing his tongue into her folds, drawing away, then pressing and licking some more.

He used one arm to keep her hips seated because she was enjoying his attentions and kept moving around, her hips arching into him. It also stunned him just how sensitive she was, more than he had thought possible, but with each lap he could feel what she was experiencing. Add to that her sweet meadow scent, and his cock was a missile again. But what he wanted still involved his tongue.

He dipped low, and as he entered her, driving deep, Grace let out a cry and a whimper all in one. He plunged now, and used the muscles of his tongue to change the position. He could feel her tight walls dragging over him, and he could feel what it was like to be invaded in that way. Her hips rocked steadily now, that motion as familiar as time, explaining the exact way he could please her.

Her gasps and cries grew steady and rhythmic. He wanted her to come. He slid his free hand beneath her waist and caught her lowest left wing-lock. Her cries turned low and guttural. "Yes" came out as a hoarse plea.

He rubbed first, then reached the sensitive aperture and flicked back and forth with the tip of his finger as he continued to drive his tongue ruthlessly.

He felt her come, the quick pulses deep within, the sudden jerks of her body, and the way she screamed from deep within her throat, as though his movements had set her on fire. Her body began to glow again so he drove deeper and harder. This time he pinched her wing-lock until she was thrashing on the bed, her heels pounding into his back. Her hands were now on the back of his head pushing as he thrust so that his tongue and chin slammed into her.

He loved it and only stopped when she stopped, when her body grew slack and her legs grew quiet.

"Oh, that was good," she whispered, breathing hard.

"It's amazing to feel what all this feels like to you." He was breathing hard as well but for a different reason. He was ready for her again. He wanted to take her, to thrust into her with his hips pistoning fast. But he wanted something else, he just didn't know what.

He rose up so that her legs fell to the sides, now draped over the bed. He stood in front of her looking down. The two inches of added height gave him a different perspective. She looked a little farther away, which made her appear more fragile. He loved how different they were, that she was woman, and in a physical sense more vulnerable than he would ever be. He leaned over her and planted his broad hand on her chest, his fingers spanning her, reaching easily from nipple to nipple.

He looked at her neck. He needed her blood, that much he knew, and he would take it . . . soon.

But he still wanted something more.

Using both his hands, he started at the top of her head, and in a long smooth gliding stroke swept down her body, caressing her neck, her shoulders, her arms, then back up the undersides of each to catch her ribs and rub down to her waist, her hips, the outsides of her thighs, her knees, her ankles, even her feet.

He savored doing it, but he also loved that he could feel the pleasure his touch gave her. Incredible.

He flipped her over. Ah, this was what he wanted. He wanted to take her from behind as he had that first time in the basement of his cabin. Now, however, he had control.

He caressed the back of her head, her wing-locks that were still moist, the mounds of her buttocks, which he kissed each in turn, then dragged his hands down the backs of her thighs, her knees, her heels. He stretched out on top of her, his cock pressed between her legs. He felt her laugh—a giggle really, a warm sound.

How had this come to him, this banquet of sensation? How? He didn't deserve Grace, not even a little bit. Yet she was here, with him, so completely, 100 percent. And she filled him, filled his soul and warmed him where he had been cold and dead, a metaphorical vampire, for how many decades, how many centuries?

He took her arms and spread them out, his own on top of hers. "Spread your legs," he urged.

She spread them, and he did the same on top of hers.

"We're flying."

We certainly are, she sent. *I'd say the words out loud, but they'd be muffled by the bed.*

"Are you comfortable?"

She sighed so that his chest rose and fell with her. *Very.*

"I need to take you, Grace. This body, this state, has very definite needs. I need you in this position."

Leto, you can have me in any position you want.

He shuddered. He let his legs fall between hers and—as he had done when she had first returned to Mortal Earth—he lifted her up so that she was on her hands and knees. He got behind her and made serious use of his tongue once more until she was groaning and pushing back into his face. Her meadow flavor streamed over his tongue.

He rose up and positioned himself at her opening. He held himself steady as she pushed back with her hips. He entered her an inch at a time, pressing into her, watching his cock disappear and at the same time feeling what that was like for her. The dual sensations almost made him come, so he took a few deep breaths.

The rough time in the cellar had been amazing. But this was different, taking his time, watching his beast-sized body connect with hers as only a man can connect with a woman, his cock being drawn into the well of her, into that place built for him.

When he reached the end, he took hold of her hips, kept her steady, and slowly drew back. He groaned the entire distance just as she groaned. He moved his hips back and forth, he arched his pelvis, he teased her as he drove in and out.

He paused and leaned down to reach her back. He licked the weeping wing-locks, as many as he could reach from his position. Each time his tongue swept over a lock, and took in her juices, her body shuddered and her hips twitched, which of course rolled a new sensation down his cock and into his balls.

Sex had never been like this before.

"Take my blood, Leto," she called to him, her voice hoarse. "I need you to take my blood."

He almost lost it, hearing the words spoken aloud. To offer up one's blood was a sacred gesture, the most loving, the most intimate. He licked over her neck, sustaining a slow drive into her body at the same time.

She rose up on one arm and swept her hair away from her neck. She had done the same thing the first time he'd taken her, and somehow that memory rushed forward—of how rough he'd been and how good it had felt—and his hips started to pummel her.

She was vampire-strong and stayed with him, so that when his lips found her neck and his fangs emerged, she held her head perfectly still. He struck, and the taste of her blood brought him in a sudden rush. He groaned and cried out as he sucked, the sounds garbled against her neck.

But he felt her grasp him and pull deep as she held her upper body still so that he could drink and shove himself into her and come and come and come.

Grace felt all this muscled warrior slamming into her and coming and sucking hard at her neck. She was hurting, but it was a good kind of hurt, and it seemed to intensify the sensation of her own orgasm as she held herself immobile. She screamed, long and loud, pleasure streaking through her like flames burning and shooting along every nerve.

Her body seemed so strangely fit for Leto in his beast-state, as though all previous encounters had been paltry. She felt alive, as she'd never felt alive before, as though he was beating new life into her with each heavy thrust. As though with each draw on her neck as he continued to drink, and continued to pulse into her, the act of giving of herself was strengthening all that she was.

The color blue rushed at her from all sides, enlivening her soul, enriching her heart, her thoughts. Her mind was swept with blue and more blue. She felt as though she could soar in this position, take to the skies, with Leto servicing her from behind and taking her blood, as though she could speed straight to the stars and explode into a fireball of blue light, as though she could take her place among the heavens as in the myths of old.

This was ecstasy, oh, yes, a blue heaven of ecstasy.

Later that afternoon, Greaves folded to the Seers Palace, straight to the pit. He needed another hard look into the immediate future so that he could plan his next moves, but what he found was a mess. He wasn't generally given to profanity, but in this moment he let loose with a couple of very sincere, very descriptive words.

Stannett lay completely naked, his body crusted with red, pink, and white residue. Greaves approached his mind slowly and felt the man's usual massive shields.

But Greaves wasn't who he was for nothing. He shaped his mind into a missile and punched hard. He almost fell inside and found a wide sweeping vista of bliss and *nothing*, as though the man's mind had been erased.

He didn't think that was possible, so he began to prod around and found the remnants of more orgasms than a man should ever have. Stannett was in some kind of sexual coma and of no use at all.

All six powerful Seers were dead on either side of him.

Greaves grunted his displeasure. Stannett was one of the most gifted men, the most preternaturally powerful men, he'd ever known. But he had an addict's psyche and would always let his need for mental relief outweigh his rational mind. Stannett had recently forfeited a perfectly elegant setup at the Superstition Mountains Seers Fortress, not because he couldn't keep his dick in his pants, but because he couldn't make sufficient use of his rational mind to keep his schemes on the down-low.

So here Greaves was, cleaning up another mess. He needed pure vision now more than ever. He'd almost succeeded in tearing Grace away from her *breh*—and had he done so, all of his plans would have finally clicked into place. The value of this expensive Seers Palace was proven in his mind, but not with Stannett in his state of excess.

He drew his phone from the inside pocket of his suit jacket and called his command center at the Estrella Mountain Complex. He spoke with an aide, who suggested sending one of his more sadistic Section Leaders over to get Stannett on board. He knew the one, a woman with real potential and strong preternatural power, physically capable of dominating Stannett.

Greaves thought it an excellent plan.

A few minutes later, the woman arrived, a female Militia Warrior with her red hair cut short and pressed flat against her head. Both his army and Thorne's had the same components: Division and Section Leaders and Militia Warriors. Greaves had added generals at the top so that he need only deal with a handful of military men himself.

Greaves swept a hand in the direction of the pit. The woman moved forward and glanced down. Her lip curled. He had the feeling that if she'd been alone and seen this sight, she would have spit. "Is this the man who raped all those women out at the Superstitions?"

Greaves smiled. Apparently the woman had issues, which meant she would be quite perfect for this task. "The very one. I'd like you to whip him into shape, and I do mean literally. He tends to give himself to pleasure when he should be working."

The curl of her upper lip turned into a smile, and the hard light in her eye deepened. "With pleasure, master."

Lovely manners.

He gestured to the corpses. "These will need to be disposed of and more strapped in. You'll find the cells are full of excellent replacements."

"Very good, master."

"As for Stannett, I need him awake and sober. Whatever you need to do to get him to that state—feel free to do."

"Yes, master." She jumped down into the pit and folded into her hand a leather whip with silver spikes hooked to the tip.

The sounds of Stannett's sudden screams accompanied Greaves as he lifted his hand and folded once more to Estrella Mountain and his Command Center.

When he arrived, one of his aides hurried forward with good news. "We have most of the colonies mapped. The rest are close to discovery."

Greaves had gone over the electronic grid that showed the entire globe of Mortal Earth. He had identified an almost invisible signal that marked the hidden colonies. Once he recognized the signature, his team had created the transmitters as well as the system by which each colony was being mapped using negative space. The process had been more successful than he'd hoped.

This was good news indeed.

"Excellent." He moved to the deep end of the room, which held several large screens constantly in play. One showed the Mortal Earth colonies; another showed the various locations of his army. A third screen detailed troop movement based on his most recent orders, including minute-by-minute status updates.

He scanned the numbers. Below him, in the underground tunnels of his complex, the bunkers were filling up. He had been a visionary, and right now it was paying off. He had tens of miles of bunkers, drilled deep into the mountain range, large enough to house and feed half a million Militia Warriors for several weeks at a time.

He had seven ambitious generals, all committed to the Coming Order. Each had been chomping at the bit for a real battle for decades. The spirit in the room said everything. There were no squabbles; just a wonderful tense excitement, like a storm building and building.

The Seers reports out of Bogotá showed a battle over White Lake and another odd kind of spectacle event, both of which would take place within the next two to three days.

He smiled as he watched the screens, as he moved from general to general and listened while each orchestrated the movements of the army, either to the bunkers here in Estrella or to several key places in the world for easy dispatch to annihilate the Mortal Earth colonies.

Despite the presence of the obsidian triad and that Casimir was making it almost impossible to kill Leto, Greaves found he was breathing more deeply than he had in a long time.

And, yes, he was smiling.

Grace sat in the kitchen at the villa island and sipped her coffee. Leto stood opposite her near the sink, mug in hand. His hair was loose and shiny all down his shoulders, arms and back. He wore a black tank, jeans, and no shoes. Though he was no longer in his beast-state, he looked . . . edible.

Her lips parted but no words came out. Just air, a sigh full of desire. Had the *breh-hedden* done this to her, made her want him like she'd never wanted any man before? Probably, and yet she'd always desired him.

His eyes were so blue and clear now. Five months ago, they'd been clouded with pain and despair, the remnants of his life working with Greaves.

Had the *breh-hedden* worked this miracle as well? His healing both within and without?

She eased up on the mug and set it down with a clink on the stone surface. He seemed preoccupied, which didn't surprise her given the task set before him.

"You're so quiet," she said at last. "And you've been staring at the faucet for at least a minute. Should I be worried?"

Leto glanced up from his own mug. He chuckled, at least for a moment, then his expression grew somber once more. "I've just been thinking about Greaves's army—or more accurately, the kind of logistics required to bring his army under my command. What I fear is that if I move the divisions in bits and pieces, Greaves will catch wind of what we're up to, and then all hell will break loose. We'd lose a huge portion of the ranks, and maybe even provoke a battle we would absolutely lose."

"How many Militia Warriors we talking about? I know you spoke with at least a hundred Division Leaders."

At that, Leto smiled. "Grace, I'm almost afraid to speak the words out loud, but I honestly think I could bring over a million."

Grace's brows rose. "*Half* Greaves's force?"

Leto nodded. "I just can't seem to figure out a way to fold that many troops to safety without Greaves knowing."

Grace wanted to help. It was a simple as that. She stared at her mug, wondering if obsidian flame could be of use to Leto. She had thought her involvement in the war would somehow mean physical battle. Yet as she sipped and pondered, her thoughts turned to Thorne and his aides bent over the grid tracking the enemy's movements; to Marcus launching web PR all over the world about the attack on the Seattle Colony; to Leto's training of the colonial militia.

Overt battle was only one facet of war preparation. Right now, the logistics of how to move a million warriors had become the focus.

He rounded the island, setting his cup down as he drew near. He sat on the stool next to her and rubbed his fingers over her arm. She could feel what that felt like to him, the softness of her skin beneath his fingers. She sighed again. And she felt grateful.

"You are a hard thinker, Grace. Even the muscles of your cheeks feel tense."

She met his gaze and touched his face with her hands. He'd shaved, and his skin felt so smooth. She could feel how warm her fingers felt to him. "I've always been this way. You need to know that about me. I think about everything."

"No problem," he said, searching her eyes. "Just try not to shut me out."

She frowned. "What do you mean?" She set her cup on the island and shifted toward him, one knee between his legs.

He tapped her forehead with his index finger. "Here. I suspect when you think this hard you believe you've spoken aloud, but you haven't."

"Oh. You may be right."

"So . . ."

She blinked, and once more felt her brow furrow. Enlightenment dawned, however slowly. "I should share more." Maybe that was part of her ghost ways: Her life was internal, and she rarely communicated her thoughts with anyone.

"Please." But his eyes were lit with laughter so she did the only thing that made sense. She leaned into him and kissed him on the lips. As she drew back, he followed and captured her mouth, kissing her back and catching her around the waist.

She could feel his body light up. How quickly his maleness responded to touch, to sensation, to his tongue deep in her mouth. And because she could feel the pleasure riding him so quickly, she melted against him. In a way, his pleasure had become hers.

I feel your nipples against my chest and my chest against your nipples. This is so strange. Wonderful, but strange.

She drew back and planted a hand on his chest. How quickly sex could fire up between them. She kept her hand firmly in place and at the same time set up a quick succession of blocks to stop from feeling all that his body experienced.

"I'm feeling you very low," he said. "How your body responds to me."

"Hush," she whispered.

"What's wrong?" This time he frowned.

"Leto, I could so easily fall back into bed with you, but for the last hour I've been thinking about the doe that I saw on the villa lawn this morning."

"You have?"

"Yes, because the moment I saw her, that was all I could see. She's not the usual desert sight, a deer out in the open. I kept watching, completely distracted from everything." Her obsidian flame power vibrated from deep in the earth.

Leto gasped and even looked down at the floor. "I don't know if it's because you have your hand on my chest, but I can feel that."

She smiled. "I think it means I'm on the right track." Chills chased up and down her arms. "I have an idea that might be exactly what's needed. It would put pressure on Greaves on several fronts at the same time."

He overlaid her hand with his own. His lips curved. "What's on your mind?"

"Remember how, in Moscow Two, Greaves tried to have a military review?"

"Yes. Thorne and the Warriors of the Blood stopped it right in the middle."

Grace nodded. "What if we had something similar, only featuring obsidian flame, a large very flamboyant spectacle event. We could demonstrate the triad's power, we would give Marcus another PR tool for holding on to Endelle's High Administrators . . . and . . . we could do some serious folding."

His eyes widened. "The doe on the lawn."

Grace smiled. "Do you see? While we're giving a demonstration in public, which would be a huge distraction to the enemy, we could also be folding your divisions wherever you wanted them."

"Dear Creator, it's a brilliant idea. But can the triad do something like that?"

She opened her obsidian power, letting all that rumbling power flow up and over her.

Leto enfolded her in his arms. "What you're experiencing is incredible. So much power. I can feel the vibrations along your skin." He drew back slightly and kissed her.

I think your idea is brilliant, he sent.

Grace felt something deep inside her begin to warm. His praise meant the world to her. She could help. She wanted to help.

Of course, with so much power now rippling from her and with his mouth sealed to hers, Grace started forgetting about the topic at hand. Her hands slid up his back and his body curled around hers until his embrace was all that she cared about.

Leto. She whispered his name through her mind.

Grace.

He drew away slightly to look into her eyes. Her breathing sped up, but not just because she wanted him. His eyes were on fire, a blue fire that spoke to her. "What is it?" she asked. She wanted him to say the words out loud.

He caressed her face, kissed her lips again. "Everything seems to be changing. You are. I am. Do you think it might be possible . . ." He kissed her again slowly, then once more pulled away to look at her.

Grace's heart thumped heavily in her chest. He hadn't finished his thought, but she understood him. Would love be possible between them? Something deep and real, something not clouded by the war or his fractured state or her ghostliness. All these years, all these centuries, she had moved like a spirit through the world, much like her apparition-self, always studying and hoping, but for what she didn't know.

Yet as she looked into Leto's eyes, hope soared. Could she become real in his life? Could he give himself to her despite the ugliness of the war or his guilt over the past century of serving a monster?

If every step she took from this point forward brought her closer to a true union with Leto, she vowed that if called upon, she would throw herself into the depths of hell just for the chance.

"Let me call Thorne," he said, releasing her. "We have a strategy to put in place, but at some point, I want to sink inside you, all the way, to find out what this can be between us."

"All the way," she returned.

CHAPTER 13

Leto watched Thorne pace Endelle's sitting room. This time Endelle sat in one of the large purple chairs opposite Leto. Grace stood behind him, her hands resting on his shoulders. He loved it.

Thorne shoved a hand through his hair, stopped mid-stride, and turned to Leto. "I don't like it. Obsidian flame is untried, and you're talking about combining a spectacle event with a series of massive folds?"

"You've got it," Leto said. He took one of Grace's hands in his. "Your sister has got some serious chops. And even you, as the anchor to obsidian flame, must have a sense of what the triad is capable of. Remember what it was like when Grace, while in possession of Fiona, battled Jean-Pierre with the sword?"

Thorne shook his head. "I am remembering. But the timing would have to be so precise, the locations fixed. Do you have any idea of the sheer logistics that we're talking about? Obsidian flame would essentially be in flight during the military part of the review and at the same time doing all this secret folding of masses of warriors. How could it possibly work?"

Leto would have answered him, but Endelle rose to her feet. She still wore her leathers and a weapons harness, no octopus tentacles or badger pelts. She was strangely subdued and serious. "Thorne, what the fuck is the matter with you? This plan is genius, and you're acting like a little girl."

At that, he turned to her and laughed. He put a hand to his forehead. "Shit, I think you're right. I guess it doesn't help that we're talking about my *breh* and my sister being involved in something incredibly dangerous." He threw his hands in the air. "We'll make it work." His gaze slid to Grace. "You think you're up for this?"

Leto rose to his feet at these words. "Hell, yeah, she's up for this. You've been her overprotective brother too long. Grace can do anything."

Thorne's brows rose. He looked from one to the other.

Leto felt Grace's hand slide into his, warmth against his palm. She gave his fingers a squeeze. He looked down at her and winked. She grinned. My God, had he ever seen her smile like that? He got lost for a moment just looking at her until he heard Endelle make a gagging sound.

When he glanced her direction, she said, "This goddam *breh-hedden* shit gives me the scratch. If I see one more couple making goo-goo eyes at each other, I'm gonna toss my cookies."

"Goo-goo eyes?" Leto asked. "Really?"

She jerked a hand to encompass both Leto and Grace. "What would you fucking call that?"

"I was letting her know that I respect the hell out of her."

"Fine. Whatever." But a smile replaced all that disgust as Endelle held Leto's gaze. "It's a good plan. And do you really think half of Greaves's force will come with you?"

Leto didn't quite recognize the sensation that sped through him, but dammit, it felt like pride. "Yes. I do."

"Hot damn. Well, it seems to me we've got some work to do, and I want Marcus in on this pronto." She laughed. "He's gonna have a field day with this one."

The next hour was spent conferring with Marcus via video cam. As predicted, Marcus went into hyperspeed. Even while on the line, he left his station and started barking a dozen orders at his staff.

Leto sat beside Endelle, sharing in the conference. He met her gaze. "See what I mean?" she said. She crossed her arms over her chest and smiled some more, turning once more to stare at the screen as she waited for Marcus to come back.

He had never seen Endelle so relaxed. He got it. He really did. Much of the past twenty-plus centuries had been spent building to this moment.

Marcus returned, his eyes almost feverish. He demanded specifics, and Leto told him what he needed to know.

"We're moving fast on this," Marcus said. "Tomorrow night at eight, the triad will be in the air."

Marcus then stated exactly what he needed to have happen before anything else. "I've got to have a photo op with the triad in full mount. A back view of the wings with the different-colored flames."

"I'll get on it," Leto said. "We'll use the Apache Junction Two workout center."

"Good. That's all for now." Without saying anything more, he clicked off, and the screen went blank.

Endelle snorted then laughed. "Marguerite's going to love this," she drawled.

Leto frowned. "What do you mean?"

"Have you been around many pregnant women before?"

"Not really."

"My suggestion, then, is that you stay the hell away from that photo op."

Leto wasn't sure what she meant, but he wasn't too concerned. Not when right now he had to grapple with where to move a million warriors during a spectacle review.

An hour later, Grace hid her smiles behind her hand. She stood in the large workout center of the Militia Warrior HQ with her obsidian sisters, and Marguerite was very unhappy.

The meeting with Thorne and Endelle had ended with Endelle barking her orders. Obsidian flame would train at the workout center, Marcus and Havily would put the spectacle event together and begin a PR web-release campaign, Leto would contact his Division Leaders, and Thorne would help Leto establish endpoint fold locations for the troops.

But before the triad could begin practicing, Marcus had commandeered the women, insisting on a visual spread that focused on the triad's unique wing coloration. Grace knew he was right to insist on it. The dark flame pattern and colors of each woman's wings would make a striking display.

"I know I shouldn't care," Marguerite said, fluffing her short platinum curls, "but right now my pregnancy ass is the size of Arizona, and Marcus wants the wings photographed from *the rear*. Hell, no one will even see the wings. They'll just ask why there's a blimp supporting the black and red flames."

Grace tried not to laugh, but Marguerite was so funny. On the other hand, when had a pregnant woman ever not been extra conscious of her figure?

Marguerite had on maternity flight gear that showed the full curve of a six-month-pregnant belly that held twins. From Grace's point of view, she looked beautiful.

Marguerite splayed her fingers over her stomach. "And what about this? What's Marcus going to do about this?"

"Marcus said he just wanted a shot of the wings from behind."

"Ugh."

The photographer set up her tripod and had a team with her who managed the lighting and staging. They'd brought a dark backdrop lit softly from below with a row of dim lights.

Grace took both of Marguerite's hands. "You look more beautiful than you know, my idiot obsiddy sister."

But Marguerite just rolled her eyes. Very much in Endelle's mold she said, "Whatever."

The photographer called out, "If Ms. Dresner will stand on the center box, Ms. Albion and Ms. Gaines can stand to either side. First, however, you'll want to mount your wings." Grace understood the need for the box for the picture. Marguerite was much shorter than either Grace or Fiona; having her elevated would give the photo a more balanced look.

Grace stepped a good ten feet away from everyone in the room, as did both Marguerite and Fiona. With advanced powers came enormous wings. She also turned away from everyone from a certain amount of natural embarrassment. Mounting wings was similar to sexual release; even thinking about it had her heart rate climbing, her wing-locks weeping fluids, and her skin breaking into a sheen of sweat.

Her thoughts turned to Leto, of course, which so did not help. Desire began to spread through her. She was about to release her wings when Leto's voice was suddenly in her head. *Are you okay? Oh, my God, Grace, what are you doing over there? I can feel your wing-locks, and I had to excuse myself from this latest meeting. Should I come to you? Do you need me?*

Uh . . . no. we're getting ready for the photo shoot. Marcus wanted a back view of all our wings, since they're uniquely flame-based. We're in black leather flight suits. Leto?

He didn't respond right away, but she could sense that he was breathing hard. As she lowered the blocks, she kept in place so that she wasn't always experiencing his external sensations, she was hit with what she could feel was a painful erection. Which aroused her even more. When she felt his forehead suddenly hurt, she asked, *What was that?*

Oh, sorry, this is all just so weird. I'm in the bathroom at the palace. I was just drying my hands when I felt all you were feeling. I slammed my forehead into the wall a bit too hard. Shit, I cracked a couple of tiles. Grace, are you sure I can't come to you?

She smiled. She couldn't help herself. *No. We have to finish this shoot. But when I see you again, I think we need to manage some alone time. Maybe with wings.*

She heard a growl, or at least she thought she did. Could he communicate a growl telepathically?

Is that a promise?

Oh, yeah.

I'll leave you to it then. I'll have to block your sensations.

Same here. Bye.

She felt the connection break. It was so strange being so close to Leto at any given moment.

She took a few deep breaths and let her wings fly. She put her fingers to her lips because she'd almost orgasmed. She hadn't realized how close she was, but then she'd felt everything Leto was feeling.

Yes, she definitely had things to *discuss* with him later, or maybe just things to mount. Many things to mount.

She closed her eyes and resorted to some serious deep breathing.

The room had grown very quiet.

When she was finally in command of herself, she turned to find, first of all, that Marguerite had a wet towel slung around her neck.

Fiona was blinking rapidly.

"Well, that was interesting," Grace said.

Fiona laughed. "I haven't been mounting my wings very long, but that was really strange. I realized I had only mounted my wings when Jean-Pierre was around." Of course, her cheeks started to grow very pink. Then she laughed. "Oh, this is just too embarrassing."

When Fiona turned in Marguerite's direction, Grace had a full view of her wings. "Oh, Fiona, your wings are magnificent. All that black and gold and the flame pattern is so evident."

For the next few minutes, they spent time examining one another's wings. Marguerite's were a deep cherry red, with black flames at the base. Grace had seen hers while on Fourth with Casimir. There had been plenty of mirrors to look into, unlike in the Creator's Convent.

As she took her place to the right of Marguerite, an order that seemed fitting because Fiona had been the first to discover the nature of her power, Grace began to gain some confidence. She really was obsidian flame. Her wings matched Fiona's and Marguerite's. She really did belong here.

Of course, the proximity of the triad kept a certain level of power flowing among them, but as long as they didn't form a circle together the power remained a pleasant vibration over her skin.

As the photographer worked them, most of the comments came from Marguerite and generally stayed close to the topic of how well acquainted the photographer was with Photoshop and did she truly think she could shave at least four inches off her bottom.

The photographer assured her repeatedly that she could have final approval of the photo.

When the photographer and her crew took off, Marguerite contacted Thorne and asked him to join the triad because they were ready to begin practicing.

When Thorne arrived, Grace addressed obsidian flame's biggest concern. "So, we need to figure out how to do the mass folds." She turned to Fiona. "You were able to channel Endelle's ability to fold. Does that mean you have the same ability now?"

Fiona shook her head. "There is always a residual effect, something learned, but it's not the same thing. So, no, I don't have her level of power."

"So I need to acquire Endelle's ability."

Fiona smiled. "That would follow."

Grace knew why she was smiling. There was one woman on the planet with the ability she needed to acquire, but it was never an easy thing to work with the scorpion queen.

She glanced at Thorne. "Would you contact Endelle for us?"

He smiled. "Of course." He whipped his phone from his pants pocket. Grace had forgotten that he'd broken the mind-link with Endelle all those months ago. Now he had to contact her the usual way. He probably could have used telepathy, but Grace had a feeling Thorne wanted it this way. Maybe having a *breh* made a difference as well.

Grace waited and tried to calm her heart. Endelle was never easy to take, but this was new territory and she was already nervous. Thinking about being within Endelle's soul was like thinking about swimming with sharks.

Suddenly the alarms started shrieking like mad, after which Endelle appeared. She looked around, clearly not understanding why the alarms were ringing.

Thorne lifted a hand and shouted over the shrill signals, "I'll take care of this." Once more, he was on his phone. He spoke quickly and a moment later the alarms stopped, thank you, Creator.

Endelle scowled at Thorne. "Didn't you tell them I was coming?"

He laughed. "You didn't exactly give me a lot of time."

"I suppose not. You could say I'm a little anxious about what's happening here." She glanced from one woman to the next, finally landing on Grace. "So you have the ability to acquire any of my skills."

"That's right."

She smiled. "You're very sure about it."

"Yes, I suppose I am." She explained about practicing with Alison and about reading souls.

Endelle actually smiled. "Okay, so tell me what to do."

Grace felt uneasy. "I think I should warn you that I'll have to go deep to get to this particular power—as in, I'll be descending into your soul."

"Fine."

"You mean, just like that? You don't mind?"

"Hell, no. Just do it, Grace. What the fuck do I care? All I want is to finally get the upper hand over Greaves, get his fat balls in my hand, squeeze hard a few dozen times, then send him to perdition. If that means you do some soul diving, it'll be worth it." When Grace still hesitated, Endelle added, "Aw, for shit's sake, just jump inside my mind, or wherever the hell my 'soul' is"—she made air quotes—"and let's get this damn thing done."

"Okay, fine." Maybe not the most brilliant response, but Grace was very surprised. She had thought that the Supreme High Administrator of all of Second Earth would be more protective of her deepest parts. But then Endelle wasn't exactly known for her boundaries.

She moved just a little closer to Endelle, closed her eyes,

then pushed into Endelle's mind. She hadn't expected the entrance to be so easy, but then Endelle had motivation to cooperate right now.

Grace allowed herself to sink through the deepest layers of Endelle's thoughts. Because the entrance into her mind had been so easy, Grace had thought she would move swiftly into the woman's soul. But this layer of her mind was deep and it was dark.

She continued to sink. At last, she found what turned out to be a brilliant turquoise field of light that seemed as broad as it was high. There was so much beauty in the center of Endelle's domain that she could hardly contain her wonder.

She focused on Endelle's folding ability, and as before a kind of lock appeared. Grace focused her thoughts, shaping them into a blue key, and inserted.

With a powerful rush, Endelle's folding ability covered her. There was so much power that she was thrust out of Endelle's soul. She flew outward so that when she opened her eyes she was ten feet away from Endelle and flat on her back. She opened her eyes to stare up at the enormous steel girders that supported the roof.

She took deep breaths, but closed her eyes. She thought about Endelle, how beautiful her turquoise soul was, how vast, as though it would take millennia to know her, really know her.

She saw Endelle's stilettos, then looked up to smile at her. It was strange knowing her in this way, the loveliness of her soul, all that beauty covered up with her odd fashion choices, her profanity, and her deep cynicism.

"I take it you were successful?"

"I was." Grace rose to her feet. "But I wanted to tell you that your soul is very beautiful. I mean it's an elegant turquoise color, which I realize makes no sense, but you have surprising depths."

Endelle's mouth turned up on one side. "You mean, for a scorpion queen?"

Grace grinned. "Yes. Exactly."

Endelle chuckled. "Just don't tell anyone. It would ruin

my rep." She glanced at Marguerite and Fiona. "I guess I'm done here."

She lifted her right arm. Thorne reached out for her, to stop her, but she vanished anyway with a smirk and an "Oops."

Grace covered her ears because the alarms were incredibly shrill and loud.

Thorne rolled his eyes and withdrew his phone from his pocket once more.

When the alarms stopped, Grace knew the time had come to begin practicing the mass folds. Her heart thumped now. This was what she had put into motion, a spectacle event featuring obsidian flame as a subterfuge for stealing Greaves's army away from him.

But could the triad carry it off? Could she really do what she had promised? Only one way to find out.

Leto stood in the palace command center and glanced at his watch. Six-thirty. Thorne had promised him that he'd call a halt to the obsidian practice by seven-thirty. He had only an hour left; then he could head to the villa and make sure everything was ready. He had a certain plan in place involving wings and an empty house. Having checked in with Parisa, he knew she was working at the rehab center through the night, and of course Medichi was working the Borderlands with the rest of the Warriors of the Blood.

It felt strange not to be including the rest of the brothers in the war plans, but Greaves hadn't let up on the Borderlands and a constant flow of death vampires was keeping the WhatBees and the Militia Warrior squadrons working hard every night. And that had always been a significant part of Greaves's strategy: to wear down the most powerful warriors on the planet, thereby reducing their effectiveness. The plan had worked well until the *breh-hedden* started bringing strong women to the warriors, changing the focus of each of their lives and adding all sorts of new powers to Endelle's arsenal.

Leto had lived a long time, and he had noticed that when

evil tried to forge a wall against that which was essentially good, then life would respond and provide a countermeasure. Maybe it was spiritual in nature, or maybe it was just the immense life force inherent within the spirit of man to ensure survival above all things. In his opinion, the arrival of the *breh-hedden* was one of those countermeasures.

And he and Grace were part of that.

He focused once more on the separate grid that Thorne had brought in for the purpose of mapping that portion of the army that would submit to Leto's command. Leto was satisfied with his progress. His biggest concern involved those warriors among the ranks who would prefer to be with Greaves. Most of his conversations with the Division Leaders ran along that line, but the general consensus was that each leader would remove those warriors to a separate area for a specified duty. That way, when the time came for the mass fold, then those staunch supporters of Greaves would remain behind.

Because he had trained the army, especially the leadership, the troops had tremendous loyalty to their Regiment and Division Leaders. Those whom Leto contacted chose pretty quickly to align with Endelle. The generals had caused so much suffering among the divisions that the five months since Leto had left Greaves's service had created exactly the right atmosphere for a mutiny.

Leto had asked Endelle to create two large areas on the planet that she could cloak in mist, to which Leto could begin sending the support staff and materials any working army needed: latrines, tents, an abundance of food and water, and weapons.

The logistics of his part in the battle plans had finally come together. All that needed to be done now was to make sure that the triad could locate each misted area with ease. From what Grace had told him, she would simply need to see the location in her mind, something that could be accomplished as soon as the locations were set up.

Grace. Sweet Christ, his heart had expanded over the past few days. And how his life had changed. Was it only days ago that Grace had come back to him? During that time, he'd made peace with his beast-self and learned to make the transition with ease and without putting anyone in jeopardy. Incredible.

He wanted to give her more, to give of himself fully. And he was trying. But he also knew himself, that the war had taken something from him, had made it almost impossible to give all that he had to give. He wondered if that would ever be different.

He felt the hairs at the back of his neck rise. He turned, and sure enough Casimir made himself visible. "You are really starting to bug the shit out of me."

Casimir's smile was rueful. "I need a word with you."

"Okay." Leto frowned. He didn't know what to make of the Fourth ascender. He recalled doing battle with him in the Convent when Casimir had been acting on Greaves's behalf. Casimir's purpose had been to destroy both Grace and Leto, but then the *breh-hedden* had gotten hold of Casimir and changed everything.

Casimir drew in a deep breath. "I wanted to apologize for that Convent mess and for my behavior."

Leto didn't know what to say, but he felt angry all over again. "You took Grace to Fourth. You somehow persuaded her that you needed her. Don't think for a moment that I don't know how you worked to manipulate and seduce her, because I do know. She deserved better than you." His hands were balled into fists. He wanted to hit Casimir, but the damn man just stood there—no cocky smile, just sincerity in his dark brown eyes.

"I should never have taken her," Casimir confessed. "But I was a different man back then and I'd made a deal with Greaves. The prize was Grace."

Leto knew it wasn't as simple as that. Grace had explained to him a dozen times that her intuition had told her she had to be with Casimir if she was to save Leto's hide.

But he was a man and Casimir had walked off with Grace as pretty as you please, and he'd been too lost in his dying blood fiasco to do a thing about it.

"I don't know what you want from me," Leto said.

Only then did Casimir smile. "Your forgiveness."

"Aw fuck."

Fortunately, Endelle showed up and ended what would no doubt have turned into one of those really awkward moments.

Casimir greeted Endelle but then made his excuses and left.

Leto watched him leave, thinking that he didn't know what to make of the man. But it was getting harder to stay mad at him when he admitted he should never have gone after Grace, and even apologized for it.

When he turned back to Endelle, he did a double take and he couldn't help but laugh. For a while, Endelle had actually worn a flight suit and a weapons harness, showing that her warrior side was ready to do battle.

But the other side of her that had fully embraced the spectacle aspect of their plans had clearly taken over. She wore some kind of strange spotted-fur bustier that looked similar to leopard but the spots were too small. Civet cat came to mind. Probably. A large red pendant bounced against her breasts.

She wore black-and-white-striped, and very snug, leather pants.

When she reached him, he said, "Thought you'd given up your fashion sense for the duration."

Endelle smiled. "Are you kidding? We've got a spectacle to put on. This is just the beginning. I have my seamstresses working on a coat with several trains, perfect for flight." Endelle was leading the review. Unlike Greaves, who had waited ceremoniously in his concrete grandstand, Endelle meant to be the opening act.

For some reason, he found her enthusiasm comforting. Endelle had always taken the war with Greaves in stride, something necessary for a conflict that went on for centuries. Her pleasure in her absurd clothes had no doubt been a tremendous release for her, perhaps even a passionate avocation.

"How's the army-hunting going?"

"Good. Real good."

She met his gaze and, for a moment those ancient lined eyes filled with compassion. "Damn, I missed you Leto. You and Marcus had been with me longest, and for decades both of you were AWOL. But now you're here. And you're bringing me an army. I'll bet James's announcement wrenched your heart."

"More than you'll know." Leto was moved. He would never have believed that his service to Greaves would have taken this turn.

Endelle added, "And you know that if any of the other generals had built the army, this couldn't have happened."

"I've been thinking about that. I think you're exactly right. Greaves's generals are almost as power-hungry as Greaves is. They won't have treated their Division and Section Leaders well."

"So, what do you think Greaves's strategy will be? You probably know him better than anyone."

"Thorne and I have talked about Greaves a lot. Over the decades, I heard a number of scenarios discussed. However, because I'm in your camp, he'll probably change things up. One thing I'm convinced he'll do is attempt to eliminate the hidden colonies, because he has no idea what threat level the colonial militia presents. By now, he'll have learned that I trained the militia force and he'll do what he can to neutralize it."

"How do you think he'll do it? I mean what's your take on it?"

"At some point, he'll attempt to move his death vampire force into place all over Mortal Earth, burn the mossy mist away, and attack all at once. And trust me, I know this because that's how I would have advised him. He doesn't do anything without measured thought. That's why he's still around."

"Have you got any idea about how to handle the colony sitch?"

"Every colony has a militia force ready to fight, but you know the odds: one death vampire against four militia warriors. He's been building his death vampire force for decades, feeding them from his blood slave facilities, so that they are a very powerful force. Our effort must be to keep him from burning away the mist. The death vamps can't get in otherwise."

Endelle nodded. "You're thinking the triad will have to help."

"Facing Greaves on multiple fronts when the time comes will absolutely require that the triad protect the colonies. And it makes the most sense. Grace is like Alison. Neither is built for straight-on battle. Tell me you know that."

"Yeah, I do." She sounded resigned.

Endelle released a deep breath. She rubbed her chest. "Wish I had my weapons harness back on. As hot as that damn thing was it gave me more comfort than I realized."

He glanced at the oversized red pendant. "What's that made of?"

She looked down and flipped the pendant up and down with her index finger. "Dead ladybugs. Don't worry. Kaitlyn, who's been working with me, is into all that organic shit. She actually went to a ladybug farm and collected some dead ones. Fucking waste of time if you ask me, but, hey, it's her time. Besides, this pendant rocks."

Grace stood in the desert beside Thorne, looking at the warriors the triad had been moving from place to place, just to practice the mass-folding skill. Everyone was taking a break. Marguerite had headed to the rehab center to check in on her Seer teams, to make sure they kept blocking every aspect of the spectacle event from Stannett. Fiona sat in a camp chair talking quietly on her phone to one of the blood slaves she'd been counseling for a few months now. The warriors were rehydrating.

For the past several hours, Grace and the triad had been working with her newly acquired mass-folding ability, and she was still astonished. Seriffe had ordered a thousand of his warriors to be at the triad's disposal for the afternoon, and Endelle had created her own version of the dense mossy mist to sustain the secrecy of their practice here in Apache Junction Two.

In addition, Endelle had set up a second location in North Africa Two, also cloaked beneath a mossy dome of mist. It was to these two separate locations that half a million warriors each would be sent. Right now, Gideon was at the second location, with Brynna reporting in constantly over the success of each practice fold. Everything had gone perfectly, which of course made Grace nervous.

"I wish we could try a larger force, just once."

Thorne nodded. "I know what you mean. But I can feel the power, Grace. It's there."

"I know, but . . ."

He slipped his arm around her waist. "I'm with you. Let me see what I can do." He stepped away from her and made a phone call. When he returned to her, he smiled. "Will another five thousand do? Seriffe has them on maneuvers at the desert below Endelle's palace."

Grace's heart skipped a beat. "Yes. Five thousand would be great. Do we dare try the fold from that position?"

"I don't think a single fold of a large contingent will arouse too many suspicions. Greaves will probably think Endelle was trying out her skills."

"But I don't want to bring them here. I think we should send them to North Africa Two."

"Good idea."

With the plan set, Thorne made his phone calls in order to ensure that the five thousand were in a solid formation, everyone standing in squads of four and ready for a fold. He then folded straight to the McDowells so that he could mentally share with Grace the location and structure of the five thousand warriors.

Grace sent a quick message to Marguerite via their shared obsidian pathway, then let Fiona know what was going on.

A few minutes later, after Marguerite had returned, Thorne returned to download the location and image to Grace. Once she could see exactly what they would be doing, she placed her hand on Marguerite's shoulder and Fiona's.

Thorne moved several feet away. This was the biggest change that had occurred. After working together through the afternoon, the massive obsidian power had settled down and Thorne no longer needed to touch any of the women in order to dissipate the excess power.

This time, as the circle closed and the power began to build, Grace let it flow. She focused on her folding ability and could sense when Fiona was ready to receive her. She slid easily within Fiona, taking possession, and with a single mental effort the massive fold began. Even though the triad was at Apache Junction Two, and the five thousand warriors were in the McDowells, Grace could sense the fold as it happened.

The shared obsidian power grew stronger and stronger, flowing upward toward the dome of mist. Grace could actually see within her mind's eye as the fold took place, all five thousand warriors being moved to North Africa.

Thorne's voice spilled over all that power. "Seriffe reported that the fold was successful at the McDowells. Gideon just reported in as well, and the warriors have arrived in perfect formation."

Grace cheered. Fiona and Marguerite joined in.

"Shall we do the reverse?" Thorne asked.

"Yes," Grace said.

Both Marguerite and Fiona responded in the affirmative as well, and without a single break in the flow of power, Grace reversed the fold.

Afterward, though Thorne gave his confirmation report from Seriffe, Gideon, and Brynna, Grace already knew the mass fold had been successful. She could feel it.

When she disengaged from Fiona and reentered her body fully, she drew back from both Fiona and Marguerite. "Did you both have a sense of what we'd done? When it happened?"

Marguerite nodded. "Yes. For the last few folds, I could feel it when it happened."

"This is new," Thorne said.

Fiona added, "It came on gradually, but Grace is right. I could feel the fold. I could feel the landing in North Africa, then the return fold to the McDowells."

Thorne smiled. "Shit, that's the best news of the day." His head bobbed and he glanced at his watch, then at Marguerite.

She moved quickly in his direction and slid her arm around his waist. "Tell me we're done for the day. I'm ready to put my feet up. Really ready."

He kissed the top of her head. "We're done and it's now seven thirty. I did promise a couple of warriors I'd get their *brehs* home."

He started herding them in the direction of the landing platforms. Even though the team had been doing this work outside, Seriffe had a strict policy in place about folding. If you were anywhere at Militia Warrior HQ, inside or out, you had to use the landing platforms.

On the way, Leto was suddenly in her mind. *Coming back to the villa anytime soon? It's seven thirty-one.*

Even though she knew his sudden presence in her mind was the result of the *breh-hedden*—and because of it, much stronger than telepathy—she was startled. *Hey, how about a warning. You weren't there, then suddenly you were practically shouting inside my head.*

Sorry. It's just . . . well, I'm at the villa. Did she hear a low growl again? How could he do a growl telepathically? But it made her smile.

She realized she'd been blocking his physical sensations, so she lowered her shields. Too fast, apparently, because she was overwhelmed by the feel of his bare feet on the wood floor of the villa, the muscles of his legs tight and tense, his body in partial arousal, his arms flexing and unflexing.

She even stumbled. Thorne caught her arm. "You okay?"

She looked up at him and felt a blush on her cheek. "Yes, of course," she said quickly.

But he looked concerned so she added, "I'm getting used to the *breh-hedden*'s quick form of communication. Leto suddenly jumped inside my head, and he surprised me."

Thorne smiled and let go of her arm. "I know. It can be jarring when you're not used to it."

"You can say that again." *Jarred* was the least of what she felt.

To Leto, she sent, *Heading to the landing platforms now, but this is a long walk.*

Can't wait.

Because she felt him shudder, she blocked him once more so she could finally breathe. But she walked faster.

He spoke the vows that moved my heart,
I turned and opened my robe.
He split the continents wide once more,
And took the spoils he had won.

—Grace of Albion, "The Convent Years," from
Collected Poems, Beatrice of Fourth

CHAPTER 14

Greaves arrived at the Illinois Two Seers Fortress, and, yes, the situation with Stannett seemed to be well in hand, at least for the present. The redheaded Militia Warrior clearly hadn't spared her whip. Stannett had only his leathers on, and his upper torso was still cut up if not bleeding. But at least Stannett looked sobered.

Still, Greaves really needed to impress on his servant the critical nature of the hour that fast approached. He backhanded him and sent him flying across the room so that he landed hard against one of the black marble walls. Stannett crumpled to the floor.

Greaves strode to his position and looked down at him. "Do I need to explain to you what has happened while you were squirting all over yourself today?"

Stannett tried to blink, but he listed sideways. His eyes showed a lot of white.

"Do you wish for my assistance, master?" The female Militia Warrior's voice soothed him.

"No, I thank you. And again, I value how much you were able to contribute in so short a span of time."

He reached down to Stannett and placed a hand on the

man's thick hair. He shuddered slightly at the strange stiff texture. Despite his fury, he allowed the healing waves to flow. He needed Stannett's brain functioning so that he could get back in the future streams and do his job.

In quick stages, Stannett pulled himself upright and began to focus his eyes. When he looked up at Greaves and flinched, Greaves removed his hand and stepped back.

He folded a document into his hand and waved it at Stannett. "Do you see this paper?"

Stannett nodded.

"Good. I'm going to show it to you, and I want you to absorb what you see." He lowered the sheet to Stannett's eyes. It was a printout of the obsidian triad photo, all three women in full-mount, displaying the unique flame pattern of their wings.

The Seer scanned it thoroughly. A frown between his brows grew deeper and heavier with each passing second.

"Over the past few hours, have you seen anything about this in the future streams?"

Stannett blinked several times, but the frown never left his face. He shook his head slowly, his chin sinking. "Marguerite and the teams she created are very powerful. No doubt they've been blocking the images."

"Undoubtedly, which means I need you to try harder. This event is scheduled for tomorrow night, yet I've heard nothing of it from you and your bound Seers. How is this possible?"

"I humbly beg your forgiveness."

"I'm not here to dispense absolution. I'm only here to try to get you to understand that we're on the verge of a major battle. And let me remind you that if your failure causes my failure, it means that Marguerite, as the Supreme High Seer of Second Earth, will have your ass in a sling. Do you understand?"

Stannett finally met his gaze and some of the false humility he'd been showing disappeared. He even looked frightened.

"Good. You're beginning to get the bigger picture." There

was only one real way of dealing with Stannett. If he didn't understand exactly how he could be hurt, he would continue indulging his Seer joyride.

The Militia Warrior seemed to have succeeded in reining him in for the most part, but she didn't have the power to know what he was doing in the future streams. Only Greaves could do that.

"And now, please select your next set of Seers extremely well. I want you to spend the night hunting for information about this event. My senses tell me that it's not what it appears to be."

"Yes, master," Stannett said.

Satisfied, at least for the present, Greaves folded back to Geneva and paced his office from the desk to his black leather couch and back. One thing was clear: If Greaves survived this whole damn turn of events, he was going to have to get rid of Stannett and figure out some other way of getting the information he needed.

If he survived.

For the first time in centuries, he'd begun to doubt the outcome of the war. He stared down at the printout once more. Above the three women were the words OBSIDIAN FLAME SPECTACLE EVENT AT THE CAMELBACK PARADE GROUNDS, BY PRIVATE INVITATION ONLY. AIRING ON ALL MAJOR NETWORKS WORLDWIDE. CHECK YOUR LOCAL LISTINGS.

By the time his public relations department had alerted him to the news, the photo had gone viral. Obsidian flame was now being discussed in every corner of the globe.

So with one press release, his plans had been turned upside down.

He rubbed his chin, then his slick bald head. He rubbed his chin some more.

He couldn't quite bring his emotions under control, but he understood them. He was close to panic because it was the smaller print at the bottom of the page that disturbed him the most: AN HONOR GUARD WILL ACCOMPANY THE REMARKABLE OBSIDIAN TRIAD. *Honor guard* was code for a military review. But of what magnitude, and what had prompted Endelle to put obsidian flame on display? Unless of course it was to try to woo back some of the High Administrators he'd already hooked on dying blood.

He wadded the paper into a ball, tossed it into the air, then aimed a controlled hand-blast at it. The paper ignited, exploding into a ball of flames. He watched it land on the black marble of the floor and burn to ashes.

He had come so close to getting Grace to come with him back to Geneva, at which time he would have had her killed and none of this nonsense would even be happening. There would simply have been no triad. But she had been more powerful than he had thought possible and had resisted him.

He mentally shut off all the lights in his office, turned off the various electronic devices, and stretched out on the floor.

He needed to relax. He needed to think about how he would bring pressure to bear on Endelle's coming spectacle.

His first thought was a number of well-placed bombs that would take out her administrative headquarters as well as the Camelback Parade Grounds, but that was illegal.

On the other hand, with his plans on the tipping point of annihilation, what did he care for legalities? He would think about that. If he struck first, if he bombed the spectacle, he would gain an enormous advantage because obsidian flame would be destroyed.

His thoughts grew more and more focused on this concept so that within a few minutes, he'd made the decision to move forward with his plans.

Leto had taken great pains to get Medichi's house ready for Grace. He'd been in a state of partial arousal for the past several hours. She knew it, too, since she could feel all his external sensations. And just a moment ago, she'd sent, *We had a long walk, but I'm almost at the landing platform. Wings coming up.*

He shivered in anticipation.

Parisa was definitely out of the house, just as she had said she would be. And Medichi was on duty at the Borderlands.

He and Grace would have the house to themselves.

Because Militia Warriors patrolled the villa grounds constantly, Leto had shuttered all the windows. And for what he had in mind, he definitely required some privacy.

Needing to make sure that he had enough room for wingmount, he'd cleared the hall nearest the bedroom he shared with Grace. All that remained was the heavy rectangular oak table he planned to make use of, now cleared of decorative debris. Ever since he'd felt Grace mount her wings, and he'd cracked those tiles in the bathroom at the palace, he'd been thinking of this moment.

He felt Grace fold into the entryway.

He felt how much she ached.

"You need me," she said, hurrying toward him.

She was in his arms, and he planted his mouth on hers as though he intended to remain there forever. She groaned against him. He felt her clothes disappear, and his hands touched her wet wing-locks.

He groaned and lost his clothes. He was hard as a rock.

She pushed away from him suddenly, held out her arm, and brought the comforter from their bed into her hands. She threw it on the table and leaned over on her stomach, spreading her legs wide.

Oh, God.

He held out his hands, reaching for her, wanting to touch, yet knowing he was too damn close. He felt dizzy with desire. He could hardly move. He also felt all of her need, and the strange thought flitted through his mind: How the hell do the bonded warriors stay away from their *brehs*?

He moved forward stiffly, both knees and cock, until he could reach her. By now her entire body trembled, so he trembled.

I can feel you, she sent. *My, God. The* breh-hedden *is amazing.*

He planted his large hands on her hips, and she tilted for him so that her ass rose in the air. Sweet mother of the Creator, he nearly lost it.

"Take me now," she whispered. "My wings are ready to explode from my back."

"I can feel that," he said, but his voice was hoarse and deep. He didn't even sound like himself.

He positioned himself against all that beautiful wetness and began to push. She cried out, her fingers grabbing the comforter and shaping into fists.

"Leto, I want to come as I release my wings."

"I know. Me, too. I'm too damn close."

"Me, too."

But he worked at holding back as he pushed inside her. He loved being in this place with her, connected, on the edge of orgasm, of giving her pleasure as her body pleasured his.

With great effort, he was able to calm his body down just enough so that he could establish a rhythm. She panted now, holding on to the sides of the table.

His wing-locks were a mess, the moisture trailing down his sides in rivulets. He felt what it was like for her to have his cock stroking all the sensitive internal nerves just as his cock grew harder with each thrust.

He grunted now, holding back, holding back.

"Leto," she cried. "Now."

He moved faster and began to feel both her wings come and his, her body clench around his cock, and his balls release firing up and out. It was all so much, her sensation and his. Her wings fanned out below him while his floated in the air around them both. The ecstasy—oh, God, the ecstasy—like a wave shining around him as he continued to plunge and drive.

It didn't end, and he could feel a second release coming. "More," he whispered, kissing her back between her wings.

Yes, she sent, filling his mind.

He plunged into her again, his hands low on her hips as he pulled her toward him. Her wings flapped, and the air moved over him, adding yet another layer of sensation.

This time, however, he focused on what she was feeling as he drove his cock into her. "You like pulling on my cock."

"Yes. And I love what it feels like. So beautiful. We're connected, Leto. You and me."

"Yes." He could feel her breasts rubbing against the stiff cloth of the comforter, another sensation. She had full breasts and every push of his scraped the sensitive nipples and gave her pleasure.

He drove harder now, arching over her. He was tall enough that he could plant his arms above her shoulders so that he made a wave of his back, his hips, his buttocks. With each thrust she gave a cry.

He felt her shift, and her arm appeared next to her head, beside her wing. She turned and presented her wrist to him.

The angle was awkward, but like hell he was going to turn that down. He supported himself with one arm and took her wrist, carefully as he positioned his fangs then bit her. Again, she cried out.

As he began to drink, her blood powered him further so that now he was slamming into her, a hard missile. Her cries turned to heavy grunts and grew louder until her wings moved with every quick thrust. When he could feel her coming again, his body reacted as though she'd taken her fingers and pulled on him at just the right pressure.

He released her wrist, arched his back, and shouted at the ceiling. He came and came and came.

By the time his body settled down, Grace was completely lax on the table. Her wings even drooped toward the floor. She giggled. "Oh, that was perfect" came in a rush of air out of her mouth.

He didn't want to leave her body, but he also wanted to make sure that he didn't accidentally hurt her wings. They were strong yet fragile. Plucking a feather hurt like a bitch.

He slipped out of her, and her knees buckled for a moment. She caught herself and carefully began drawing her wings in. When her back muscles had thinned out, she finally stood upright.

She folded a towel into her hand, and without apologizing or showing any sign of embarrassment, she cleaned up.

He stood smiling at her, like an idiot, his wings still at full-mount and flapping lazily.

He was happy, so goddam happy.

She grinned in response.

He spent the next hour with her in the bathtub, soaping

her up, rinsing her off, kissing her, and making love to her all over again, but this time very slowly. Even then, he ended up sloshing most of the water onto the floor.

When he helped her out of the tub and passed her a towel, he realized she'd grown quiet, almost still. She was thinking hard again.

"What is it?" he asked.

She met his gaze as she dried off. "Just thinking about our last conversation in the kitchen and about becoming more real in your life. I keep thinking how we completed the *breh-hedden* so early in the process. I worry that in not connecting fully we've made ourselves vulnerable, if that makes sense."

He tossed his towel onto the sink, crossed to her, and took her in his arms. "I think about it as well, and I agree with you that we're vulnerable. I feel it, too."

"We've both had it rough," she whispered.

Death vampires had disrupted their lives early on, perhaps forcing each to draw inward, to fail to connect on a deep level with others.

He squeezed her again, and she grabbed his arms and returned the hug. "We'll stick close right now," he whispered, kissing her hair. "And just keep talking to me. I'm here."

The next morning, Greaves paced the long conference room in his Command Center at Estrella Mountain. He'd come to consult with his generals once more, but the level of vampire testosterone bouncing around the room had given him a headache.

For the first time in months, he missed Leto. He hadn't really understood the warrior's value until precisely this moment when his generals were shouting one another down and crying for blood, insisting on launching every weapon within the Estrella Complex right now, at this very moment, to blow the Camelback Parade Grounds all to hell so that the spectacle event would have to be canceled.

He wanted to torch the room, burn them all alive, and start over, maybe create a new life for himself.

He rarely felt like this, as though he needed to question every aspect of his life and, yes, to start over. His mother, Beatrice of Fourth, had invited him to partake of her baptism program and be redeemed through her graded pools in the way Casimir had. If he'd understood the process, he would experience within these baptisms every wrong he had ever committed against another human or ascender, followed by searing remorse.

He smiled at the idea. That would be a lot of remorse, indeed.

He glanced briefly at the men shouting at one another across the table. One of his generals threw a sheaf of papers into the air, another who was much given to profanity let loose with a string of beauties, while a third had been yelling so long and so loud that his face was beet red and his eyes were bulging.

Greaves continued his pacing. The bombast and railing fell into a muffled background noise as he pondered what he should do about the forthcoming obsidian flame spectacle.

His generals wanted him to attack, but would that be wise?

What would Leto have recommended? Patience, then more patience, to be wary of a trap, to be careful with public relations, and to never underestimate Endelle.

But Leto wasn't here and Endelle had chosen this moment in history to make a very public demonstration of her latest preternatural good fortune.

The trouble was, he still didn't know what the triad could do. If he attacked, could obsidian flame respond with equal force?

When the shouting of his generals once more pierced his mind, he simply raised both hands and, using several carefully combined resonances, said, *"Enough."*

Two of his generals passed out. The rest gripped their heads and grunted in pain. Resonance combined with mindspeak had wonderful applications.

At least the bombast had ceased.

"I know you would all prefer to torch the planet, but we

need to be a trifle more restrained than that. I think limiting our destruction to the Camelback Parade Grounds, at the height of the spectacle event, will accomplish all that needs to be accomplished. With luck, we'll destroy the triad, and then we can proceed with greater confidence. After that, we'll begin a systematic destruction of all the hidden colonies on Mortal Earth."

Now that a decision had been made, his staff calmed down.

"The spectacle event is scheduled to begin at eight o'clock this evening, as you know. Please have rocket launchers in place and be ready to fire on my orders. Are we clear?" He didn't wait for an answer. He lifted his right arm and folded back to Geneva.

Julianna dipped down and smelled the roses Owen Stannett had sent her. The fragrance was lovely. Too bad it didn't help her present mood.

She reached for the note again. How many times had she read then reread his tidy little message? How many times had she screamed at the ceiling of Greaves's bedroom?

So Grace was back, beautiful, perfect, little-miss-spiritual Grace of Albion was back. Whoop-dee-fucking-doo.

She stretched her arms overhead, then reached for a long-handled, bamboo back scratcher. The thing about having so much destructive sex with Greaves wasn't the pain, it was the frequent itching as her skin healed.

She closed her eyes and lightly rubbed the narrow tines over the her middle wing-locks. She cooed and sighed.

Greaves had gone crazy with his claw again. And again.

She really did belong with the Commander. And though she had no serious interest in Casimir anymore, her delicate female vanity was wounded. She needed relief from that wound, just as the bamboo tines were giving her relief from her itchy wing-locks.

She wanted justice because Casimir had walked out on her.

No man had ever walked out on her before. Ever.

Well, one had, a century ago, but she'd made him good and dead with her special hand-blast ability, so he no longer counted.

The truth was she didn't really blame Casimir, at least not nearly so much as Grace. She wanted to hurt Caz, of course, but her true desire was to see Grace dead. But how and when to attack?

She had Seer contacts in the highly corrupt Mumbai Seers Fortress. Her first conversation with the High Administrator of the Fortress provided her with the simple information that little could be retrieved about Grace in the future streams because she was being blocked by more powerful Seers that were now attached to Madame Endelle.

Of course perfect Grace would have Endelle's protection.

Realizing that she'd used the back scratcher too vigorously and was now bleeding, she set it down on her nightstand. She fingered the soft petals of the roses and pondered her present conundrum.

"Oh," she murmured, as a new thought struck.

No one would be looking for Casimir in the future streams, and if Greaves was to be believed, he was out and about protecting Leto as his Guardian of Ascension. Grace might be beyond her reach, but maybe, just maybe her Mumbai connection could discover something about Casimir. She kicked herself for not having thought of it sooner.

She made her call to Mumbai. "Forget what I said about keeping after Grace in the future streams. I want you to look for Casimir of Fourth. Apparently, he's on Second right now. And the moment you have word, you're to call me. Do you understand?"

"Yes, Julianna," the deep masculine voice returned. "And you will of course tell your master how obliging I have been."

"Yours will be the first praises I sing when he returns. And I will be sending the usual packet of rubies."

She heard the deeply satisfied sigh before the obligatory farewells. She hung up before he'd finished his assurances of dying fealty to so important an ascender as she.

She decided to dress, then fold to the Sahara, where she could be alone for an hour or so to practice her hand-blast abilities.

As she sweltered in the hot desert, each time she drew her energy into her hands and released the blast, she pictured Grace's brains exploding all over the sand.

The image made her seriously content.

CHAPTER 15

Destiny, I have found, is one of the strangest phenomena in
any dimension, for it consistently works against common
sense and every practical goal man can conceive.

Memoirs, Beatrice of Fourth

CHAPTER 15

Grace slipped on a simple white linen gown, something
she'd made for herself while on Fourth Earth. Leto snored,
a sound that pleased her more than she could say.

She left the room and crossed the narrow hallway to a
second guest bedroom. The sun was rising on the opposite
side of the house, so as she dropped to her knees in front of
the window, the very tops of the White Tank Mountains were
lit in a rosy glow. Militia Warriors still patrolled, a constant,
slow, vigilant movement back and forth.

She saw a fainter movement past the tree line that separated the desert-like mountains from the traditional villa
landscaping.

She extended her vision and saw that the same doe waited
patiently for breakfast. She smiled, lowered her head, and
closed her eyes. By long habit she ran through a litany of
prayers, most of which she had constructed throughout the
centuries. They eased her heart and mind and seemed to
settle something deep within her so that she could move
forward with the day's enormous challenges.

Today she would practice once more with the women,
and at eight o'clock, the spectacle event would take place.

Because she hadn't put any blocks in place, she felt Leto rise from his bed. When he found her, he didn't speak but sank to the carpet behind her, joining her in her meditation.

She continued to pray until her soul felt at ease.

Her last thoughts were a basic giving of thanks for the simple gift of life.

When she opened her eyes and turned, she found Leto still on his knees behind her, one hand shading his face, his shoulders bowed. She saw in an instant the weight that he carried as a powerful ascender, as a warrior, as a trainer of Militia Warriors, as a gifted leader. She had often seen this same demeanor in Thorne.

Leto, she sent, *thank you for joining me.*

He lowered his hand and met her gaze. He pulled her back toward him and cradled her, his head bent over her shoulder as he nuzzled her face. He smelled so beautiful, of the forest.

She shifted in his arms and put her hand on his face. "What is to become of us?"

He kissed her and rocked her. "I will love you, I will work hard for you, and I will do everything I can to bring the stars down for you to hold in your hands. And I will strive to make this world a finer, better place for you."

His vows, he was speaking his vows to her.

She could offer no less.

"And I will love you, Leto. As long as I draw breath, I will love you. I will do everything I can to bring the earth up to possess your heart. I will try to stay alive that we might know each other properly in the coming months and years."

He thumbed her cheek, then kissed her. She felt his desire for her rise. In a soft voice, he asked, "What time do you have to be with the others at the workout center?"

"Eight."

"Then we have some time."

She saw the hopeful look in his eye, but her nerves were on edge. "You wanted me to share, right?"

"Yes, absolutely. Anything."

"I'm afraid, Leto. There, I've said it. I'm afraid of what

will happen tonight. I mean, I know the triad can do the mass folds. I'm not worried about that. But I fear everything else that can go wrong. And what if Greaves decides to attack at the spectacle?"

He kissed her, and she swallowed her fears, or tried to.

He drew back and petted her head, sweeping his hands down her hair, her shoulders, her back. "Every warrior feels this way before a battle. This is normal. I promise you." He smiled and cupped her chin. "Let me ease you, Grace. Let me take care of you. Let me make you less afraid."

The room suddenly smelled of the forest and Leto, and because she wasn't blocking his sensations she could feel his arousal and what it was like to hold all her soft femaleness in his arms.

And because the war loomed so close and no one knew the outcome, she simply rose from the floor, took his hand, and led him back to the bedroom.

Endelle stood on a tall platform before three full-length mirrors in her large bedroom.

She knew how to rock the spectacle, and she wasn't holding back now. She was having her final fitting for the hastily constructed regal costume she intended to wear for the event.

Poor Marcus would throw a bitch-fit, but it couldn't be helped. He had wanted her to rein it in a bit, but this was her passion, what had helped keep her sane, especially in recent months since Thorne had broken his mind-link with her. As the administrator in charge of public relations for her, Marcus had done an amazing job. He'd single-handedly cleaned up her image all around the world and had somehow even gotten rid of those unfortunate Mardi Gras photos in which she had, oops, lost her top.

But beyond the superficial crap, he'd built up her image as primarily a ruler of independent territories, confirming that her most important goal would always be to make certain each Second Earth Territory existed in a state of complete autonomy. Greaves had an opposite vision, and this was something Marcus punched at hard in the worldwide political blogosphere, hammering away at the truth that Greaves was interested in world domination, not freedom for all ascenders.

"If you would please turn, Madame Endelle, an easy step to your right?"

She had discovered that the recently rescued blood slave Kaitlyn, a new mother, was also an excellent seamstress and costume designer. She had a gift with working a variety of materials and never even flinched when Endelle said "possum" or "cuckoo feathers." If anything, her eyes lit up. She was a hands-on kind of gal. In addition, she could work miracles with just about any medium.

She was fashioning a massive coat for Endelle, structured for wings so that it could be worn while in flight. The back had a strong central strap and was very fitted, but for the most part was bare. The bottom of the coat was made up of a number of layers, many of which would extend for several yards behind her while in flight. Those layers were constructed of traditionally lighter fabrics like lace, silk, and even netting.

She already wore her civet cat bustier and the ladybug pendant. She pressed her hands to her hips. The coat was cinched in to showcase her small waist and was composed of sequined black leather, with white sequins in zebra-like lines.

Spread out in other parts of her palace, the long trains were being hemmed by her seamstresses.

In an hour, her hairdressers would arrive.

Endelle had to admit she actually felt excited about the Camelback spectacle event, which brought one hard fact sharply into view: This was one of the first times in recent decades that she'd gone on the offensive.

And it felt fucking great.

The room's audio system came on. "Madame Endelle, Carla here."

"Go ahead, Carla. Kaitlyn is with me."

"Understood. Marguerite wishes to report in."

"She all rested up?" The red variety of obsidian flame

had endured a long night. With Stannett bound to six powerful Seers, he'd been a bitch to guard hour after hour. By Endelle's calculation, Marguerite might have gotten four hours of sleep, but hello, welcome to the shit-for-luck club.

"Send her in."

A second later, Marguerite appeared in the doorway. She hadn't been in Endelle's private bedroom before. "Love your digs," she said. "The round bed is suh-*weet*."

Endelle laughed. Marguerite had a singular quality in that she could make Endelle laugh more than any other ascender she'd ever known.

Marguerite grimaced, then flicked a finger against her belly. "You two stop fighting. I'm with Her Supremeness. Show some respect."

Endelle's brows rose. Marguerite met her gaze but smirked. "Thought I'd start early with the discipline. Don't think it's working. They're both as stubborn as Thorne."

"But not like you." She let the sarcasm roll.

"Oh, of course not." Marguerite fluffed a collar that wasn't there, as though preening.

Endelle felt something deep inside begin to settle. Some part of her had been damn worried about Thorne for God knew how long. *Breh-hedden* or no *breh-hedden*, Marguerite had caught Thorne in a beautiful deep safety net and now he was more of the vampire he always should have been. She might have still been sad that she wasn't so close to him, but she was a thousand times more grateful that Marguerite had found him.

"Okay, Supreme High Seer of Second Earth, why are you here so damn early and how did it go last night?"

"As for my being here at this hour, there's something I need to talk over with you, a concern I have. As for last night, it went like a sonofabitch. Stannett was in rare form. But my teams have some real Seer chops. I worked with them to lock Stanny down without my help, because God knows I need to be free to function with Grace and Fiona tonight, without distractions."

"Have you been able to see Greaves's plans at all?"

She shook her head. "Nope. We're at a stalemate." She frowned.

"So what's bothering you? You said you needed to talk something over with me, but everything seems to be in order."

"I've been unsettled about Greaves. And it's not that I've seen this in the future streams, because I haven't, but I have a gut feeling he intends to attack the spectacle event tonight."

Endelle grew very still. She even stepped off the platform and held Marguerite's gaze for a long moment. "The one thing I trust right now is instinct, especially from obsidian flame. So you think there's a serious risk of attack?"

"I do."

"You know, when Grace first suggested her idea of a spectacle, I really assumed that Greaves wouldn't dare attack. I mean we're filming the damn thing and putting it on the web for the whole world to see. If he attacked, it would turn a good portion of Second Earth against him.

"But I think you may be right because if I were in his shoes, with an opportunity to destroy the one thing standing in my way of taking over Second Earth—dammit, I'd take it."

She called out, "Hey, Carla, would you get Thorne over here?"

Carla's voice sounded through the room. "You bet."

Endelle smiled. "Love this security system. I have a direct line to Central Command at all times. It's voice-activated. All I have to do is say 'Carla' during the day and 'Jeannie' at night, and the women have to respond." Both Carla and Jeannie had worked at Central forever. They were Endelle's link to the Warriors of the Blood day and night.

A few minutes later, Thorne arrived. Endelle would have started in on the issue at hand, but the moment he saw Marguerite, he had to have his arms around her and give her a kiss.

When the embrace lingered Endelle made her usual gagging sounds until the two *breh*-mates knocked it off. She then told Thorne what Marguerite had shared with her and that she agreed. "So what do you think, Thorne? What's your take on this?"

"I think Greaves would be a fool not to try it." He then glanced from Marguerite to Endelle several times and finally addressed his *breh*. "Do you think obsidian flame could fold the review to safety if needed? I mean, it would have to be done with split-second timing."

"Jesus," Marguerite said. "If we're busy folding Greaves's army to new locations, I don't know. I honestly don't know."

Thorne nodded. "Then that's what you're going to practice today."

"Right," Marguerite said, but she'd paled.

He put a hand on her shoulder and held her gaze. "Listen to me. Leto knows where Greaves's artillery is. He'll know when it lights up or if it lights up. I'll get him on it, and we'll arrange a signal, okay? We'll figure this thing out."

By the time Grace arrived at the workout center, Marguerite and Fiona were already there with Thorne. "I've sent for Leto," he said. "We're going to need him."

Her gaze shifted beyond Thorne's shoulder, and she saw that the corner of the room had come alive with all sorts of computer equipment, including several large monitors.

"What's going on?" Her chest grew very tight.

Marguerite explained about her obsidian intuition firing off about Greaves, even though she couldn't find anything in the future streams about him or a possible attack at the spectacle event.

Grace. Leto's voice was suddenly in her head, and a second later she could feel him. She turned, and as he had done the day before, he strode across the mats looking like a god. Her heart seemed to flip in her chest, and without thinking she ran to him. He caught her up in his arms and held her tight, her feet dangling off the floor.

What's wrong? he sent.

Marguerite thinks Greaves will attack at the spectacle review.

When he remained silent, she pulled back and he lowered

her to the floor. She asked, "I mean, do you honestly think that Greaves would attack even though it would ruin him in the eyes of the world?"

"I know his mind. I know that right now he must feel that all his ambitions, his centuries of planning, are threatened by the triad. If Marguerite has that instinct vibrating through her obsidian power, I can only say that I think it's not just possible, but likely."

Grace lowered her gaze to the mats. "This is what I feared," she said, "that by coming back, I'd be getting this close to weapons and bombs. I don't know if I can do this. I thought it would just be a spectacle parade."

He drew her against him and held her tight, but he didn't say anything.

Grace took one breath after another. She knew it was too late to change things, and part of her didn't want to. But she'd seen the war destroy Thorne for centuries. The same war ripped her sister, Patience, out of the air, taking her who the hell knew where.

Now she was part of a power-based triad, and because she'd been so very clever, she'd placed herself at the center of what could be a bombing.

Leto's voice was once more in her head. *You can go back. You have a right to the life of your choosing. Don't let any-one tell you differently.*

Leto, you always say what I need to hear. And yet . . .

It's not simple.

You're right, our decisions are never simple.

She'd had the life of her choosing for many centuries, and during all that time she'd never really found a place to put down roots. She had searched the ends of the earth, even Mortal Earth, looking for some sort of spiritual enlighten-ment, but nothing lasted, nothing satisfied.

In the end, she'd chosen to come back to Leto and to stop avoiding the war. She thought of all that was at stake. She remembered Leto's speech at the warrior games about how everyone had a part in the war, because it wasn't just about swords and guns and bombs. It was about building a better future going forward and that all ascenders had a role to play.

She didn't like the role she'd been given to play. But what did that matter?

She chuckled softly and drew back. "I don't know what I expected when I returned, or what I thought would happen when I said we should use a spectacle event as a ruse to move an army. I think I was naive." She smiled ruefully. "I'll be okay. I just keep needing to get used to this new reality."

She turned to walk back in Thorne's direction. Leto joined her with his arm around her waist.

Both Fiona and Marguerite comforted her, which of course caused their shared power to flare. However, in this case, it helped. "I kind of lost my nerve. But now that I feel all that massive obsidian vibration, I'm okay. We can do this, can't we?"

"Of course we can," Marguerite said. "Or as Endelle would say, 'Shit yes, of course we fucking can.'"

Grace started to laugh, and her obsidian sisters joined her.

Leto drew close, kissed her on the cheek, and said that Thorne had moved computer equipment to the workout room so that he'd be nearby if the triad needed him. "I'm locating Greaves's artillery. I have one of Marcus's computer geeks, which is code for 'hacker,' to help me break into some of the Commander's files."

Knowing that Leto was working on the bombing issue also gave her some comfort. But it was her brother who helped the most when he said, "We're going to practice the rest of the day, here and out at the parade grounds as well, until all of you feel comfortable. The first thing we need to do is to find out if the triad can gather its power while in flight and without making physical contact. I feel confident it can be done, but we want to be sure.

"Also, we need to find out what happens when obsidian flame folds someone while in flight, which would include the swan and geese handlers, Endelle, and any of Marcus's in-flight video operators. Though I have a feeling that the triad's power will protect everyone, we need to know what we're dealing with.

"Finally, I want to do an emergency run while in flight, to simulate Greaves's firing his artillery. I want to be assured that I get a signal from the computer operator, and that I can alert the triad that an emergency mass fold is necessary for the parade grounds, then have Grace perform one very fast. How does that sound?"

Somehow having her brother break the challenges facing obsidian flame into specific skill sets and practice drills helped Grace a lot. She could even take a deep breath without feeling like she was being strangled. She realized that she was working with warriors who knew a lot about the value of regular workouts and drills on every level.

The first thing the triad did was to separate and focus on the obsidian flame power, causing the vibrations to rise without making physical contact. After a few false starts, a simple form of telepathy, from Grace to Marguerite then to Fiona, set the necessary sequence. Marguerite even suggested they use the word *scorpion* to focus on in order to prompt the experience. After an hour of practice, *scorpion* brought the power flowing within seconds each time the word passed from woman to woman.

Once the power could be brought without physical contact, Thorne moved everyone outside to continue the in-flight practice. Leto even suggested that he be the guinea pig for the first folding experiment. He and Thorne argued, but in the end Leto prevailed when he said, "The hell if I'm allowing any of the Militia Warriors to be hurt because of this. And you know I'm strong as hell and powerful, which means that if anything goes wrong, I'll heal fast. Get Horace over here if it will make you feel any better."

Grace watched him stare Thorne down. Marguerite hooked her arm through Grace's. "We have two tough hombres, don't we? Sweet Christ, is it bad of me to want to see them get into a fight? Thorne's closing his fist. Look at his arms. Those muscles."

Grace could not have cared less about her brother's arms,

but Leto's shoulders were hunched and bulked up. Her mouth watered. She blinked several times.

Giving herself a shake, she approached the men and grabbed each by the wrist. "Hey, knock it off. The last thing we need is the two of you locking horns."

The men backed down, which meant each took a few steps away from the other. She met Thorne's gaze. "I happen to agree with Leto. And just in case, Horace should be here."

"Fine," Thorne said. He whipped his Droid Ascender from his slacks and started hitting the screen. A moment later, he said, "Hey, Carla, we need Horace at my position at Apache Junction Two, and, no, no one is hurt, and, yes, I do know he's probably asleep, but get him to me anyway as quick as you can, at this position. I'll let security here know."

He tapped again and spoke to security. "Horace is coming to my position."

Grace wasn't surprised when about two minutes later, Horace materialized next to Thorne. He squinted against the bright sunshine.

"Sorry to disturb," Thorne said.

But Horace bowed slightly. "No problem, *duhuro*."

Thorne opened his mouth as though to say something then simply shrugged, smiled, and clapped the tall, thin healer on the shoulder. "Thanks for coming." He then explained what they were doing.

Horace's eyes grew wide. "I'm ready if you need me, but I really hope you don't." A fold could trash a pair of wings, even the strongest wings.

Leto removed his shirt, which caused Grace to put a hand to her chest and to weave on her feet. She didn't think she'd ever get over what the man looked like.

He met her gaze but shook his head. He looked so serious, just as he should given the circumstances. And she knew she wasn't helping because she knew that he could feel all the desire she was presently experiencing. The next moment, she felt his mental shields slam into place.

At the same time, she started setting up her own blocks like mad because all she could think about was what it had been like the night before with Leto at the villa, his body slamming into her from behind and both sets of wings mounted.

As he turned away from her, however, she was lost all over again as his wings unfurled. They arrived in a blue flurry of movement and suddenly all four panels of his unusual, exquisite wings were just there. He drew them in to close-mount and shot into the air.

Thirty feet up, he unfurled and flew above them, turning in a slow arc and flying over them once more.

She put her hand to her chest. In flight, he was, as Endelle might have said, fucking magnificent. He began to plow through the air, even making another full loop that must have been a hundred yards in diameter. She didn't move as she watched him, and she sure as hell couldn't have looked away. She wanted to be up there with him.

A hand gripped her arm. "Hey." Thorne's voice broke through, and she turned to him startled.

"What?" she asked.

His stern expression softened. "Didn't you hear me calling to you?"

She shook her head and pointed into the sky. Thorne's gaze followed. "He's your *breh*."

Grace turned once more to watch Leto make another pass. His *cadroen* had come loose, and his long black hair flowed behind him. "Yes," she said. "He's my man."

She heard Thorne chuckle, though she wasn't sure what he found amusing. "Shall we see what happens when the triad folds him out of the sky?"

Oh, that. "Yes, of course."

She turned to Grace and Marguerite. The latter sent the word *scorpion* into Grace's mind, the telepathic link formed, and the obsidian power flowed.

Thorne's thoughts were suddenly present as well. *Leto's ready. Fold at will. Bring him next to Horace.*

Grace went into split-self mode, took possession of Fiona, then focused on Leto, now a hundred yards above the triad. She thought the thought.

She could feel the fold happen. The next moment she separated from Fiona, returning to herself. She wasn't surprised when Leto appeared beside Horace, smiling, his hair wild, his blue eyes shining with pleasure and triumph, and his full-mount wings completely intact.

He met her gaze. "The fold felt like being wrapped in cotton and just set on my feet on the ground. Beautiful."

Grace went to him, unable to contain all that she felt. She slid her arms carefully around his waist, and like a dream, his wings enfolded her. What a miracle all of this was, being here with Leto and her brother and with obsidian flame, feeling Leto's arms around her. She felt overwhelmed and blessed.

She remained like that for a long time, just savoring him, savoring life, savoring the love she felt for him, the soft movement of his feathers over her skin. He was safe and uninjured, and he was hers.

Of course, the practice had to continue, but she thanked Thorne for letting her have that moment with Leto.

The rest of the morning involved practice and more practice, folding individual Militia Warriors in flight, then groups of them just to make sure that if the triad had to fold the spectacle handlers out of the air, it could be done safely.

After that, Grace took to the air and worked with Marguerite and Fiona doing the same thing all over again, but bringing their obsidian power online while in flight, then folding more Militia Warriors also while in flight.

The success of the venture was mind boggling.

With the most critical issues settled, the final trial run had been set up. The entire obsidian flame triad, including their *brehs,* was now in flight, and Grace would perform her final feat before tackling the spectacle review at eight.

It was now three o'clock in the afternoon, and Grace flew beside Marguerite and Fiona. Leto, Jean-Pierre, and Thorne flew behind each of them, for protection and for support. Thorne was taking no chances with this part of the practice.

Grace felt very connected to her obsidian sisters.

Leto's voice penetrated her mind. *You can't believe what*

your combined wings look like. The flames of all three are exquisite. The colors are bold. You'll get to see when we land because there's a video-bot flying above us.

For herself, Grace had forgotten the joys of flight. She didn't fly often enough. It was important to mount the wings at least once every two weeks to keep them fit and healthy. Ten days was even better. But flying was a different experience altogether, one of the real benefits of ascended life. She could see the various regiments below her, some receiving instruction over loudspeakers, some practicing marching. All wore flight battle gear, which gave a formidable unified appearance—and of course the black leather kilts were a great look.

She flapped her wings steadily, moving forward in an easterly direction along the parade route. Endelle's beautiful graded administrative building, with terraces of hanging plants, was off to the south, Camelback Mountain to the north. A thousand tanks anchored the route, and stands were lined up in set intervals. The spectators, however, had been strictly limited to Militia Warriors in casual dress, no civilians allowed.

All along the route, the video cameras were in place, with their operators, everyone testing and retesting their equipment. She was amazed at all that Marcus, Havily, and their teams had created within a brief twenty-four hours. Large stands of stadium lights were already part of what was a traditional parade grounds.

Landing platforms had been set up at both the east and west ends of the route. It was strange to watch hundreds of warriors arrive then literally run off the platforms so that the next squadrons could fold in right behind them.

Leto, she sent telepathically, avoiding the com.

I'm here.

The organization is phenomenal. Have the hidden colonies sent their regiments?

No, they've remained within the colonies to protect the citizens. We're still acting as if Greaves intends to attack at any given moment.

Thorne's voice came over the com. "Grace, do you see the warriors at attention?"

Grace glanced down and to her left. There they were, in massive blocks of five hundred each, ten blocks total. "I see them."

"That's your mass-fold target. We've gathered ten thousand for practice."

"Copy." It was so strange to use such formal com-speak.

Marguerite's voice broke over the com. "Banking left."

Grace could feel the other two women turn just as she turned, their movements functioning as a solid group. They were a triad now. Maybe there were a lot of bumps yet to overcome, but for now they were obsidian flame.

Traveling up Scottsdale Boulevard Two, Marguerite happened to pull forward from her center position. Right afterward, Thorne recommended they keep the stronger, arrow-like formation because it would allow for greater visibility from the wing position.

He was right. Grace could see Fiona straight across from her now and could even catch her eye. Fiona nodded and smiled. The woman looked euphoric, but then she had only been flying for a few months. Nothing was more exhilarating. She flew like a pro, using her arms constantly to help make slight wing adjustments with every current of air that whipped over her or hit her broadside.

Two more miles and Marguerite spoke into the com, "Bank right. Folding endpoint site in one mile."

Now heading east, Grace saw the massive area cordoned off with more rows of tanks. The tanks were Thorne's idea to help substantiate the rumors Marcus had sent around on the web that Endelle had a bigger army than anyone knew about.

Grace's heart began to hammer in her ears. Thorne came on the com. "Is 'the flame' ready?"

"Ready," Grace responded. *The flame* was Thorne's idea for abbreviated radio-speak.

Both Marguerite and Fiona called out, "Ready."

"Execute at will," Thorne ordered.

Still in flight, Grace didn't hesitate. She took possession

of Fiona, and as the shared obsidian flame power vibrated heavily through her, she focused on the mass of troops back at the parade grounds.

Grace pictured the formation square containing ten thousand warriors, and she simply thought the thought.

She felt a tremendous vibration through the air as well as movement, very swift. The next moment, the entire force appeared below the triad, next to the tanks.

She glanced at Thorne. He smiled at her and winked. Yep, ten thousand Militia Warriors, all in perfect formation, were shouting, punching the air with strong fists, and whooping it up.

Grace's smile was so broad her cheeks hurt.

The breh-hedden *never arrives at the opportune moment. But then in life, there rarely is such a thing as an opportune moment.*

—Collected Proverbs, Beatrice of Fourth

CHAPTER 16

Stannett sat up and vomited into the bowl the female Militia Warrior had provided him. His eyes rolled in his head. He'd been working most of the day, and he didn't know how much longer he could sustain the blocking maneuvers. The hour had to be nearing six in the evening, and the spectacle event was set for eight. As for discovering what Endelle was up to, or her now famous obsidian flame triad, he couldn't even get close in the future streams.

Greaves stood on the deck opposite Stannett's chaise longue, arms crossed over his chest. "Anything new?"

He shook his head. He felt weak, sick, discouraged. Coming to the Illinois Two Seers Fortress, and heading up Greaves's entire system, was supposed to have been a pinnacle in his life, something to be enjoyed and celebrated. Now he was a quivering mass of nausea, with a raging headache, and he felt weaker than shit.

"No change," he said. "I can't reach the spectacle event. Marguerite has it blocked off."

"How can she perform both functions?" Greaves asked.

Stannett shrugged. His cheeks cramped. He'd be losing it

again soon. "My guess is that she's been training Seers to work in teams."

"My on-the-ground surveillance near the Camelback Parade Grounds says that they've done a couple of mass folds. What do you make of that?"

What did he make of that? Why the hell was Greaves asking him questions better suited for his generals? "I don't know." He brought the bowl close, took several deep breaths, and threw up again.

"You shouldn't have indulged, Stannett. Now, when I need you the most, you're at your weakest."

With his chin low, he looked up at Greaves. "I truly regret my indiscretion." Of course, right now he would have said anything to appease Greaves.

"I'm glad to hear you say so. But what I need—besides the blocks against Endelle's Seers—is any information about when to attack the spectacle parade. Do you understand?" Greaves levitated, then slowly descended into the pit until he stood at the foot of Stannett's chaise longue. Greaves waved the bucket away.

The female Militia Warrior stepped back, saying, "I'll be back shortly with fresh Seers." Greaves nodded. She vanished.

Stannett took deep breaths. It didn't help his nausea problem that Greaves smelled of lemon furniture polish.

Greaves glanced left and right. "There is blood on the leather."

"The women tend to bleed from various apertures, including their wing-locks, when the process overwhelms them."

"I see." He glanced back at Stannett. "So, how are you keeping our plans blocked in the future streams right now if the women keep dying on you?"

Stannett smirked. "I have power. It sometimes doesn't show as much as perhaps it should, but I'm holding it steady. The effort has given me a monstrous headache, which is why I'm puking."

Greaves's smile softened. "Let me help with that." He rounded the side of the chaise and put a hand on Stannett's forehead. The pain drifted away like fog beneath the sun.

He looked up at Greaves and released a deep breath. "Thank you, master."

"Keep blocking our side of things, and if you can find an inroad to secure the intentions and timing of the opposition, let me know."

"Yes, master."

Greaves lifted his hand and was gone.

Stannett released a deep breath. He had grown sick of this endless pressure to produce and perform. Greaves didn't understand his need for autonomy. Yes, he'd lacked control, but he was doing better now and he didn't like being hemmed in.

The Militia Warrior returned and changed out the Seers, whipping them on the legs when they uttered even the smallest sound. She struck one Seer across the face with her whip when she dared to ask where she was. The welt would last a long time.

Stannett followed his jailer's movements. Certain ideas had taken root in his mind of a profound sense of ill usage. Once the female Seers were strapped in, Stannett put them in the usual stupor. Afterward, he rose from his chaise longue. Time to make a change of his own.

"Is there a problem, Seer?" the woman barked. She wasn't a woman, not really. Very flat-chested, proud of her muscles. She probably wished she were a man.

"No problem," he said. He levitated to the viewing platform just a few feet from her. He kept advancing toward her.

She narrowed her gaze. "What the fuck do you think you're doing? Get back down into the pit and get back to work. Or did you not hear the master, not understand his critical need for your services right now?"

"I heard him and I understood him." Stannett hadn't planned out exactly what he intended to do.

He lifted his hand and sent a blast soaring through the air straight for the woman. She didn't really have time to react.

She flew backward and hit the wall with a loud thudding sound. She fell to the floor.

Stannett's brows rose. Her entire chest was caved in and smoking. He'd killed her.

He wanted to feel bad, he really did, but his appetites had reasserted themselves. He left her where she was and returned to the pit and to his chaise longue.

He stretched back out. He looked inward and physically ascertained what he already knew, that the blocks held. Now to get the relief he needed.

He slipped into the future streams, joined his power with the six women, and let the pleasure flow. The first orgasm hit him before fifteen seconds had passed.

"I want a shower," Grace whispered, sitting on the black mats at the Militia Warrior workout center once more. "Dear God, I long for a shower."

Leto smiled. He sat behind her and rubbed her shoulders. It was almost five thirty—not even three hours till the spectacle. He had spent the day securing the location of Greaves's artillery through his computer and put Gideon in charge of making sure Thorne was alerted when any of the sites lit up.

All during that time, he had taken numerous breaks to watch obsidian flame work as a team. He saw Thorne's role clearly, the same one he performed as the leader of the Allied Ascender Forces, Endelle's army. He kept everything headed in the right direction. Thorne held things together, or—as he liked to say—he was the anchor to obsidian flame.

With such a massive undertaking, the triad critically needed an anchor, someone with a com who could make split-second decisions, someone who had preternatural power of his own to do whatever needed to be done.

It was the one thing that gave Leto some peace in what had become his own battle of worn-out nerves as the afternoon advanced. However, right now they all needed some downtime.

Thorne finally released the triad and made it possible for

all three couples to return to their homes. He also let security know so that the folding could be done straight from the workout room.

Leto rose to his feet with Grace, took her hand, and folded her back to the villa bedroom. He laughed, because before he could say a word he heard the water running. She'd flipped the levers using a little kinetic manipulation. "Yeah, I guess you do want your shower."

Grace laughed. "You should probably know this about me." She gave him a quick kiss, then headed into what was now a roll of steam coming from the bathroom.

Of course as soon as he thought of her in the shower, naked, certain ideas flooded his mind.

He followed after her but frowned when he felt her no longer standing but sitting on the floor. Yeah, the sharing of external sensations always provided a lot of data to process.

He found her seated in front of the toilet, her arms around her knees.

He looked around and drew his sword, but they were alone. No death vamps this time.

"What's the matter?"

She looked up at him and blinked a couple of times. "What if I can't do this?"

Oh, that was all. Just a little pre-battle jitters. Of course, Grace wasn't a warrior. She wouldn't know just how normal this was.

"The whole time I was practicing," she said, "I was fine. Really fine. Now all I can think is, *Two hundred thousand at a time*. And what if Stannett breaks through in the future streams and discovers our exact plan? What if Marguerite's teams can't sustain the blocks she's put in place?"

Leto sat on the floor next to her and put his arm around her. This was where millennia of service as a warrior could be of use. "You're not doing this alone, Grace, not by a long shot." He rubbed her shoulder gently.

"It feels like it's all on me."

"Do you think Thorne feels any differently right now? Or Endelle? How about Fiona or Marguerite?"

She turned to look at him. After searching his eyes for a long moment, she let out a deep breath. "I see what you mean."

"What you're experiencing is perfectly normal."

"Really?"

"Of course."

"Are you worried?" she asked.

The question surprised him, not because she asked but because he had to dig around for the answer. "I'm not sure. Maybe after so many centuries I'm immune. But I also know that it's a waste of energy to fret like this before a battle. You'll need every ounce of your strength while in flight."

She pressed his arm with her hand. "I still couldn't believe we were able to fold all those Militia Warriors while flying. How did it look from your view?"

"I have to admit, I wasn't looking at the troops on the ground. My view was so exquisite that my gaze was fixed right here." He drifted his hand down her back to cup her buttocks.

Grace laughed. "I don't believe you for a second but . . . um . . . how much time do we have before we're needed back at the parade grounds?"

"Marcus wants us at the palace by seven fifteen."

He leaned close, nuzzled his way toward her neck, then sucked above her vein. *That means we have at least an hour and a half. We can accomplish a lot in that amount of time,* he sent. *A lot.*

He felt her shiver and her body start to unwind. Even so, she pushed him away and rose to her feet. "I still want my shower. I am so not doing anything without getting clean first. And I do mean *anything.*"

His eyes fell to half-mast. A shower didn't have to take long, especially if he helped. And the thought of her really clean in various places forced him to get rid of his clothes and join her.

By seven fifteen Leto stood with the rest of obsidian flame in the central rotunda, waiting for Endelle before folding to the parade grounds. He was jumpy, but then they all were. On the other hand, this was a solid team, all the coordinates had been laid in for the mass fold of Greaves's army, and obsidian flame had proven they could get the job done.

The only real unknown was whether or not Greaves would actually bomb the spectacle parade. But Leto had his own team, led by Gideon, watching the monitors, which now had a heat-sensing fix on the location of all the local artillery. The moment anything went hot, Gideon would know and in turn would relay the information to Thorne's com.

Perhaps for all those reasons, even Casimir had arrived to wait with the obsidian flame team. Though a couple of times Grace had drawn near and chatted with him, Casimir was very respectful. Leto admitted it helped that he looked so different with his bald head and his long white linen robe. He looked more of a monk than a seducer of women.

Could Leto forgive him?

Did it even matter?

Thorne nudged him and spoke in a low voice. "Not sure I could tolerate having him around."

Leto chuckled softly. "It's kind of hard to complain when he's fought off Third Earth death vampires twice on my behalf."

"See your point. Still."

"Yeah . . . still." He sighed.

"Any clue yet about this ascension of yours?"

"Nope. And I'm not feelin' it, so I don't know what to tell you. Of course, all I really care about is being with your sister. So it wouldn't matter to me whether that was here on Second or on Third . . . I just need to be with her."

"Well, it's not the usual process for an ascension, that's for sure. I mean, have you been having dreams at all?" The hallmarks of an ascension always included dreams of the new world and often inexplicable longings as well.

"Nothing. No longings to be on Third, no dreams of ascending. Nothing. Just Casimir showing up saying he was my Guardian of Ascension."

"Well, like everything else, I'm sure it will sort itself out." He shifted slightly, then murmured, "Oh, my God."

Leto turned, as did the entire group.

Endelle had arrived.

Her hair rose to an enormous height and width, teased to a full madness, but drawn in at the center with a crown that bore about a hundred sparkling gems. Probably not real, but holy shit.

Her bustier was the same spotted fur he'd seen the day before. The rest of her costume was layer upon layer of fabric with a panel of peacock feathers serving as a kind of apron. Two smaller women, each in simple black flight gear, carried the train.

"I'd twirl for all you gape-mouthed idiots, but we haven't got time." She turned to Thorne. "We ready?"

He nodded, then finally closed his mouth. "Uh, yes."

She glanced at the triad, all in simple black leather flight suits and black flats. "You ladies ready?"

"Yes, ma'am." All three obsidian flame responded as one.

"Then come stand by me. Bring your men with you, then let's do this thing."

Timing is everything.

Some truths are so universal as to be dull. But Grace had never known this truth to be quite so relevant as it was now. The entire success of the mission depended on getting the timing exactly right.

She had a death grip on Leto's hand, but he stood fast. He seemed oddly relaxed, maybe because he knew she was so wound up.

A Sousa march blared from the loudspeakers, a lively sound and appropriate for the spectacle. But the music seemed to keep her nerves on fire, and every sixteen bars she would jump.

Fiona leaned back against Jean-Pierre's chest. He had his arms wrapped around her, as usual. Grace didn't think being held so tight right now would help her at all.

So Leto allowed her to keep squeezing his hand.

At the same time, she kept glancing up at Thorne on her right. His jaw worked. He touch his headset frequently and continued talking quietly, this time to Gideon, making sure that the artillery-locating files were up and humming at the workout center where Leto had set them up.

They all wore headsets hooked over one ear, which made communication easier. Thorne had a companion piece on his shoulder that allowed him to change frequencies. He had reports coming in steadily from Marcus, who had command of the entire communications system. He was also connected to Colonel Seriffe, who was in charge of security and the two hundred thousand Militia Warriors here at the parade grounds.

Where the defecting army was concerned, as soon as obsidian flame was airborne and moving down the parade route, Leto would give the order to begin the secret mass folds of Greaves's army. Brynna waited in North Africa to confirm the success of the first two folds. The second two were destined for Apache Junction Two.

If all went according to plan, the first fold would take place in ten minutes.

Once more, she squeezed Leto's hand hard.

Because he couldn't reach Stannett, Greaves was flying blind, a state he despised more than anything else on this advanced ascended earth. He had lost contact with the Militia Warrior he'd put in charge of Stannett, and he was unwilling to leave his Estrella Complex to see what was going on. He had hoped to get that slight edge he would need to be victorious tonight.

He was almost dizzy with the potential of what could be accomplished in one bombing raid. He would destroy not just obsidian flame, but also Thorne—who led Endelle's army—and Endelle herself. He felt almost giddy with the sheer potential so close at hand. If he could do this, all he would have to do is march his army over to Endelle's palace and take over.

He paced his war room, trying to still the excitement that coursed through him. He had excellent visuals of the Camelback Parade Grounds, of tens of thousands of Endelle's Militia Warriors in full black-leather flight gear, of rows upon rows of tanks, of the usual spectacle nonsense ready to take to the skies, and even a close-up of Endelle looking like she belonged in a circus.

He had but to say the word, one general would hit the GO button, and the parade ground as well as Endelle's nearby administrative HQ would be dust.

But the one thing he'd relied on to guide him had failed. Stannett was offline, and Greaves had a really sick feeling that he'd killed the Militia Warrior.

Even if that were true, it was too late to do anything about it now.

Whatever happened from this moment forward was all up to Greaves and his limited information. He was tempted to just let the artillery take out the parade grounds now; some part of him knew that was exactly what he should do.

But the cautious part of him as well as the strategist held back. If he wiped out obsidian flame in the middle of the spectacle, the world would understand his intentions and would submit more readily. After he decimated the area, he'd finish off the colonies, eliminating all points of threat in the space of a very short evening.

The fireworks boomed and lit up the sky.

Showtime.

Grace drew in a deep breath, then glanced once more at her brother. He had really changed over the past several months. He was a new man in every sense. She hardly recognized him now, and not just because his eyes were no longer red-rimmed, but because his stature had altered. He stood with his shoulders well back, his head high. He had always been a leader of men, but now he seemed to be more. There were even rumors that he would one day become the Supreme High Administrator of Second Earth, replacing Endelle.

Not tonight, though.

She heard Leto draw in a quick breath. She glanced at him, then saw that he was looking at the monitor. Endelle was airborne, her massive train flowing behind her. Grace smiled. Whatever else the woman was, with fireworks blasting in the background, with the music blaring, she gave good spectacle. She was fit for her world and for her times.

She waved at all the spectators as her gown trailed behind her, a comet speeding by, on enormous wings, a great, glorious, irreplaceable, profane, feathered comet.

Another monitor showed the parade grounds. The troops were already on the move, marching in strict formation, making strong turns en masse, with the occasional unified shout. All the warriors knew the order of events, and it said a lot about Thorne and Seriffe's training of the Second Earth Militia Warriors that all the men and women proceeded down the parade route as they did. Everyone understood the real possibility that Greaves would attack and that only the perfect timing and power of obsidian flame would be able to remove everyone from harm's way before complete annihilation.

There were five huge grandstands, but all were full of Militia Warriors in street clothes. No civilians had been allowed to be present in case things went wrong.

Grace pressed a hand to her stomach.

The swans and geese and their handlers flew in from the northwest. Grace could see them in the air, but the cameras gave a much better visual so she ended up watching the monitors. This would be one fine webcast once the event was edited.

If all went well.

Oh, God. If all went well.

To Leto, she sent, *I know you've told me, but is your army ready to fold?*

He looked down at her and smiled. *Hells, yeah,* he sent.

Thorne called out. "Obsidian flame, mount up."

Grace felt her stomach take a spin. This was it. Leto stepped away from her, and despite the ferocity of her nerves, and because of the practice of two millennia, she let her wings fly.

Much to her surprise, suddenly she could breathe. Something about the simple act of mounting her wings had steadied her. She even chuckled.

She glanced at Fiona, who in turn winked at her.

Marguerite also turned back and smiled first at Fiona, then at Grace. She stood two feet in front of them, in the position they intended to sustain while in the air.

Grace nodded and smiled, even though her heart raced.

Yep, showtime.

She looked once more at the image of Endelle on the monitors. She was clearly glorying in her trip down the parade route. Maybe it was for that reason—that Endelle could enjoy a moment so fraught with danger—that Grace finally let go of her nerves and began to focus on her obsidian power.

With a whisper of a thought, she could feel the rumble beneath her feet, feel the earth-based power ready to flow through her and enable her to do things no vampire should ever be able to do. She flexed her wings, just feeling them.

She glanced at Thorne. He turned toward her and offered a curious frown. *You okay?* he sent.

She nodded. "I'm good."

He smiled, then returned his attention forward. He touched his headset almost continuously now, shifting from one entity to the next, speaking softly the whole time. He was fully in command.

With that, he gave the order to take to the dark night skies.

Grace reached out in her obsidian way, touched her obsidian sisters, felt the answering response, and as one they launched.

Grace's wings plowed air. The fireworks still boomed, lighting up the sky in an array of colors and patterns. Every once in a while, she'd watch a dragon-shaped series of lights pass by her peripheral vision. Motion was good. The music wasn't as loud now that she flew above the amplifiers and the marching warriors. The DNA-altered swans and geese flew in front of their group and behind. She could occasionally hear the handlers calling to them.

Spectacle.

One of the best parts of ascended life.

If Endelle was right, if Grace had been right in suggesting this scheme in the first place, then another kind of spectacle was about to hit the air.

Her com lit up and Thorne's gravel voice said quietly, "You may fold the first section at will." Which was code for the first part of Greaves's army.

Grace let the coordinates move through her mind, and she held her mass-folding ability in the forefront. She apparitioned, took possession of Fiona, and without hesitating let the fold begin. She felt the mass movement of a quarter of a million Militia Warriors, from Mongolia to North Africa, as obsidian flame folded them. She felt dizzy with excitement.

Leto came on the com, something she could perceive even in her split-self. "Brynna confirms."

She wanted to give a shout, but Thorne came on softly and said, "Prepare for the second fold. Grace, when ready proceed."

She focused on the second group, from the Australian Outback. She felt the power flowing in an almost constant loop from Marguerite, to Fiona, then herself, even split as she was. She concentrated on the coordinates, and once more she let the fold just happen. It was an amazing sensation, and all this was happening as the fireworks continued to boom, the warriors below marched, and all the swans and geese kept the focus on spectacle and not on a war-changing secret folding operation.

"Brynna confirms the second group arrived," Leto said. "She's folding to the Superstitions so that she can confirm the third fold." A moment later. "She has arrived at the Superstitions. She's ready to receive the third fold."

Thorne's voice once more spoke softly. "Grace, fold your third group when ready."

* * *

Greaves heard Thorne's voice over the com. He stared at the parade ground but couldn't see any special movement of troops. They all moved in formation and had remained constant in number the entire distance, so what could Thorne have meant by "fold your third group"?

He had heard both Thorne and Leto talk about obsidian flame folding something somewhere, but if they were doing so right now, it wasn't on the parade grounds.

He glanced at the monitors and spoke to his staff. "Do any of you see movement, like some kind of mass movement of the troops?"

When he received a general negation, he peered once more at the monitors. What he was seeing looked like plain old spectacle to him.

An aide approached. He would have brushed him off, but he held a piece of paper, was sweating like a pig, and had a wild look in his eyes. Greaves got a really bad feeling. "What?" he barked.

The aide shoved the paper at him. "Your . . . your Mongolian army is gone."

Greaves blinked. He looked at the paper. Glanced at the aide. Shifted to stare at his generals, who wore blank looks. He didn't bother asking what the aide meant.

To his staff, he asked, "Has Thorne made another fold request?"

The aide that kept the monitors alive with ongoing footage, said, "Warrior Thorne just spoke of a fourth fold to his sister, Grace."

When Greaves saw another aide flying at him from down the hall, Greaves knew.

Leto. Fucking Leto.

His army.

The fold wasn't on the parade route. The spectacle was one big fucking distraction.

"Launch the artillery now."

Approach the gates of rapture with wonder,
Lay down the past,
Then fall.

—*Collected Poems*, Beatrice of Fourth

CHAPTER 17

Grace had just heard Brynna confirm the fourth and final fold when Thorne's voice intruded again, this time with an edge. "Obsidian flame, get us the hell out of here."

Grace's heart rose in her throat. This was it. She was still in possession of Fiona and she needed to do the mass fold of the parade route, but she couldn't calm down. Then Leto's words filled her mind: *Ease down, Warrior, and focus on the coordinates. You can do this.*

Grace took a deep breath and turned her attention to the spectacle performers in the air, to the slow flap of Fiona's wings, to the troops on the ground and in the stands. She took another deep breath and simply let the fold begin.

She began the slide through nether-space just as the first bomb exploded.

Her mind swirled around and around. Her head hurt. Then her mind went blank.

After a long moment, she opened her eyes and blinked. She was on her feet, and Leto was holding her upright. Her wings flapped slowly. In the distance, she could hear bombs exploding.

She gave her head a shake. Leto was in front of her, his hands on her waist as he looked into her eyes. She could tell he was worried. "Are you all right?" he asked.

"Did we make it? Was I too late? Is everyone safe?"

"Obsidian flame got everyone out, to the last swan. You've been dazed for about five minutes, which is why you feel disoriented right now."

"Dazed?"

"Yes. I think it happened because you folded while in your split-self configuration and within half a second a shell exploded as we were all mid-fold."

"That was close." She looked around, but all she saw was the row of tanks. She was alone with Leto in the desert. "And are you sure all our troops got away?"

"Yes. As soon as the fold took place, and because of all the training that Seriffe has demanded of his Militia Warriors for years, all two hundred thousand of the parade troops, as well as the warriors that held civilian places in the grandstands, started folding to prearranged barracks around the world. The spectacle performers, the birds, and their handlers are in Apache Junction Two."

"And Greaves's army—or rather *your* army?"

"Brynna confirmed. We have one million warriors on our side."

She rubbed her forehead, but she smiled and her heart expanded. "That's fantastic. Now, tell me what the parade grounds look like?"

"Like a battlefield."

"Did Greaves show up with his troops and tanks?"

"No. It looks like he meant only to blow the site all to hell with his artillery. Fortunately, Marcus got it all on film. No doubt he'll have this flying around the Web right away, along with obsidian flame's mass fold."

"And everyone's really safe?"

He nodded slowly. "Everyone's safe."

"We did it," she said softly.

"Yes, we did. Now retract your wings so I can get you back to the palace."

She looked around, then called out, "Casimir, show yourself. I can feel that you're here."

Casimir became visible and he was smiling. "That was a beautiful show you just put on. I'm proud of you, Grace."

"Thank you."

Casimir glanced at Leto and waited.

"What?" Leto snapped.

"I won't leave until you're both out of the desert."

Leto scowled. "You would have taken me out of the air if you'd had to, wouldn't you?"

Casimir merely dipped his chin, but he added, "I didn't need to, though, did I?"

"No, you're right. You didn't." He put his hand on Grace's shoulder. "To the palace."

With her wings safely retracted, Grace smiled, and was once more flying through nether-space.

Greaves still couldn't believe what had happened. He had even viewed the disastrous results on the Internet. The ruse had been perfect. All he'd thought about over the past twenty-four hours was when and how to obliterate obsidian flame with a bombing; it never occurred to him that he was looking at a massive fucking deception.

But to add insult to injury, the Web was full of Marcus's propaganda about how Greaves had attempted to do harm to the women of obsidian flame and to a bunch of swans and geese. PETA Two was in an uproar. Talk about spin.

He might have found it amusing that he'd actually been duped, but he was far too angry and the stakes had been way too high. The terrible reality had already begun sinking in that Leto had taken back at least half the army he'd built on behalf of the Coming Order. *Half.*

He couldn't say he was heartsick. You had to be in possession of a heart to be heartsick. In this sense, he was a true vampire, the kind of Mortal Earth mythology, the creature without a heart.

He didn't even particularly feel *despair.*

No, what possessed him so strangely in this moment was

a rage so pure, it was like a flame in his soul expanding, growing hotter, burning brighter, and most of all demanding recourse.

He needed recourse.

Action.

A hunt.

A devouring.

Now.

This night.

If he'd been interested in sex in that way, he would have killed someone right now for the pleasure of it and orgasmed hard.

But what he needed was different. He needed destruction of that which he believed had caused his failure. His dreams for the future were everything. He had a vision for the world, for Second Earth and for Mortal Earth, and once he had accomplished this goal, he meant to tackle the cesspool that he knew Third Earth to be.

He would transform three worlds, then over time continue to move upward until he saw the fulfillment of everything, a transformation of all six known dimensions.

That something so ridiculous as a beast and the blue variety of obsidian flame had gotten in his way seemed the height of absurdity. He understood now so well just why it was necessary for the true ruler to begin his reign with murder and to sustain that level of killing so long as opposition presented itself.

He was forbidden by the rules of COPASS to kill anyone outright, just as Endelle could kill no one outright. These rules had been designed to serve him, because he knew that Endelle had more power than he did and that if she was ever unleashed upon the world, she could cast a net of dominion far wider than he.

But she just didn't have the right frame of mind.

He believed in his cause, but he also believed in the law. He just wanted a greater command of the creation of the law so that his purposes would always be served.

Therefore, he could not kill outright.

But that didn't matter.

He had many arms to do the deeds that needed doing.

And a killing this night was required.

He gathered a squad of four powerful death vampires, then folded with them to the Seers Fortress. He found Stannett, just as he suspected, naked again, all the women dead, and the man covered in his own juice.

Following a peculiar stench, he turned to his right, and there was the Militia Warrior, her chest gone and her internal organs spilling out of her body, all very charred.

He ordered his death vampires to hold the still-unconscious Stannett upright. He then folded all of them to the basement and strung him up in chains.

He put his hand on Stannett's head, letting healing waves flow, until the bastard came around.

Stannett blinked and squinted, then said, "Forgive me. I don't know what happened."

Greaves clucked his tongue. Already his temper was settling down. "You know precisely what happened. You killed the woman so that you could do as you pleased."

"It was all too much," he whined. "I'm not used to working that hard, and my head hurt."

"So you are saying that you've been suffering terribly?"

"Yes, very badly."

"Well, let us take care of that."

"Thank you, master. And I am sorry."

"As am I."

Greaves signaled to his squad. "Please, take what you need from him."

"No," Stannett cried. But Greaves was done with the man's pleadings, whimperings, and failures.

And now Stannett was done.

The vampires moved on him as by great practice, each choosing a vein. One sank to his knees and struck one of the lower access points. Another moved behind him and struck one side of his neck. The other moved in and attacked the other side. The fourth grabbed an arm and punctured Stannett at the inside of his left elbow.

Stannett cried out repeatedly to Greaves, begging for a second chance. As his blood left his body, he continued to call for mercy. The sound of his pleading voice as he was drained of life was exactly what Greaves had needed to calm his rage and his frustration.

The death vampires were killing machines and did their job systematically.

Within two minutes, Stannett's head slumped.

Another two minutes brought the death vampires rising from a very white body. Each made a fist to exhibit arms bulging with muscles. Their eyes were manic with pleasure. Dying blood was a glorious thing.

Feeling much calmer, Greaves sent the squad back to their bunker beneath Estrella Mountain, then folded to Geneva. Julianna welcomed him with open arms and gave a squeal of delight as he released his claw from his left hand.

Her screams further eased his soul so that by the time he had finished deep inside her, he knew what steps to take next. He focused first on Casimir. Because Greaves had been associated with him recently, he had a sense of the man. Using his voyeur window, he was able to locate him at the portal to Third Earth.

He knew that Casimir was making use of his own voyeur window to keep track of Leto, and right now he needed Casimir to focus on something else.

Greaves created his own little deception: Using a trick he'd been developing lately, he messed with Casimir's window reception so that images of Leto would fade in and out. Casimir would assume it was his own difficulty, which hopefully would buy Greaves enough time to get the next job done.

And he would not wait until morning to do it.

Back at the palace, Endelle was having a great time. The hour was past ten, and the celebration of such a profound victory, without one casualty, was one of the most pleasurable moments of her life. Marcus and Havily already had the Web full of the stories of obsidian flame's ability to do a mass fold, which also featured a video that showed the folding-away of the entire spectacle event, including swans and geese, followed by Greaves's illegal bombing of the empty parade grounds.

Endelle had asked that the video be kept on a loop so that at any time she could look over her shoulder at the monitor and laugh.

Fighting a battle without a single loss, and at the same time bringing over to her side half of Greaves's army—well, damn, she was in a state of bliss.

She had her own bottle of Silver Patrón and filled her shot glass to the rim for about the tenth time. She stood up and lifted it high. "This toast is for Grace, for coming back to us, for taking her place as obsidian flame, for coming up with the most awesome strategy ever, and mostly for having the courage to enter my own twisted soul and pluck my mass-folding ability right out of what she says is a blue flame lock, whatever the fuck that is. To Grace."

All her warriors were present, all nine WhatBees. She'd freed up the rest of them from Borderland duty so that she could celebrate with her elite Warriors of the Blood, the men who had kept Second Earth safe for all these centuries.

The men, as well as the women bonded to Kerrick, Marcus, Medichi, Jean-Pierre, and Thorne, all gained their feet and held up a variety of glasses in Grace's direction. The woman blushed at all the praise.

"To Grace" resounded to the top of the dining hall rotunda, then back again.

The sound, made big because of so many masculine voices, pleased Endelle's soul.

She sipped her tequila, smiling as she drank. Goddam but she felt good. She couldn't remember the last time she'd felt this fantastic, this free, this satisfied, and sex hadn't been involved at all. But this had been as good as a good lay, flying like that, knowing she could pose for the cameras and show off her costume, heading up her army, leading obsidian flame. Yeah, damn good.

But that fold! Especially while in full-mount and not one

feather out of place once she hit the ground. Shit, that had been something else. The power had rolled along the parade route starting at the back, like an all-encompassing wind that passed through her body yet caught her up at the same time, and shunting her in a quick ride through nether-space. Her wings had held—another miracle provided by obsidian flame. No way in hell would she try it on her own. Wings could get thoroughly trashed during a fold, and that kind of destruction would hurt like a motherfucker.

She glanced at Grace. The woman had truly surprised her in about every way possible. That she'd left the Creator's Convent in Prescott Two to shack up with Casimir-the-Hedonist on Fourth Earth had been one of the shockers of the century. But that she'd come back so changed was another shocker, wearing loose clothing, lots of makeup, and her hair curled. A lot of her restraint was just gone. Maybe Casimir had done that for her, or maybe being with Beatrice, or maybe it was the *breh-hedden*.

So Grace was back, the third leg of a now über-powerful obsidian triad, and all cuddled up with Leto. Endelle had extended her hearing a couple of times, because eavesdropping was just plain fun. Grace kept whispering to Leto that she wanted him to "go beast." Endelle was pretty sure she knew what that meant, and if she'd been in Grace's shoes, she would have done the same thing.

She sipped her tequila, then laughed again, no less so when Leto called out to Thorne, "Hey, how about having Jeannie fold us back to my cabin."

Thorne frowned slightly. "The cabin in Seattle?"

"Yes," Leto said. "The colony is secure, and I'm going to create my own dome of mist over my property." He glanced at Medichi and smiled. "Besides, I think the villa will be crowded tonight."

Medichi laughed. "Very crowded." He leaned close to Parisa and kissed her full on the lips.

Thorne opened his mouth, probably to argue with Leto's request some more, but Leto already had his tongue in Grace's mouth again.

Endelle met Thorne's gaze, but she understood the need for some alone time. "I'll add my own dome of mist over the cabin." She then called out to Jeannie and gave the order.

Leto and Grace vanished.

Endelle was almost tempted to open her voyeur window and have a brief look-see at the couple, but she really was trying to work on her boundaries. Alison kept preaching to her about them, and she supposed she was right. So, instead, she poured another shot of Silver Patrón and savored the moment.

Tonight had been a major victory, maybe not the final one that would end Greaves's plans for good but a solid step in the right direction. She had no doubt that *the little peach* would retaliate, but she doubted it would be in the next few hours. Would he want a straight-up battle, now that he'd lost half his force? She honestly didn't know.

"Go beast for me," Grace whispered, licking at Leto's neck.

Leto was in agony. She'd gotten him worked up at the palace, but each time she said, "Go beast for me," he swore he almost came.

Maybe it was the way she said it, kind of pleading with an ache in her voice. He could also feel just how aroused she was, her nipples in hard beads against his palms. So strange to feel her sensations at the same time he pressed his hands into her breasts.

He leaned against the wall by the fireplace, and she leaned into him, her hips pressing upward in a sensual roll, stroking the full length of him with her body.

"Go beast for me, Leto."

He wanted to, but he also wanted to take his time with her. "You were wonderful tonight," he said. "You were amazing."

She stopped licking his neck and looked up at him. Her gold-green eyes glittered. "It was an incredible experience," she said. "Have I thanked you for supporting me like you did? I'm not sure I would have gotten through it without your help. You calmed me enough to get the fold done."

He kissed her. "You're welcome . . . again. For about the hundredth time."

She smiled and kissed him back. "Don't you think I deserve a reward?"

"Oh, I don't know." But he pressed her bottom with both hands and flexed his hips.

She hissed, and her hips responded so that she rolled over him again. She licked his neck, but this time she began to suck. A shudder went through him.

Go beast for me, Leto. I want you big . . . everywhere.

Leto closed his eyes and just let the pleasure of her mouth on his neck ride him. He could feel how much she enjoyed her lips on his skin, and sucking at him. But it was all too much.

The only question he needed to answer was simple: *Where?* Then he remembered how much she liked water. He groaned and tried to calm down.

He pushed her away. "I have an idea, but you need to be naked."

She nodded. Her lips were so swollen. She waved a hand, and her flight suit disappeared.

He had to close his eyes again for a couple of reasons. One of them involved how easy it would be to just spill all over the floor, but the other was much more critical. The hidden colony was still covered in mist—Endelle had seen to that, and she'd covered his cabin as well. But not the hot spring. Mentally, he got the deed done. Yep, power was great.

"How about a soak?"

She drew in a deep breath. "Your bathtub might fit us both, but not if you're in a beast state."

His woman had a one-track mind. "I'm thinking about the hot spring." He waved his own hand this time, and his clothes disappeared.

Her turn to shudder. Her knees buckled, so of course he had to catch her. "I'm going to fold us both to the edge. You ready?"

She nodded. "Uh-huh." Then she kissed him.

He landed on the rocks, and because her lips were still

pressed to his, he barely kept his balance. He drew back and smiled. "You're so anxious."

"I'm hungry," she whispered.

"Well, let me feed you then."

She listed sideways, so he did the only sensible thing: He fell sideways, pulling her with him straight into the pool.

The warm water helped to calm things down. For a reason he couldn't explain, some inner desperation perhaps, he really needed this time with her to last. He felt oppressed with things he didn't understand. Yes, they'd had a victory tonight—and yet had they done anything more than just infuriate a tyrant, a man with no conscience, who had a vast army?

"Leto," Grace whispered against his ear. "Why so distressed?"

He looked at her. "You can feel that?"

"Yes. Your whole body has grown tense. I want to make love to you, and your thoughts are practically shouting at me."

He shook his head. "I'm not sure exactly what's bugging me. I've been uneasy ever since seeing the southern sky lit with those bombs. Greaves will want revenge. We've wounded something far worse than anything physical."

"His pride."

"Yes, at the very least his pride. But we've stripped him of his advantage."

She pushed away from him and threw herself backward into the water only to rise and float, her breasts like two small islands, her eyes closed.

Leto watched her float. Dammit, he'd ruined the moment for her. He had only been thinking of his own fears and concerns. But Grace was the one who had done the heavy lifting tonight, and her success should be celebrated.

"I feel like an ass."

"Well, then come feel my ass but not until you're ready. I can wait."

He stood up and pushed through the water to get to her. She stayed floating on her back. She was looking up at the dark night sky.

"The mist you created over the pool is beautiful. You have a small swirl that's quite elegant."

He dipped down and put his hands beneath her back to support her, then he moved her in a circle faster and faster until she was giggling. But the restraint was there, within him, almost screaming at him: *Don't get involved, don't get close, don't give your heart, don't forget how quickly a war can rob you of everything.* Would he ever be free of this terrible holding back, this unwillingness to engage fully with her?

He feared the answer.

And he was definitely being an ass.

So he gave her the one thing he could give her, but this time all he had to do was think the thought and he began to transform.

Grace felt the movement in the water, like gentle pushes here and there. Leto had released her back. She sighed. But her eyes were closed, and she was trying hard not to be so disappointed.

All she had wanted was to be with Leto, and have him go beast for her, but he seemed lost in his worries and she couldn't fix that. So, she floated and tried not to think about him or the tangible space that seemed to always be between them despite the fact that they were fully bonded.

Then she realized what that pushing sensation was.

She popped her eyes open and stood up in the water.

She gasped. "How did you do that? I didn't know except the movements in the water felt a little different."

He looked down at her from his increased height. His fangs had emerged. All that former desire came rushing back to her, especially since the moist air of the hot spring smelled heavily of the forest and man, Leto and beast.

Her nostrils flared as she took in his scent. At the same time, she put her hands on his massive pecs and began to fondle him. She loved his body in this state. She could hardly explain it. But he was just more of himself: more to touch, to feel, to experience from both his sensations as well as hers.

She slid her hands around his waist intending to hug him, but she felt his wing-locks and they were dripping.

She drew in a sharp breath. "Turn around," she commanded.

His eyelids sank low. "Meadow scent."

"Just turn around."

He obeyed, and the water sloshed from his heavy thighs; small waves washed over her. She began at the lowest wing-lock and rubbed back and forth. He arched his back and roared.

The sound gripped her low, which caused him to roar again.

She glanced around the pool and found a large boulder that was smooth as it angled into the water. She took his hand and guided him over to the rock. "You must let me do this to you. I want to. Will you let me?"

He chuffed his response and spread himself out on the rock facedown. The water came up to the tops of his thighs.

Her lips trembled as she moved into him. He was a visual feast, and he was hers, both to command right now and to enjoy.

She moved behind him and pressed her hips against his buttocks. He groaned.

She leaned over him and licked a line straight up the center of his back. She stroked the sides of his hips from his waist down to as much of the thigh as she could reach below the water, then she came back up. The whole time she moved her hands closer to the front of his thighs, slower and slower until she wrapped her hands around the base of his stalk. At the same time, she started licking his wing-locks.

He chuffed against the rock, breathing hard.

Grace, you're killing me.

Good.

She leaned close and focused her attention on the mid-point wing-lock on the right side of his back. The lock was big, like everything about him right now, including what she held in her hand. She rubbed her cheek along the lock and felt moisture at the aperture. She glided her left hand up his cock and felt moisture at the tip.

She flicked her tongue over the end of his wing-lock. The pleasure he felt, which she could experience because of the *breh-hedden,* tightened her internal well. He tasted of the forest and man. *I wish I could lick both tips at once.*

His hips pumped, and he groaned. He planted his forearms on the rock and buried his face between. *I wish you were under me right now.*

Grace released him and sank beneath the warm water, spreading his legs wide and pulling them away from the rock. She pivoted and carefully rose up, taking great pains not to clunk her skull on the hard rock.

He kept making room and growling. As her head breached the water, she licked his cock ever so slowly as she continued to rise until she could take his crown in her mouth. He was big and filled her mouth. She sucked.

Grace. My God. Grace.

Her body clenched because she could feel how her mouth felt on him while at the same time enjoying the pleasure of him in her mouth. The *breh-hedden* might have been many things, but *erotic* defined this part. She could feel what he felt, the way his forearms braced his forehead, the way the water felt sloshing around his thighs, and the way her fingernails felt pressing into his buttocks.

She sucked harder and his hips flexed then pulled back. He was close. Hell, she was close.

She released him, and he groaned long and loud. She pushed his stomach away and worked her way up until she was reclining on the rock beneath him. "Is this under you enough?"

He was so beautiful in this state: Leto and so much more. He stroked her face with his big hands, then leaned down to kiss her. When he drew back, he said, "When I enter you, I'm not going to last long."

She smiled and reached up to kiss him back. "I won't, either."

"This whole pool smells like I'm walking through a summery meadow."

"No it doesn't, it smells of the forest and man, of you, of Leto the beast." She smiled and petted his cheek.

"Leto the beast. The way you say it makes me want to be this way forever."

"I wouldn't complain."

He pushed her legs apart. She worked with him. The smooth rock at her back could still cause some problems if she wasn't careful.

But he hadn't reached several millennia in age without having learned a thing or two. "That rock is too damn hard for what I need to do."

"What do you need to do."

"Slam into you, as fast as I can, for about thirty seconds."

"Oh, I don't think it will take that long."

He smiled, then chuckled. "I'm going to fold us back to my bed."

"I'm all wet."

"I'm counting on that."

He kissed her as she glided through nether-space. The next moment she was flat on her back, on his bed, and what do you know, there was a towel beneath her. He found her entrance and pushed, but, yeah, she was wet and he glided all the way in, as deep as he could get.

He groaned.

The dual sensations about killed her.

He planted his hands above her shoulders, and looking down at her began to pull his hips back, then thrust. She felt like she couldn't catch her breath, even if she wanted to. He moved faster and faster, and as soon as she started to come, all that he was experiencing brought her orgasm crashing down on her. She screamed. He roared. The sound of his voice drew the orgasm out so that she writhed beneath him.

He grunted and gathered her up in his arms, but his hips didn't quiet down. "Shit, I'm going to come again," he shouted.

He moved faster again, faster than before. She pushed her mind against his and felt his shields falls. She dove within and sank, then dove into the center of his soul.

He cried out over and over. *Oh, my God, Grace.*

She felt how her presence changed all his physical sensations, enhancing them. Pleasure began driving up her body, over her flesh, up into her well, tugging and pulling, higher and higher, invading her abdomen and her chest until this sweeping orgasm even flew through her mind.

She saw stars, the pleasure was so intense.

On and on, it cascaded through her mind, through her body, his body, hers, until she lay slack and Leto's body was a heavy weight on her.

He moaned. *So good.*

She was still moving through his soul, the part of him that was his truest self. She felt deeply content, then he was just suddenly there with her, his soul engaging with her soul.

He moved with her like a dance, flowing around her, over, through, under, above. She responded and felt overcome with a profound sense of peace. Maybe there were holes in their current relationship, things neither of them could define very well, but in this moment she felt one with him. And it was beautiful.

Two souls merge,
Life flutters anew.
Oh, my beloved
Open for me,
Bid me welcome,
Not adieu.

—Grace of Albion, "The Convent Years," from
Collected Poems, Beatrice of Fourth

CHAPTER 18

At midnight, Grace lay across Leto's chest, his massive arms surrounding her. He was still in his beast-state and she kept petting his body, savoring how big he was, and that he was hers. She kissed him and loved on him.

He squeezed her shoulders and sighed. "That was amazing."

"Yes, it was. I'm glad you brought us back to your bedroom. This has been one of the most wonderful nights of my life. I feel very free and relaxed, more myself than at any other time I can remember." Which seemed strange, since she was still convinced that she was holding back. But was she? Maybe the limitation she experienced was somehow different than she imagined.

He squeezed her again and kissed the top of her head. He chuckled. "I loved what you did in the pool when I was stretched out on that rock, when you slipped into the water and arranged my legs so you had to come up underneath me. I think I will remember that moment as long as I live."

She giggled and smiled. "We should spend a lot of time in the hot spring. I love being in the water."

"Grace, when you were in my soul, it felt like heaven."

She drifted the tips of her fingers over his pecs. He caught her hand and kissed her fingers.

"But this frightens you," he said.

"A little, but I'm not sure why. It's all so new, I guess."

"You mean the *breh-hedden*?"

She pivoted to look up at him. "Not just that. Everything. These powers that just seem to keep expanding and being part of obsidian flame. I still can't believe we folded over two hundred thousand warriors—"

"—and don't forget the birds."

She laughed. "And the birds. But we got everyone to safety. I mean, who can do that?"

"A team of powerful ascended women, that's who."

He leaned down, caught her lips, and kissed her. She kissed him back, pushing herself a little farther up his chest, wondering just how far down this road they really were.

She loved Leto, so very much. Her heart was given, that much she could feel within herself. Maybe she did have parts missing, but she had a powerful instinct that time would make those ghost-like parts of her more real. At least, she hoped so.

She was about to make a comment on how much everything was changing when a sudden light filled the room. A moment later, Greaves was just there, standing at the foot of the bed, his hands behind his back.

"My, Leto, how you've grown?"

"Greaves. What the fuck are you doing here? And how the hell did you get through two layers of mist and one of them Endelle's?"

The Commander simply lifted a brow. "Are you kidding?"

Then he began to pace.

Grace couldn't reach the sheet to cover her body so she huddled next to Leto. He sat up, leaning over her, shielding her with his massive chest. Her heart started thumping.

She couldn't believe the enemy was in Leto's bedroom.

She waved a hand, and now wore yoga pants and a tank top. Good enough. She put her hand on Leto's shoulder. *I'm clothed,* she sent.

He didn't relax, not even a little. Clearly, nudity wasn't their biggest problem.

"I think I've been amazingly forbearing and gracious," Greaves said. He slid his hand along the smooth edge of the footboard. "Nor did I need to announce my presence. I could have struck and slain you both, but that hardly would have been gentlemanly, now would it?"

"You won't kill us," Leto said. "COPASS, by law, would be forced to take action. Endelle would insist on it. You still don't have a majority of Second Earth Territories in your camp. CO-PASS would have had to submit to the majority's will."

He shrugged. "Perhaps." He wore his usual immaculate dark wool suit. His bald head gleamed. He stopped pacing and turned toward Leto. "Perhaps I don't care anymore. I think you and I both know exactly what is at stake in this room right now. Do you think I don't know that you took half my army away from me? Or that Warrior Marcus has turned my less-than-successful bombing attempt into a PR nightmare?" He waved a hand toward Grace. "Or that her return hasn't made my life a nightmare?

"But there is something more, Leto. You wounded me. I trusted you and you betrayed me. I had wanted to believe in our friendship, I even had thoughts at times that we could become more than friends. I know it's foolish of me, but you hurt my pride and that is the truly unforgiveable sin."

Grace extended her thoughts to Casimir. Why wasn't he here? He was supposed to be Leto's Guardian of Ascension. Yet she could tell he wasn't in the cabin, wasn't anywhere near.

Greaves rocked back on his heels, then smiled. "No, my dear Leto, I'm finishing this tonight. Don't bother trying to fold or use your telepathy. None of it will work. I didn't just add my mist, I shrouded your cabin. No one in. No one out. Not even Casimir, I'm 'fraid."

Grace still had her hand on Leto's shoulder. He was still in his beast state, but his body had heated up, almost burning beneath her fingers. She could feel his rage vibrating along his skin. Even if he had wanted to hold back, to try to reason his way out of the situation, she knew that he had suffered too much, endured too much, to do much more than engage in battle with Greaves right now.

Leto rose from the bed, his chin low. He folded on battle gear without flexing a single muscle. He lowered his body into a fighting stance. "Bring it," he growled.

Greaves had thrown down the gauntlet, and because Leto was a warrior first, he had to do battle by every honorable code in his body. But he was no match for Greaves.

He would die in this battle.

And Grace would die with him.

Worse yet, the world would fall to this monster because obsidian flame could not function without her. With the triad out of the way, Greaves would gain the advantage. Over the centuries, he had gathered enough weaponry, turned enough death vampires, created a big enough army, and garnered sufficient support from enough territories to complete his dominion of Second Earth.

Grace felt her obsidian flame power rumbling deep within the earth. She sat up and allowed the power to flow up through her legs, inhabiting her more forcefully than ever before.

She wasn't sure yet what she meant to do or even what she could do, but before she could act or even contact her obsidian sisters, Greaves threw something at her and a searing pain sliced through her shoulder.

She turned to look at the source of the pain, but movement was incredibly difficult and hurt like hell.

Her right shoulder was now pinned to the wood headboard with a long thick dagger.

A loud, heavy growl flowed through the room, a beast enraged, and Leto began flinging powerful hand-blasts at Greaves one after the other. But Greaves barely broke a sweat as he met each one with the open palms of his hands, apparently absorbing all that energy.

My God, the power Greaves had.

Get out of here, Grace! Leto shouted within her mind. *Do what you can to escape. Now.*

She reached for the knife and, grinding her teeth, pulled it out. She screamed and fell forward. She tried to fold but couldn't, just as Greaves promised. She didn't know what to do, or what else she could do given the situation. And she was in so much pain her mind had turned to mush.

But she had to focus. She worked at ordering her thoughts. What about her power to acquire abilities? Could she somehow make use of it now, in this terrible situation?

Maybe if she joined forces with Leto, but my God her shoulder her hurt. She could barely move her arm.

She reached deep for her healing abilities. Her obsidian power amplified them so that the wound began to close. She whimpered in relief.

And what of obsidian flame? Could she bring her obsidian sisters through Greaves's shroud?

She sent a telepathic message to Fiona, but even though her obsidian power was in play, it couldn't pass through the shroud. The same with Marguerite.

She looked up. Leto seemed to be holding his ground, still flinging hand-blasts, but for how long?

Leto hurled the hand-blasts one after the other, as though his desperation to keep Grace safe had amplified his power. But for all that, Greaves met each blast effortlessly. At least the swiftness of the blasts did keep Greaves from attacking Grace again. But why did she remain on the bed?

"I see you have a new form," Greaves said.

Leto didn't answer. Anger fed his power, and he flicked his wrist three times and rushed power at Greaves.

But his former master shunted them aside. "Your abilities have expanded."

"Yes. So has my motivation. I want to live now. I didn't before."

"You should always be prepared to die."

"Fuck off." He shunted a couple of Greaves's hits aside while powering up. But he felt Grace's presence suddenly and simply allowed her to enter his soul very deep. He knew what she was after and felt her acquire the same power.

Good thinking, he sent as he flipped another blast at Greaves.

As soon as she left, and he could sense her reshaping her powers, he hit Greaves with all he had. Grace joined him.

Grace's unexpected blasts struck Greaves in the chest, and he flew back against the wall by the fireplace. Leto knew better than to stop, and Grace must have had the same idea because they advanced on him and rained hand-blasts at him in quick succession. His body jerked and started to smoke until finally he fell limp.

Leto moved to stand over him. Was this possible? Had he and Grace together defeated the monster?

Grace approached him. "Is he dead? I can't believe we might have actually killed him? Is he dead?"

The answer came swiftly as the body vanished and Greaves called to them. "Come, come, my children. Did you think killing me would be so simple? Or that even together you had enough combined power to destroy me?"

As Leto turned, Grace with him, the next blast flowed over Leto's body like a sheet of molten ore, heavy and burning hot. This time he was thrown against the same wall, and Grace with him. He had no illusions about what had just happened. This blow would finish them both. All Greaves had to do now was bring in his death vampires.

So was this how it would end for him and for his woman, smashed up against the wall, in the same place Greaves had just inhabited?

He opened his eyes to slits. He could manage nothing more. Grace was in a heap next to him, her limbs bent at weird angles and blood flowing from her nose and mouth. He smelled burning flesh. He tried to reach her mind, but nothing was there.

The pain was beyond Grace's comprehension or tolerance.

Before she could make sense of what she had done, she apparitioned and the moment she did, the pain was gone. At least Greaves couldn't prevent her from doing this.

Her first thought was again of Casimir. Maybe she had

sufficient power to bring him through the heavy shroud that Greaves had created over the cabin. She focused on him, and her ghost-self flew through the cabin and the dense shroud all the way through nether-space, past Second Earth, to the portal to Third.

She found herself in a room that had a wall of windows. Casimir was pacing the length. She called to him.

He turned toward her. His eyes went wide as he looked her up and down. "I saw you like this in Moscow Two when you took Leto away."

"Yes, this is my apparition-form."

"What's happening? I just realized that something is wrong with my voyeur window. Is Leto all right?"

She shook her head. "Greaves has us trapped in Leto's cabin, beneath a shroud of mist that no one can penetrate. I can leave in this form, but neither of us can fold out of the room. I'm hoping I can bring you back."

"Let's go."

He moved toward her, and she put her apparition-hand on his shoulder. She thought the thought, but nothing happened. She tried several times, but she couldn't move him back with her.

She shook her head. "This isn't working. Just . . . let Endelle know. I've got to find some way to do this. I'm going to Beatrice. Maybe she can help."

"Yes, go. I'll do what I can here."

She focused on Beatrice and began to glide past Third; then she was at the palace. Beatrice sat in her chair, the lavender yarn in a ball at her left elbow.

"My son has hurt you, hasn't he?"

Grace explained the situation. "Can you help me?"

"Try to take me back with you." Beatrice reached for Grace's arm.

Once the connection was made, Grace once more attempted the return trip—but she couldn't do it, not with another ascender.

Despite her apparition-form, she fell at the philosopher's feet. She didn't know what else she could do. She laid her head on Beatrice's lap. "Did you know this would happen, that your son would take my life?"

"No, but it seemed like a logical thing for him to do. You are one of the greatest threats to his plans."

"I learned Leto's hand-blast skill just now."

"You're very powerful, Grace."

She frowned as she fingered the silk of Beatrice's skirt. She felt the woman's gentle hand on her head. "I don't want to die. I want to live and be with Leto, to share his bed. I want to bear his children, but I'm barren. My life has been so barren, so useless."

"Don't say that. You were always beloved wherever you went."

"And yet I held back from love. Even after I completed the *breh-hedden* with Leto, it was as though I was still a ghost with him. He could be outside of me or in me, and yet could he really embrace me and hold me? Hold who I was? Oh, Beatrice, I didn't want to be a ghost with him, an apparition. How do you make the apparition real when you've been a ghost your entire life?"

And there it was, the hard truth, the deep understanding that finally came to her. She had been a ghost in her life from the time she'd given up her baby for adoption. She'd lived in the shadows of life, always keeping herself safe, keeping herself from harm.

Now she was near death, as was Leto, and she had no way to help him or herself. How had this happened? Why had this happened? "I've lived in the shadows all my life."

Beatrice spoke softly. "My dear, you don't even know, do you?"

"What?"

"You stepped out of the shadows the moment you folded three dimensions and made love to a beast-man in the basement of the Cascades cabin. You've been out of the shadows at least that long. You just lack experience. So go. Make more experiences."

Grace blinked. Had she moved out of the shadows? Was she more than a ghost?

And yet, as she thought about all that she'd done over the past four days, she realized she had never been that person before, taking charge, formulating enormous plans to alter Greaves's ability to take over the world, then actually following through with the spectacle event and the mass fold of a million warriors. She was no longer the woman who'd lived in a convent for a century.

She was obsidian flame.

Which meant . . . that she already had the tools in her possession, had been learning them for the past several days, all that she would need to defeat the monster.

What came to her was so pure and so simple that she rose up in her apparition-form, kissed Beatrice on the cheek, then folded, not to the cabin but to the palace. This time, she wanted Endelle.

Beatrice had said she needed to make more experiences. Well, who had more experience than the scorpion queen?

Grace found her walking through the rotunda nearest her rooms, where she stopped and stared at Grace.

"So you can see me?" Grace asked.

"Of course I can see you. What the fuck are you doing here? I thought all you cared about was getting Leto to go beast for you."

She told her about Greaves and how he had them both trapped and dying. Endelle put a hand to her forehead. "That bastard. Okay. What do you need me to do? I can try blasting through the shroud."

Grace wasn't convinced anything external could help at this point. "I need something from you."

When Endelle once more suggested an assault, Grace said, "Just trust me right now to take care of this, Endelle. Please. I can do this. I just need something from your soul, and once I've acquired that ability, I'll want you to bring the rest of obsidian flame here to the palace. And then, as soon as I can, I'll bring Leto to you."

Endelle became very still. She grew relaxed, her shoulders dropping. Opening her hands wide, she said, "Take whatever you need." No more questions, or suggestions, no complaints, just *take what you need*.

And here was the truth about the hard-bitten ruler of Second Earth: Endelle always came through.

"I need to capture your skill of living out loud. I mean, I think I'm already getting the hang of it, but I'd like a booster just in case."

Endelle laughed. "You sure you're ready for that?"

"Oh, yeah. It's time. It's been time for two millennia."

"Then hit me, baby."

Grace pierced Endelle's mind and once more sank deep toward the woman's soul. She found the lock she needed all lit up and inserted her blue flame key. The lock gave way, the door opened, and it was as though all of Endelle's life poured over her: all the ways she met every challenge head-on, all the ways she could be cunning, all the ways she manipulated with sarcasm.

Grace drank it in.

Street smarts. That's what Endelle had. And courage, mountains and mountains of courage. But mostly, Endelle had experience, that which Grace lacked the most, experience dealing with Greaves.

She thanked Endelle telepathically and sped back to the cabin. She moved to stand in front of Greaves. He still couldn't see her or even perceive that she was near him, and he still sat in that chair, as if he had all night to finish them off.

Good. Although in this moment, she had to resist a very Endelle-like desire to slap the bastard silly.

She smiled.

Then she looked around. She let all of Endelle's experience flow through her mind. She picked up one strategy and threw it out. She picked up another and turned it over in her mind. She felt more substantial in herself, more weighted, more real, as though having all of Endelle's experience backing her up had sharpened her focus.

She apparitioned across the room to stare down at Leto. She blinked. She needed to do something with him, but what?

* * *

Greaves sat in the chair near the head of Leto's bed. He'd barely broken a sweat and two powerful vampires lay facing each other in a tangle of burned and broken limbs. Neither was dead yet, and he would need to bring in a few death vampires to get the job done, but not just yet.

He savored this precise moment in his life, in his long career, in the brilliant path of his ambitions, because with just a little patience, he would see this pair good and dead; obsidian flame would be eliminated as a threat, and he could at last allow his plans to unfold.

He leaned his head back and he smiled.

Life was good.

Leto wanted to lift a thumb to touch Grace's cheek, but he didn't think he could. He didn't know exactly how many bones of his were broken, but the pain was staggering. He couldn't move, couldn't even lift a finger. Her eyes were open, but there was little life present, if any.

How had it come down to this? What had he done wrong? How had he failed to keep Grace safe?

He had known she was at risk. The fact that she had out-maneuvered Greaves had put her in danger.

However, during the past several days with her, it hadn't occurred to him even once to share his experience with her, and now that he looked at the situation, he felt like a complete fool. What could Grace have become if he had said to her: *Take what is mine, take all that is mine; all that I have experienced, I give to you freely and fully. Learn all that I have learned.*

But maybe it wasn't too late. He was a vampire of tremendous power and ability. More important, he could communicate all that to Grace, if there was even the smallest spark left inside her.

Grace, he sent. His voice sounded thin, even within his own head.

I'm here. I'm safe in my apparition-form. I'm not feeling

any pain. But I need something from you, I'm just not sure what.

I think I know. I finally get it, how I held back from you. Grace, I have within me all that you need in terms of skill and experience, even power. Just glide within me and feast.

I think you're right. In fact, I know you're right, but you're in so much pain.

Pain doesn't matter. Pain means life. Come to me. Take me now.

He felt her slide against his mind, then drop in and down. She knew the way to his soul where all his abilities lived, where he held all the deepest memories of action and forward motion, of decision and analysis, of strategy.

He felt her move within him and it was like heaven all over again, yet even more complete. She found the key to his vast experience as a warrior and as a leader of men. She opened the door, and he felt all that learned wisdom and understanding flow over her and through her. She caught it and held on.

Grace flew up and out of Leto's most essential self, and when she'd departed she looked around. She stared at Greaves, so at ease in the chair. He still couldn't see her.

She recognized what he was feeling: a deep satisfaction that he had vanquished them both, that now he could continue with his plans.

She accessed all that Leto had just shared with her, the analytical processes of his mind, how swiftly he would create strategies but toss them aside if they didn't seem right, then his lightning-like ability to formulate new ones.

She did the same now.

She assessed the situation: her broken body, Leto's as well, Greaves's enormous power, the shroud he had placed over the cabin. She and Leto could never fight him and win, so this could never be about acquiring enough power to battle Greaves.

She could also sense that Leto was near death, so her most critical task involved healing and escape.

And now it all seemed so simple. She leaned down and kissed Leto while still in her ghostly form.

I'll be back in a moment. I need to reach Fiona. I think I'll be able to bring her back because I can possess her. I will need to see Horace as well, to acquire his healing ability. Stay alive, Leto.

I'll be here returned to her strong and steady. How different from the man in despair she had left five months ago.

Fiona, who had the ability to enhance power, would be able to amplify Horace's healing power once Grace had Horace's advanced ability.

Because she was still functioning within her obsidian power, Grace focused on Horace and her apparition-self began flying through space. She found him just finishing up with one of the Militia Warriors at the New River Borderland. She called his name. He turned toward her, but he couldn't see her.

She explained where she was and what she needed. He nodded, saying, "Of course. I have heard of what you've been able to accomplish. Please do what you need to do."

Grace took as few words as possible to explain her process. Horace, the most powerful healer on Second Earth, nodded and closed his eyes.

She dove within his mind, then fell into his soul, which was, as she knew it had to be for such a kind man, very warm and very beautiful. She found his healing lock, inserted her blue flame, and acquired the ability.

She drew out and thanked him.

She then apparitioned to Fiona, moving swiftly and smoothly through nether-space. When Grace reached her, she was in Endelle's palace because Endelle had done as Grace had asked and brought her obsidian sisters to the central rotunda, ready for action. Thorne stood next to Marguerite, and Jean-Pierre was pressed close to Fiona, his arms surrounding her.

Grace took as few words as she could manage to explain the Greaves predicament.

"What do you need from us?" Endelle asked.

"I need to possess Fiona in this form."

"Do it," Endelle said softly.

Fiona moved toward her by way of assent. "Yes, do whatever you need."

Something deep inside Grace blossomed, a sense of belonging and of hope, of being very present in her life and less ghost-like than she'd ever been before.

She focused for just a moment on her variety of obsidian flame power and let a new wave flow from the earth, up into her soul, even into this apparition-form that was as much a part of her as her corporeal self.

She thought the thought and simply took possession of Fiona. Her obsidian power flowed.

Together Grace sped with Fiona back to the cabin. Just as she suspected, because she was part of Fiona, she passed through the shroud of Greaves's mist and into the bedroom. Her body and Leto's lay crumpled and burned.

Oh, God, Fiona murmured.

It's all right. Now, I'm going to concentrate on the healing ability I learned from Horace. Are you ready to enhance the power?

Yes.

Grace just let the thought take form in her mind, and healing began pouring toward the bodies on the floor.

Leto drew a sudden deep breath and rose, his own body knitting together at lightning speed, miraculously, unbelievably. He wasn't even sure exactly how this was happening, but he could feel Grace's presence.

He turned Grace's body and watched her re-form, though she remained inert because Grace was in her apparition form. He glanced around and saw the strangest sight: Fiona in a ghost-like form, glowing in streaks of gold and blue. It meant of course that Grace was with her, and that together they were doing the impossible.

And now all his pain was gone.

In a sudden heartbeat, the dual apparition-form vanished, and he heard a thump behind him.

Grace rose, laughing. "I stood up too fast and hit my head on the wall." Her gaze shifted beyond Leto. "Oh, shit, we'd better get out of here."

"How?" he asked.

"What the hell is this?" Greaves shouted, rising from his chair. "How did you heal?"

Leto feared the worst, that though Grace had worked her miracle, Greaves would now bring fire and brimstone down on their heads and wipe them from the face of the earth.

But the moment these thoughts flew through his mind, he realized Grace had already split into her apparition-form and once more Fiona returned, glowing with blue and gold streams of light swirling around her.

Fiona winked. Or was that Grace? Then he heard Grace's voice in his head: *Sorry for the delay, but I had to access Endelle's folding ability. Ready?*

Yes. Make it quick.

He felt Greaves's power ramping up again. He stiffened, waiting for the blow, but before the blast hit he was gliding through nether-space. When his feet touched down in the palace, he felt Grace beside him as well, though a little unsteady on her feet since she was only partially inhabiting her body. He steadied her with a hand beneath her arm.

He was still in his beast-form, so she might as well have been a feather. He drew her into his arms and held her close. He felt the moment when she returned fully to her body. She slid her arms around his neck. "We made it," she whispered.

He kissed her again, but his warrior concerns returned as he drew back. "Greaves. We should prepare in case he follows us here."

"Fiona and I blocked the trace."

He let out a deep breath. "Good." He kissed her again, long and deep. *I have things I need to say to you, my darling.*

Me, too. So much.

Endelle's voice cut through their telepathic conversation. "Okay, you two, knock it off. We have things to discuss."

Leto released Grace and set her on her feet.

Grace, however, turned toward Fiona. "Thank you," she said earnestly. "Thank you, for all that you've done to be able to work with me as you have just now. We would have died otherwise. Fiona, how will I ever repay you?"

Fiona shook her head, and her cheeks turned a rosy hue. "I don't feel like I did anything except lend a hand."

Grace laughed. How like Fiona to diminish her contribution.

But Endelle was tapping a stiletto. "All right, Grace, enough with the chitchat. Where's the Geneva bastard, and what do you think I should do about him?"

The entire group fell silent.

Leto couldn't believe his ears. Endelle asking advice of anyone? Especially of Grace?

"Uh," Grace murmured.

"Oh, for Christ's sake. You did good, and so I'm asking, what do we do next?"

Grace blinked a couple of times, then turned to Marguerite. "I think this might be a job for your Seer skills. My intuition is yelling at me that we fire up obsidian flame and use the power this time to look into the future streams."

Fiona seconded the plan, and the three women moved together at once.

Leto could feel the surface changes that Grace experienced, the flow of vibrating power over her body. Beyond that, he watched and waited.

The women looked peaceful with their eyes closed as they worked through the process.

He also felt the moment the triad completed what they'd set out to do because the soft rumbling vibrations disappeared, flowing back into the earth.

Leto turned to Grace. Her eyes were wide as she met Marguerite's gaze then Fiona's.

"All right," Endelle said. "Cut the suspense. What are we up against?"

Marguerite moved to stand beside Thorne. She took his hand and held on hard. "First, Stannett isn't blocking the future streams anymore. He's just *not there*. I think he might be gone, as in dead."

Silence held the room for a moment, then Endelle said, almost somberly, "Well, thank the Creator for small favors. So, what did you see?"

"Greaves is preparing to attack the hidden colonies, all of them, in about fifteen minutes. He succeeded in mapping every single one so he knows where they're located. In the vision, he's using his own power to sequentially torch the colonies, after which he intends to fold his death vampires to each location to attack the colonists. It's very organized."

Leto struggled to breathe. He had always known it was a likelihood that Greaves would go after the colonies, but now that the moment had come, he felt sick in his gut. The logistics seemed impossible. How could they get enough Militia Warriors to each site at this late hour?

He was ready to contact Seriffe and to start issuing orders to gather the necessary squads at Apache Junction Two, but Grace put her hand on his arm. "Hold on, Leto. I think this might be something obsidian flame can help with. Marguerite has already seen what we need to do. We're to set up as a triad in Diallo's courtyard so that we can be as close to the mossy mist as possible."

"What exactly are you going to do?" he asked.

"I'm not sure, but once we engage as a triad I have no doubt we'll know what needs to be done." She turned to her brother. "And, Thorne, it appears you will have a larger role in the process as well. Just wanted to give you a heads-up."

At that, Thorne smiled. "If it means saving the colonies, my pleasure."

Circles are the ultimate perfection.

—*Collected Proverbs*, Beatrice of Fourth

CHAPTER 19

Greaves felt the future flow toward him like a dark wave, foreboding but exciting. Stannett was gone, so he had no one at the helm at the Illinois Seers palace to block his next moves. His only shot was to act quickly.

He contacted the war room at Estrella and had his generals ready to initiate the attack on the colonies once he was assured that he could burn all the mossy mist away.

Grace and Leto had somehow made their escape. He still wasn't sure how, except that suddenly a miraculous healing had occurred. Even then he should have been able to blast them all to hell, but they just disappeared and he had no idea how they'd gotten past the shroud he'd created.

Unless of course obsidian flame was involved in a way he still didn't understand.

He thought about folding back to Estrella, but the location within the Seattle Colony served his purposes better and he could monitor the results of his efforts right away.

He sustained the shroud over the cabin, settled back in his chair, and redirected his hand-blast energy. With great care, he began gathering kinetic energy; in a few minutes he'd be able to ignite the moss-based mist of the Seattle Colony.

He'd worked out the sequence, and once he fired this special hand-blast, the burning would ignite all the colonies, one after the other, in quick succession.

He had only a couple of minutes, and then this part of his plan would unfold.

Grace stood on Diallo's patio, her hand tucked into Leto's. He was still in his beast-form, and she loved it. He kept looking down at her from his increased height, looking into her eyes as she looked back.

The world was new, different, better, brighter, even though she still wasn't sure what had happened between them.

I love you, she sent.

I love your hand in mine, the beats of your heart, your smile, your infinite worth.

Love flowed from Leto now as it never had before. She could feel it, a warm, almost liquid sensation of caring and belonging. That was the difference—or at least one of them, since she felt changed as well.

Whatever strange shields had existed before now lay flat, dissolved, obliterated.

He leaned down and kissed her, apparently still not caring that everyone gaped at either his size or his affection for her. When he drew back, he whispered, "I love you so much."

Her heart expanded, and she sighed.

"I love you, too."

"Grace," Thorne called softly.

She could hardly tear her gaze from Leto. She blinked and turned. He put his hand on her shoulder, the expression in his eye tender. "Marguerite has had a second vision about the colonies. It's time."

She nodded, but she wasn't sure she could feel her feet. As she relinquished Leto's hand and turned toward her obsidian flame sisters, though, she felt her power vibrate deep in the earth and once more rush up her legs and into her being.

She reacted swiftly, opening her mind to Marguerite, who shared the vision with both her and Fiona at the same time. Her breath left her body in a swift rush.

"He's begun his torching sequence. The colonies will begin to ignite in a little over a minute."

Grace glanced at Thorne. "How do we proceed?"

He shook his head. "I can only support you. Grace, this is your call. I anchor obsidian flame, but what I understand now is that you lead it."

She could not have been more shocked—and yet it made sense in terms of the allocation of gifts. Marguerite could only indicate the direction. Fiona's power could only support what Grace could offer. But Grace could find the location, then learn and amplify the ability needed to fix things.

In this case, what did she need to do? What needed to happen?

Her mind whirled swiftly. She needed to stop the process at the core, at the place where it would begin, where the moss would first be lit on fire.

"The mist," she said. "The key is with the mist." She shifted slightly toward Thorne. "And you know how to make the mist, right?"

"Yes."

"Then may I enter your soul and find the formula for the mist?" She smiled as she said it.

"With pleasure."

Grace dove and felt Thorne jerk back in surprise. He was very powerful and almost prevented her from sinking. But a moment later, he relaxed and relented.

Grace had finally come to understand that she wasn't second to him or to Patience, but an equal in power and in purpose. She dove and fell through the deep cloudy space between the mind and the soul where the key to many, many things existed.

Thorne's landscape was multihued but in subdued tones, like the facets of his eyes that were also multihued in soft golds and greens, light browns and blues, even grays, a perfect hazel. *Magnificent,* she sent to his mind. *You are magnificent, my brother. And so beautiful. I can feel that you are whole and that Marguerite has done this for you, given you peace.*

It's a strange thing to feel you within me. I love you, Grace, and I'm so proud of you and what you've accomplished. I can feel your power. It's amazing.

She smiled and focused on the mossy mist. A memory glowed a vibrant blue color, of Diallo teaching both Marguerite and Thorne how to make the mist that protected all the colonies. She found the lock and inserted her blue flame obsidian key. In a flash, she drew from him what she needed, then swiftly pulled out.

As she opened her eyes, she realized she needed more than just Thorne's ability to make the mist. "There is another key. Excuse me. I must go get it right now." She had to act fast and couldn't stop to explain.

She apparitioned to the hospital on Second, then sought and found Diallo. He was still bruised. *Diallo, forgive me.*

He turned his head in her direction. *I can see you, Grace. You look lovely. What form is this?*

A sort of split-self.

Ah. But I can feel your discomfiture. Tell me what I can do.

First, she relayed as swiftly as she could all that was happening. *I have the key to the mist, but there is something more I need. I felt it within Thorne, but he doesn't have the key to the rest of the colonies. I need to acquire the ability from your soul.*

His brows rose, but a smile tugged on his lips. *I have been wondering how to be of use when my body is broken. Now I know. Please, take from me what you need.*

She explained in more detail what she would need to do, and when he gave permission, she dove as she had with Thorne.

She marveled at how different each person was. Diallo felt as though he carried great riches within, and when she sank into the clouds separating the mind from the soul, she landed in a place of the brightest gold. She gasped and she felt him laugh within his mind. *I can see what you are looking at, Grace. I am equally surprised, but I believe that my wife may have created all that beauty. I can account for it in no other way.*

Grace wanted to stay and to savor, but she had a mission to accomplish. She focused on the mossy mist and the lock came forth, almost blinding in its beauty as well. She put her blue energy within, and the gate to his knowledge opened. What she saw astonished her—the sheer simplicity of how Diallo had created the interconnected mist that sustained the secrecy of so many hundreds of colonies all over the globe. She took the secret into her soul and flew from Diallo, nodding to him in her apparition-form as she swiftly returned to the courtyard garden.

"I've got it," she said the moment she reconnected with her physical self.

Thorne stood behind Marguerite, his hands on her arms. Jean-Pierre moved in to support Fiona in a similar way, and Leto wrapped his oversized arms around her. She looked up at him and smiled.

I'm with you, he sent.

She felt it again, a wave of love that hadn't been there before. She nodded, then turned back to Marguerite. "What's our timing?"

"Twenty seconds."

Grace looked up. "The mist is still intact," she said. Everyone looked up.

"But not for long," Marguerite said. She continued the count down, "Nineteen, eighteen, seventeen . . ."

"Fiona, I'm coming to you," Grace said.

"I'm ready."

Grace opened her obsidian flame power, which flowed quickly and easily now after so much practice. She focused on the job at hand, on protecting all the colonies. She let Diallo's knowledge of the interconnected mist flow through her as well. She apparitioned to Fiona and slid inside. She felt Fiona's ability to enhance a skill take over so that the obsidian power was responding to the event about to unfold. How different this was from the mass-folding experience, as though this time a whirlwind flew around the garden at tremendous speed.

"Hold steady," Marguerite said aloud. "Eight, seven, six . . . Hold. Hold." Then finally, "Now."

The energy began to flow upward in a swirling stream of silvery light. But with the light, Thorne began to levitate as though part of the stream.

"Thorne," Grace called out, although the voice was Fiona's since she was possessing her. "What's happening?"

"Thorne?" Marguerite added.

"It's okay. I'm safe within the stream of energy, but I must go on this ride." Then he was smiling.

Suddenly the stream of light whipped through the dome of mist and stopped the charring effect. The mist began to knit back together. The light sped off into space, carrying Thorne with it.

She could feel him traveling almost at an incredible speed as the obsidian power moved from dome of mist to the next, and the next. Each time the burning was stopped and the healing of the mossy mist commenced.

"This is amazing," Marguerite said. "My Seer vision is tracking him. He's flying to every colony and watching as the fire on each dome is quenched by the power we just released."

Unbelievable, Fiona murmured within Grace's mind.

Grace gloried in the achievement. How glad she was she had returned to serve as obsidian flame. Greaves had been so close to decimating all the hidden colonies, and the triad had stopped him.

Thorne was over the hidden colony above Nigeria One and watched the same miracle occur that had been happening all over the world. When obsidian flame had released the answering power that would counter the burning and destruction of the concealing mossy mist over the Seattle One colony, he'd been swept along in the wake.

Initially, he hadn't understood why he was the one moving through space, but now he knew he served as a witness to what was happening. His report would further anchor the triad and support their power and reputation before the world. This alone would enhance Endelle's reputation with all her allied High Administrators.

Watching the obsidian power quenching each dome of mist, then rebuilding what was burned, made him smile. This was a new world, a new beginning for Second Earth. He was sure of it.

The hot humid air rose from the continent beneath him as he continued to be caught in the stream of obsidian flame's power. His silver aura glowed all around him. If he'd been visible to human eyes, he would have looked like a strange comet streaking through the dark night sky and even in the lightening dawn that appeared farther east.

When at last the stream of power brought him full circle back to Diallo's garden, he explained what had happened and what the experience had been like. "Of course the most important part is that the colonies are safe once more."

Leto had his arm around Grace's waist, a natural place now for him to be. He listened to Thorne's explanation of events and marveled at how different life was now among the Warriors of the Blood. Even Jean-Pierre looked relaxed as he leaned down to kiss Fiona on the cheek.

Marguerite had her arm around Thorne's waist. She was beaming, as she should have been. The triad had done all that they'd needed to do and had saved all the colonists tonight, even more cause for celebration.

The air changed suddenly, as though charged with a new energy.

He looked around. *Casimir?* Leto sent.

The Fourth ascender returned. *Let them know I'm here, and I'll go visible.*

Leto made the announcement, and Casimir materialized.

"Is something wrong?" Thorne asked. He looked from Leto to Casimir.

Casimir also glanced around the garden as though sensing someone was there. "Yes. But I'm not sure what's going on? I don't sense Greaves, though."

Grace turned toward him. "My obsidian power is rising again." She took a step past Leto, peering into the foliage near the south end of the patio. "Who's there?"

Suddenly, swords were in hands as a figure materialized.

A woman, a very beautiful woman with cat's eyes, appeared. She wore a provocative gown in a deep shade of peach. Her dark hair was dressed in waves. She looked harmless.

"It's just me."

Leto knew the woman, but not well. Her name was Julianna, and she was known to be Greaves's companion. His uneasiness grew, especially when her gaze settled on Grace, so he kept his sword in hand.

"I have a score to settle, Grace of Albion. You know I do."

"Julianna," Casimir said. "You must leave. Nothing good can come of this."

She turned toward Casimir, who was on her right. "What I will never understand," she said, "is how you could have chosen Grace over me. You and I were soul mates, we understood each other, but as soon as you caught her scent, you were hers body and soul."

"I used you ill," Casimir said. "Blame me, not Grace. I pursued her when I should have attended to the woman sharing my bed. But I was a bastard then, and I'm trying to do better now. How can I make it up to you?"

"So that's the way of it then?" Julianna's eyes were wide. "You wish to redeem yourself? Greaves said you were immersing in water and trying to get yourself clean. But how does that make up for what you did to me?" Her gaze shifted to Grace. "For how that woman stole you from me."

Leto's uneasiness grew.

"Julianna," Grace said. "I beg you to leave. If you do, all will be well and you can continue your life as it is now."

"My life?" Julianna said, turning slowly to face her. "You dare to speak to me about my life? Casimir was mine, and you took him from me. You have done this, so you must die."

Everything happened at once.

Julianna's wrist flicked, and power flared, more power than Leto had ever seen a Second ascender deliver before. He threw Grace to the pavers and stepped over her body into the blast.

Oh, God, he would die.

But at the last moment, Casimir streaked in Leto's direction, moving with his Fourth ability, protecting Leto as he had promised to protect him. Casimir took the full blast in the abdomen.

The air smelled of burned flesh.

Julianna screamed long and loud, "No." Her voice echoed around the garden as she ran toward Casimir.

Leto lifted Grace up. She turned to stare at him. "Are you all right?"

"Yes. Casimir protected me."

She turned slowly in Casimir's direction. She put a hand to her mouth, then moved to drop down beside him. "Casimir, you must not die." She began to weep.

Casimir shook badly as he turned to look at her, then at Leto. He nodded. "Good. You're all right." His eyes closed.

Leto glanced at Grace. This was what she had meant, the task that Casimir had been destined to fulfill. Leto would not have survived the blast, and the only way Casimir could have been here to act as a shield was if he had taken Grace to Fourth and been changed by her presence in his life. What had she said? Something to the effect that the only way to keep Leto was to love Casimir.

And now Casimir was dying.

Leto knew he had less than minute to change the future if he could. Whatever animosity he had felt toward Casimir a few months ago had died in the past few days.

He touched Grace on the shoulder. She turned to him weeping, but he said, "Obsidian flame. You can do this."

She straightened suddenly, as though remembering. She reached toward Marguerite and Fiona. Both women came running and joined her on the ground next to Casimir. Thorne and Jean-Pierre moved with them. "I acquired Horace's healing ability earlier. I want to try it now."

Julianna was still kneeling nearby and crying hysterically. But a moment later, at Thorne's instigation, two Militia Warriors arrived and hauled her away, one on each arm. The trio vanished.

She would see prison time for doing harm against a fellow ascender.

Grace was trembling as she put one hand on Marguerite and one on Fiona. As the triad had proven during the spectacle event, touching wasn't necessary, but right now that's what Grace wanted. She was freaked; she needed to calm down.

But with the touch, the obsidian power rose, vibrating beneath all of them as they sat grouped around Casimir. She split-self, then jumped inside Fiona who, thank God, was waiting and ready.

The amplification of the healing power began, so that Fiona, possessed by Grace, turned and held her arms above Casimir. He was unconscious now, his body still. Grace felt little life in him—but if ever a power had been designed to do the impossible, obsidian flame was that power.

Healing flowed not in gentle waves, but in massive dips and swells so that Casimir's body floated above the patio pavers. The smell of burned flesh disappeared first. Then Grace watched the organs re-form and the skin knit together. She remembered her own healing in Leto's cabin, how swift it was because of Fiona's ability to enhance a power.

Barely a minute later, Casimir's eyes opened and he rose to his feet. He stared at his hands and fingers. He felt his stomach. He said something, but she couldn't quite hear him.

"Casimir, what did you say?"

He turned to her. "Patience."

Grace shook her head. She wasn't sure what he meant, but then his eyes were wide. He was still in shock. Suddenly he grabbed her and held on to her. She felt that he was weeping.

Leto moved to look at her, but for the first time since Casimir had returned, he wasn't jealous. Leto put a hand on Casimir's shoulder. "Welcome back, brother."

Casimir reached for Leto as well, so that Leto was caught in the same embrace as Grace. "You've both given me so much, I who deserved nothing. Thank you. And I promise that I will spend the rest of my life atoning for how I hurt each of you."

When Grace drew back, it was Leto who held on to Casimir a little longer. "You saved my life. Repeatedly. I owe you everything. I could not have withstood Julianna's hand-blast. So thank you, Caz."

When Leto finally let him go, Casimir wiped at his face and nodded. "I was just doing my job." But he laughed, and Leto laughed with him.

Grace stood beside them, wondering at this long journey that had brought both amazing men into her life: Leto so deeply fractured by his service and Casimir twisted in his hedonism because of centuries of sexual slavery.

She was moved and content and shaking with the remnants of the obsidian power.

Leto must have felt her trembling, because he slipped both arms around her and held her close. *You were brilliant*, he sent. *Thank you, my beautiful Grace. Thank you for saving him.*

Yes, everything was changing.

When Casimir folded back to the observation deck, he used his Fourth ability and reached out to Patience. He wanted her near him, he wanted to speak with her, he wanted to lay his life before her.

Death had come to him and he'd been spared.

Casimir? He loved her voice in his head. How quickly the *breh-hedden* could make such a small thing as the voice of a woman seen like the most important element of his life, as though his next breath depended on it.

Will you come to me? he returned. *There is something I want to say to you.*

Of course.

He smiled. She hadn't argued; she had simply said, "Of course."

She arrived within minutes, wearing her jeans, just like his jeans. He used to wear leather, but no more. Leather had been all that he'd been allowed to wear for centuries, then later all he'd worn to sustain his seductions. Jeans were so down-to-earth.

She smiled. "You smell like wine, and it's getting to me." But her eyes narrowed and her head tilted. "Something has happened?"

"Your sister just saved my life."

"Grace? How?"

He asked her to sit beside him on the sofa. For the next hour, he told her everything about his life, about his association with Grace, about the redemption pools, about serving Greaves, about Leto, even about his early centuries often chained to a bed and passed from master to master. Everything.

She touched his fingers gently and with compassion. Later she rubbed his arm. She shed tears with him. She kissed his cheek and neck. She embraced him.

She told him about her reckless life, her lack of focus, the dangerous choices she had made over the centuries, then her journey here on Third. "I've never felt I belonged anywhere. And now you're here. I hardly know what to think."

"Will you date me?" he asked. "I mean, the *breh-hedden* will be difficult to withstand anyway. But if it's okay with you, I'd like to date you, go out with you. I don't want to just hop into bed with you."

"I want to apologize for the last time I saw you. I kind of panicked and left you standing at the observation deck." She drew a deep breath. "I'm not good with relationships. I never was. I've often thought it was a warrior kind of thing. I don't know."

"All I've ever known is how to seduce a woman. But I don't want that with you, even though I know the *breh-hedden* would make it so easy."

She nodded. "Tell me about it. All I can think about right now is how to get you out of your jeans."

He laughed, but his expression sobered almost as quickly. "I want you so badly right now that I ache. But I think it would be wonderful to wait. I want you to trust me as I've seen Grace put all her faith in Leto. I haven't been trustworthy for most of my life. I think it's something that has to be earned.

"Also, I intend to complete Beatrice's redemption program. And that will take time."

Patience took his hand. "Casimir, I'd like nothing better than to date you. And I will wait as long as you need me to wait before we share a bed."

Casimir felt his heart open as it never had before. He couldn't believe this was happening to him. He felt as though an angel had taken pity on him, had believed in him, and had given him a method by which he could transform.

Of course, in reality, that angel was Grace.

All the walls had come down. That was the truth that Grace knew as she slid into bed beside Leto. They were back in the villa guest room and wouldn't return to the cabin until the Seattle Colony was safe from Greaves permanently.

Something mysterious and magical had happened during the time that she and Leto had battled Greaves in Leto's cabin. She had passed through some kind of veil that had given her new insight into herself. She had embraced Endelle's ability to live out loud, and Beatrice had helped her to see that by returning as she had to Leto, to serve as obsidian flame, she had already begun the process of becoming real in her life, of giving up her ghost-ways.

Leto, it would seem, had experienced something similar. He was fully present when he looked at her, when he touched her face, as he did now, when he kissed her.

She slid beneath him and parted her legs. She wanted this moment with him more than anything, to have him make love to her with both hearts wide open.

"I love you so much," he whispered.

She looked into his clear blue eyes. Her heart strained toward him. She would never get enough of him, of being this close, of looking at him. "Everything is different now, isn't it?"

He smiled a very soft smile. "Yes. That separation I felt is no longer there. Earlier in my cabin, facing death, somehow I began to see things more clearly, especially my relationship with you. I let go of my holding back. I realized that if I had been fully engaged with you, Grace, if I had shared myself with you in a deeper, more profound way, we probably wouldn't have ended up in that situation."

"I know what you mean. And because of my ghost-ways, I didn't have enough life experience to do battle with Greaves. In that sense, I was as much to blame that the situation devolved as it did. But I'm here now, Leto." She squeezed his buttocks, and his smile broadened.

"Me, too." His gaze fell to her neck, and what do you know, his fangs emerged.

Her back arched.

He smiled a little more. She lifted her hand to touch the sharp tip. She punctured her thumb, then let the blood pool. She slid her thumb into his mouth and let him taste. He closed his eyes and groaned. He pushed his cock up against her hand. She squeezed his crown.

I'm too close, he sent.

She released him, and he shifted his hips. He found her entrance and pushed. She savored both sensations: what it was for him to feel how tight she was as he made his way inside her, and how much pleasure all that pushing gave her.

I love the connection, she sent. *I love being this close to you, feeling you, then enjoying the pleasure you feel. It's extraordinary.*

He moved slightly and began licking her neck above the vein. Her voice caught in sharp little gasps. *Do it, Leto. Please. I'm in agony now because I feel how close you are and now I'm close all over again.*

He struck and began to pull heavily on her neck. *Oh, God, your blood, Grace. It's sweeter than I remember, and the power is heady, a rush everywhere.* He groaned, and she felt that he would change for her, become the beast that she loved, which made her grow lax and smile.

He kept pulling at her neck and making short jabs within her body, but the entire time he swelled and transformed.

She petted his arms and shoulders, relishing the size of him, thrilling at the massive growth of his muscles.

Even his cock was bigger, broader, so that with each new push, she arched in pleasure.

I'm here, he sent. She knew what he meant because his powerful mind was suddenly pushing within hers.

Everything had changed.

That was what she thought the moment Leto pierced her mind.

She surrounded him with her arms and savored. His right hand drifted up her thigh, her waist, and squeezed her breast. She felt tears start to her eyes. She had never felt so possessed, never felt like she belonged so much as she did right now with Leto stretched out on top of her.

She overlaid his hand with her palm and pressed that she might feel the pressure of his hand once more against her breast.

He groaned.

I love you, he sent. It was so different when he was deep within her mind and spoke telepathically, as though his words had resonance. But it was also different because there were no more walls. The intense physical sensations began to blend with all that she felt for him and with all that love that he was pouring into her.

She took his hand and lifted his wrist to her mouth. With the practice of two millennia, she brought her fangs forth and struck.

She felt the piercing because she could feel his external sensations. It hurt yet felt so good at the same time.

His blood hit her tongue and thirst was all she knew. She drank, and somehow the power of his blood eased back the closeness of her orgasm, holding it just offshore. The *breh-hedden* hovered at the edges as well, like last time, yet it all felt so very different because his love was like a constant wave pulsing over her now.

And in the same way, she let her love flow toward him.

Leto, I want to go deep into your soul this time.

Yes, please, yes.

She pushed against his mind, then fell in, because he wanted her there. She dove to the limits of his mind, then fell again through the cloud that separated his soul.

But once inside his soul, it was as though an iridescence surrounded her and covered her—and she knew it was his love, newly birthed in the past few hours. She let him feel her love as well, and the iridescence brightened.

I love you so much, he sent.

Delight filled her, a layer over the physical pleasure, a gentle coloring over the depth of the love that now flowed back and forth, two waves meeting and passing through each other, returning to meet and pass again.

Then suddenly the *breh-hedden* struck, so unexpected, like a wonderful fire that erupted to great heights.

The iridescence burned bright; pleasure filled her deep within her soul, then her mind, then shooting outward to wash in heavy waves over her body. She knew she was screaming, and Leto's cries wrapped around her own, rising high into the sky.

She felt his pleasure as he began to come, which ignited hers. All the years of loneliness and separation burned away in the face of the *breh-hedden,* as though a fire ripped through her and through Leto. On that fire burned, forging a rapture that simply exploded.

She withdrew her fangs. He withdrew his.

"I'm coming again," he cried against her ear. He pumped into her, that great hulk of him, hard and fast and true and honest and beautiful.

She received what he had to give. Her body responded with ecstasy again and again, pleasure flinging her into the stratosphere, waves of heat driving her back to be flung wide again until her screams resounded through the room and his roars could be heard all the way to the edge of the universe.

After a time, she floated back into her body.

She felt him float back into his.

He lay on top of her, sated, beyond sated; she could feel in him the intensity of his satisfaction.

She was moved beyond words as she embraced him. His wing-locks wept. She was damp beneath her back as well.

"The gates of rapture," she said.

"What?"

"It was something I read in one of Beatrice's collections, something like, 'Approach the gates of rapture with wonder, Lay down the past, Then fall.'" She chuckled. "I fell hard."

"Me, too."

Only the deepest, most unexpected changes
Can conquer great evil.

—*Collected Proverbs*, Beatrice of Fourth

CHAPTER 20

The following morning, Endelle stared at James. She sat on her purple couch, her heart now pounding in her chest. "We're that close?"

"Yes," he said. "Very nearly home on this one."

"You really believe that, don't you? That the war against Greaves could be over soon?"

"Yes."

She couldn't believe it.

Thorne had come to her suite a few hours ago to report that obsidian flame had successfully stopped the torching of the colonies. His account had been extraordinary. Adding to the fact that shortly afterward the triad had healed Casimir after Julianna blasted open his stomach, and Endelle couldn't believe her fucking ears.

Grace's return had done this, had created some kind of magical effect on Second Earth. She didn't know how else to think of such a wonderful string of wins for her side.

And now this. James wanted to get Leto ascended within the next couple of hours, because soon afterward Alison would open the portal to Third as had been prophesied from the beginning of her ascension.

"But we have to act quickly," James said. "Greaves is getting very discouraged by all his setbacks, and he's spoiling for war. Wake your people up, then let's get both Alison and Leto over to White Lake. It's time to move things along."

She rose to her feet and called out, "Carla?"

A slight pause, then the security audio system came on. "Yes, Madame Endelle?"

"I need all the WhatBees here to my palace, ceremonial dress, their *brehs* included. Make sure that Alison wears flight gear and obsidian flame as well. Got it?"

"Yes, Madame Endelle."

Leto slung his purple cape over his shoulder. Warrior formality demanded that he wear a traditional brass breastplate over a short black leather tunic. On the breastplate was the emblem of the Warriors of the Blood—a silver sword crowned with a green laurel wreath. He had always thought the emblem simple and quite beautiful, even powerful.

He sat down in the chair near his twig bed and buckled on a sleeker, more formal version of battle sandals.

"You show a lot of thigh in that tunic," Grace said, but she was smiling.

He worked on the last buckle, looking up at her as he gave a final tug. She stood near the entrance to the bathroom, brushing a long curl around her finger, then letting it fall.

"You like?" he asked.

"Can't you tell?"

"Oh, I can tell. Your scent has this room clouded, and I'm not blocking any of your physical sensations." He could feel her nipples pushing against her bra. He took a couple of deep breaths because he was so close to throwing her back on the bed and taking care of business . . . again. But with five minutes left before they were both expected at the palace, he'd run out of time. "You look beautiful, by the way."

"Thank you." She glanced down at her flight suit. "But I feel underdressed for the occasion."

"Carla was adamant," he said, rising to his feet and turning toward her. "Endelle wanted Alison and obsidian flame ready to mount wings if necessary."

"I know, but still. This is your ascension ceremony."

"Sort of an ascension. I wouldn't worry about it." He put his hands on her arms. "And in case you haven't noticed, I'm not complaining about the flight suit at all. It fits your curves perfectly." He drew her close, then ran his hands from her waist over the curve of her bottom.

She laughed. "Now your scent is filling the room."

He released her because he was feeling way too much. "Are you ready to go?"

She folded her brush away and nodded.

He put his hands on her arms once more and thought the thought.

Grace arrived at the landing platform in the palace and was immediately overwhelmed by the sight of all the warriors dressed in the same garb as Leto. They were gathered in small knots, just talking, but they were a massive physical presence given their height and general physique.

She had known these men for a long time, some of them her entire life—like Marcus and of course Leto. Others had come later: Kerrick, Luken, Santiago, Medichi, and Zacharius. Jean-Pierre was the youngest, having ascended out of France during the revolution years.

And Thorne was one of the men as well.

They looked magnificent, all powerful, muscular warriors, the shortest six-five.

James appeared in the doorway and called out, "Ah, the man of the hour. Leto."

So, this was to be an ascension ceremony attended by a Sixth ascender. That was a surprise. His appearance brought a knot to Grace's stomach. Something was going on, something big.

He waved everyone forward. "The ladies are in the central rotunda, and we'll have the ceremony in there. If you'll come with me."

James led the way. Casimir, as Leto's Guardian of Ascension, was already present and stood near Endelle. The warriors who were bonded joined their *brehs*. Luken, Zach, and Santiago stuck together, the last bastion of bachelorhood in their small group.

Moving to stand near the terrace, James waved Grace and Leto forward. She stood off to Leto's right, a foot back as was the usual position for those supporting the ascendate.

James took his place in front of the terrace.

In a typical ascension ceremony, the officiate would offer thoughts on service to the dimension, usually reading from a book. In this case, James began very differently as he addressed Leto outright.

"Your ascension, Leto, as I'm sure you've noticed, is very different from the usual process since you've not been *called* as an ascender. You'd normally be called by the appearance of dreams detailing the new world and longings for a different life. The only aspect that resembles a typical ascension is that you've developed the ability to morph like a Third Earth warrior. Would you agree that all of this is true?"

"Yes, absolutely."

James drew a deep breath. "That's because you're not officially ascending to Third Earth."

At that, Leto turned and met Grace's gaze. She saw relief in his eyes. They had both been worried about what would happen if he actually did ascend to Third.

James smiled as Leto turned back to him. "There will be no disruption of your *breh-hedden*, you may trust me in this. Sixth wouldn't have allowed it. But I digress. There is a specific purpose in your ascension. We need you to take over my role as the gatekeeper of Third Earth. My duties call me elsewhere, and I'm not allowed to make war in your dimension, to use force to protect the gate. And we feel it's necessary for the securing of peace on Second Earth that a warrior be stationed at this critical gateway."

This pronouncement brought a hum through the group. Grace had no idea what Leto would do as a gatekeeper or why it was necessary at all.

Endelle stepped forward. "I don't understand, Shorty. I

thought Alison would be opening the portal and we'd have access to Third Earth society, customs, even their wisdom and knowledge."

"You should know by now that nothing in the ascended world is simple. One day I'm sure that the sharing of cultures will happen and that this will be true among all six dimensions. But right now we have to deal with a situation that Greaves has caused. It needs to be locked down before we can go further."

"What situation with Greaves?" Endelle asked, her voice sharp.

"The commander created an invisible breach in the portal to Third that has allowed him to bring Third Earth death vampires through at will *and* without you or your warriors aware of what he's been doing."

Endelle frowned. "Somehow I thought Greaves had found a way to create those vampires himself, making his usual squads bigger and better. It never occurred to me that they really were from Third Earth. Not that I could have done anything about it had I known."

"Exactly. Their origin would have changed nothing. But the real danger is simple: Greaves is ready to bring a hundred such vampires through the breach in the portal as soon as he engages you in what we believe will be the forthcoming battle over White Lake. Not even you could have fought a contingent of that size; they would have decimated your Warriors of the Blood. You would have lost the war that fast."

This brought a number of heated expletives from all the warriors against Greaves and his machinations.

But it was Leto who asked the next logical question. "So are you saying that by opening the portal and sealing the breach, we end the possibility of Greaves sneaking these bastards through during a battle against him?"

"Precisely. The portal will once again be secured—but it will need to be guarded by a warrior. May I ask if you are willing to accept the assignment?"

"There is no question. Of course, I accept. But what will it entail? Will I reside on Third?"

"No, on Second, but the ascension that I initiate here to-day will give you a permanent mind-link with the portal. You will be alerted when anyone approaches, no matter which dimension, and because of the demand inherent in the mind-link, you will need to respond to each approach. Are you willing to engage in a mind-link of this sort?"

Grace felt the sudden tension in Leto's thighs, back, and neck. She understood his reaction. He had served as a spy for a century, always at Greaves's beck and call as well as James's. Now he would be bound, or so it would seem, to the portal, with no real guarantee how easy or how pressing that duty would be.

But she also knew Leto's character, the essential element of his warrior's soul. Above all things, Leto was a man of duty, something he would always do and something she treasured about him. She was not surprised when the tension eased from the same parts of his body and he said, "I am willing."

James smiled and even approached Leto to reach up and clap him on the shoulder. James couldn't have been more than five-eight, so he had a ways to reach. "Good man," he said quietly. "And I'll always be there, Leto, to be of service to you. This isn't a duty we would expect you to perform without our being available to you at will."

"I'm grateful for that," Leto said.

James stepped back to his original position and added, "There is an observation deck as well as living quarters at the portal, which you will have access to at any time." His expression softened. "I confess that when certain political situations on Sixth Earth became *irritating,* I would stay in the portal suite for weeks at a time, at least until my temper cooled. But you will see the situation for yourself before the morning is out. Or you can ask Casimir. He has been staying there while he served as your guardian. And of course Grace can accompany you whenever you wish as well. Does all of this sound acceptable to you?"

Leto nodded.

Grace released a deep breath. Leto could remain on

Second Earth and as needed she could travel to the portal with him. She had been uneasy from the time that Casimir had shown up and made it clear he was serving as Leto's guardian.

James made the rest of the ceremony very simple. He offered a brief prayer to the Creator, wishing many blessings for Leto in the coming decades. He then placed his hands on the sides of Leto's head and essentially installed the mind-link.

Leto felt the weight of his new responsibility, but for some reason he didn't feel burdened as he had in times past. Instead, something inside him now rose to the challenge. He glanced at Grace and smiled. She had done this for him, her acceptance of him and her belief in him. Her love had made all things possible.

James ended the ceremony by extending his arms into the air to encompass everyone in the room. "And may the Creator grant each of you strength in the coming hours to fulfill each given destiny. So be it."

"So be it" passed around the group, and a moment of silence rested upon the rotunda.

After at least a minute had passed, Endelle asked James what was next on the agenda.

James went straight to Alison and took her hands. "The time has come to open the portal to Third."

Leto glanced at the woman he had fought in the Tolleson Two arena. And now both of them had a connection to the portal.

"With Stannett out of the way," Endelle began, "we have a slight advantage in the future streams. I want to see a block set up, on Alison's behalf, so that as much of the opening of the portal as possible will be kept shielded from Greaves. We know that he's had some of the best Seers in the world under his command. I don't want to assume that just because Stannett is gone, we're home free."

"Agreed," Thorne added. He glanced his *breh*.

Marguerite smiled. "I'll get on it." She reached within her flight suit pocket and withdrew her phone. Leto heard her make the arrangements with her Seer teams.

Everything seemed to be coming together, except for one small thing. Leto felt sure that Greaves had something else up his sleeve, something unexpected that could still turn the tide of war against Endelle. However, he kept that suspicion to himself. Even if it was true, what could anyone do about it at this late hour?

He turned to James. "So what's our timing here? Do you know?"

James smiled. "You'll leave for White Lake in fifteen minutes." His gaze slid over the group. "Warriors will want to change into flight battle gear. Obsidian flame will serve in support of Alison." He turned to Thorne. "You'll want to have Colonel Seriffe shut down all the hotels and gardens for the morning. Declare a state of emergency."

Thorne immediately whipped his phone from his tunic pocket. Turning away from the group, he let Seriffe know what was happening.

To Endelle, James said, "I'm not allowed to be present, but I will be watching."

Endelle retired to her sitting room for a few minutes just to gather her thoughts, even to savor what was happening. My God, it looked like everything was all but settled, or would be within the next few hours, especially since Greaves would be denied his Third Earth death vampires.

After all these centuries, everything was moving so fast and at each step along the way, over the past few days, Greaves has steadily lost ground. Half his army was gone, and he'd failed to destroy either the colonies or obsidian flame. With the breach repaired, he would lose another part of his strategy as well.

Yet even as she wanted to exult in this turn of events, this narrowing down of Greaves's chances to actually win this war, she couldn't. The bastard had never fought fair, not one day of his fucking ambitious life. What if he'd saved his best for last, something unknown and therefore unpredicted.

Still, her adrenaline was flowing.

The end truly was near—or at the very least a major battle that would change the face of things on Second Earth.

She heard the door to her suite close.

She turned and there was Braulio, the vampire who had been her lover a few millennia ago, who had served once as the leader of the Warriors of the Blood and who had supposedly died in her arms but magically returned to chap her ass over the past few months. He was somehow connected with James in this whole mess with Greaves and more than once had tormented her by sinking his tongue into her mouth, which made her want him to sink other things as well.

He wore a dark blue silk shirt and tailored slacks. His belt had a silver buckle with a scorpion detail.

She smiled. An homage, no doubt. She rose to her feet.

He moved toward her, looking her up and down. "I thought you'd be wearing squid tentacles or clamshells today."

"Sorry to disappoint."

His smile was crooked and all male. "A snug black-leather flight suit becomes you."

She reached up and touched the scars at the back of her neck. She saw his gaze follow the movement, and she got a sick-gut feeling. "Aw shit," she said. "You're here to tell me what you did to me."

He nodded. "It's time. Like everything else right now."

He moved in close and slid a hand up and down her arm. "First, I want you to know that I'm sorry that I did this against your will. I hated doing it, but I was under orders. And in this case I actually agreed with the decision because I believe it will save your life."

"Ominous."

"It is." He'd never looked more serious, which increased her uneasiness.

"Spill it, asshole. The suspense is killing me."

"A lot of nasty shit has come out of Third Earth, including experiments with viruses built just for vampires. Greaves has that virus living in him. And now you do as well."

She thought for a minute. "Are you saying you put a virus in me?"

He nodded. His eyes narrowed, but he didn't add to his announcement.

Then she understood. "You gave me the virus by biting deep into my spinal cord."

"It's the best delivery method."

Her breathing shifted, and her face grew hot. She listed on her feet.

He kept her upright, but she pushed him away and sat down again. She rubbed her neck and felt ready to weep like a baby. But something else occurred to her. She snapped her head in his direction.

He moved to sit on the coffee table in front of her and planted his hands on her knees. He met her gaze dead-on.

"If you gave me the virus," she said, "then you have it, too."

He nodded.

She sat back in her chair. "Before you tell me what the ramifications of this virus are, I need to know how you got the virus."

"I volunteered. I wasn't about to inject you with something that I didn't understand."

She put a hand to her chest. What the fuck had he done to himself? To her? And why was it so damn important?

Endelle had lived a long time, but everything that had ever happened to her had been her choice, not forced on her by another ascender. Even becoming the Supreme High Administrator of Second Earth had been an assignment she'd agreed to. Of course Luchianne had put her in a headlock, but still Endelle had said yes.

"So what does this virus do?"

"The upside is that you can shape-shift, or morph if you like, into any biological form you like, you can add appendages, you can change your DNA and grow things like claws."

"Greaves has a claw he brings out on his left hand."

Braulio nodded.

"Well, so far so good, but I take it there's a downside."

"A big one. Have you ever noticed that Greaves's left hand is a just a little weak?"

"Yes, I've seen that. I figured it had to do with the claw."

"It does. Changes become permanent."

Endelle took a long moment to digest this aspect of the virus. She thought of herself, of becoming something different. She also thought of Greaves. "So is he some kind of crab monster because of that claw of his?"

"I don't know. He may only have experimented with the claw."

Endelle looked away from his dark blue eyes and the compassion she saw within them.

"Do you have changes that are permanent?"

"I have one."

"Can I see it?"

"You've seen it repeatedly."

She wrinkled her nose. "Is that a double entendre?" She glanced at his crotch—then her brows rose. "So you can change the DNA, huh?"

He rolled his eyes. "My cock is big enough as it is, as you well know."

Yeah, she knew, and thoughts of that powerful aspect of his anatomy, despite the dark nature of their present conversation, sent shivers down her neck. "You're right. You're plenty big."

He smiled and looked very male as he nodded.

"So, what's this other form of yours?"

He didn't say anything. He just changed.

Her mouth dropped open. "Shorty?"

Light blue eyes twinkled at her.

"Well, I'll be damned. So you were serious that one time you told me you could be anything I wanted you to be."

"Pretty much."

A moment later, James began to disappear, and Braulio re-formed. James was Braulio, and Braulio was James.

"Holy shit. Well, this isn't so bad. And, hey, Thorne can morph like this."

"Unfortunately, there's a big difference," he said, sitting on the coffee table again. "I have to become James at least once a week to release that part of my altered DNA, or I start to go insane. This is always true, for me and for you. For Greaves as well."

"So, if you don't like the form you take, too bad, you're stuck with it?"

"Exactly."

"But why did you choose 'James' then, for an alternate shape?"

"A lot of reasons. James is a harmless persona and has served me well in approaching Alison, for instance, while she was in her rite of ascension. I've also served more recently as the gatekeeper to Third Earth in James's form. Again, the less threatening shape has given me a strong advantage when challenged by powerful Third Earth entities."

"You've battled on Third Earth?"

He shrugged. "*Battled* isn't quite the right word since I'm not allowed to battle. I argue and threaten, and when provoked, I offer a display of power that is sufficient to turn away any Third aggressor."

"You've been busier than I thought."

"I do my part."

"But now I have this virus. I suppose next you'll tell me this has something to do with the little peach."

Braulio dipped his chin. "And the ability within the next hour to become whatever you need to be in order to survive."

"The next hour," she repeated. She didn't ask him to explain. She knew. She felt it in her bones. She'd be facing off with Greaves over White Lake, probably not long after Alison worked her magic with the Third portal.

She stood up and held his gaze for a long moment. "You going to tell me how this battle ends?"

"We've seen several outcomes. But I'm not allowed to interfere and I won't. Just take everything I've said into consideration. I'm sure right now Greaves is plotting what to do with his morphing ability."

"Fuck."

His expression grew even more serious. "Exactly."

Then he smiled, and before she knew what he intended, he blurred toward her, took her in his arms, and kissed her. She didn't fight him this time because she was a woman going into battle and she wanted the feel of his arms around her.

His voice was suddenly in her head with resonance. *Endelle, Endelle, Endelle.* He kept whispering her name until her lips parted.

He groaned heavily as he pierced her mouth and began plunging his tongue into her just the way she liked it, the way she remembered him doing all those millennia ago.

Sweet Christ, the vampire had her number. His hands roved her flight suit. She was just about to fold the suit away, or tell him to rip it off her, when Braulio drew back.

"Sorry, sweetheart. Time to rumble."

Greaves stood in his peach orchard and flexed his claw. He held several Seers reports in his right hand and alternately moved from reading them to snapping his claw, then trying to figure out his next step. And back again.

He might not have Stannett's help anymore, but the reports out of Mumbai and Johannesburg were similar enough to give credence that a war-changing battle would take place over White Lake this morning.

He had already informed his generals and ordered his special death vampire regiment to be ready to fold at his command.

These elements were clear in the future streams: an army at the ready, and a death vamp force poised to engage in battle. According to the Seers reports, he would soon be flying over the lake, with his death vampires supporting him, and engaging his number one foe all these years: Endelle.

Yet in the past several days, he'd lost so much ground that he felt as though the pavers beneath his feet were made of quicksand. He'd started sinking when Grace returned, and the more he'd tried to pull himself out of the quagmire, the faster he'd gotten dragged under.

He still couldn't believe that he had failed to destroy the colonies. Somehow he hadn't imagined obsidian flame being able to stop the burning away of Diallo's interconnected mist—yet the triad had done exactly that.

He shuddered. The dark wave of his future was still pounding him, despite the care he had taken to gain every advantage in his bid for world domination.

He still had two serious advantages in hand. The first was his secret force of Third Earth death vampires that he would be moving very soon through the breach in the portal. The other was his ability to shape-shift. The latter, however, had a serious drawback in that whatever choice he made would be permanent. Whatever he decided to become in the next few hours, he'd be forced to continue each week for the rest of his life. Yet these two elements had the possibility all by themselves of wresting Second Earth permanently away from Endelle and her allies.

The claw had been an experiment, but it had fit with his lifestyle, since he liked to do a lot of hurting when he made love.

However, a claw was one small, manageable appendage. If he chose, during this battle to risk everything by engaging Endelle at last mano a mano, then he might just have to choose a larger form that guaranteed a win against her but would be an unfortunate choice for a weekly transformation.

The only question that remained was simple: How badly did he want to win this war?

When he folded back to his Estrella Complex, he found his generals clustered around the largest screen at the end of the room.

Greaves got an uneasy feeling. "What's going on?" he called out.

His aide moved toward him quickly. "We're not sure. Parts of White Lake have disappeared from view."

Mist. Then he felt it. Endelle's mist. Fuck.

He glanced at the papers in hand. Nothing had been prophesied about this. So what the hell was going on that he didn't know about? What critical information had Marguerite's teams blocked from him in the future streams.

He felt the quicksand around his ankles again. Maybe he'd been hasty in killing Stannett after all.

* * *

As Alison floated in the air just above the blue-green waters of White Lake, she realized that the dreams she'd had of the lake had shifted over time. But perhaps that was a reflection of the nature of life. Paths were chosen and discarded. The journey branched and new roads were taken.

One dream had showed her backed by nearly twenty women; opposite the women were almost twenty warriors at Warrior of the Blood status.

But in recent days the dream had changed to involve obsidian flame, one of the most powerful elements to have emerged in Endelle's administration ever.

As she flapped her emerald wings and set her gaze above her, the blue vortex appeared. Kerrick floated opposite her, a protective presence, her original Guardian of Ascension. His white wings were magnificent in the midday light. Imagine vampires living fully beneath a strong desert sunshine.

Leto floated beside Kerrick, ready to assume his duties as the new gatekeeper to Third. Her throat grew tight looking at him, so different now. He was deeply fulfilled and more powerful than ever. She knew that look. Kerrick had become this man when he'd completed the *breh-hedden* with her, more determined than ever to do his duty and to be all that he could be.

She remembered her battle with Leto, how frightened she'd been at the impossible task of fighting a Warrior of the Blood with three thousand years of experience. Kerrick had downloaded his battle memories—that was one of the reasons she'd won the battle. The other reason had been more complex: She had relied on her own gifts and abilities so that in the end she had defeated Leto and saved his life, by reversing a pocket of time and creating shields that his sword could not penetrate.

Now she was here, a vampire and a *breh,* executive assistant to Madame Endelle, and saddled with the ominous task of opening the gateway to Third Earth. She was a healer of the mind and had been during her adult years on Mortal Earth.

She could see the blue vortex now swirling above her,

calling to her as though from the time of her ascension the portal had been living inside her, a task to fulfill when the time called.

James had explained what needed to be done, yet how strange to think that she was the one to do it, of all ascenders, the youngest, the least experienced.

Her nerves, however, felt like a car with the revs too high. She took numerous deep breaths.

Behind her, obsidian flame waited to support her.

Finally, she felt the timing was exactly right. She turned and nodded to Grace.

This was it.

Grace had already dipped within Endelle's soul and acquired her levitation ability.

Alison felt obsidian flame's power come to life behind her. She rose in the air and a moment later she was speeding toward the vortex, a stream of power lifting her up and propelling her at the same time.

She opened her mind, focusing on the portal to Third. She spread her arms wide and, as though the portal had always been part of her, she held her power open.

She then invited Grace to enter her soul and to acquire the same ability to connect with the portal.

Grace dove within, which made Alison smile because the woman had incredible gentleness as her blue flame power slipped into Alison's soul. She could feel the slight pressure deep within as Grace found the lock to her portal ability, inserted her preternatural blue flame key, and acquired the same ability.

A moment later, Grace departed, leaving behind a strange emptiness. Grace then sent, *What would you have us do?*

Alison took a deep breath. She knew instinctively what needed to be done, so she returned, *Do what you normally do. When the triad feels the need to connect with the portal, just let the power flow.*

Understood.

Alison waited, but it couldn't have been more than seconds before she could feel the rumbling beneath her. The obsidian power began to stream like a vast wave of energy, moving through Alison and past her, amplifying the connection to the portal until a slivery stream of light shot in the direction of the gateway.

The result was music, like a heavenly choir humming the most beautiful harmony she had ever heard. The music swirled around her and through her. She cried out in a kind of spiritual ecstasy.

The blue vortex spun faster and faster and suddenly blossomed, for she could describe it no other way. She could feel that the portal was opening—and at the same time she could also see the breach that Greaves apparently had created to bring his Third Earth death vampires through.

Though it has not been my privilege to travel to either
Fifth Earth or Sixth, it has been the experience of
my several millennia as an ascended being that the truism
The grass is always greener has never been more
accurate than in our dimensional world.

—*Memoirs,* Beatrice of Fourth

CHAPTER 21

Greaves reached White Lake in time to see Alison, supported by obsidian flame, open the portal to Third. He saw the breach he had created with his own substantial power now fully exposed.

He tried to fold his death vampires through at that moment, but he couldn't reach them.

Then the worst happened as the breach sealed itself, reforming with the now open portal, a beautiful blue blossoming aperture ready to move ascenders freely between the two dimensions.

Again, he located his hundred and tried to fold them, but then he felt it, a Sixth ascender blocking Third. At almost the same time, the portal began to close up.

"No," he screamed long and loud, so that waves of energy pulsed from his body, radiating in a large circle around him.

Alison hadn't just opened the portal as his Seers had foreseen over a year ago. She had closed it as well, allowing no breach, no means by which he could continue to secure Third Earth death vampires.

He watched as obsidian flame and Alison began to sink slowly back to earth, back into Endelle's mist.

When Greaves understood that he would be unable to bring his force through the now healed portal, he knew that his last chance at winning this war without invoking his virus-based morphing ability had just disappeared.

He folded back to Estrella.

All his generals and aides turned toward him, waiting. For a long moment, he couldn't speak the words. He was stunned at what had just happened.

Finally, he told his staff the truth. The elevated spirits began to dissipate, just like his own. He would change that in a moment, but even he needed time to digest the ugly reality that he would not have his Third Earth force with him today.

At last, he waved a hand over his body. He changed from his elegant Hugo Boss suit into very basic black sweatpants and nothing more.

His generals backed up. He could see the shock, even the disapproval on their faces, so of course he had to give them a small demonstration of things to come. He let his claw emerge.

He smiled as the same group took another step back.

"Don't worry, my friends. All is not lost."

He then closed his eyes, and oiled up his body, top to bottom, in order to facilitate the coming change.

"I want a formal presentation at once," he ordered.

His generals fell into line, each now restored to composure, eyes intense and focused on him.

"All begins and ends here," he said, his voice filling the space with a faint resonance, nothing to harm his men this time but sufficient to build determination within each soul.

He glanced from face to face, warriors all, each having given himself fully to the Coming Order.

Greaves was not a man of sentiment, but he moved forward and went from man to man, cupping each at the back of the neck with his palm. No words were spoken as he passed down the line.

When he was done, he stood back and said simply, "You have your orders."

The line broke as each man moved to his station in the

room to sit before a computer screen and to monitor the ranks under his command. If so moved during events at White Lake, he would order an outright attack.

As it stood, however, mobilizing the entire army served no purpose since Leto had stolen half his force. For the moment, Greaves had lost the military advantage he'd worked so diligently to create, but he saw no sense in expending warriors when he might have need of them later. If during the coming battle he actually failed, he would fold to his Geneva stronghold, recover, then rebuild.

He had made his decision about how he would morph during the coming battle. He would hold nothing back. By the rules of war, approved by COPASS, both he and Endelle could do their worst.

And so he would.

He was therefore taking a small contingent to White Lake, not even a full regiment, just five hundred seasoned death vampires. They were an exquisite force of pretty-boys, all with blue-tinged skin and glossy black feathers when in flight. His force, if nothing else, would be a beautiful, terrifying sight to behold.

With him, he also had his diminished squad of three remaining Third Earth death vampires from the original lot he had snuck through the breach in the portal over the past six months. The majority had already died—some at the hands of Thorne five months ago in Moscow Two, and the rest more recently because of Casimir and Leto's combined efforts.

When an aide called out that the mist from White Lake had just disappeared, Greaves bid his generals to await his orders, then folded to his landing platform at the mouth of the vast Estrella Mountain underground barracks. His death vampires stood in formation, lovely to behold in black kilts and maroon weapons harnesses. He'd ordered his own form of the *cadroen*, so that his men presented a uniform appearance.

He smiled. Using a form of mass telepathy, he communicated in a firm mental voice, *Today we vanquish our enemy.*

As one, each right fist pumped the air and a deafening battle cry filled the cavern.

Endelle stood on the bank of White Lake, her mist withdrawn. She felt deeply sobered by watching Alison fulfill a destiny that Alison had predicted at the time of her ascension. Obsidian flame, Leto, Thorne, Kerrick, and Alison flew toward her, and landed one after the other in an arc in front of her.

Each ascender was equally sobered, as though in some mystical way, they knew as a group that what happened next would be pivotal.

By prior agreement, she folded everyone to the Apache Junction Two landing platforms. Once down the ramp, she turned, let the group gather around her once more, and ordered obsidian flame to use Marguerite's Seer ability to have a look at White Lake.

Fiona, Marguerite, and Grace faced one another. Endelle could feel the power flow from deep in the earth. Thorne stood near them, ready to anchor all that power as needed.

Endelle knew the moment when Marguerite entered the future streams; it was as though a switch clicked. The same switch got flipped again as Marguerite withdrew. But her face was pinched, and her eyes wide, as she met Endelle's gaze.

Endelle knew that Marguerite had seen something about the battle that horrified her. She had a split-second decision to make about what the group should know and finally called out to Marguerite, "Come here and show me what you've seen. Just me, do you understand?"

She nodded and moved past the other two women to reach up and put her hands on Endelle's face. Marguerite let the vision flow.

When Endelle watched the images pass by in a swift wave, she watched the nature of her own transformation. She saw Greaves as well. She didn't understand how her new form could battle his and possibly win. She was still herself, except without flight gear, and her wings had changed, morphing to enormous, ethereal, floating panels without feathers; more butterfly than bird. Her hair floated in a mass of iridescent pastel shades. Her naked body, while still very female, also bore what looked like a flame pattern of the same pastel shades and very iridescent. The effect was beautiful but not exactly the lethal presence she would need to defeat a monster.

In the vision she flew in Greaves's direction; then the prophetic images faded to nothing. Was she flying to her doom? Because Greaves looked like a man now covered in impenetrable plates like a medieval knight, yet made up of his biological material.

She squeezed her eyes shut for a long moment absorbing what she had seen.

She simply couldn't believe what would be required of her or how the form she had chosen could actually battle Greaves.

When she opened her eyes, she drew a deep breath and told Marguerite to remain silent and not to share the images with anyone.

"Endelle," Thorne called out. "This isn't right. You should tell everyone."

"Perhaps I should," she said, straightening her shoulders. "But there is part of the vision that concerns only me, which I intend to keep private between me and Marguerite. The rest, however, I can communicate, but I want all the Warriors of the Blood in the folding hangar as quickly as possible, in flight gear, their *brehs* with them."

Thorne got on his com and started barking orders one after the other.

Endelle didn't wait to watch anyone arrive. She turned instead and walked in the direction of the hangar.

Once through the broad doorway, she inclined her head to Gideon, who stood on the elevated command platform that overlooked the enormous room. She noted the tension in his eyes and in his stance.

Everyone felt the proximity of battle.

She moved to stand near the extensive folding platforms, her back to the room. She could feel her elite force arriving

one after the other, as well as Havily and Parisa, who were
bonded with Marcus and Medichi.

When everyone had arrived, she turned around—and the
sight took her breath away. All nine of her beloved Warriors
of the Blood, all in battle gear and ready for war, waited for
her, shoulders back, spines straight, eyes alert.

These were her warriors, the men who had been with her
for centuries, battling death vampires at the five major Borderlands in the Phoenix Metro Two area. Her throat felt
tight, her eyes burned, her heart ached.

Each had suffered while striving to do right by Second
Earth, to keep mortals and ascenders safe from the killing
inherent in the soul of the death vampires.

She loved them all, but she wondered if her warriors
knew how much she valued them. She let her gaze move
from one to the next, starting with Kerrick who had bonded
with Alison, the first of the men to be struck down by the
breh-hedden. Marcus was next, his slash of brows over
light brown eyes. He gripped Havily's hand. Medichi was
the tallest, his arm tight around Parisa's shoulders. Jean-
Pierre, as was his habit, stood behind Fiona, his arms
wrapped around her; Fiona's head cradled against his neck
and shoulder.

Thorne leaned down, saying something tender in Marguerite's ear. She smiled up at him and kissed him.

Leto met Endelle's gaze and gave a brisk nod, his arm
hooked around Grace's. Luken stood next to Grace, one of
three remaining unbonded warriors. He had the biggest
shoulders she had ever seen, bigger than even Braulio's. He
was her new leader of the Warriors of the Blood, having re-
placed Thorne.

Zacharius, with his thick curly hair that drove the women
wild, smiled crookedly. Santiago stood next to him with all
his Latin charm, flipping a ruby-studded dagger.

Her men.

Her warriors.

"Madame Endelle," Gideon called out.

She turned toward him and nodded.

"I just received word that Greaves and a large contingent of death vampires are now in flight over White Lake, just beneath the Trough to Third Earth."

Her heart rate kicked into high gear. "Do we have visuals?"

"Coming." Gideon spoke quietly into his com. He tapped on his computer keyboard and a moment later the huge screen behind him came to life.

The visual left nothing to the imagination. In a vast line, from the vortex and gathered in row upon row to the south, were hundreds of death vampires, the bright sun of the desert glittering off the gloss of their wings and exposing the pale skin tinged with blue. Each wore a maroon weapons harness, the signature color for Greaves's army.

Greaves led the parade, but he hadn't mounted his wings. He merely levitated at the head of his force and he seemed to be wearing only a pair of pants. His body gleamed with oil, which confirmed what she and Marguerite had seen in the future streams.

Greaves would change shape, and she would be forced to as well. She would have to morph into something that had a chance of subduing what Greaves would become.

"Dear Creator," she whispered.

And for the first time in millennia, Endelle knew fear. She could hear her warriors murmuring.

Thorne drew close to her. She met his gaze and asked, "What do you suggest?"

"We'll need a Militia Warrior force five times that size."

Endelle saw the glitter in his eyes. "You have the force ready, don't you?"

Thorne met her gaze and smiled. "Damn straight I do."

"And you'll need healers on the banks and Militia Warriors in speedboats to pull the wounded out of the water and get them to shore." Wings could easily get caught in water and drown an ascender.

At that, Thorne smiled. "Already done. They're a mile from the vortex, in a flotilla ready to engage."

Endelle shook her head. "I keep forgetting that you've been planning every contingency for months." She drew a deep breath and said, "You have command of obsidian flame. Do with them what you see fit on every level. I know they're not warriors so if you can help it, don't put them into battle. Find some way to use them that will support me or your troops."

"I agree wholeheartedly."

"Then let's do this thing. Let's see if we can't finish off that bastard right now."

But Thorne took her arm gently in his. To her mind, he sent, *I saw the vision as well. It flowed into my head as Marguerite saw it. I could also sense that there was something permanent about the change, unlike what I am able to do when I morph. Are you sure you have to do this thing?*

Yes, Braulio explained it to me.

He searched her eyes, *I'm so sorry that this is on you, Endelle. You deserve so much better. Regardless, I've got your back.*

Endelle nodded. *I know.* Just his nearness calmed her fears. *Thank you.*

After Braulio had told her the difficult truth about her new ability, she had known she was facing one of the toughest moments of her life, to choose to become something she would have to morph into the rest of her ascended life.

But the hour was too late for regrets or for making other decisions. There was nothing to be done or to be undone. Apparently Greaves was going all-in, pushing his last chip onto the table and expecting to win because of his little secret.

Of course, he had no way of knowing what Braulio had done to her.

As she pondered the vision of herself in her altered state, she wondered why the hell she would have chosen something that looked so vulnerable. A ruse of some kind?

Then she remembered something about scorpions. Some carried a poison that could kill a human being but couldn't harm a cat. She thought about adding a fine stinger tail to what would otherwise be a quite beautiful transformation, but the vision hadn't included anything like that, just an odd almost continual shedding of perspiration, probably to keep the wings flexible. If nothing else, she would be quick in the air, much more agile than with her usual wings.

She gave her orders and with obsidian flame, including Thorne, backing her up, as well as her Warriors of the Blood, she folded to White Lake. She now levitated in the air fifty yards from Greaves. And because Thorne had built the army, and had made sure his force drilled a variety of maneuvers every day, she could sense her force move into place behind her: twenty-five hundred seasoned Militia Warriors, male and female.

Greaves was suddenly in her mind, busting past her mental shields, a reminder that the bastard had power. *You can surrender now and live,* he sent.

There was resonance and force behind his words, as though he shouted into a canyon. His voice hurt.

She sent back her favorite phrase, however, and added her own resonance. *Fuck you.*

With pleasure, she watched Greaves list, ever so slightly, midair.

A faint mist suddenly surrounded Greaves, and Endelle knew the time had come to morph. Her throat grew tight as she also swirled her mist. She got rid of her flight suit, took a deep breath, then let the morphing begin.

The physical ache returned from the time Braulio had first infected her with the virus, deep in her muscles and bones, as everything began to stretch and reshape. She kept the future stream image firmly in mind and, despite the pain, allowed the new being to come forth from her body.

But dear Creator, help her to understand how this shape could slay a monster?

Thorne saw Endelle's mist, as well as Greaves's. He knew what was transpiring, though he could hardly believe the transformations that would take place. At the same time, he had to get his army poised for battle.

He turned to face what was essentially a full regiment of twenty-five hundred warriors, which meant five warriors against every death vampire, a necessary equation. He touched his com and spoke to his twenty-five Section Leaders, each of whom had charge of a hundred men and women.

Like a ballet corps, the force split vertically, forming five layers, one above the next, in the air, thirty feet between each layer so that Thorne's gaze now traveled up and up.

Wings flapped sustaining positions. He spoke again, and the force now spread across the width of White Lake, bank to bank, another means of allowing for battle maneuver.

He glanced at both sides of the lake and noted how the hotels and gardens were completely empty of people. Colonel Seriffe had done his job well and evacuated everyone against the battle now shaping up on the lake.

He turned to face Endelle once more and saw in the distance that Greaves had completed his transformation and was hovering near the surface of the water. According to the vision, the battle between Endelle and Greaves would take place just above the surface.

Thorne extended his vision to see Greaves better.

Jesus H. Christ. The monster had become more of himself but with what looked like a biological suit of armor. He was twice Greaves's normal size. His face was still there, but his body had heavy plates that could probably withstand hand-blast capacity. He looked physically powerful. If Thorne could guess, then blow for blow Endelle would have to become something similar to be able to battle him, and according to the future streams, she would not be anything close.

Endelle's mist evaporated and what emerged was like something from a massive chrysalis: an angelic butterfly that glittered beneath the sun. Thorne had to put a hand up to shield his eyes. It was as though she were covered in gems that reflected the light.

She was so beautiful.

Though he had a sinking sensation that what she had chosen to become could never battle a fully armored Greaves, he thought wryly that Endelle had created one helluva spectacle costume, something that must have pleased her soul.

As he saw Greaves's death vampire force—and because

Endelle had given him complete command of the army—he made a quick decision.

He touched his com and ordered his regiment to perform one of his favorite drills, a massive group flight, at an angle rising into the air in order to achieve a superior advantage over the enemy.

A split second later, his Militia Warriors, *as a unit*, began to flap every shade of wing imaginable at an upward angle that within less than a minute, if unimpeded, would place them above Greaves's death vampire force.

He marveled at the sight his force presented, flying in perfect formation as a well-practiced regiment could do, up and up, still stacked five high, still the breadth of the lake below.

As they passed overhead, moving between him and the direct sight line of the sun, shadows rippled over him.

Pride swelled his heart.

Whatever the results of the forthcoming battle, he would never forget this moment as long as he lived.

He tapped a second com and reached Luken. "There are three Third Earth death vampires behind Greaves. Only your warriors will be able to take them. As soon as Endelle engages Greaves, attack only those vamps."

"Understood, boss."

Thorne smiled. How many times had he heard Luken call him "boss" while he had been the leader. A hundred? A thousand? More than that, no doubt.

He knew when Luken had communicated with the warriors, because as another unified group, they launched high into the air, but still below the Militia Warriors that were now almost in place.

Greaves's force remained static, submissive to his will. But he had apparently been so focused on Endelle that he'd failed to observe Thorne's maneuvers. When several shadows passed over him, he looked up and seemed to weave in the air for a moment as though surprised.

He must have issued orders, because his pretty-boys suddenly began an upward drive in the direction of the now descending Militia Warrior force. A few seconds later, the battle in the air began as swords clashed and maroon-vested death vampires began fighting squads of Militia Warriors.

Thorne turned to face north and could see the flotilla in the distance. He touched his com and spoke with Horace, directing him to begin an approach; the battle had commenced and healers would be needed soon.

As for obsidian flame, he pivoted in the air and said, "I want you to stay back with Horace and the support line of warriors. If you're needed, I will call you forward. But even Endelle would prefer that you remain separate from the battle."

The women nodded gravely. But it was his sister who drew close and said, "If you need us to fight, we will." Both Marguerite and Fiona nodded in agreement.

They were brave, these women, none of whom was built to wield a sword. But each had the same spirit as his warriors, willing to do all that was required of her.

"Thank you," he said, looking from face to face with great affection. "I promise I will summon you as needed." But he was relieved as he watched them fly north in the direction of the flotilla.

Endelle allowed herself to feel the being she had become. She flexed her new wings, grateful that she still had her arms and legs and wasn't in too different a shape from her usual flight arrangement.

She experimented for a moment, flapping the butterfly-like panels. Just as she suspected, she could move quickly and make much sharper turns. She also found that because the change was genetic, her body knew what it needed to do.

What bemused her, however, was just how much she perspired from every cell of her skin as well as her wings.

Greaves began to advance on her, a satisfied smile on his face. He moved through his advanced levitation and gained speed.

Shit, if he plowed into her, he could knock her into the water, and she had the worst feeling she would never get out. Wings and water did not mesh at all.

Her genetics began to speak to her about the fluids she shed. They had a purpose, but she couldn't quite make it out.

Greaves had completed half the distance.

On he came, his protective plates writhing as he floated. His eyes were almost black as he stared at her. He lowered his chin.

She knew what would happen. He was a bull charging her, and only speed would get her away.

Greaves drew within fifteen feet, formed a missile with his body, then charged.

But she had the ability to flit in this form. She twisted a couple of times with her wings and was suddenly thirty feet away and to the southeast. She flapped her new wings, hovering. She smiled. Damn, she liked this form.

She waited for Greaves to charge her, but for some reason he didn't move as he watched her from a distance. He looked as though he was injured as he held a hand over one of the plates. But exactly how had she hurt him?

His hand fell away as he straightened and looked up at her.

Endelle wondered if when she'd twisted and whisked away, she'd struck him with her foot, but she didn't remember making contact.

All around her, Thorne's force battled death vampires. She could hear dozens of war cries sounding again and again. She heard the flapping of wings, sword rasping against sword, and occasionally a scream of pain.

She also heard water splashing and the rumble of speedboats below her.

When Greaves once more sped up his levitation and came barreling toward her through the air, her perspiration increased. It came from every part of her body, wings included.

As he drew near, she moved but not quite fast enough. He caught her right hip and sent her spiraling. She moved her wings but couldn't quite catch air. She tumbled in the direction of the water. She calmed her mind and allowed her new body to right itself so that her wings went through a new wicked twist.

She now floated just a few feet above the water. Her heart was a jackhammer.

She searched for Greaves, but couldn't find him.

On instinct she began to fly straight up. As she did, hands clamped around her feet and began pulling her down once more toward the water.

She looked down. Greaves's morphed body looked strange, as though he'd been pelted with baseball-sized balls of hail.

Down he dragged her. As hard as she flapped her wings, she had no strength to withstand his physical and muscular superiority as the being he had become.

If he got her under the water, she would drown.

But there was something more, something that worked at her subconscious mind.

She sweat profusely now, but the flapping of her wings sent all that perspiration into a spiral above her.

Then she understood.

She drew her wings in, which of course plummeted her more quickly to a sure death. At the same time, she focused on the fluids leaking from her, increasing the volume and letting them flood Greaves.

He screamed and released her. She flitted back into the air, barely escaping the lake's surface. She glanced down. Greaves was writhing in the water. It wasn't sweat that she perspired, but droplets of acid. How grateful she was to have trusted the image in the future streams.

Greaves thrashed in the lake for some time, but it was clear the water wasn't helping and that his protective biological plates were being eaten away. She couldn't imagine the pain that he experienced right now.

Endelle remained in her elevated position. She wouldn't go near him until she was sure he was completely subdued.

At last, Greaves's plated form floated on the surface, faceup. His eyes were closed. He was still alive, but barely.

Thorne, I need you, she sent.

A few seconds later, as he approached, she added, *Not too close.* She then explained about her acid-based, built-in defense mechanism.

He kept his distance. Glancing at Greaves, he said, "That explains the deep pockmarks and oozing blood."

"I can't believe he's still alive."

"What do you want to do with him?"

Endelle thought about summoning obsidian flame to make use of some serious hand-blast capacity and incinerate him on the spot. She also thought about having him tried for war crimes.

"Can we even contain him?" Thorne asked. "Or will he just dematerialize and go heal himself somewhere?"

A number of boats arrived. She glanced to her right and saw that the triad was in one of the foremost, all eyes cast in Greaves's direction. Fiona had her hand to her mouth and finally looked away.

But it was Grace who called out, "Madame Endelle, would you consider relinquishing him to Beatrice? Can you give Greaves a choice?"

Grace was suggesting that Greaves be granted something he had never granted a single person whose life he'd been the means of ending.

Fury filled her. She wanted to pluck Greaves out of the water and continue to bathe him in acid until his flesh and bones were completely dissolved.

Behind her the sounds of battle had grown fainter and more distant. Thorne's regiment had done its job.

She stared down at Greaves. She wanted him dead for two thousand years of misery that he had brought down on her, on her warriors, on all of Second Earth.

She lifted her wings and felt the perspiration forming once more. But Grace was suddenly in flight and hovering above Greaves. She called out, "I promised Beatrice I would try. Let Greaves go to his mother, to enter the redemption program. It will be punishment enough. Then he can become what he might have been if he had not been tortured and abused as a child. Please, Endelle, let Beatrice try."

Endelle didn't want Greaves reprieved. She wanted him to pay for everything he had done.

She looked at Thorne, but he just shook his head. *Your*

call on this one, he sent. *But you need to make the decision quickly. Every warrior here will want him dead. Soon, you won't have a choice.*

So this was to be her call. She had seen Casimir's change. He was a new man, and his conscience would demand penitence for centuries to come. She knew that the redemption program was its own form of punishment that essentially lasted a lifetime because of the rebuilding of the conscience.

Greaves would suffer.

He was also beginning to recover. Greaves had powerful self-healing abilities. He began swimming to shore, lumbering through the water. She called out to the triad, "Once he reaches the bank, cast an energy field over him while I figure this out. Alison has that ability."

As she pondered what had to be the hardest decision of her life, she watched the triad pull together. Only by shifts of shoulders and arches of necks could she see the early part of the process. Once Grace took possession of Fiona, the earth-based power rumbled and began to stream, a silver river of energy above them.

Greaves reached the bank and started to rise to his feet, even with all the deep pits and rivulets of blood. Fiona turned in his direction. The next moment he lay flat on the grassy bank, a beautiful gold, red, and blue field of energy pinning him down.

Endelle turned away from the flotilla, rising higher into the air. She needed to think.

The lake was full mostly of dead or dying death vampires. Colonel Seriffe and Thorne had trained the warriors well.

Even the Third Earth death vampires were dead. Santiago flew above their bodies. She could sense that he was stationed there to make certain they didn't have an unknown power to rise. If any of them did, he was ready with his ruby dagger in one hand and sword in the other.

The rest of the sky was full of Militia Warriors patrolling back and forth. Occasionally she could spot her Warriors of the Blood. Just a few knots were still battling over the lake far to the south.

Retrieval boats zoomed past below, and by order, Militia Warriors flew down to escort them in case any of the death vampires in the water weren't really dead.

She began to feel weary in her new form. Of course all her battle adrenaline was gone. She even felt a pressing need to get to solid ground and morph back to her ascended form.

She returned to Greaves's position, created some mist, and went through another painful morphing process.

By the time she was done, she had little energy to do more than sit in her flight suit and stare into Greaves's eyes.

He had changed as well, but his body, as to be expected, was pitted in many places to the bone. Even parts of his skull were exposed. He lay naked and trembling, his eyes full of pain. But he was healing, that much was clear to her.

"I'll give you the choice, Greaves. We can try you at COPASS in Prague for war crimes that Marcus has well documented and to which many, many people will testify and for which you will undoubtedly be executed. Or I can send you to Fourth, to your mother, and to the redemption pools. Which will it be?"

He lay shaking as he closed his eyes. She knew him. He was one manipulative bastard and was no doubt trying to figure out which course of action would give him the best advantage going forward.

When he finally opened his eyes, he sent, *Beatrice.*

"As you wish." She focused her thoughts on Fourth Earth. She and Beatrice had been friends for millennia. When she gave Beatrice the news, the woman grew very silent.

Endelle added, *You have Grace to thank for intervening.*

I am coming to you returned to her, and a split second later Beatrice appeared in an elegant peach-silk gown and beautifully coiffed red hair, looking as Grecian as ever. She nodded to Endelle, but it was to Grace that she said a soft thank-you.

She waved her hand over the monster that had tormented Second Earth for so long. He now wore a long white robe. Endelle was just about to have obsidian flame release the energy field when Beatrice took him exactly how he was, prone and caught by the field.

Endelle sat with her hands clasped around her knees. She was exhausted from morphing and trying to stay alive as she battled Greaves. Her hip ached where he'd struck her.

And now he was gone, taken away to Fourth in an energy field.

She couldn't believe it. After all this time, after centuries of being unable to deal effectively with Greaves, suddenly he was just gone.

She hardly knew what to think or to feel.

She remained on the bank of White Lake and watched her team perform all that they needed to do. The speedboats rescued dozens of wounded Militia Warriors from the waters, those who had been injured during battle against the death vampires. The healers moved from boat to boat and worked on the injured.

The September sun rose high in the sky, shining down on the great victory over White Lake. Her Warriors of the Blood remained in the sky, moving back and forth, helping where each was needed. Thorne floated in the sky twenty yards away, fully in command, speaking into his headset almost constantly as he directed the show.

In stages, she began to relax. The scourge of Second Earth was gone and would never be back.

She tried to figure out what she was feeling. Much to her surprise, she was at peace.

There would be work still to do in the future. At the very least, she would need to start negotiations with Greaves's generals, to do all that she could to end the possibility that one or all of them would decide to pick up where Greaves had left off.

But beyond that, her Warriors of the Blood as well as her Militia Warriors would continue to hunt down the last of the death vampires until Second Earth was free of their horrifying and constant threat. Without Greaves to create new death vampires as he had been doing all these centuries, the threat would diminish day by day.

When at last she made it back to the palace, having left White Lake in Thorne's oh-so-capable hands, she walked into her sitting room and found Braulio seated in the farthest oversized purple velvet chair.

"You did good, Endelle."

"I did, didn't I?"

He smiled, and she held her hand out to him. "Come make love to me, and afterward, I want to sleep for about a century."

He rose from his chair, and as he moved toward her, he said, "I've been waiting for this day for the last five thousand years."

A family is a fluid thing,
Changing shape with each birth and each death.
Take care to celebrate the simple joys of each day.

—*Collected Proverbs,* Beatrice of Fourth

CHAPTER 22

A week after the battle over White Lake, Grace sat several yards away from an enormous bonfire smack in the middle of the desert. Marguerite had suggested the gathering for fun, as well as to celebrate that Second Earth had a new future.

Grace had her arm around Thorne's and leaned her head against his shoulder. She sighed. She swore her happiness knew no bounds. Leto was checking on Kendrew and Sloane and would return anytime. Casimir had returned to Fourth to continue his journey through the redemption pools but had left his sons in Leto and Grace's care. He would be returning at least once a week to spend a few hours with them and to reassure them that he was still alive and would be a proper father to them once he had completed Auntie Beatrice's special healing program.

The boys were confused but not nearly as agitated as Grace had seen them in former times. Leto had proved to be quite good with them, so that even he was gaining favor.

She heard the sound of an ax against wood and shifted to look in Santiago's direction. Once he'd learned that there would be a desert party, he'd started hauling and chopping enough logs to feed at least ten bonfires.

Most of it was stacked off to the side, but some of it was in the shape of huge logs that either Santiago or Zacharius would take to chopping just for fun.

As it was, the fire rose at least thirty feet into the dark night sky.

Marcus and Havily were sitting side by side to the right of Thorne. They were seated on a huge log, arguing about something, until Marcus dragged her into his arms and kissed her. Havily laughed and leaned against his chest. He rubbed her back, then kissed her again.

Kerrick and Alison sat on a blanket well back from the fire. Helena was with them, but because she was so active and very powerful, Kerrick had created a dome of mist over the child so that when she mounted her wings, she couldn't just take off. The baby had learned to fly before she'd taken her first step. What a challenge.

Grace smiled. But when had parenting ever *not* been a challenge?

As for Medichi, he'd taken Parisa off into the desert at least a couple of hundred yards away. She couldn't see them or hear them, thank the Creator. Maybe they'd further disguised their position by sneaking behind a massive saguaro or setting up their own mist. Given the distance and the darkness, a vampire could accomplish a lot with his *breh*.

Zacharius slammed his ax into a log, leaving it there, then moved to stretch out on a blanket on his side. He threw small bits of something into the fire. The bits would flare and more sparks would rise. Santiago walked over to him and handed him a Dos Equis.

Grace couldn't help it. She extended her hearing in Santiago's direction. "It's just you, me, and Luken, *hermano*."

Zach smiled up at him and clinked Santiago's bottle. He smiled. "Yep, just the three of us. I'll want to hit the Blood and Bite in a few."

"I'm with you." Santiago dropped down to sit beside him. He sipped his beer, and he, too, had that dark look.

But Grace had a sudden strong impression that the

breh-hedden wouldn't be far behind for either of them. And why would it be? They were Warriors of the Blood, some of the finest vampires on the face of the earth, some of the most powerful both physically and preternaturally.

Which made her think of Luken. He had politely refused to join the party. He insisted that at least one WhatBee show up at the Borderlands, that it wasn't right for Seriffe's Militia Warriors to shoulder the burden alone, even for one night. But Grace knew the truth. Luken still had a thing for Havily, and in this kind of environment, where *brehs* would be affectionate—well, Grace wasn't surprised he'd made his excuses.

As for obsidian flame, they were accounted for. Jean-Pierre sat on a log, off to Grace's left, with Fiona on his lap, his long fingers stroking up and down her bare arm. He kept whispering things into her ear, and she would giggle, looking very young, almost carefree. The word was that Fiona was pregnant, though the pair was keeping it quiet for now.

Grace thought the couple ought to have children, a dozen of them, and maybe they would over the centuries to come. The war looked to be over, though there was massive cleanup to be done, with thousands of death vampires still roaming Second Earth.

Despite that, a new spirit was everywhere: hopeful when a few days ago it seemed impossible to win a battle against Greaves. Now he was on Fourth Earth and no longer a threat.

She watched Marguerite approach the bonfire. She had fashioned a very long stick for herself so that she could prod the wood-based coals at the bottom of the bonfire, dragging some out and building smaller bonfires. She seemed to be enjoying herself immensely. But then why wouldn't she? Her young life had been filled with horror, and she'd never really gotten to be a child. Apparently, Thorne encouraged her to just play, in the same way Marguerite in turn encouraged him to relax and let things go.

She was so happy to be in the same circle as her brother. She would be an aunt to Thorne's children and couldn't wait. Thorne would one day serve as the ruler of Second Earth—that much she felt in every bone of her body, though no official announcement had been made nor had Endelle given a hint that she was stepping down. And Marguerite, as Supreme High Seer of Second Earth, was almost single-handedly overhauling the entire global Seer process, beginning with what she was calling her Seers' Bill of Rights. With Owen Stannett dead, very little stood in the way of Marguerite's reforming the corrupt Seers Fortress system.

Grace patted Thorne's arm. "This is a great group, you know."

He smiled down at her, looking deeply content, a warm light in his eye.

Oh, Creator in heaven, she thought, *thank you for giving him peace.* His hazel eyes were clear and beautiful, especially in the flickering light of the bonfire.

He nodded. "Yep, some of the finest men and women you'll ever know." He glanced around. "Isn't Leto back yet?"

"He wanted to make sure that the boys were all right. We got a babysitter, but he said he just wanted to check things out. He feels very protective of them. I never thought I would see this, but he and Casimir seem to have formed a bond."

Thorne shook his head. "We've entered a time of miracles, that's what I think."

Grace smiled. "And Marguerite has become your miracle."

"In every possible way." His gravelly voice had dropped at least half an octave, so it wasn't a surprise that Marguerite turned to him, the long stick quiet for a moment, her brows raised.

Grace could tell they were communicating telepathically. Marguerite dropped her stick and launched herself into his arms. Grace had the good sense to shift to the end of the log just to give the couple some room, laughing as she did so. Marguerite kissed him. It was such a beautiful sight, to see her worn-out brother so restored and so deeply in love.

She sighed. Leto hadn't been gone very long, but she missed him. She was almost ready to go to him, but a shimmering in front of her brought Thorne to his feet his sword in hand.

But there Leto was, having returned to the bonfire, and near him was Casimir and . . . Patience.

Grace blinked at her sister, who stood smiling beside Casimir, her arm hooked around his.

"Patience?"

Thorne folded his sword away and drew close to Grace. "Is that you? Patience?"

She nodded. Tears swam in her hazel eyes.

"I can't believe it," he said. "I thought you were dead. I found so much blood in that gully that I was sure you were dead."

Patience shook her head, and as tears tracked down her cheeks she told of James having ripped her out of the sky to serve on Third at the portal with him. She had been able to tell James when Greaves created the breach and just how many Third Earth death vampires he had ready to help him in his bid to take over Second Earth. "I wish it could have been done differently, because I know my sudden disappearance wounded you both."

Grace reached out to her and took her hand. "I knew you weren't dead, but you're right, it hurt so much to lose you." She glanced at Marguerite and reached for her hand as well. "But you see how everything has turned out. We have a new sister, and we will become aunts to her twins."

Patience admitted that one of the advantages of her situation was that she had been able to know the significant events of her siblings' lives. She couldn't have stayed on Third helping James without some information.

"I suppose now that Greaves is contained on Fourth, James allowed you to come here."

"Yes."

She then looked up at Casimir. There was such a soft light in her eye that Grace said, "Am I seeing what I'm seeing?" She glanced from Patience to Casimir.

He covered Patience's hand with his own. "The moment I arrived at the portal, I scented her."

"Oh, my God." Grace put her fingers to her mouth as her eyes filled with tears. She felt Leto's arm surround her shoulders.

Are you okay with this? he sent.

She turned to him. "More than okay. Don't you see how perfect this circle is?" Of course, she had one concern and shifted her gaze to Patience. "But you do know that Casimir and I—" She found the words impossible to say.

But it was Patience who rolled her eyes. "Grace, I was never celibate like you. And I've had many wild centuries. Casimir knows that. We've talked it all over. As for your relationship with him on Fourth, we've agreed that without you having taken him there, he would never have entered the redemption pools and would never have agreed to serve as Leto's Guardian of Ascension. I met him, essentially, because of you, so I regret nothing."

Grace looked from one to the other. She could see the *breh*-bond forming between them. Once more her eyes filled with tears. She just couldn't believe that Casimir, of all ascenders, had brought Patience home.

A long series of embraces followed. Patience would return to Second Earth, and Casimir stated without hesitation that he wanted to make his home on Second, not just because of Patience but because of his boys as well. "After all," he said, "I promised Kendrew and Sloane that Auntie Grace would always be in their lives."

Grace smiled. "You know, I always promised to take them camping in the Cascades." She took Leto's hand. "I hope we can do that soon."

Leto pulled her close. "Absolutely."

Casimir frowned. "And the new school term is about to start. I'll need to get them enrolled right away."

Grace stared at Casimir for a long moment. It was hard to remember the man he had been. Never in a thousand years had she thought she'd hear him speak about enrolling his kids in school.

She thought of Greaves. If Casimir could be redeemed, maybe it was possible that Greaves could be transformed as well.

Beatrice sat in her favorite chair in her living room, the one with the footstool that Grace had occupied while helping Beatrice to roll her balls of yarn. She missed Grace and wished the younger woman was here. She needed some comfort.

She leaned forward and covered her ears. Tears began leaking from her eyes. She was trying to be strong, but her son's screams could be heard all over her floating estate. His agony, his rage, his remorse had erupted from the moment he'd touched the water of the first pool, the gentlest pool, the one that was meant to ease the sinner into the process.

Instead, Darian might as well be bathing in fire.

How great were his sins.

More than could be numbered.

He was the author of blood slavery, he had led countless ascenders into addiction to dying blood, and he'd used his squads of death vampires to kill any who stood in his way.

Her son had no conscience.

And so he screamed.

Beatrice covered her ears and wept, unable to fathom how many years or decades or even centuries would be required to wash away the last ramification of all his evil deeds.

Grace had forgotten the trials of childhood. A vampire's long life had created a nearly infinite distance between the sufferings of the two decades required to reach adulthood and the almost boundless challenges of living as a mature ascender.

She glanced at Leto, who stood on the opposite side of their small campsite, in a clearing in the forest on Mortal Earth, deep in the Cascades. He'd built a large campfire that had roared and crackled and was only now settling down.

She sat with Kendrew on her lap. He was the elder of Casimir's boys—six years old now. Sloane sat in his kiddie camp chair, but he had drawn as close to her as he could get and held her hand tight.

These boys had had a rocky beginning, but their lives were beginning to smooth out and Grace was part of that, as she had promised.

But it was Kendrew who had brought up the current offense. He had entered the first grade in the Seattle hidden colony's school and—children being what they had always been—one of his schoolmates had already brought up a supposed past crime of his father's. He had told Kendrew that Casimir had been the instigator of a bomb attack in Las Vegas Two that had nearly killed twenty thousand people.

"I know for a fact that is completely untrue," Grace said.

Kendrew twisted in her arms and looked up at her. "My papa didn't do that terrible thing?"

"Not at all, and you can tell your friend that Fiona was there, Warrior Jean-Pierre's *breh,* and she told me that it was Greaves who had ordered his death vampires to blow up the building. Your father hadn't even known about it." Greaves had intended for Casimir to die as well, but Grace didn't think Kendrew needed to hear that.

Kendrew smiled and turned back around to face the fire. Sloane now leaned against her arm. It was getting late, and the boys were tired.

Grace shuddered inwardly on Kendrew's behalf. Maybe the six-year-old who had attempted to malign Casimir had gotten the facts wrong in this case, but one day someone would speak the truth about his crimes; then what would Grace say? Casimir's list of wrongdoings was long, horribly long, and the truth one day would be out.

She leaned down and kissed the top of Kendrew's head. He had curly hair like his father. "Your father is one of the bravest men I've ever known because he saved Leto's life and almost died doing it. There is nothing greater on earth than laying down one's life for another."

At that, Kendrew once more turned into her and looked up at her. "He is brave."

"Oh, yes. And smart, so very smart. And he has the funniest sense of humor."

Sloane's hand grew slack in hers. She could feel his body sinking against her.

"And now, my darlings, time for bed."

Kendrew didn't protest, but slid off her lap. Sloane, on the other hand, at three, could barely walk he was so drowsy.

She called to Leto. He turned and smiled that beautiful smile of his, now full of affection for her, of love. She inclined her head in Sloane's direction. He moved swiftly and lifted the three-year-old as though he were a feather.

The boys' tent was at a right angle to theirs and held two cots. She tucked Kendrew in and kissed him. She put her hand on his forehead and offered a prayer and a blessing.

She left the tent and Leto performed a similar ritual with Sloane, though the younger boy's eyes were closed when he put his large hand on the small forehead and offered another blessing and a prayer.

When Leto zipped down the front of the tent, he led her back to their larger tent. Before going inside, he glanced around. "I was going to put a dome of mist over our campsite, but then I realized it wasn't needed. The colony is safe, and the one vampire powerful enough to break through Diallo's mist is corralled on Fourth Earth."

In the distance, she heard wolves howl, a long plaintive cry in the dark. She loved that sound. She loved Mortal Earth, where all life had begun, humankind and vampirekind alike. She loved the hidden colony as well. She would have been content anywhere, in any dimension, with Leto, but she confessed she was happy in this quiet, secret ascended world, happier than she would have been on Second Earth.

This was a good place to begin her life with Leto, camping with Casimir's boys. She wanted to have children, and maybe one day she would.

An hour later, Leto was buried inside Grace and trying not to laugh. Making love to her and attempting to keep as quiet as possible in order not to awaken or frighten the boys had given his woman the giggles.

"I'm just not used to this," she whispered, laughing all over again.

"Hush," he said, but his smile was broad. "You're not helping, and if they wake up we'll have to stop."

At that, she grabbed his bare ass and sunk her nails. "Oh, please don't stop," she whispered back.

He thrust hard into her just once, which made her entire body arch and her mouth fly open. He crushed what he knew would be a loud moan, by kissing her and driving his tongue into her mouth.

She gave up her laughter then, and with her own hips met his pelvis in answering grinds. But her moans started anyway. Ah, well, it couldn't be helped. Grace was very vocal, and he loved it. Better to just make it quick.

By now he knew her body well. Because of the *breh-hedden* he could feel her responses, the pleasure she felt with each thrust, just as she had to be experiencing what it was like for him to have her body encase him and pull on him.

Heaven, he sent.

Yes, oh yes. I'm so close.

I can feel that you are.

He felt her orgasm ride through her body, which caused him to speed his thrusts just a little bit more. Sharp cries left her mouth. So much for keeping their lovemaking a secret from the boys. Hopefully they were sleeping deeply enough.

He came then, pleasure streaking through his cock so that even he, despite his self-control, uttered a long low moan. But his pleasure brought her again, so he sustained the rocking until her body grew quiet and slack beneath his.

Her hands were on his face, something she had done from the beginning. "I love you, Leto."

"I love you, too."

"You've made me happier than you'll ever know."

But he thought he knew. If she experienced even a tenth of what he felt, the joy, the deep sense of peace, and even a feeling of purpose in their *breh-hedden* union, then he did know something of her happiness.

Later, as Grace fell asleep in his arms, Leto gave thanks for the life he'd been given, for a life that had been returned to him in full measure. How far he'd come from Moscow Two when he was on the brink of death. Now he stood, and perhaps would forevermore, at the gates of rapture.

ASCENSION
TERMINOLOGY

AAF pr. n. Allied Ascender Forces, Endelle's army.

ALA pr. n. Ascenders Liberation Army, the name Greaves assigned to his army.

answering the call to ascension n. The mortal human who experiences the hallmarks of the *call to ascension* will at some point feel compelled to answer, usually by demonstrating significant preternatural power.

ascender n. A mortal human of earth who has moved permanently to the second dimension.

ascendiate n. A mortal human who has answered the *call to ascension* and thereby commences his or her *rite of ascension*.

ascension n. The act of moving permanently from one dimension to a higher dimension.

ascension ceremony n. Upon the completion of the *rite of ascension*, the mortal undergoes a ceremony in which loyalty to the laws of Second Society is professed and the attributes of the *vampire* mantle along with immortality are bestowed.

the Borderlands pr. n. Those geographic areas that form dimensional borders at both ends of a dimensional pathway. The dimensional pathway is an access point through which travel can take place from one dimension to the next. See *Trough*.

breh-hedden **n.** (Term from an ancient language.) A mate-bonding ritual that can only be experienced by the most powerful warriors and the most powerful preternaturally gifted women. Effects of the *breh-hedden* can include but are not limited to: specific scent experience, extreme physical/sexual attraction, loss of rational thought, primal sexual drives, inexplicable need to bond, powerful need to experience deep *mind-engagement,* etc.

cadroen **n.** (Term from an ancient language.) The name for the hair clasp that holds back the ritual long hair of a *Warrior of the Blood*.

call to ascension n. A period of time, usually involving several weeks, in which the mortal human has experienced some or all of, but not limited to, the following: specific dreams about the next dimension, deep yearnings and longings of a soulful and inexplicable nature, visions of and possibly visits to any of the dimensional Borderlands, etc. See *Borderlands*.

Central pr. n. The office of the current administration that tracks movement of *death vampires* in both the second dimension and on *Mortal Earth* for the purpose of alerting the *Warriors of the Blood* and the *Militia Warriors* to illegal activities.

the darkening n. An area of *nether-space* that can be found during meditations and/or with strong preternatural darkening capabilities. Such abilities enable the *ascender* to move into nether-space and remain there or to use nether-space in order to be in two places at once.

death vampire n. Any vampire, male or female, who partakes of *dying blood* automatically becomes a death vampire. Death vampires can have, but are not limited to, the following characteristics: remarkably increased physical strength, an increasingly porcelain complexion true of all ethnicities so that death vampires have a long-term reputation of looking very similar, a faint blueing of the porcelain complexion, increasing beauty of face, the ability to enthrall, the blackening of *wings* over a period of time. Though death vampires are not gender-specific, most are male. See *vampire*.

dimensional worlds n. Eleven thousand years ago, the first *ascender*, Luchianne, made the difficult transition from *Mortal Earth* to what became known as Second Earth. In the early millennia four more dimensions were discovered, Luchianne always leading the way. Each dimension's ascenders exhibited expanding preternatural power before *ascension*. Upper dimensions are generally closed off to the dimension or dimensions below. See *off-dimension*.

duhuro n. (Term from an ancient language.) A word of respect that in the old language combines the spiritual offices of both servant and master. To call someone *duhuro* is to offer a profound compliment suggesting great worth.

dying blood n. Blood extracted from a mortal or an *ascender* at the point of death. This blood is highly addictive in nature. There is no known treatment for anyone who partakes of dying blood. The results of ingesting dying blood include, but are not limited to: increased physical, mental, or preternatural power; a sense of extreme euphoria; a deep sense of well-being; a sense of omnipotence and fearlessness; the taking in of the preternatural powers of the host body; etc. If dying blood is not taken on a regular basis, extreme abdominal cramps result without ceasing. Note: Currently there is an antidote, not for the addiction to dying blood itself but to the various results of ingesting dying blood. This means that a *death vampire* who drinks dying blood, then partakes of the antidote will not show the usual physical side effects of ingesting dying blood; no whitening or faint blueing of the skin, no beautifying of features, no blackening of the *wings,* etc.

effetne n. (Term from an ancient language.) An intense form of supplication to the gods; an abasement of self and of self-will.

folding v. Slang for dematerialization, since some believe that one does not actually dematerialize self or objects but rather "folds space" to move self or objects from one place to another. There is much scientific debate on this subject since at present neither theory can be proved.

grid n. The technology used by Central that allows for the tracking of *death vampires,* primarily at the *Borderlands* on both *Mortal Earth* and *Second Earth.* Death vampires by nature carry a strong, trackable signal, unlike normal *vampires.* See *Central.*

Guardian of Ascension pr. n. A prestigious title and rank at present given only to those *Warriors of the Blood* who also serve to guard powerful *ascendiates* during their *rite of ascension.* In millennia past, Guardians of Ascension were also those powerful ascenders who offered themselves in unique and powerful service to Second Society.

High Administrator pr. n. The designation given to a leader of a Second Earth *Territory.*

identified sword n. A sword made by Second Earth metallurgy that has the preternatural capacity to become identified to a single *ascender.* The identification process involves holding the sword by the grip for several continuous seconds. The identification of a sword to a single ascender means that only that person can touch or hold the sword. If anyone else tries to take possession of the sword, other than the owner, that person will die.

Militia Warrior pr. n. One of hundreds of thousands of warriors who serve Second Earth society as a policing force for the usual civic crimes and as a battling force, in squads only, against the continual depredations of *death vampires* on both *Mortal Earth* and Second Earth.

millennial adjustment n. The phenomenon of time taking on a more fluid aspect with the passing of centuries.

mind-engagement n. The ability to penetrate another mind and experience the thoughts and memories of the other person. The ability to receive another mind and allow that person to experience one's thoughts and memories. These abilities must be present in order to complete the *breh-hedden*.

mist n. A preternatural creation designed to confuse the mind and thereby hide things or people. Most mortals and *ascenders* are unable to see mist. The powerful ascender, however, is capable of seeing mist, which usually looks like an intricate mesh, or a cloud, or a web-like covering.

Mortal Earth pr. n. The name for First Earth or the current modern world known simply as earth.

nether-space n. The unknowable, unmappable regions of space. The space between dimensions is considered nether-space, as well as the space found in *the darkening*.

off-dimension n. An expression referring to an *ascender* not being on his or her prime resident planet; e.g., an ascender from Second Earth who goes rogue and lives on *Mortal Earth* would be considered off-dimension.

preternatural voyeurism n. The ability to "open a window" with the power of the mind in order to see people and events happening elsewhere in real time. Two of the limits of preternatural voyeurism are: The voyeur must usually know the person or place, and if the voyeur is engaged in *darkening* work, it is very difficult to make use of preternatural voyeurism at the same time.

pretty-boy n. Slang for *death vampire,* since most death vampires are male.

rite of ascension n. A three-day period during which time an *ascendiate* contemplates *ascending* to the next highest dimension.

royle **n.** (Term from an ancient language.) The literal translation is: "a benevolent wind." More loosely translated, *royle* refers to the specific quality of having the capacity to create a state of benevolence, of goodwill, within an entire people or culture. See *royle adj.*

royle **adj.** (Term from an ancient language.) This term is generally used to describe a specific coloration of *wings:* cream with three narrow bands at the outer tips when in full-span. The bands are always burnished gold, amethyst, and black. Because Luchianne, the first *ascender* and first *vampire,* had this coloration on her wings, anyone whose wings matched Luchianne's was said to have *royle* wings. Having *royle* wings was considered a tremendous gift, holding great promise for the world.

Seer pr. n. An *ascender* gifted with the preternatural ability to ride the future streams and report on future events.

Seers Fortress pr. n. *Seers* have traditionally been gathered into compounds designed to provide a highly peaceful environment, thereby enhancing each Seer's ability to ride the future streams. The information gathered at a Seers Fortress benefits the local *High Administrator.* Some believe that the term *fortress* emerged as a protest against the prison-like conditions the *Seers* often have to endure.

spectacle n. The name given to events of gigantic proportion that include but are not limited to: trained squadrons of DNA-altered geese, swans, and ducks, *ascenders* with the specialized and dangerous skills of flight performance, intricate and often massive light and fireworks displays, as well as various forms of music.

Supreme High Administrator pr. n. The ruler of Second Earth. See *High Administrator.*

Territory pr. n. For the purpose of governance, Second Earth is divided up into groups of countries called Territories. Because the total population of Second Earth is only 1 percent of *Mortal Earth,* Territories were established as a simpler means of administering Second Society law. See *High Administrator.*

Trough pr. n. A slang term for a dimensional pathway. See *Borderlands.*

Twoling pr. n. Anyone born on Second Earth is a Twoling.

vampire n. The natural state of the *ascended* human. Every ascender is a vampire. The qualities of being a vampire include but are not limited to: immortality, the use of fangs to take blood, the use of fangs to release potent chemicals, increased physical power, increased preternatural ability, etc. Luchianne created the word *vampire* upon her *ascension* to Second Earth to identify in one word the totality of the changes she experienced upon that ascension. From the first, the taking of blood was viewed as an act of reverence and bonding, not as a means of death. The *Mortal Earth* myths surrounding the word *vampire* for the most part personify the Second Earth death vampire. See *death vampire.*

Warriors of the Blood pr. n. An elite fighting unit of usually seven powerful warriors, each with phenomenal preternatural ability and capable of battling several *death vampires* at any one time.

WhatBee pr. n. Slang for *Warrior of the Blood,* as in WOTB.

wings n. All *ascenders* eventually produce wings from wing-locks. *Wing-lock* is the term used to describe the apertures on the ascender's back from which the feathers and attending mesh-like superstructure emerge. Mounting wings involves a hormonal rush that some liken to sexual release. Flight is one of the finest experiences of ascended life. Wings can be held in a variety of positions, including but not limited to: full-mount, close-mount, aggressive-mount, etc. Wings emerge over a period of time from one year to several hundred years. Wings can, but do not always, begin small in one decade then grow larger in later decades.

Y pro nai-y-stae **n.** (Term from an ancient language.) The loose translation is, "You may stay for an eternity."